Graveyard of Empires

Empires

Book I

by
Lincoln Cole

Published by Lincoln Cole, Columbus, 2015
admin@LincolnCole.net
www.LincolnCole.net

Cover Design by M.N. Arzu
www.mnarzuauthor.com

Table of Contents

"The universe seems neither benign nor hostile, merely indifferent."

- Carl Sagan

Prologue
Sector 4 – Tellus
Alaina Naylor

1

Thunder rumbled outside the soccer stadium: a deep roar as storm clouds gathered in strength, the prelude to a ferocious storm.

Alaina absently twirled her father's curly auburn hair between her fingers, glancing around at the gathered crowd with poorly hidden trepidation. The five-year-old girl was perched high atop her father's shoulders and held a good vantage of the rally, but it also made her stick out above the masses. So many people; so many, many bodies, all clustered together with nary inches of separation.

The soccer venue was immense, holding well over a hundred twenty thousand fans for a sunny afternoon match, but there weren't any games scheduled for today; instead, a raised dais sat on the central circle of the field, silent and empty, waiting amidst the sea of curious onlookers.

The stadium was filled well past capacity for today's event: people were clustered as close together as possible, butting up against the sides of the stage and threatening to spill atop it. The seats were being ignored by all but the weariest of onlookers.

Excitement was in the air; people stood in aisles ad on plastic seats, jockeying with futility for better positions. A gentle din of murmuring hung in the air: whispers on the wind, a million insignificant conversations.

It was cloudy—it was *always* cloudy this far inland—and warm today. Little Alaina let out an exaggerated yawn, stretching her arms to the sky the same way her mom always did in the mornings. She would rather be playing tag with her brother Tommy or dressing dolls with her sister's Jessie and Eva than sitting here waiting for the rally to start.

She would much rather be back in bed, nestled close with Mr. Snuggles, her bunny rabbit, listening to the pitter-patter of rain. But father woke them up early and told them that they had to get dressed right away before he brought them here. He was as happy and excited as she had ever seen him.

He didn't tell them why, only that it was important. That it would change the world. All of the worlds, even. Alaina didn't see how or why that should matter. *Her* world wasn't that big and consisted of family and friends and bunnies.

Right now she was just bored from sitting around and hoped it would sprinkle soon. It looked like it was going to, and felt like it was going to, but as yet the sky hadn't opened up.

"How long must they keep us waiting?" Kate Naylor—Alaina's mother—asked. She was a willowy woman, dressed in a loose fitting pink blouse with blue pants. Her brown hair was tied in a bun with a few loose strands fluttering against her cheeks. It was windy.

Her eyes were smeared with hastily applied makeup, something she described as a *raccoon*. Alaina didn't know what a raccoon was, but her mom didn't seem to like them very much.

There hadn't been time for her to do a complete job. Carl, her father, had rushed them out half-dressed and bleary eyed while it was still dark. They finished waking up and dressing in the car. Tommy had forgotten his drawers and Alaina her right shoe—another detail for which mom was mad at dad. Alaina didn't actually mind not having both shoes: it just meant she got to be carried while her older siblings had to walk.

"Not much longer," Carl answered. A repeated sentiment they all heard many times that morning. "It won't be much longer now."

"This is a hazardous gathering if ever there was one," Kate replied, her voice bitter.

"It's not as if—"

"How are we supposed to get out if something happens? What if someone starts a panic? The children will be trampled."

"Nothing is going to happen," Carl said.

Kate narrowed her eyes at him. "These people are fostering a rebellion," she said quietly. "Something is going to happen, and I want no part in it."

"I'm hungry," Alaina said, yawning again and resting her little chin on her father's head. He reached up with his left hand and squeezed her arm. His right stayed on her leg, keeping her firmly in place atop his shoulders.

"Won't be much longer," Carl repeated. "And then we'll all go to the Sunny Side for breakfast. How's that sound?"

"Okay," Alaina said, happy to agree. "I want eggs."

She loved eggs. They were her favorite thing for breakfast and Sunny Side always had the best eggs.

"Then you shall have eggs, my little princess," Carl said, squeezing her leg.

"I hate that place," Tommy said.

He was sitting on the ground between his parent's feet, picking at the faux grass of the field under their feet.

"You never hated it before," her father said.

Tommy's legs were curled up against his chest. He was seven years old, thin and wiry for his age. "Can't we just go home?"

"Soon," Carl said.

"Why did we have to come so *early?*" Tommy asked. "Nothing is even happening!"

"We had to get a good spot," Carl explained with waning patience.

"For all the good *that* did us," Kate mumbled. Alaina couldn't help but agree: they *were* really far back the stage. She felt her father sigh beneath her.

"It won't be long now. I promise."

"We could have just watched the speech at home," her mother said, adding insult to injury. "It's going to be shown on every channel in the country. Probably the world."

"It's a declaration. Not a speech."

"It's a speech," Kate reiterated. "And it's tantamount to treason."

"It isn't treason. It's freedom. This is going to be an auspicious day," Carl said, ignoring her. "The day that everything changes. This is the day that—"

"I know, I get it," her mom interrupted angrily. "And I agreed to come for *your* sake. And for *their* sake. But I didn't plan on getting here *four hours* early. The kids are freezing."

Alaina glanced down at her siblings. Jessie and Eva were clutching their mom's black pants and shivering. They were wearing their best school dresses and looked like twins. They weren't, though, and were actually two years apart. Her big brother Tommy was too busy pouting to even notice the chill in the air. And she...

Well, Alaina had never really been bothered by cold weather. Or hot weather for that matter. She enjoyed extremes and was kind of hoping for some snow. Not the right season, but she didn't care. Or a storm. Thunder was one of her favorite things, the primal thrill of it as it rolled across the countryside.

She sympathized with her mother's complaint, though. They'd arrived a little after five in the morning and hustled to find a place, yet there were still hundreds of people between them and the stage.

It could be worse, though. There were thousands upon thousands of people behind them. It was even more cramped the higher up the stadium seating they went. There simply wasn't enough room to sit and relax. Not if they wanted to see anything.

"If I'd known it was going to take this long for things to get started I wouldn't have made everyone come," her father said, "but this is going to be an important day for a long time and I thought it would be good..."

His voice trailed off as a few people shushed him from farther up the crowd.

Like an ebbing wave, the stadium fell quiet as one. There was a heaviness in the air, thick with anticipation. It worked its way from the stage to the far reaches of the crowd as a tingling shiver brushing along a spine. Fingers pointed forward, people were tapped on shoulders, and suddenly everything was still.

Someone had walked atop the stage. A short man, rail thin and gangly, walking with long, even strides toward the center podium. Behind him rested an empty line of bleachers two rows high.

"Who's he?" Alaina asked. A dozen people made shushing sounds and glared at her. Her father just squeezed her leg gently.

The man stopped in front of the oak podium and rested his hands upon it. He was ugly with a silver goatee and deep gray eyes. His face was young but lined with intensity. Right now, he was wearing a charcoal button-up suit that hung off of his lanky frame and black shoes polished to a sheen. He looked like some sort of animal, poised with tension and ready to strike.

All eyes faced front. Alaina felt tension ripple through the crowd, punctuated by an occasional cough. Waiting, anticipation, fear; it all hung in the air like incense.

The speaker wasn't as old as Alaina's father, probably only in his late teens or early twenties. His eyes swept back and forth from face to face, daring anyone to meet his gaze. To match it and stare back. No one tried. Alaina waited for him to speak.

But he didn't.

Not right away. He stood alone upon the stage, studying them as they waited. Seconds ticked past with hesitant ambition. The crowd shifted like an angry beast, murmuring to itself.

And still he waited.

The murmuring intensified.

"Daddy, why isn't he talking?"

"Shh," Carl said, squeezing her right leg. She toyed with a strand of his curly brown hair, frowning.

The murmuring rose to an angry fever pitch.

After an eternity the man leaned into the microphone and spoke.

"My name is Darius Gray. And today, our world is free."

There was a euphoric pulse in the air, cutting through the tension like a knife. The crowd erupted. It wasn't a slow burn but rather an explosion of raw emotion and joy. People screamed, whistled, and shouted just to be heard.

Alaina covered her ears with her hands and closed her eyes. It was so loud. She'd been to the stadium before to watch a soccer game with her father, but it was nothing like this. She could feel her father, yelling along with the crowd.

The speaker—Darius Gray—leaned back from the podium. He waited politely for the crowd to settle, a light smirk curling his lips. It continued for several more seconds and then gradually faded out as stillness settled back in.

A few outliers whistled, a ragged cheer could be heard way up in the stands, but the noise finally dissipated until the stadium was once again silent.

10

Someone laughed. The sound echoed.

Once they were silent, Darius cleared his throat. He spoke calmly in a low voice. The microphones were not turned very loud. Everyone strained, leaning forward to hear him.

"It feels good to say that. God knows we have suffered long enough. However, saying it only proves the intention. It does not make it fact. Not yet. Here, in this moment, our journey begins. And it will not be easy.

"You see, there are those who will seek to weaken our resolve; to diminish our freedoms; they will seek to reinstitute the bonds and chains of poverty that we have clung to for these many years. There are those who would see us harmed. But I say no, they cannot touch us. No, they cannot break us. We must stand strong, united, and proud; we must tell such people that we *will not* be cowed—"

The crowd rumbled with a growing throb as he spoke, rising to a slow heat. Darius's voice was thick with emotion, his eyes filled with pleading but also with steel. His hands never stopped moving, weaving gracefully in the air and holding everyone's attention. Every fifth word he slammed his fist into the podium for punctuation.

"—and we will *not* be denied. We must throw off our chains. We must escape from our bonds. We will rise up and claim our destiny as a free world, undeterred and unmolested by those who would sup with injustice—"

She heard a soft '*amen*' from nearby and saw heads bobbing. The speaker's voice was filled with passion and lyricism, raising the energy. Faces were drawn with concentration and consternation as he spoke, his words touching the deepest recesses of their hearts, igniting hopes and dreams they'd locked away generations before.

"Today we declare our freedom. Today we clasp it in our hands and refuse to let go. Today we buy our freedom in blood so that our children and our children's children can grow up in a just world. A glorious world. A world where everyone is equal and all are loved. What we do today is for a new tomorrow. A better tomorrow that will come with the rising of our sun."

Darius hesitated, his face a mask of focus. The crowd was restless, hungry. They were devouring his words, yet left wanting. Here, during the lull, a large group of people strode onto the stage with practiced efficiency.

They lined up behind Darius in two separate groups and took their places on the vacant bleachers. Each was wearing extravagant clothing to represent many different nationalities from around the world.

Darius pitched his voice lower, leaning into the microphone:

"I ask you…no, I beg of you, my brothers and sisters: I beg that you fight with me. Fight for your freedom. Fight for your neighbor's freedom, as they will fight for yours. We will not rest until every man, woman, and child is granted those God-given rights we were born with. Join me, and together we will build our lives anew; under new governance. We will form a Union whereby all planets are equal and all citizens free.

"This future is in our grasp. Have faith and be strong. And know that one day our dream will become reality."

Then he stepped back. The crowd was thrumming with excitement. Alaina heard a noise overhead, a sort of humming sound. She looked back and up, behind the crowd, and saw approaching aircraft. They were trailing lines of smoke, leaving green and gold lines in the sky.

They swooped in low, just over the stadium and restless crowd. Alaina heard the roaring of their engines, and it reminded her of thunder. It was heavy, pressing down with the weight of its wake, and euphoric. She was grinning and excited though she had no idea why.

She felt the wind wash over the crowd. It buffeted them forward, knocking them into one another. It was a strong enough gust that even her broad-shouldered father stumbled. But he didn't fall. A few people caught him, steadied him, making sure he was okay. That Alaina was okay. That everyone was okay. They were in this together now.

The sound and wind dissipated, leaving colored streaks floating in the sky, separating into drifting plumes. The crowd went wild, cheering and whooping and shouting. Alaina felt the excitement and emotion. The release. She didn't understand what was going on, but that didn't matter. The passion was in the air, in her blood. She could feel her father, bursting with energy as he hollered and *whooped* beneath her.

Darius leaned forward to the microphone again. His voice was steady and loud.

"My name is Darius Gray. And today, our world is free."

2

"I think he's crazy," Alaina's mom said, scrubbing pasta sauce off of the plate and down the drain. They were in the little kitchen of their one-story home, packed in around the sink. Kate handed the clean plate to Alaina, who began wiping it with a towel. She liked drying dishes with her parents. She liked to help. "At best, he's crazy. Or a charlatan at worst."

Kate Naylor's movements were precise and short as she cleaned. She was angry, Alaina knew, and attempting to stifle it. Alaina dried the dish off quickly with her semi-wet rag and handed it to her father, who placed it in the cabinet on top of the stack. Then he picked up a long-stemmed glass of wine and took a sip, pursing his lips.

"He's definitely crazy," her father agreed. "But that doesn't change anything. He's right; about everything. We can't keep living like this. We can't just accept the poverty while all of our money gets shipped off to the Core worlds."

"He's going to get us all killed," Kate replied, dipping a cup into the soapy water. Her arms were shaking. "He wants us to turn our back on our leaders. To turn out back on the Core worlds and the Republic. He wants us to fight for our freedoms. It's a fight we can't win."

"We *can* win," her father said.

"How many rebellions have worked in the past? None, and there have been hundreds in the last few years alone."

"This is different."

"It isn't."

"Darius is a good man. A great leader. People are rallying to his cause and already we have millions supporting him. The International Council is already rallying to the cause."

"And you don't find that suspicious? I saw the way he paraded them on stage," Kate said, her voice bitter. "He must have some control over them. Some sort of blackmail."

"That's not fair, Kate," Carl said, moving over to rest his hands on her shoulders. He gave them a gentle squeeze. "They *want* to support him."

"Why?" Kate asked, turning around. She was half a head shorter than Carl, so she had to look up into his eyes. He was the one to flinch from the gaze, though. "Why would they support him? It doesn't make sense. He's only been here for three months. We don't know very much about him. And what we do know doesn't seem good. He served the damned First Citizen as one of his personal bodyguards!"

"So he knows firsthand how bad the man is," Alaina's father said, still looking away. "We should be grateful that he joined us. That he wants to lead us. He was one of the Shields, Kate. One of their best. And now he's one of us. He has the least to gain and the most to lose by rebelling, yet here he is, ready to fight for our freedom."

"I don't trust him," Kate said. "We're nothing to him. Just chattel."

"We need to trust someone," Carl said, reaching out and rubbing Alaina on her head. He was a big man with strong hands and a friendly face. He grinned down at her. Alaina giggled and swatted his hand away. "No one wants to live with our chains. No one wants to be slaves."

"What chains?" Kate asked, holding up her wrists. "What bonds, Carl?"

"It's a metaphor," Carl said.

"Metaphors are stupid," Kate replied. "Is it worth more fighting for perceived freedom or staying alive?"

"Can't we have both?"

"No," Kate said bluntly. "No, we can't. Tellus is just one planet. The First Citizen will bring his armies and destroy us in a day."

"More will join. Three other planets are already promising to sign our treaty once it is ratified."

"And that would make us four planets against hundreds. Thousands even. And they have the army, not us. Better not to rebel when we don't have a chance of winning."

Carl sighed. "If we don't try, we can't succeed. This has to start somewhere."

Her mother turned back to the sink. She handed the soapy glass to Alaina and leaned heavily against the counter. She rubbed her eyes and let out a deep sigh.

"Yes, yes it does. But I'm afraid it's going to end here too."

Carl wrapped his arms around Kate, drawing her close. He kissed the back of her knock and rocked her body in a slow dance. She was smaller than he was, tiny in his arms. She looked frail. Scared.

"It won't," he said. "You're right that Darius only arrived three months ago. You're right that it's hard to trust him. But look what he has done in those three months! He's given us a chance. A path to winning something our parents wanted but could never get for themselves. Freedom."

"I know Carl."

"But he's given us something even more important than that."

"What?"

"Hope," Carl said. "Until he showed up, we had no hope. It's hard to believe that freedom could be possible, but look how many people come out. The treaty isn't signed. It isn't even *written* and already millions of people are ready for it. We live in quiet desperation."

"And now we'll just be desperate."

"Maybe. But we will be free. A lot of people want to be free, not just us."

"A lot of people don't," Kate said. "No one in the Core is speaking of rebellion. Even the planets in Sector Three aren't talking about it."

"It won't matter," Carl said. "Not once the war really starts. We're drawing a line in the sand and forcing people to pick a side. And when their backs are to the wall and they have to make a decision, most will side with us."

"And what happens when they don't?" Kate asked, turning to face Carl. Her pale blue eyes searched his face. "What happens when they side with the Republic?"

Carl hesitated. "They won't," he said.

"You can't know that."

"But I do," Carl said firmly. "They want freedom as badly as we do. They will join our Union."

Kate shook her head, closing her eyes. "I can't stop this war. I don't think anyone can now. I just don't think anyone understands the real cost."

"We know the cost," Carl said. "We will win."

"Promise me," Kate said, her voice shaking, "that you won't join when they come calling. That you won't fight. I won't allow you to die for this man."

"Kate..."

"Promise me, or..." she didn't finish the thought.

Carl pulled her close and kissed her forehead. "I promise," he said. "I have a beautiful wife and four glorious children. I'm not about to put my life at risk for anything. Even freedom."

Kate nodded. A tear slipped down her cheek. "Okay."

"Okay," Carl agreed. He let her go. They stared at each for a long minute. Both looked sad. Finally, Carl stepped over and picked Alaina up off her stepladder. He took the glass and towel away from her and set them on the counter. "And now that this is settled, I think it's time for someone to go to bed."

"But dad," Alaina said, yawning, "I'm not even tired."

"I know," he said, holding her against his shoulder. "I meant me."

He carried her down the hall. They passed her siblings. Her brother was in his bedroom playing a VR game with a big headset on his face. Her sisters shared their own bedroom and were watching a show. Both were nibbling on little green crackers.

Alaina slept in the smallest room at the end of the hall. It was barely bigger than a closet and had very little floor space. She was supposed to sleep with her sisters, but they'd thrown a series of catastrophic fits when her parents proposed it: they refused to sleep with a baby in the room.

And Alaina didn't mind. Her walls were painted a deep blue and there were two windows. She could look outside and see the moon peeking down on her, silver in the sky. She enjoyed being alone.

It was also the farthest room from her parents, but that wasn't an issue either. Alaina usually slept soundly, without many dreams. It was a rare night that she slept in bed with her parents.

Alaina was gently lowered to the soft and cold sheets. She looked up at her father and yawned.

"Goodnight, honeybee," he said, tucking her into the covers and kissing her on the forehead.

"Goodnight, Daddy," she said. He turned and started walking toward the door. "Daddy?"

"Yes, Alaina?" he asked, pausing at the entrance. His body was silhouetted by the light.

"What was that man talking about today?"

Her father was silent for a few seconds, thinking. Finally, he said, "He was talking about you."

She scrunched up her nose in confusion. "Me?"

"He was talking about what we had to look forward to. The future. *You* are our future."

She yawned. "I am?"

"You are," he said with a nod. "And what a future you will be. I love you, honeybee. Sleep tight."

She closed her eyes. "Okay, Daddy," she whispered, drifting off to sleep.

Chapter 1
Sector 1 - Axis
Argus Wade

1

The revolver thundered in the courtyard below.

Argus could taste bile in his throat. It tasted like jealousy. One in a thousand; maybe one in a *million* trained marksmen could ever be as good as Patrick Uhlren with a revolver. With such monumental odds against him, it wasn't worth getting jealous over how good Patrick was: *God granted him his talent, and thus it is God's triumph, not his.*

That logic stung of falsehood, though. It wasn't a lack of sacrosanct belief for Argus, but rather a lack of personal worth. Both of them were members of the *Ordo Mens Rea*, but the similarities ended there. Argus was good with numbers; Patrick, an honorable Shield of the First Citizen, was a prodigy. Given the choice between which of the talents he wanted—guns or numbers—Argus wouldn't even hesitate.

Numbers didn't impress people, but they were safe. Argus had never been good with weapons and sure as hell wasn't a fan of putting his life at risk. The last time he used a pistol on a training range he'd nearly shot himself in the foot. Plus, numbers were important to the Ministry and the Republic.

Yet knowing he was important didn't diminish Argus's jealousy. Dozens of school children clustered around Patrick with adoring faces. These were the children of the most famous and wealthiest citizens in the Galaxy, the ones who could afford to send their children to the Core to train with the Ministry. All of the children worshiped Patrick in a way that they would *never* worship Argus.

It hurt.

Another small target, no bigger than a kiwi, flew up in the air. The shot that followed shook the glass Argus was watching through. Eighty meters, at least. That was the distance from which Patrick shot the target, and it exploded in a cloud of dust from a direct hit. Another cheer rose from the adoring crowd.

Argus Wade swallowed his bile. Petty or not, he couldn't afford to dally. He had a job to do.

"Patrick is an excellent shot," the quartermaster offered, stepping up beside Argus to look out at the courtyard.

They were standing in a glass walkway, having stopped on their way to the hangar. They wanted to see what the commotion was about—neither had known a Shield was visiting the Ministry today—and ended up watching for several minutes.

"He is," Wade agreed, "one of the best."

"To think: one of the First Citizen's personal defenders," the quartermaster said, reverently touching the glass as he watched Patrick reload his weapon. A flick of the wrist and then he rolled the bullets gracefully into the chamber. "I once dreamed of being chosen to join the Twelve. What a foolish child I was."

What child doesn't wish for that? Argus wondered. *But there can only be twelve at any time.* He turned away from the window. "You were saying?"

"I was?"

Argus waved his hand in annoyance. "About the trip. You were listing off supplies being loaded into my ship."

The quartermaster—he was short and ruddy with droopy cheeks—opened his ledger once again and ran his finger along the page. He found his spot and cleared his throat.

"Twenty-two crates of foodstuffs, including sixty-eight pounds of perishables and—"

"How many day's worth?" Argus interrupted. "I don't need specifics."

The man scanned his page again. "Forty-six."

"I thought it was thirteen days?" Argus said. "When I spoke to the Minister he said it would be a normal trip."

"I haven't spoken to him," the man replied.

"How many priests will be accompanying me?"

"Only one. Jeremiah Robinson. He's been sent an itinerary and is expected to move to the Hummingbird whenever you send for him."

Argus stifled a groan. Jeremiah was annoying on his best days. An old priest, set in his ways, and angry with anything he didn't understand. That category included most things, especially the Order to which Argus belonged. The *Ordo Mens Rea* wasn't discussed openly in the Ministry. Only a handful of people even knew it existed, let alone what it was for. Jeremiah didn't rank highly enough to be trusted, so he resorted instead to distrusting any and all priests he knew were members.

And that list included Argus.

The worst part was that Jeremiah wouldn't like that Argus was in charge. He would be quick to report any wrongdoings to the Minister.

But there was nothing Argus could do about it now. He pushed the concern away. "Very well. We will be leaving for Sector Three—"

"Six," the quartermaster interrupted, closing his ledger. "You'll be going to Sector Six."

"Six?" Argus echoed, excitement creeping into his voice. *That changes everything.* "You are certain?"

"Quite."

"Sector Six is outside Republican territory. It's an unclassified sector."

"Yet human occupied," the quartermaster replied. "Therefore, they should hear the word of the lord and receive His blessing."

"We haven't traveled past sector four in hundreds of years," Argus said. "They don't know of the Ministry."

"Only for now," the man replied. "But by the grace of the First Citizen, we will bring the heathens into the fold within the next few years. The legacy of such integration will belong to those men and women brave enough to face the savagery beyond our borders and spread the word of our Lord."

Shameless ass-kissing, Argus thought, *isn't necessary.*

Another gunshot sounded from below, but it barely registered to Argus Wade. His mind was in motion now, doing what it did best: sifting the muddy water to find the gold.

I suggested traveling to Sector Six years ago, but I never expected the Minister to agree. Sector Six is dangerous, but their technology is, at least, thirty years behind ours. Maybe more. The money I could make selling even the most modest equipment...

"I'll need protection," he said.

The quartermaster looked at his clipboard. "You will have thirty soldiers from the Capital Cruiser Denigen's Fist. Two pilots: Jack Lane and Michael Grant—"

"I have someone particular in mind."

The man lowered the clipboard and raised an eyebrow. "Yes?"

"Vivian Drowel."

"Not possible," the man replied. "She is not sanctioned to leave—"

"I don't care if she's sanctioned or not. She's the one I want. She has clearance, correct?"

"That was revoked when she returned from the Capital two years ago. She isn't allowed to leave the Ministry until she has been cleared."

Argus groaned internally. "Well then un-revoke it. I don't care what you have to do, get her clearance. If I'm being sent out into dangerous territory, I want someone with me I can trust."

The man hesitated, and then jotted something on the data pad. "I will see what I can do."

"That's all I ask," Wade lied. He felt a jolt of heat run across his temporal lobe as his implant heated up. He added just enough suggestion to his words to make the man do as he asked. Manipulating someone's mind was dangerous: if the Minister caught him, his punishment would be immediate execution. But he doubted the ruddy-faced man would ever know that anything untoward had happened.

The man nodded, making another notation. His expression was thoughtful.

This might not be so bad, Argus decided. *If they are sending me to Sector Six, they must not have high expectations for conversions to the Ministry. I can stop at Terminus along the way to stock up on goods and spend a few weeks planet hopping. With luck, I'll leave Sector Six with an empty hull and full bank account.*

Time to go find Vivian.

2

"Wade, we have a problem."

No hesitation. No greeting. Argus was kind of irked as he stepped into Vivian Drowel's chambers. It was a small and low-ceilinged room, Spartan in furnishing and completely lacking any warmth or personality.

Come to think of it, he was always kind of irked when Vivian was around. She wasn't exactly the friendliest person alive and she was notorious for being straightforward and direct. He trusted her with his life and loved her like a sister, he just didn't enjoy spending time with her.

"What sort of problem? I didn't think they would get word to you that quickly about coming with me to sector six. But don't think of it as a burden. It's an opportunity."

She looked up. "What?"

"The mission trip. I thought you would be excited to go."

"What mission trip? What are you talking about?"

"What are *you* talking about?"

Vivian held a data pad out to Argus. He took it and glanced at it: it was currently displaying a list of names.

"New students," he said, offering it back to Vivian. "What of it?"

"Look again."

Wade bit back his annoyance and glanced at the pad again. *Christian Blain, Anthony Walton, Georgia Winterton.* He scanned through the names but didn't see anything immediately strange about it.

"A lot of high profile students," he said. "And a lot of very rich families sending their children here to study. This is the new group arriving next week, correct?"

"Number twenty-nine."

Wade scanned farther down the list and read the name.

Abigail Walton.

He read it again, feeling his stomach sink.

"Oh..." he mumbled. "Oh no."

"You said they wouldn't find her," Vivian said. "But they have, and she will be arriving in six days."

"I didn't think...I mean..." Argus said, fighting down a surge of panic.

It wasn't possible, especially not on a day like today when everything was going so well.

"And yet, there she is."

"I can't let them have her," Argus said. He clenched his fist in fear and rage. "How the hell did they find her?"

"I don't know, Wade."

"She's not some cattle for them to do with as they please. She's *my* daughter!"

He hadn't meant to yell, yet the words hung in the air. Vivian stared at him, her expression unreadable, and Wade took a few deep breaths. His face felt flush and his muscles were tense.

"Are you done?"

Wade didn't know. He said, "Yeah, I'm done."

"Good, now explain what you meant."

"What?" Wade asked.

"About the trip. You said something about Sector Six."

He didn't care anymore about the stupid trip. He'd just been punched in the gut and had more important things to deal with.

Was this why they'd agreed to the trip? Were they trying to keep him away until they could get verify that she was his child? Was this all part of an elaborate plan?

Get ahold of yourself, he chided himself. No sense jumping to any crazy conclusions just yet.

"We're going on a missionary trip to spread the Word," he explained, distracted. "We leave in a few hours, so pack your bags."

"I'm not sanctioned to leave the Ministry grounds," she said. "I can't go anywhere until I've been cleared."

Wade waved the concern away. "It's been handled. I know you need a chance to get away from the Ministry for a while, and I need a bodyguard."

"Weapons?"

"You still aren't allowed to have any," Wade replied, "and I'm not even going to try and fight the Minister on that one."

"How am I going to serve as a bodyguard if I am unarmed?"

"I'm allowed pistols and blades. I'll give them to you as soon as we are off world."

"Fair enough," Vivian replied with a nod. "So what are you going to do about your daughter?"

"I don't know," Wade replied, biting back his fear. "But she can't stay here. She was supposed to have a normal life away from all of this."

"Her mother must know. She hasn't contacted you?"

"I told her not to reach out. I contact her."

"Maybe you should," Vivian said. "And find out what went wrong."

Argus bit back his annoyance. Of course he was going to contact Samantha and find out what had happened. "I'll do that," he said, forcing his voice to sound amicable.

"They will implant her within a month. And then her education will start."

Wade winced, unconsciously touching a long scar under his chin. It had long since healed over, leaving little trace that it had ever been there, but it was still noticeable when he turned his head.

It was the only scar he couldn't hide with clothes: a slip from an overly rambunctious teacher.

No child deserved to go through that.

Especially his child.

"I'll send her away," he said.

"Where would you send her that the Minister cannot find her?"

"I don't know," Wade said.

"The Minister won't allow it, not if he knows she is yours."

Wade knew that was the truth. If Abigail exhibited the genetic traits sought by the *Ordo Mens Rea*, then she would be kept at the Ministry because of her value to the Ministry as a servant and possible soldier.

And if the Minister knew who her father was, then she would be held out of spite. Argus Wade and the Minister didn't really see eye to eye on a lot of issues, and Givon Mielo was always looking for a way to diminish him.

"One problem at a time," Wade decided. "I still have a few hours before my ship is loaded and we can leave the planet. I'll think of something."

"What about Darius?"

Wade furrowed his brow. "What about him?"

"I heard he gave a speech on Tellus. Riled up the population; he's planning to start a rebellion. He wants to bring down the Republic."

"He's a rabble rouser."

"You know as much as I do what he's capable of," Vivian said. "It won't be long before he has an army at his disposal. Especially with Maven and Alyssa working alongside him. Those two are dangerous."

Wade shrugged. "It isn't my problem."

"The Minister still thinks you helped them escape."

"Then the Minister is wrong," Wade said. "I warned Darius against leaving. And I sure as hell didn't want him to start his own private war. What does he think he can accomplish? There are always rebellions. At least, four were started just last week."

"Not like this," Vivian said.

"*Exactly* like this," Wade countered. "They crop up, fester, and are crushed. One Capital ship can bring down an entire Sector, and we have thousands. There is no chance of Darius succeeding, so why would I help him escape and risk myself in the process?"

"So you aren't planning on joining them?"

Argus hesitated. "So that's what this is about?"

"I know *you*."

Heat rose in his cheeks. "You *think* you know me," he replied, "because we're friends. But don't pretend like you understand my mind."

"You were close with him," she said. "He looked up to you as a mentor, and you helped teach him."

"That doesn't mean I'm responsible for *his* mistakes," Wade said. "I know my place, and I'm content with my lot in life. Now, if you'll excuse me, I have some *actual* problems to deal with without you lecturing me."

Vivian nodded. "I'll gather my things and be at your ship in three hours."

Wade didn't reply but instead walked away. His hands were clenched and he felt anger. But, just as much, he was terrified. He was afraid of what would happen to his daughter, but he was just as afraid of what would happen to him when the Minister found out he'd been hiding her from the Ministry.

Best case scenario, they would just kill him.

Most likely, however, things would be far worse.

3

Two hours had passed and Wade had nothing to show for it.

He sat in his study—it was a plain gray room with a desk stacked with forms and data pads—and listened to the silence. His palms were sweaty, and he couldn't seem to get enough air into his lungs. He'd felt lightheaded and weak ever since Vivian told him the Ministry had found his daughter.

It was an intractable problem, something he'd always known was possible but believed couldn't happen. His stomach was upset, and he was fighting back panic as he thought out possible solutions to his problem.

Potentially, he could refuse his daughter admission to the Ministry. He had that authority. She would be sent home, but that would generate a report directly to the Minister and it would have Argus signing off on it. That would be as big a red flag as Wade could manage to raise, and the Minister could easily overrule his decision and recall Abigail.

He could also fabricate an illness for her, which would have her sent to the hospital for treatment, but that would be just as ill-advised. Best case scenario it would buy him a few days' respite while they ran tests on the young girl. She would end up here anyway, and the Minister would again have a report on his desk when they found out she was fine.

In fact, virtually anything he did would generate a report that would get him killed.

He pushed the worry aside, trying to calm his mind down. He turned to the stack of minor problems on his desk that had been piling up over the last few days. Forms he had to sign, requests to fill, hundreds of little problems that were easier to manage: flowers for the funeral of an important Aristocrat, coronation ceremonies for new buildings that were requesting Ministry presence at their coronation. He signed a few forms and let out a deep sigh.

"I don't know what to do," he mumbled, rubbing his face with his hands.

As if on cue, there was a ping on his communicator.

"Yes?" he asked, clicking it on.

"The Hummingbird is ready," Gary said on the other end. Gary was one of the Ministry mechanics and one of Argus's oldest friends. A regular guy; something rare to find here at the Ministry.

"Okay," Wade replied. "I'm on my way."

He clicked off the communicator and leaned back in his chair. He was out of time, and there was nothing he could do except wait it out. Maybe the Minister wouldn't find out that Argus was Abigail's father.

He hated the idea of what they would do to her here at the Ministry, but there was no way he could stop it without making it worse.

He grabbed a few datasheets off of his desk—the pressing issues that couldn't wait while he was away—and headed out the door. The halls were empty. Most of the students were in class this time of day, learning about the galaxy or their place in the universe. With their rich and important parents, that place was high on the food chain.

Most of them didn't even know Argus Wade or the *Ordo Mens Rea* even existed. They didn't know about the beatings or the implants or the ones who didn't survive training. They didn't know about the odd manifestations members of the Order could create that couldn't be explained.

They saw the Keepers, sure, but they had their own stories for what had happened to them and why: bad students who angered the Ministry, heinous criminals being given a second—albeit brief—chance at life. The children at the Ministry who weren't members of the *Ordo Mens Rea* didn't have a clue that some of their students wandering these halls were different.

Argus hated them.

He passed a group of girls clustered around a classroom, giggling to themselves.

The sound of a choir singing hymns spilled out of another doorway. Argus couldn't help but grind his teeth.

Argus found himself in the hangar, still absorbed in his thoughts and feeling lost and confused about what he was going to do. He was usually good at compartmentalizing, but this was too much.

He could go about his day like nothing was wrong and pretend he was happy. He could blend in, pretend to be normal. But this was the first time he had to face the idea that he might be out of time. This might be the end of everything.

He pulled out his communicator and dialed a number. It wasn't saved into the device, but one he had memorized for just this occasion. The call was answered almost immediately on the other end.

"Thank God you called," a woman said immediately. Wade winced. He could tell Samantha had been crying. "I've been worried ever since they took her. What are we going to do, Argus?"

"I don't know," Wade said. "I wish I knew, Sam. How did they find her?"

"The tests," Samantha replied. "They administered them at her school, but they didn't tell us it was going to happen. I didn't know or I would have kept her home that day."

Wade rubbed his face. "Do they know?"

"About us? No. They never even asked any questions. They just came while we are at home having dinner and took her. I...I would have called but..."

"I know," Wade said. If she had communicated with him on an unsecured line the Ministry would have discovered their relationship immediately.

He heard Samantha start crying again. "Wade..."

"I'll look after her, I promise."

"Will they...Will they hurt...?" she couldn't complete the question, but Wade knew what she meant. She'd seen his scars.

"Yes," he replied. "It's part of her training."

The Hummingbird ramp was open and waiting. He saw Gary appear at the top, a rag in hand. The mechanic waved and started walking toward Argus.

"Listen, I have to go."

"Wait? Can't you just send her home? Or away? Anywhere but *there*."

"I can't. If I do, they will kill both of us and they will still find her and bring her back to the Ministry."

"Then send her somewhere outside their reach!"

"*Nothing* is outside their reach," Wade replied.

"Sir," Gary said, nodding as he approached.

"Listen, I really have to go. I'll call you as soon as I can," he said. Then, lower he added, "I love you."

He hung up as Gary got closer and slipped the communicator in his pocket.

Gary was old and freckly with a receding hairline and large eyes, and Argus had never seen him without gray coveralls and carrying one tool or another. He was a good man, someone that Argus really respected and enjoyed being around. They often talked about ships and mechanical work.

But right now Argus didn't want to talk to anyone. "Not now, Gary."

"Something wrong, sir?"

There was no way Argus could explain anything that was going on to Gary. "No. Never mind. What do you need?"

A data pad stuck out of Gary's pocket. He rubbed his hands on a rag, then pulled the pad out and flicked it with his finger. "The ship had a thorough washing and is loaded. The engine looks to be in top shape."

"Good. The crew?"

"Your pilots are already on board. One is from Sector Six so he's also your guide," Gary said. "Guy named Jack. Other one's an ass, and I didn't catch his name. The soldiers are prepped, and they'll need to be picked up off of Denigen's Fist on your way."

"They aren't being dropped off here?" Argus asked. Protocol dictated that the warship delivered them to the Hummingbird personally, not the other way around. It wasn't an inconvenience, exactly, but it could be seen as a slight to the Ministry or Wade. *A more prickly man might be offended that the Captain—*

"Captain Schmidt died this morning. Denigen's Fist closed all operations until after his funeral. No ferries running so they can't get the soldiers out here like they are supposed to. You'll have to pick them up if you still want to take them."

"Dead?" Argus said, frowning. "He was fifty-eight, wasn't he?"

"Seventy-three, sir," Gary replied. "Sickly for years."

Seventy? I remember his inauguration ceremony. I didn't realize he was so old. Argus swallowed and shook his head. I didn't realize I was that old. "God grant him mercy," he prayed.

"God already did," Gary said with a chuckle. "Guess he went peacefully in his sleep. When I get that sick, I'd want some of that mercy, too."

"He was a good man."

"Wonder who will get sent up as the new Envoy," Gary mused.

Argus shrugged. "No one, most likely. Envoy's serve for life when they join a Capital ship. Portia Nace is the Envoy aboard Denigen's Fist."

"Oh," Gary replied. "I thought they went out when the new Captain came in."

Argus shrugged. "Sometimes. If the Captain and Minister die in battle, then the new Captain sends out a request. Hell, once a Captain sent his onboard Minister into combat to die just so he could get a new one. Kind of barbaric, so they made a new dispensation to work around that in unusual situations."

"So they could kick Portia out of they wanted to?"

"Well, not exactly. Portia would need to be dead, and she's only in her forties, so that isn't likely to happen."

"Or they have to ask."

"Yeah, and that looks bad on the Captain since the Envoy is the spiritual leader of the ship. If that does happen, a Captain can specifically choose his Minister."

"Ah, so they ask you to send them someone. Doesn't matter who."

"Basically," Argus said. "We can't really refuse because Capital Ships are essentially sovereign planets, apart from the rest of the government. If they request someone, then that person ceases to be a part of the Ministry and can do whatever they..."

Argus trailed off.

"...want?" Gary offered helpfully. Argus didn't even notice.

"Gary, I need to go," he said suddenly.

"What's the rush?"

"I have to send a message," he said. "A very, very important message."

He didn't wait for a response but took off for the ramp to his ship. He could send the message from his Captain's quarters.

There is precedence for it, he told himself. Captains have complete and total authority over their ship, so if the Captain wants something it happens.

Captains didn't usually last very long. It was a cutthroat world with a lot of competition and high stakes, but the reward was almost inscrutable power. They were autonomous entities, capable of enacting justice on behalf of the entire galaxy with few repercussions.

A great many of them were trigger happy lunatics, bordering on paranoid, desperate to prove their value to the ruling Aristocracy and First Citizen.

Captain Schmidt hadn't been like that. He was a good man, fair and honest. A good peacetime leader. He chose Portia Nace as his Envoy, making her the religious leader of his ship. That made her the embodiment of the Ministry, and thus God, equal even to the Minister himself while aboard Denigen's Fist. Portia was friendly and matronly, prone to overindulgence and long-winded sermons.

If the Captain *did* want to remove Portia without killing her, there was a special request that had to be made. It was, essentially, a wartime edict, but one which Argus could fulfill personally. They would send Portia home and request a new Envoy.

And the only catch...the *only* requirement was that the new Envoy was a member of the Ministry.

Like his daughter.

It was unheard of, but not entirely. One of the greatest Ministerial Envoys in history, credited with spreading the world to two thousand and twenty heathen worlds, became a ship's Envoy when he was seventeen years old. His life was shrouded in rumor and exaggeration, but the root facts were incontrovertible. It happened a thousand years ago, and he also wasn't six years old like Abigail, but it meant it was possible.

Argus could sell the idea to the new Captain by saying he would have the opportunity to groom a new Envoy to the position. Acclimate her to the ship over time and have a true champion of the faith that the crew would come to treasure.

Argus pressed the button to open the door to his chambers, at least thirty times in his haste. He fell into the chair in front of his terminal and it flickered to life. He didn't know which Captain was slated to inherit Denigen's Fist now that Schmidt was gone, but he could worry about that later.

He began composing a message, addressing it simply 'Captain.'

It is with the greatest pleasure that I am able to offer my congratulations on your promotion. I regret, however, that I must be as blunt and direct as befits your position and rank.

I am aware that the current Envoy onboard the Denigen's Fist is Sister Portia Nace, an excellent and superannuated woman. However, it is my duty to ensure that the continued operation of Denigen's Fist is both satisfactory and beneficial to the Ministry as well as yourself. I would also like to inform you that, should you wish to discuss a possible replacement for the Sister, I might have a more than adequate option...

He finished drafting the message on his communication terminal. He let out a long breath of air and leaned back in his chair, torn. If he sent this, he would be committed to following it through. There was no going back. If the Captain decided to take the message straight to the Minister, then

Argus would be murdered, and his daughter would likely be tortured anyway.

But if the Captain liked his proposal...

Argus reached out gingerly and hit the 'send' key on his terminal. *This is either the cleverest decision I've ever made.*

Or the worst.

4

"What now?" Vivian asked.

Wade was in a good mood. They were only an hour from receiving launch clearance and things were falling into place. He hadn't received a reply from his message to Denigen's Fist, but he was almost certain what the response would be. It was an insane proposal, but brilliant; any Captain would be thrilled to have someone so young aboard their ship.

Envoys were considered the Captain's equal and many members of the crew deferred to them because of the spiritual aspect of their station. They represented God's might aboard a ship. A six-year-old girl would pose no threat to the Captain's authority.

The Captain would accept his proposal and his daughter would be safe. The Minister wouldn't even have reason to look into her parentage because it would be the Captain submitting the request for the girl. Argus's name wouldn't be on any of the paperwork.

Sure, it might be strange for the Captain to request someone so young, but once she was aboard Denigen's Fist she would be outside the Minister's reach. She and Argus would be safe.

Most important, she would never be beaten or tortured, and she would never receive one of those God-awful implants. She could live a normal life like little girls were supposed to.

Well, mostly normal.

"Now we travel to Sector Six. We'll make a stop at Terminus along the way for supplies, and we should be there within a few weeks."

"What kind of supplies?" Vivian asked. "I thought we were fully stocked?"

"Machinery and equipment. The people in Sector Six are living in the past. They will pay a fortune for new tech."

"Or they will kill us and take it," Vivian said.

"That's why you're here," Argus said. "I make deals, you keep me safe, and Jeremiah preaches on behalf of the Ministry. Everyone wins!"

"Everyone?" Vivian said coolly. "What about your daughter? What happens when you get back?"

"It's taken care of," Argus said.

Vivian narrowed her eyes.

"Don't look at me like that."

"What did you do?"

"I'm *not* going to do anything. But there is a very good chance that the oncoming Captain of Denigen's Fist will put a request in for a new Envoy in the next few weeks."

Vivian stared at Wade.

"Stop looking at me like that."

"The Minister will kill you."

"Maybe," Wade said. "But he won't be able to kill her."

Vivian hesitated. "No, he won't, but you'll still be dead."

"And I'm okay with that," Argus said. "When you have kids, you'll understand."

"You mean 'if.'"

"I mean 'when,'" Wade said, smirking. "Besides, if things work out how I think they will, no one will ever know what happened anyway. I'm not really planning on dying because of this."

Vivian shrugged. "No one ever does."

"Have you spoken to the new pilot yet?"

"Not yet," Vivian replied.

Wade nodded and headed out the door. The ship was sleek and compact and impeccably clean. He'd purchased it a few months ago using Ministry funds for these sort of missions, and he was careful to ensure it was only assigned to missions he was participating in. He technically didn't own the ship, but he'd be damned if anyone else was going to be allowed to use it.

"Something else," Wade said. "Do you mind bringing the Cudgel as well?"

"My ship?" Vivian asked. "Why?"

"We are bringing a lot of soldiers because its new territory. and I want to be sure—"

"You want more cargo space," she said, making a tsk-ing sound and shaking her head. "It's all about profit to you."

He raised an eyebrow. "Would you prefer I lie? I'll give almost all of the money we make to the Ministry, so it's for the benefit of everyone."

"You're something else."

"Does that mean you'll do it?"

"Fine."

He nodded. "Good, I'll send one of the pilots over—"

"No way," she said. "I'll fly my own ship."

"Fair enough," he said. He clicked open the door to the cockpit. A man in his late twenties to early thirties was sitting at the controls. He had wavy brown hair and round cheeks.

"Oh," the man said, jumping up from the chair and standing at attention. "Uh...sir."

Argus laughed. He couldn't help it. "Sir? No one calls me sir. Call me Argus."

"All right," the man said.

"And you are?"

"Jack. Jack Lane. I'm the pilot."

"I think that last detail was implied."

Jack didn't seem to have a good answer.

"Where's the other one?"

"He's, uh...sleeping, sir. I mean Argus. In his bunk."

Argus nodded. "Are you ready to fly this thing?"

"I believe so. I've never been trained on anything this advanced, but I think I understand the controls. The autopilot will do most of the work, I'm just here in case of a malfunction or abnormality."

"And you are our guide?"

"Sir?"

"You grew up in Sector Six before moving to the Core."

"Yes," Jack said. "But it's been many years."

"What should we expect?"

"There are several planets, loosely connected under a Royal Family. Geid and Eldun are farming planets, but Eldun isn't politically stable. Geid is where I grew up. Most of the crops are shipped off of that world to feed the Capital Planet, Jaril."

"Where would you recommend we start?"

"Jaril might not let us land. They don't like the Republic, and they sure as hell don't like outside Religions. They will probably attack on sight if they know you are with the Ministry. But if you go somewhere else without at least checking in at Jaril then there could be consequences."

"Is there much travel between Jaril and Sector Four?"

"Almost none," Jack replied. "But the warp routes are fickle and many ships are lost each year. Too many stars in close proximity, so every few years the gravity changes and routes need to be adjusted. Most people just don't risk it."

Argus nodded. It was what he was expecting. His government had never bothered to expand into Sector Six, marking it simply 'uncharted territory' on regional maps. It wasn't worth the risk. Terminus was a small planet at the farthest edge of Sector Four, butting up against Sector Six.

The problem was, they would need to fly close to Tellus if they were going to make it to Terminus. Tellus was where Darius was starting his little rebellion, and even though it wouldn't pose a threat to the galaxy, it would certainly be a problem for Argus's little ship.

He doubted they would notice, though. Tellus was a backwater planet, rundown and old. They probably wouldn't even have radars capable of detecting ships this small.

"In general," Jack said, "they pretty much hate the Republic back home. Especially on Jaril and Eldun. They consider us to be an Empire, expanding and stealing as we go. If they know where we come from..."

Argus thought about it and then shrugged. "So we don't tell them we're from here. We'll say we're traders from Terminus. Won't be a difficult disguise to pull off."

"Sounds good," Jack agreed.

"All right then," Argus said, smiling in excitement. He slapped Jack on the shoulder. "Let's head to Sector Six!"

Chapter 2
Sector 6 – Geid
Argus Wade

1

Geid was a smaller planet than Argus was expecting.

That wasn't to say it was small but compared against Axis it was barely a dot. Argus touched his ship—the Hummingbird—down just outside one of the larger cities, Averton. A few seconds later the other ship traveling with him—the Cudgel—touched down as well. The Cudgel was Vivian's personal ship, a little blocky merchant class vessel that had seen its fair share of wear and tear.

Argus Wade found himself to be in high spirits as they traveled; the prospect of what he had done by sending his message to Denigen's Fist was simultaneously terrifying and exhilarating: if he was caught, he would be killed, but if things went according to plan than he would be simultaneously saving his daughter and undermining the Minister, a man he hated more than most others.

They were landing in a parking lot of an abandoned robotics factory, so it would be a significant walk to meet his clients in the city. Averton had a population of just under five hundred thousand with a median age of forty-two.

"We are cleared to land, right?" Argus asked. It wasn't his first time asking the question.

"Yes," Jack said, "we are cleared."

Jack had grown more comfortable around Argus during the trip, and Argus found him to be good company despite being stiff and unassuming. They disembarked from the ship and headed out to meet Vivian, exiting her own vessel.

The air reeked. Agricultural planets often smelled terrible, and Geid was no exception. Argus found himself gagging as he stepped off the landing platform and covered his mouth with the back end of his shirt.

He heard a chuckle from nearby and shot a glare at Vivian.

"This is not bad," she said.

"It smells like manure," Argus replied.

She shrugged. "There are worse things. Lower your shirt before you offend someone. The smell will pass."

"You mean I'll get used to it," Argus said. But he did drop the edge of his shirt back down. The smell made him gag again, but he forced his mind to ignore it. "I'll get used to having little flakes of fecal material stuck in my nasal cavities. That is *so* reassuring."

"Better than flakes of dead people," Vivian said softly. Argus looked at her incredulously.

"Is that supposed to make me feel better?"

"Just perspective. No matter how bad things are, they can always be worse."

Argus just stared at her. "You are quite the ray of sunshine, aren't you?"

Jeremiah cleared his throat, drawing their attention. They were all dressed like civilians from the region (courtesy of Jack Lane, their pilot) and looked out of sorts in the loose fitting brown clothing. Especially Jeremiah: he was a man in his late fifties and had never worn anything outside of his customary Ministerial robes.

Jeremiah had shaved his head and applied a glossy substance that gave it an extra sheen. That had taken him about an hour's worth of preparation. Vivian had done up her raven hair in a bun, which had taken nearly as long. Wade's hair had that ruffled look of someone who'd just gotten out of bed; that had taken him almost three hours to prepare, though his hair was receding more than he'd remembered.

"We need to get moving," Jeremiah reminded them. "We have many people to speak to and not a lot of time."

Then, the short bald man turned and strode toward Averton. Vivian and Argus exchanged a glance and then followed. They decided to keep the soldiers on board the Hummingbird, at least for now. They didn't want to draw extra attention: as hard as it would be for them to fit in, having twenty soldiers walking by their side would make it impossible.

Plus, Geid was supposed to be a peaceful planet, so soldiers shouldn't be necessary. Worst case scenario, Wade had Vivian to protect him.

"Here," he said, handing her a stack of pamphlets.

"What are these for?" she asked.

"You give them to people and they read them. Then they give them to other people who also read them."

"I mean why are we passing out pamphlets? Did Jeremiah make these?"

"No, I did," Argus said. "Seemed like the easiest way to do our job without having to talk to people. I offered Jeremiah some but he didn't seem interested."

"He doesn't trust you," Vivian said.

Argus affected being hurt. "He doesn't? How could he possibly not?"

"He thinks you make a mockery of his religion," Vivian replied.

Wade shrugged. "I never *asked* to join the Ministry. Hell, they never asked me either. My life is just trying to make the best of a bad situation."

"And I don't judge you for that. But it's clear you don't care much about the Ministry or Jeremiah's God."

"Why do you say that?" Argus said, miffed. "I don't think it's clear at all that I don't believe."

"This is a missionary trip," Vivian explained, "and you made pamphlets."

Wade narrowed his eyes. "What's wrong with pamphlets?"

"Nothing," said Vivian, "if you are trying to dilute your religion down to the equivalent of a travel destination. This is a *missionary* trip, Wade. We have a very specific purpose, and a true believer would find your pamphlets offensive. Jeremiah won't object, of course. The Word of God is the Word, and any method of spreading it is worthwhile. But he is still offended."

"I don't get it. Why?"

Vivian sighed. "The fact that you don't get it is why Jeremiah will never trust you."

Argus frowned and looked at the picture of smiling people on the cover of his little booklet. "The Minister thought my pamphlets were an excellent idea."

"Exactly," Vivian said, then she hurried to catch up to Jeremiah. Argus trailed behind, even more confused. Enormous crop fields flanked the road on both sides, recently harvested and stretching into the distance. They passed the occasional copse of trees that hadn't been cut down for farmland.

Wade pulled one of the pamphlets out of his satchel and frowned down at the glossy cover.

"There is *nothing* wrong with pamphlets."

He stuffed it back into his bag and rushed to catch up.

Chapter 3
Sector 6 - Geid
Traq Lane

1

"**S**tupid head!"

It was the cleverest thing Traq could think of to say, but his harsh words were greatly diminished by the giant grin on his face. He wasn't mad; he rarely got *mad* at his friend, but Everett wasn't playing *fair*.

Traq wielded a curved and gnarly stick with both hands and chased after his blonde friend, swinging wildly in the air and laughing. He wasn't quite as fast as he wanted to be on his stubby five-year-old legs.

Everett was only two years older than Traq but almost twice as big in height and girth. Traq had just passed his fifth birthday a few weeks earlier but was small for his age. He didn't know that, though. He didn't, in fact, know a lot of kids his own age at all. Everett was one of his few friends.

Everett giggled as he dodged around an oak, waving his own stick in the air behind him and breathless.

"You aren't fast enough!" Everett taunted.

"That's because you cheat!" Traq said, stopping and panting. "Heroes *never* run away!"

Everett stopped and turned to face his opponent, grinning. "Heroes *always* run away from scary aliens. Especially scary aliens that look like *you*."

And with that, Everett turned and fled again. Traq took off after him, but with his shorter stride, he couldn't catch up. Frustrated, he threw his stick at Everett, watching it hit the dirt and bounce twice well short of his enemy.

Everett stopped running, rotating slowly to face Traq with a grin on his seven-year-old face.

"And now the scary alien doesn't have a weapon!"

So it was Traq's turn to flee, weaving through the towering pines and firs to ward off his pursuer.

His charge scared up a woodland bird. It squawked angrily and burst out of its brush hiding place. Traq dodged to the side with a shout and kept running.

A light breeze whispered through the trees, tasting of pine and amber.

They were in a copse of old trees and thin underbrush roughly a kilometer outside Averton, but their imaginations had drawn them far away. They'd declared this kilometer of territory to be an empty and forgotten world; the perfect location to stage their galactic battle of good against evil.

Traq ducked around another oak, bark and sap sticking to his brown tunic. He was hoping to spot another sufficiently long stick on the ground he could use as a sword. Most were too small, and the only one he found of the proper size immediately broke.

He could feel Everett gaining ground as he burst out of the woods and into a recently harvested crop field.

2

It was the middle of summer, yet Kelvin was restless. No, 'restless' wasn't the right word. *Frustrated*, was. 'Annoyed' fit too, but he wasn't annoyed with anything in particular. Just...life.

The glow of the bright midday sun warmed the woodlands outside of Averton to uncomfortable levels, but a light breeze rolled over the hills to cool it back off. They were walking in the shade alongside a wooded area. The leaves to the boy's left and stalks of grain to his right danced gently as the wind whistled past. It was one of the many sunny days of the season, reminding people why Geid was renowned for its simple beauty.

Remy walked to Kelvin's left and Scott on the right, the former out of breath and the latter practically bursting with energy. Remy had finally stopped ranting and complaining a few minutes earlier. His rasping voice had been replaced by the soothing sounds of nature around them. But Kelvin knew it was only a temporary lull.

There was always a lot for Remy to complain about.

"You should have held on better," Remy suddenly repeated for the fifteenth time. He eyed his little brother sharply. Scott lowered his gray eyes toward the ground for a brief moment and then shrugged.

"I'll do better next time," the smaller brother said.

Scott was lithe in stature with a big nose and freckles. He was filled with boundless energy. He was also nice and friendly to people, well loved by all of the adults who knew him.

At least, he was when his brother wasn't around.

His older brother, Remy, was almost ten. His features were entirely different: he was stocky like his father with wavy black hair, brooding eyes, and the face only a mother could love. *Actually, I'm not even sure,* Kelvin thought quietly, *that his mother could love that nose.*

Though he'd never say something like that out loud; the brothers looked nothing alike, and Kelvin occasionally kidded them that Scott must have been adopted.

Something rustled in the woods. Probably an animal.

"I mean you *really* have to hold on. If he bites you, he bites you, but you gotta hold on."

"I *know*," Scott said, a whine in his voice. "You don't have to keep telling me."

"You had a hold of his tail. If you just held on for another few seconds, I would have been there to grab hold."

"You were there," Scott said with an exaggerated gesture. His blonde curls bounced on his head. "You were *right* there. You *could* have jumped on the dog like you said you were going to."

"I was lining up to tackle the sucker," Remy countered defensively. "But you let go before I could."

That was as far as Scott would argue. He looked up to his big brother: if Remy said he was about to tackle the dog then Remy was about to tackle the dog.

Not that it mattered anyway. The dog got away. It didn't make Kelvin unhappy. Remy liked to hurt animals. Kelvin didn't.

There was a crash.

Someone screamed.

Kelvin Caipton jumped to the side with a sudden yelp as something small and brown crashed out of the woods next to him. He raised his hands defensively and stumbled onto his butt, heart jumping into his throat.

The 'creature' staggered off balance and landed face first in the dirt right next to him.

He instantly regretted his yelp when Remy burst out laughing.

And he felt even more cowardly when he realized his 'attacker' was a kid. A kid several years younger than himself, no less.

"You frigging wuss," Remy said, guffawing. He lifted the little kid off the ground and dusted off his shirt. "Is this big bad monster gonna get you?"

"Yeah," Scott echoed, following his brother's lead. "He gonna get ya?"

"Shut up," Kelvin mumbled, his face heating up. "I was just caught off guard, is all."

Kelvin looked over at the small kid that had almost run into him. "Hey," he said to the newcomer, hoping to change the subject. "You okay?"

Kelvin was pretty sure he'd seen the kid around somewhere. Traq, maybe. Yeah, his name was Traq. They both lived in the same city, but it didn't have a dense population. There was only one school with about four thousand students. Maybe that was where he remembered him from. He wasn't sure.

He looked to be around four years old and scrawny, with short black hair and a confused expression on his narrow face.

The confusion disappeared a moment later, replaced by a wide grin as the kid leapt over and yanked a stick off the ground. He wielded it with both hands as he spun to face the woods. "I'm not a kid! I'm a giant miniature space alien! Stand back while I destroy this scum!"

His proclamation was followed a second later by another figure bursting out of the woods and leaping into the clearing, waving his own stick. "On guard!" he shouted, oblivious to the onlookers.

Everett Wells, Kelvin realized. The only kid in school with a rich father.

Everett avoided most kids at school because they would pick on him and steal his money. He avoided Remy like the plague because Remy's father was a drunk, and Everett's father fired him from the robotics facility a few weeks earlier.

And Remy wasn't about to forget that.

"Get him," Remy shouted.

Kelvin didn't particularly dislike Everett, but he didn't like him either. He stepped forward and caught Everett's arm before he could get away. Everett had a terrified look in his eyes as he understood what he'd stumbled into.

"Get away from him!" Traq shouted, jumping to his feet and raising his stick.

Remy whirled and punched out, catching Traq in the ribs. He was almost twice as big as Traq, and at least twice as strong.

Traq fell to the ground, dropping his stick and grunting in pain.

"Get lost," Remy said.

Traq stood up slowly. "Let him go," Traq said, his voice high-pitched and squeaky.

"Or what?" Remy asked, narrowing his eyes. Traq didn't answer, just continued to stare at Remy. "Or you'll stop me from doing this?" he asked, turning and punching Everett in the stomach. Everett grunted and then moaned, a pitiful sound.

"No!" Kelvin shouted. Traq charged Remy.

It was too late. Remy spun and threw his fist, clobbering Traq just under the eye. It sent the small kid flying. Kelvin winced as Traq collapsed to the ground, dazed.

Remy stood over him, triumphant.

"Want some more?" he asked, but Traq was barely coherent. "Didn't think so."

"Remy, you didn't have to hit him so hard," Kelvin said.

Remy turned to face him. "He's just a little brat," he said, then punched Everett again. "And if he knows what's good for him, he'll stay do—"

Remy was suddenly flying through the air. He hit the ground several feet away and fell to his side with a grunt. Confused, Kelvin looked around, trying to figure out what happened.

Then it hit him, a blast to his chest. It felt like a huge weight slammed into him, knocking him back and pushing the air out of his lungs. He hit the ground and nearly blacked out, trying to suck in air.

When Kelvin was finally able to breathe, he forced himself to sit up. What he saw shocked him.

Traq was standing over the pair of brothers, small, spindly and panting with the broken stick in his hand. Scott was unconscious with blood running down the side of his head and Remy was cowering in the fetal position.

And he was begging Traq to stop.

3

The expression of pure rage on Traq's face matched—or maybe exceeded—what Kelvin had seen in Remy's eyes.

Kelvin Caipton blinked, wondering if the world had gone crazy, and tried to stand up.

"Don't move!" Traq said sharply, stepping away from Remy. He went to a small pile of rocks.

Kelvin froze in place. Traq picked up a stone, eyed the edge, and dropped it, then picked up another. *Oh god*, Kelvin realized suddenly, *he's searching for one with a point.*

"Traq," Everett mumbled, picking himself off the ground, his voice shaking with mingled fear and shock. He looked disoriented but otherwise unhurt. Kelvin touched the side of his own head, and the fingers came back wet with blood. "We should go."

"Not yet," Traq said, picking up another rock.

"Traq, please, my mom will get mad."

At the mention of 'mom,' Traq seemed to relax. He shook his head and took a deep breath, blinking repeatedly. "Yeah..." he said, absently dropping the rock on the ground. "I guess we should go."

And like that, the look of rage was gone. If Kelvin hadn't seen it he would never have believed Traq was capable of such anger.

Remy and Kelvin were still lying on the ground and Scott was unconscious. The sight of blood on his friend's forehead made Kelvin's stomach twist painfully, but he didn't dare move. He barely even breathed as Everett and Traq walked away.

About six meters farther up the wood line, Traq stopped suddenly and dove into the woods. "Yes! My new weapon!" he said, stepping out of the trees with a long stick in hand. "This is my war blade, and I'm the hero now. You get to be the space monster! You can't catch me!"

And then he was gone, disappearing into the woods like a phantom. Everett hesitated for just a second—possibly judging how the last few moments had fundamentally changed their relationship—before obediently chasing his friend into the woods.

I bet he never catches him again, Kelvin thought.

I sure wouldn't.

Another thirty seconds passed. A chickadee sang from above. It then fell silent as if sensing the somber mood. The wind whistled past, pushing his hair in his face. Kelvin gingerly picked himself up off the ground. He went over and helped Remy stand up, ignoring the fact that his big brutish friend was crying.

They stood, staring at the spot of woods the others disappeared into. A long few minutes passed before Remy turned to Kelvin. All traces of anger were gone, replaced by equal parts fear and awe. "He threw me."

"Threw you? How? He's tiny," Kelvin asked.

"No man, not with his hands. With his *brain*. His eyes...turned purple."

Kelvin didn't know what to say. He turned around to wake up Scott but froze when he saw three figures off in the distance watching them. One was a short man with light skin and wavy brown hair, one a tall man with graying hair and a mustache, and the other was a tall woman with raven black hair.

They were wearing brown clothes that looked plain and cheap, but Kelvin could tell the group didn't fit in. They weren't from around here. They were watching, shocked looks on their faces.

Kelvin watched them for a few moments and then the three turned and hurried down the road.

Chapter 4
Sector 6 – Geid
Argus Wade, Traq Lane

1

"What the hell was that?" Jeremiah asked, rushing on. The shocked and terrified look on his face would have been hilarious to Argus if it wasn't for what had just happened. "What the *hell* was that?"

"What was what?" Vivian asked mildly. She pretended like she was calm as she fell into step behind Jeremiah, but Wade could see it on her face. She was just as shocked and unsettled as Jeremiah.

"...That!" Jeremiah said, gesticulating wildly. "Whatever just happened back there?"

Argus took a deep breath. "I don't know what you're talking about," he said. "I saw some kids fighting, but it isn't our business to get involved."

"He did something," Jeremiah argued, waving his arms. "That kid flew when the little one looked at him."

"Kid was scrappy," Argus admitted. "I'll give him that."

"No way could he win that fight," Jeremiah said. "No chance."

"Well, he did," Argus replied.

"But he couldn't. Not without using some sort of..."

"Jeremiah!" Vivian said sharply. Jeremiah froze and they all stopped walking. He turned to face her. "What are you saying?"

"I'm saying that the kid..."

She stared him down and he trailed off.

"What...are...you...saying...?" she repeated softly.

Jeremiah looked helplessly at Argus. "You saw it?" he mumbled.

Argus shook his head slowly. "I didn't see anything strange," Argus said. "Just a few kids fighting."

"Just a few kids fighting," Vivian agreed.

Jeremiah shook his head weakly. "But..."

"You think you saw something strange," she said, "but it was your mind playing tricks on you. Nothing else."

He didn't respond.

"If you say you saw something different, and it gets back to the Ministry, how will they take it?"

The look on Jeremiah's face was utter defeat as he realized what Vivian was saying. If Jeremiah told the Ministry what he saw, they would think he was crazy, and probably kick him out. There was no way anyone would believe him because something like that wasn't possible.

At least as far as Jeremiah knew.

"It was a crazy fight," Argus added. "Happened so fast."

Jeremiah hesitated, then said, "Yeah, really fast. The little one probably just hit him really hard."

Argus stifled a deep sigh of relief and started walking again. "Just a fight," he said. Then, he added lower, "Just one hell of a fight."

<h1 style="text-align:center">2</h1>

It took almost an hour before Jeremiah had fully calmed down, and by then his own mind had put its internal filter to work. He fully accepted that he'd just missed a part of the fight and nothing untoward had happened. Certainly no child had gone flying through the air for no reason.

Argus envied his ignorance. Jeremiah grew up in the Ministry but knew nothing about the tortured souls he worked alongside. He didn't know that Argus and Vivian had a guillotine resting casually on their necks, and one wrong move would send it slicing down. Unlike Jeremiah, Argus knew *exactly* what had happened in the fight, what the little kid had done to his attackers.

The only problem was he also knew it was impossible.

Argus and Vivian finally found an excuse to slip away, explaining that they would pass out pamphlets while he preached in the center of town. He looked disgusted by their suggestion and didn't even offer to accompany them, saying he could find his own way back to the ship in a few hours.

"It isn't possible," Vivian said as soon as they were alone.

They found an empty stretch of road with stumps and rocks and sat down. Fields of barley swept into the distance, dancing on the breeze.

"Not at all," Wade agreed. "Not without an implant."

"Do they have implants here?"

"The Ministry doesn't stretch this far from the Core," Wade said. "I bet they don't know anything about them. We need to find him."

"That might be dangerous," Vivian said.

"Doesn't matter. What he did...what he is able to *do* defies everything we know about the implants and the Ministry. He could be worth everything."

"To the Ministry?"

"To us," Wade said. Then he winced and looked around. There weren't any people nearby, but he pitched his voice lower. "He means so much to us."

"We have to turn him over."

"We can't," Argus said.

"You know the laws."

"To hell with the laws," he replied vehemently. "After *everything*, you think I care at all about *their* laws? This is different. This changes *everything*."

"It changes nothing," Vivian said. "He's only a child, and our duty is to bring him to the Minister for education and training."

"We can't," Argus said. "He's different, and they will be afraid of him. You know what they will do to him if we bring him in."

"You know what they will do to *us* if we don't."

Argus couldn't disagree. "I know what they will do. We will be Keepers as soon as they find out."

"Exactly."

"And that's it? That's all there is for you? Let them destroy this child as long as were safe."

"Argus..."

"Who cares what happens to him as long as—"

"Argus, stop," she said quietly.

"We can't take him back," he said. "No child deserves that."

"So what, then?"

"We leave him. Pretend it never happened."

She shook her head slowly. "What if Jeremiah says something?"

"He won't, he doesn't even think it happened anymore. He just thinks it was some child's game."

"But what if he mentions it. Just in passing or as a joke. He won't know, but they will. Then they will find the child, know we withheld it from them, and we will be punished even more harshly."

"So what then?" Argus asked.

Vivian spoke quietly. "We handle it."

"We what?"

She stared at him.

"No," he said, vehemently. "No way are we murdering a little kid. He hasn't done *anything*."

"You said yourself what they will do to him. What we can do is far more humane," she said. "And we don't have a choice."

"There is *always* a choice," Argus argued. "We can't sink to that level."

"Then you prefer we all suffer and die?"

He was silent for a long moment. "I'll think of something."

"You always say that."

"And I *always* think of something," he replied. "Maybe our guide can help figure out who this kid is. He used to live here."

He clicked on his communicator. The pilot answered after a few beeps. "Hello?"

"Jack?" Wade asked. "We are looking for a kid we saw earlier. You might know his parents. He was small, maybe seven or eight years old. Curly black hair. Maybe he—"

"Oh, you mean Traq?"

Wade raised an eyebrow. "Traq?"

"Yeah. Not a lot of kids out here. It's mostly adults and elderly because young families move closer to the city. You must mean Traq Lane."

Argus coughed. "*Lane*? Any relation?"

"He's my nephew," Jack replied. "I haven't seen him in about a year. I can find my sister for you, or give you her address. She's outside Averton, and I'm sure she hasn't moved."

Argus glanced over at Vivian. "Yeah. Sure. Give me the address."

3

Traq's house was a squat one-story affair with patched gray siding. It was constantly damp with mildew and faded with age, but impeccably clean. His mother took good care of it.

There was no restroom or shower, but instead, each room held a chamber pot for when the public facilities were closed. Such facilities consisted of a communal outhouse with two attached showers and a hand pump. The ten surrounding houses shared it.

Traq bounded into his home, pushing aside the crimson curtain blocking the doorway with a big grin on his face. It only took a second, though, to realize his mom was upset.

"Did you hurt those kids today?" Rica asked.

The question didn't sound like an accusation, but it was tinged with worry. Her eyes were puffy, but her voice was calm.

It was then he noticed the two other people in his house. A man in a woman in brown clothes sitting in their living room chairs. The man was overweight, barely fitting into the chair, and one of the legs was wobbling. The woman had sharp feature and gray eyes.

"I...I don't know," he said. He wasn't lying, not quite. He *had* wanted to hurt them at the time, but he didn't remember why. At least not anymore. It had been a sudden urge he couldn't and didn't want to resist, and he'd just started using the broken stick like a club. "I think I might have."

It took her a long time to reply.

"Why?" she asked, her voice wavering.

"They wanted to hurt Everett. And then they started hurting another kid. I just..." he didn't know how to explain.

"You did right," she said. "We have to protect our friends."

A tear fell down her cheek, and she brushed it away. Her face was round and always red, and her hair was tousled. She gave him a hug. "Come on, let's go get you cleaned up."

She led him outside, leaving their guests alone in the living room.

4

Argus let out a sigh once they were gone.

"*More*," he said. "She said there were *more* occasions. This wasn't the first time something like that happened."

"No," Vivian replied. "But you saw her face when we told her. This was the worst."

"He can't control it," Argus said. "And it's only going to get worse."

"She knows," Vivian said. Wade shook his head.

"She can't know anything," he said. "Like I said before, the Ministry doesn't reach this far out. All she knows is he's angry."

"She knows something is wrong," she replied. "And that is enough."

"He doesn't understand what he is doing," Wade replied. "It isn't his fault."

"No," she said. "But it is our responsibility."

"I know."

She hesitated and then sighed. "What do you suggest?"

"I'll stay with him."

"What?" she asked, shocked.

"They won't care if I don't come back for a while because—"

"Hang on, what the hell are you talking about?"

Argus was silent for a moment. "I can watch out for him and make sure he's okay, and I can teach him how to control the outbursts."

"You're in charge of half of the Ministry finances," she said. "You think they won't notice when you don't show back up."

"I know it's risky—"

"You're damn right it is."

"But it's the best plan," he finished. "More people will come, and eventually, someone will find him. If I watch the kid for a few years, keep him hidden while the Ministry and Republic explore out here, then we can figure out a more permanent solution."

"There is a more permanent solution," she reminded him, her voice low.

"Then kill him!" he replied angrily. Gesturing, vehemence and disgust in his voice. "Murder that innocent child. Prove that the rumors about you were true!"

Vivian tensed and Argus regretted his outburst. His words hung in the air

"I'm sorry," he said. "That was uncalled for."

"No," she said, "you're right. I'll watch him. Keep him safe."

"Vivian..."

"I don't have anything to do on the Ministry grounds anyway. My absence will be easier to hide."

He hesitated. "I *could* put in a requisition and have you posted out here for a few years. It would be good exposure for the Ministry to have a permanent station in the region..."

"Damn you," she said. "You planned this."

He held up his hands. "It *is* the best option."

She sighed. "I don't know anything about children," she said. He shrugged.

"Neither do I. I think they work the same as puppies. Feed them, make sure they don't poop on the carpet, and you're good."

"Wade...I'm being serious."

"I know," Wade replied. "If you do this, I can't thank you enough."

"You'll owe me."

He nodded. "I'll owe you until the end of my life. Which, for a great number of reasons, might not be too far in the future."

She chuckled. "What are you going to tell the Minister?"

"That you needed some time away to yourself, so I gave you a post out here to keep our supply lines open."

"He'll believe that?"

"He'll believe in the extra money we bring to the Ministry. I'll get you a trading certificate. Start exploring nearby planets and figure out what people need, and I'll have it all shipped to you."

Vivian thought about it. "Okay, Wade. I'll do it."

"Thank you," he said. "I'm sorry, because I hate asking you to leave your home."

She turned to face him just as the curtain opened and Rica stepped back into the room. Vivian spoke low so only Argus could hear. "The Ministry was never my home."

5

"We would like to offer your son a scholarship," Argus said.

Rica was skeptical. "A scholarship? For what?"

"We want to give him an ideal education in one of the greatest cities in the galaxy, on the greatest world in the galaxy."

Rica stared at him. "Why?"

"He deserves it," Wade replied. "He will have the greatest of educations, never want for anything, and one day he will be making decisions that impact the entire galaxy."

"I mean why would you do that? Why him?"

Argus didn't miss a beat. "He's a bright child, full of life, and at the Ministry, we seek to train the best and the brightest to be the next generation. This education is sought after by the richest members of society and costs as much as a small planet, but we want to offer this to Traq for nothing. He will fit in perfectly."

"I...um...I need some time..."

"Of course," Argus said. "Take all the time you need. Of course, there will be sponsored visits for him to come visit you, as well as for you to visit him. Now, if you'll please excuse us, we will return tomorrow for your answer."

He stood up, shook Rica's hand with a bright smile, and headed out into the warm Geid air. Vivian followed, leaving Rica and Traq alone in the little home.

6

As soon as the guests were gone, Rica called her brother. He said he would be right over, and as soon as he was off the communicator, she started crying. She gave Traq a hug.

"They are going to steal you from me..." he heard her say under her breath, her voice trailing off. It was raspy and thick with emotion. "After everything..."

"Mommy," he said, and she set him down on her bed. Traq's eyes fell to his hands, bundled in his lap before him. "Did I do something wrong? I'm sorry I made you upset."

She shook her head. "No, honey. You didn't. I'm just..."

"I'm sorry I hurt those kids."

"I know you are, sweetie."

Traq didn't know what else to say. He was used to his mom being angry with him, but he didn't know how to react to her being sad. There was a whistle at the door, saving him from being so far out of his depth. Rica drew in a deep breath to steady herself, rubbing her eyes with the bottom of her palms.

She made a sniveling coughing sound laden with such depression that it made Traq wince. She walked toward the front door. Traq followed her a few steps behind.

When she pulled the curtain open Traq's uncle stepped inside. "Jack," his mother said, throwing her arms around her brother and breaking out in tears again. "Oh, Jack, I don't know what to do."

Jack Lane gently pushed Rica back and picked Traq up in a big hug. "Hey, little man. How you been?"

Traq hugged his uncle and whispered. "Mom's upset."

He didn't dare show how happy he was to see Jack. He was sure that he was supposed to be sad too. But it was hard to hide his grin.

Jack was a hero and a legend around the city Averton. Someone who not only made it off their forsaken little planet but made it all the way to the Core Worlds.

"I know," Jack whispered back. He set Traq on the ground. "I need to talk to your mom alone for a few minutes and then we can go play Piollo if you want."

Traq nodded and headed off into his mom's room, but he kept the curtain open a tiny bit so he could hear what was said.

"I came as soon as Argus told me. They want to take Traq?"

"They said for a scholarship at the Ministry," she replied. "I almost said 'no way in hell' but then I heard about what he did today. They told me he attacked another few kids."

"Attacked? Was it bad?"

"Very," she said, her voice thick. "He put Remy in the hospital."

"Was it...did he...?"

"Yes," Rica said. "He had to have."

Silence.

"Do they know?"

"They didn't seem to know anything. They said they only caught the tail end of the fight and didn't see what happened."

Jack sighed. "Thank God."

Traq heard his mother sob, and a long minute passed before his uncle spoke again.

"We can't keep him here. You know that."

"But if I keep him inside..."

"Like a prisoner?"

"Jack..."

"He's a kid," Jack said. "What happens when people start asking questions?"

"How does he do it?" she asked. "I've seen him do things..."

"I don't know," Jack said. "If I'd known, all those years ago that he would be like..."

He fell silent.

"I don't know what I would have done."

"I don't care," Rica said. "They can't take him, Jack. He's my child."

"I know, but..."

"After all this time, there is no way I'm just going to—"

"I know, sis."

Rica rubbed her face. "What do we do, Jack?"

"I don't know."

Jack held out his hands and lowered his chin. Traq wasn't sure what they were talking about.

"He was the sweetest baby I've ever seen," Jack said. "But he's different, now. Something changed."

"They said I can come visit."

"You'll like Axis. It's a beautiful planet. Crazy, but beautiful."

"Can they take care of him?"

"If there's anywhere in the galaxy he will be safe," Jack said. "It's on Axis at the Ministry. Safest place in the world for little kids, especially different ones."

"And you'll watch after him?"

"Every day," Jack said.

She was quiet. "Okay, Jack. I'll start packing his things."

Chapter 5
Sector 4 – Alderson
Jayson Coley

1

"That's it?" Jayson Coley asked, staring out the train's circular window into the forest beyond. A squat building had just appeared through the canopy of trees, ahead and above them on their path through the forest. It was the first sign of humanity they'd seen in almost eight hours since debarking on the train. "That's where we are headed?"

"That's it," Richard Dyson agreed with a nod. "The famed Silvent Academy."

Jayson eyed it for another moment. "I thought it would be bigger."

This was starting to feel like a wasted trip. This entire planet was small and uninviting with very little in the way of civilization. They had landed at a small backwater spaceport and ridden a train out into the forest. He'd come here because Silvent Academy was supposed to be the best: it was a military boot camp known for training spies and saboteurs as well as the famed Fists of the First Citizen.

It wasn't open to the public but rather invitation only. Jayson had been surprised and a little suspicious when he got his invitation, and to be honest he wasn't totally sure why he had come out here at all. Jayson wasn't even sure if he would agree to join the academy if they offered it to him. He'd just turned nineteen, and after two years away from home, he was starting to think it might be time to go see visit his family.

Back when he lived on his home world, Eldun, Jayson used to think he was tough. A real badass, and he always planned on leaving and proving that he could make it on his own. He thought he could handle anything the galaxy threw at him.

Nothing dispelled *that* illusion as fast as having his own gun taken from him and pointed at his face.

Jayson stretched out his shoulders and fidgeted in his seat. His legs were cramping from the extended trip, and he had the beginnings of a headache developing behind his eyes. Allergies, most likely. This was a new planet, and it would take his body time to acclimate.

"And I also thought maybe it wouldn't be so far from civilization. Are there even any cities on this planet?"

"I don't think so. It's a training planet. But don't let the size and lack of amenities fool you," Dyson replied, yawning. "It's come by its reputation fairly."

Jayson watched the Academy slip out of sight once more behind the trees and let out a sigh. Huge pines, thick with memories and shadow. Right now they were skirting the side of a great mountain, following a switchback trail ever upward. The peak of the mountain disappeared into the clouds, buried in snow.

"Eight hours on this damned train with nothing to eat but stale peanuts, and the academy looks like a damned hotel."

"I'm telling you, kid," Richard said. "Looks don't tell the story. They only accept a handful of students a year to get the best training possible. Most of us will probably be on the same train tomorrow heading home."

Jayson leaned back in his chair.

"How did you get roped into this?' Jayson asked.

Richard Dyson shrugged. He had a trimmed black beard and cropped hair. His clothing was expensive, a blue silk shirt and tailored pants. He was muscular and athletic, quite a bit bigger than Jayson.

"I grew up on Terminus. Spent my youth on the streets. Learned how to fight. The military wouldn't take me," Richard replied, leaning back and folding his hands behind his head. "Then Darius showed up and I liked what he had to say. I talked to some people, heard about the academy, and hopped the first shuttle here."

"You think they'll take you?"

"I think there's only one way to find out. What about you?"

Jayson thought about it for a second. "I was working with a group. Just a bunch of private contractors doing odd jobs. Mostly security."

"Pays well," Richard said.

"It does," Jayson agreed, "until your client gets murdered. Then no one wants to work with you. Friends disown you. You become a pariah."

Richard whistled. "That's harsh. Do you know who paid for the hit?"

"The guy was an arms dealer on Terminus. All kinds of enemies," Jayson said. "We never figured out who paid to have him taken out. But I do know who pulled the trigger."

"You didn't stop him?"

Jayson was silent for a few seconds. "It was a woman. She did it right in front of me with my gun. Shot him twice from up close. She wasn't at all concerned with me seeing her face or watching it."

"You saw her face?"

Jayson ignored him. "I drew my gun. Or tried to. I'm still not quite sure what happened, but I ended up on my ass with a gun to my head. My gun."

Richard's eyes went wide and then he burst out laughing, slapping his knee. "Wait, wait, wait. You got your ass beat...by a *girl?*"

2

Jayson smiled and shook his head. "I should have gotten my ass *killed*. But she didn't kill me."

"Was she hot?" Richard asked.

Jayson scrunched his nose. "How is that relevant?"

"It's *always* relevant."

Jayson shook his head and sighed. "I don't really know. I closed my eyes and tried not to wet myself."

"You're...what...sixteen?"

"Nineteen," Jayson answered, chagrined.

"Then how could you *not* have noticed?" Richard asked. "Even if she was about to kill you, even if she'd already *shot* you, you should have noticed whether her ass was nice or not?"

"What can I tell you?" Jayson asked, shrugging.

"The truth. Come on, you had to notice *something*. Big breasts, little breasts?"

"You don't give up, do you?"

"Hell no," Richard replied. He scratched his beard. "The last time a woman tried to kill me, I asked her to be my wife."

Jayson snorted. "Did she say yes?"

"I think she eventually would have. It didn't end well."

"Why not?"

Richard shrugged. "She tried again." Jayson laughed. "Come on, man. Give me something. You have to remember *something.*"

Jayson sighed. "Fine. She had little breasts. Green eyes. Shoulder length red hair. Athletic build. Perfectly smooth skin with freckles on her chest because she was wearing a black low cut 'V' blouse and skin-tight pants and...holy hell, I guess I do remember a lot."

"Told you," Richard said. "Even when a woman is about to murder you, there's always time to notice."

"Anyway," Jayson said. "She didn't pull the trigger. When I looked up again, she was gone."

"An angel of mercy."

"Not likely," Jayson said. "She wasn't much older than I am. Maybe she just felt sorry for me."

Richard nodded sagely. "I know I do."

"Anyway," Jayson said, "two days later I got a message. A location and a date along with an invitation card for Silvent Academy. Didn't say why, but once I researched the Academy I figured it out pretty quickly. Anyway, here I am."

"You think it was her?"

"I don't know."

"You're hoping it was her," Richard stated, his voice flat.

Jayson didn't reply. He didn't need to. He adjusted in his chair and looked out the window.

"So you're telling me a girl beats the hell out of you, doesn't kill you, and then *maybe* passed you a message to come to Alderson and join the Silvent Academy, and you *do* it?"

Again, Jayson was silent.

"Wow, you got it bad," Richard said, settling back in his chair and studying Jayson. "You need to let this crush go before it gets you killed."

"There's no crush. She didn't kill me, and I want to know why. I don't like being toyed with."

"Whatever helps you sleep at night," Richard said, chuckling. "I wonder if I was that ignorant ten years ago. I'm thinking yes. Definitely. Hell, I'm probably just as bad now."

"How long has the Academy been here?" Jayson interrupted, changing the subject.

"Six hundred years," Richard replied. "Give or take. And that's if you believe all of the stories. I'm a little bit skeptical. Thinking two hundred sounds more reasonable."

"Still a long time."

"True enough," Richard agreed. "But until a few years ago it was still a Republic training center. Now it's Union and belongs to Darius Gray. Bet your crazy chick didn't tell you that?"

"Is that going to change things?" Jayson asked. "Like how they operate?"

"New management," Richard said. "But otherwise, I doubt it will change much. Maybe the color of our uniforms."

"I doubt you'll wear uniforms," Jayson said. "But I'm not sticking around. I came here to check that message out. I want to know who sent it and why. I'm not trying to get in."

Richard laughed. It was a rich sound, full-throated, and contagious.

"If you think they're going to let us leave," Richard said, "then you're either wishful or a fool."

Jayson blinked. "What do you mean?"

"Whoever told you about this Academy must have left a few things out. When you make the trip to the Academy, it is a trip for their *consideration*. Whether or not they accept you is irrelevant."

"But when I got on the train—"

"They told you that it makes two trips a week, one into and the other out of the Academy. They never said you would get be on both."

"I don't understand," Jayson said, ignoring the sinking feeling in his stomach. "I'm just going as a guest."

"We're all here as guests," Richard said. "But let me tell you a secret. There are no guests at the Academy. Once you board this train, you're only leaving one of two ways. The first is as a graduate of the Academy."

"And the second?"

Richard grinned. "In a bag."

Jayson let out a sigh and leaned back.

"Though, to be honest, that's probably not true either," Richard said thoughtfully. "I'm sure that if you die they just leave you for the animals."

"You're making this up," Jayson said.

"I wish," Richard said.

"Then why didn't you tell that me back at the station," Jayson said. "You *knew*, and you still didn't say anything."

"I figured you knew, too," Richard said with a shrug of his shoulders. "And to be perfectly honest, would it have changed anything?"

Jayson hesitated.

"Didn't think so," Richard said. He leaned forward and patted Jayson on the shoulder. "Look, kid, if it's any consolation, I think you'll do well here. You might even survive a few weeks."

Jayson pointedly chose to stare out the window. He considered trying to jump off the train and escape. But he had no idea how to get back to the spaceport, and even if he did there were no ships there. Sure, he could follow the tracks, but that would be an incredibly long trek, and if they caught him...

And, to be honest, he was fairly certain Richard was lying to him. He'd come out here as a guest, not an applicant. Surely they wouldn't begrudge him the opportunity to *see* the Academy and investigate the message the woman had given him?

Right?

3

They finally came to a stop in front of the Academy. It was a sprawling building, only a few floors high, and rather bland. No observable patterns. No outlandish colors. Just uniform gray bricks and wooden beams. A pockmark on the mountainside.

The seven passengers filed out, dragging bags behind them. The only one Jayson had met was Richard. At the station, he'd introduced himself to one other person: Tricia Jester, a thirty-something black woman with almond-colored eyes and slim figure. She walked with a dancer's grace and kept a holdout pistol tucked in her left boot. She was somber and quiet.

None of the passengers were over forty. Expressions varied from excited to apprehensive. And they all, except Jayson, looked prepared for an extended stay. Jayson hadn't even brought luggage.

The train only waited long enough for its passengers to unload. As soon as they were clear it kicked into motion again, gliding in reverse back down the mountain.

They waited, formed into a line watching the doors. After a few minutes, an old man with a cropped gray beard and leathery skin stepped out into the sunlit clearing. He was shorter than Jayson, only a few inches, and squarely-built. He walked with a limp and leaned against his white cane. His clothes were ivory and loose fitting.

He moved at a glacial pace, stopping in front of them He closed his eyes and took a deep breath through his nose as though in preparation for delivering a great speech.

"Welcome," he said, his voice wheezy. He tapped his cane thrice against the ground before finally opening his eyes. They opened to slits and he smiled lazily at them. It was a friendly smile; a fatherly smile. "Thank you all for coming."

The gathered passengers exchanged glances. Jayson wasn't sure what he had been expecting, but this old welcoming party was definitely not it.

He tapped his cane against the ground again, three times.

"My name is Desmond Eppard. If I could ask a favor, please leave your belongings on the ground behind you. They will be brought to your rooms during the duration of your stay. Supper has been prepared; something to welcome you after your sojourn."

"Thank you," a few guests murmured. The old man smiled wider, his grey eyes twinkling.

"You are most welcome," he said, tapping his cane again and spinning on his heel. It was a graceful motion, unexpected.

He began hobbling the other direction, using the cane for balance. The seven guests exchanged another glance. They dropped their bags and moved to follow Desmond.

Jayson was the last to follow, more than a little cautious. The hairs on his arms and neck were tingling. The woods were thick with shadows. Forbidding. Now that they were outside the train, they also felt deeper.

Standing outside in the clearing alone, he began to feel isolated. He was sure he was being watched, but a quick scan around the area revealed nothing.

Just because he couldn't see anyone didn't mean he was alone.

The thought scared the hell out of him.

Jayson rushed to follow the others inside. They passed the threshold into a lavishly decorated antechamber. Symmetrical staircases climbed to the second level. Thick wooden doors ornamented with silver trim opened into an enormous hall in front of them.

It could hold four to five hundred people if they packed in tightly, but right now it was vacant. Eerily so. The walls were egg-shell white and devoid of decoration.

Inside the hall were interlocked gray benches, very plain and small in the room. Right now those tables were barren, except one near the center.

Jayson could smell food as they approached. His mouth began watering and he could feel his pulse speeding up. A packet of peanuts—complimentary on the train—was the only thing he'd had to eat today, and the spread smelled heavenly.

Desmond sat down first, resting his cane on the bench and easing down. Jayson picked a spot on the opposite side and slid into it.

An old fan spun lazily overhead. Otherwise the mess hall was quiet.

"Please," the old man said with his lazy half-smile. The sound echoed. He gestured toward the dishes and trays spread before them. "Enjoy."

54

Hesitantly, the guests began picking at the various dishes: smoked venison strips swimming in brown gravy, slices of roasted turkey with leafy greens, a thick yellow cream (lemon flavored) poured over cold spinach and kale, a bowl of quartered potatoes bathed in butter and smothered with chives, and spiced sausage wrapped in yeasty bread.

The atmosphere was subdued. At least at first. For drinks there was a pitcher of spiced red wine, a flagon of honey wine, and a sweet green juice that tasted of mangos and passion fruit. There was also a pitcher of water.

Jayson decided to stick with water. Most went right for the wine.

It only took a few awkward minutes before the trepidation evaporated from the atmosphere. The food was delicious, everything cooked to perfection. Jayson helped himself to a thick soup with floating chunks of white fish that dissolved in his mouth.

Silence was replaced with murmuring, the murmuring with conversation. More dishes were uncovered: grilled onions and stuffed green peppers, thick slices of a soft blue cheese, chunks of hard bread fresh from the oven.

Jayson ate slowly. The ostentatious meal should have put him at ease—if they were planning to kill or enslave him, why feed him first?—but it actually had the opposite effect. What Richard said was weighing heavy on him, and he was starting to feel on edge.

There were two things that were wrong: first, no one else came into the room. He would have expected a server or attendant at the very least. It was almost night, around supper time, and yet they were completely alone.

But the more disconcerting fact was that the old man never touched the food. He smiled at his guests, murmured politely when a question was asked, and watched them eat.

Twenty minutes slipped past. They were gradually becoming more boisterous. Many were red faced from the wine. A few were even drunk.

Except for Tricia Jester. She was sipping the green juice, eyes locked on her plate. *She's as worried about this as I am,* Jayson decided.

"What's the game here?" he asked, folding his hands. He stared at the others around him and spoke quietly, in a businesslike tone. It cut through the carousing atmosphere like a knife.

The conversations died slowly. Everyone exchanged confused glances, eyes settling finally on Jayson.

He ignored them, focusing instead on the old man. Desmond was sitting at the end of the table, idly stroking the handle of his cane.

"What game?" he asked wheezily.

"You haven't even told us your name."

"I did," the man countered. "My name is Desmond—"

"I know a lie when I hear it," Jayson said. He heard a few sharp intakes of breath, but he paid them no mind. "I grew up with liars. I want to know your *real* name. And while you're at it tell us the truth. What are we doing here?"

"You were all invited..."

"...to tour the Academy. But that isn't how this works, is it? We're not interviewing you, you're interviewing us. So, if you would allow me to return to my first question, I ask again, what is your name?"

Silence, then, "You have to earn my name," the man said, his voice hard. The twinkle was still in his eye, but there was something else there now. Not anger. Not exactly. But something close to it. Jayson peered into those eyes and saw the soul beneath.

He didn't like what he saw.

"And how do we do that?" Jayson asked. He kept his voice calm, but his heart kicked up a notch.

The man eyed Jayson for a few seconds, his lazy smile disintegrating. It was replaced with a feral grin that showed entirely too many teeth. He let out a long breath, closed his eyes, and whispered, "You survive."

4

Desmond was up in a flash, swinging the cane with two hands like a club. It smacked into the jaw of the closest reveler. A short balding man with a ferret's face. One of the drunkest members in the group. The man collapsed backwards with a yelp, sliding off the bench and thudding onto the floor.

The long table squealed as it was jerked in various directions across the cement floor. The other six applicants all tried to extricate themselves simultaneously, tripping each other up.

Jayson slid his legs free and dropped into a defensive crouch. He wished like hell for a weapon. He wished even more that he hadn't come.

The old man spun his cane. It whistled into motion toward a drunk twenty-something kid with bulging muscles. The first blow landed on the right shoulder and was followed with a sharp *thwack* on the left hip. Both blows echoed through the cavernous hall.

The kid screamed in pure agony, collapsing.

A drunk man laughed, failing to extricate himself from the table. His foot was stuck under one of the bars. The laugh didn't last long, though, before the cane whistled in.

By now the rest were clear. Two people still stood between Jayson and the old man, and he considered making a run for it. He could go for the door before the man could dispatch the others.

He quickly dismissed the idea, however. Where was there to go?

Richard Dyson was still up, Jayson saw. He was backpedaling slowly, but he hadn't turned to run yet. He was apparently having similar thoughts.

Tricia Jester was standing as well, a look of cool concentration on her face. She held one of the serving trays—a metal one, not plastic—as a shield and was circling, keeping a few meters between herself and Desmond.

The only other person still standing was a blonde woman with a sleeveless shirt. She was tall and willowy. She had the face of a badger and teeth bared in an ugly snarl. She'd gathered a butter knife from the table and was brandishing it before her. She passed it from hand to hand. Jayson could tell right away that she was an amateur.

She was the closest to Desmond. He planted the tip of the cane into the ground and leaned on it, staring at her. "Well go on then," he said wheezily, grinning. "I don't have all night."

She feinted low and then attacked high, going for his neck. She overextended, and even if she'd been stabbing a bag of potatoes her attack would have been little more than an inconvenience.

Desmond swiped his left arm up to deflect her clumsy attack and swung the cane in a low arc. It collided with her left knee with a sharp *crack*.

Her mouth opened, releasing an agonized gasp. She fell to the ground, clutching her torn cartilage. The knife fell harmlessly beside her and the old man casually kicked it away.

He rolled the cane over the back of his hand and caught it. "I would not recommend running," he said, pointing the make-shift weapon at Richard. Fifteen meters separated the two men. "Not yet, at least."

"What is this?" Jayson asked. There were a few short utensils—all dull, he realized—that wouldn't do him a lot of good against the cane. He didn't pick one up; that would be tantamount to issuing a threat.

"As you said," the man replied, the smile briefly returning, "It is an application process."

"And what if I'm not interested in applying."

"Then I'll cut your throat and leave you to bleed on the floor," he said. "But that is not the preferred solution."

The woman on the ground was still screaming, clutching her broken knee. Without taking his eyes from Jayson's, Desmond brought his cane down on her forehead in a precise *whack*.

The room fell silent.

"So you're just going to kill us?"

"No, of course not," the man replied. "It is rare that we kill an entire group of recruits. This is simply a lesson. Those four—" he said, nodding at the ground beside him "—had best take it to heart. This is a dangerous place."

"So now what?"

"Now you try to kill me," the man said, taking a step forward. He tapped his cane against the ground and smiled, his eyes twinkling.

"Three against one," Richard cut in. "That hardly seems fair."

"You can attack me one at a time if honor demands it," Desmond replied.

Richard shook his head. "No, no. I meant not fair for us. Can we call in backup?"

The old man didn't respond, just looked at the unconscious bodies around him.

"How about stretching?" Richard asked. "Can we at least stretch first?"

The man scowled at Richard. "Does the lion stretch before stalking its prey? Does a bird stretch before taking flight?"

57

Richard scratched his chin. "So, is that a no?"

"Fight me," the man said.

"And if we don't?" Jayson asked.

"Then this will be quite easy," the man replied.

Jayson let out a sigh and shook his arms out. Tricia was circling with nimble steps, moving so that they were flanking the old man in a triangle. She had a knife in hand and was using the serving tray as a shield.

Jayson moved to the table and grabbed a pair of ceramic plates. He thought to dump food off of them but changed his mind. The plates would be difficult to throw and easy to deflect, and flying food might actually be the best distraction he could hope for.

A few seconds passed and then Tricia attacked. She was quicker than Jayson expected, moving with fluidity and ease.

Her tray came up as a visual distraction. She anticipated the old man knowing she was approaching and used it to break his line of sight. She jabbed low with her knife, aiming for his thigh.

The old man waited until the last possible second before countering. He ignored the shield, spinning his cane in a quick deflection. He knocked Tricia's hand away and launched an attack at her head.

She ducked away from the attack, leaning at an awkward angle. She quickly stepped onto the bench and skidded her butt across the table to create more distance. The attack missed by inches.

Jayson attacked. The old man still had his back to him. Jayson stepped in, kicking at the back of his knee. He moved as quietly as possible and grimaced in satisfaction as his kick landed. It wasn't a clean hit, but even a glancing injury was better than nothing.

Then he jumped back and ducked, anticipating more than seeing the old man's counter. A heavy backhanded swipe whistled past, flying right above Jayson's head.

And that was just what he was waiting for. Jayson stepped in and threw his plates.

From such close range he couldn't possibly miss. He flipped them in the old man's direction, lobbing them as easy targets. In response the old man brought his cane in to deflect. But Jayson had chosen ceramic plates: instead of batting them away the plates shattered, spraying the entire area with broken ceramic chunks and pieces of food.

Jayson used the distraction to sweep his leg. He caught the old man just below the knee and tripped him. Desmond hit the ground with a thud as broken plates landed everywhere, scattering wildly.

Richard chose that moment to wade in, rushing in and aiming a kick at the man's head. Tricia flanked in the opposite direction, going instead for the man's legs. It was a good strategy, difficult to counter.

They had him right where they wanted him.

But they never even came close.

The old man kipped up, landing nimbly in a crouch. He swept the cane through three quick arcs. The first disarmed Tricia with a jolt to the back of her hand. The second hit Richard hard in the foot he was kicking with, and the third landed on Tricia's right temple.

She dropped like a sack of potatoes, unconscious before she hit the ground. Richard stumbled, hopping on one leg while holding his foot and cursing.

Jayson took a few steps back, creating separation. He couldn't believe how fast the old man was, how precise. No motion wasted.

Jayson had spent two years in the militia on his home world of Eldun, learning hand-to-hand combat and weapons training. He would have considered himself moderately skilled, but against this man he knew he was outmatched.

The old man stepped limped away from Jayson, gingerly testing the weight on his left leg. His expression was grim; the twinkle gone from his eyes.

"Bum knee," he explained, letting out a low sigh. He grabbed the knob on the end of his cane and twisted. It rotated ninety degrees and clicked. Then he drew the knob away from the cane, sliding a long and thin blade out of the wood.

It looked sharp.

The old man held the wooden shell in his left hand and the blade in his right.

"I thought this was an initiation."

"It is," the old man said. "But we don't need all of you."

The old man went for Richard first, swiping first with the blade. Richard dodged clumsily, hopping on his one good foot. The feint was followed by two quick jabs with the cane.

The first landed on Richard's thigh and the second thudded on his shoulder. Richard went down with a grunt of pain.

He started to stand back up. A quick kick to his head ended that plan, knocking him unconscious. Jayson was the last one standing, and he knew that if something didn't change he was in a lot of trouble.

He used the momentary distraction to mask his approach, needing every advantage he could get.

Jayson launched a kick, aimed for the man's midsection and kidney.

The naked steel dipped low, moving to intercept his kick.

Jayson barely stopped his leg in time. His leg hit the blade. It sliced through his pants and drew a deep cut along his shin.

The man turned, facing Jayson and holding the weapon at ease. Jayson tested his leg. He felt blood running down the calf, pooling in his shoe, the leg seemed to hold his weight with only a mild throbbing.

Jayson moved to attack again. The old man raised the blade to parry the attack and Jayson was forced to back off again.

"I can't fight against your blade," Jayson said, gritting his teeth against the pain.

The man's smile was brittle. "You can't *win* against a blade."

"Then what's the point? Of any of this?"

"Respect."

"Respect would be you lowering the weapon," Jayson replied. "And letting me walk out of here."

"You aren't leaving," the man replied. He twirled his blade and took a few steps closer. "Until you are finished training. Or dead."

Jayson backed up a few steps, leaning against the table. His hand closed on one of the metal serving trays. His left shoe was squeaking and leaving little globs of blood behind. "Can I take option three?"

The man hesitated. "Option three?"

"The one where I kill you and walk out of here."

The man barked a laugh, stroking his beard. He bowed ever so slightly. "You are more than welcome to try."

Jayson rushed forward, whipping the tray around in an arc. He didn't aim for the man, but instead attacked the air in front of him. The man backed up, not bothering to deflect, and Jayson swiped again.

Another feint. The man ignored it. Jayson cursed and quick stepped forward. His opponent took another step back, but Jayson was quicker. This time the attack that came aimed for the man's head.

It was easily deflected by the blade. Jayson twisted his wrist as the two pieces of metal collided, turning the tray ninety degrees. He let the blade slide along the tray, holding it between him and his opponent. He didn't have any moment for an attack, but that wasn't his intention. He put the large flat tray right in the man's field of vision, breaking line of sight.

The old man jabbed out with the wooden cane in his left hand. Without sight, however, the attack was misguided. Jayson caught the cane with his right hand and yanked hard. The man stumbled forward off balance, pulling back hard on the wood so that Jayson wouldn't disarm him.

Jayson let go, releasing the tension, and then shot in at his opponent's legs. He shouldered into his thighs and caught the calves before the old man could sprawl, then used his lower center of gravity to lift him into the air.

And then Jayson brought him down as hard as he could, slamming him onto his back as hard as he could. It should have been enough to knock the air out of his lungs. Then he could take the man hostage and use him as a bargaining chip to get out of here.

Jayson leaned forward and raised his head...

...and saw the pommel of the cane-sword coming at his face.

It hit Jayson right in the temple. Even without good positioning the close quarters attack hurt. He saw stars fly as his head jerked back and cursed his stupidity. He punched out, aiming for the man's ribs, but too slow. The old man rolled with surprising agility, twisting his leg and pushing Jayson off.

Another jab of the sword hilt hit Jayson in the cheek. He managed to turn his head enough to make it a glancing shot, but it still hurt like hell. Jayson ducked and shoved, trying to extricate himself and get clear, but the old man held on. Now his takedown was working against him. The old man launched two more precise hits on Jayson's shoulder, sending agony rippling down his left side.

Then he slipped free. Jayson forced himself to a knee and then wobbled to his feet. His head was spinning and his face hurt.

The old man stood five feet away, red faced and breathing in short, ragged breaths. The mirth was gone from his eyes. So was any forgiveness. Jayson watched, the world spinning and stars exploding in his vision, as the old man stalked in. His white beard was mashed against his face and his bright clothes were stained with blood.

Jayson's blood.

The sword came first. No feint. No games. Just an attack meant to kill. Jayson threw himself to the side, and the attack meant for his chest drew a long gash on his side instead. He ducked and weaved away from the man, but it did no good. His opponent was relentless. A cut on his arm was followed by another on his leg. He was moving slowly and his right arm wouldn't work very well. He couldn't raise it any higher than his chest.

But that didn't matter, he couldn't see well either. Blood as running from a cut above his eye. *I can't keep this up for long,* he knew.

It didn't matter. Jayson side stepped, and his footing betrayed him. The bloody shoe slipped on the smooth marble floor and he landed on his hip. A groan came out his lips as pain flashed through his body.

One hit on his arm knocked him to the floor, and a second hit his diaphragm, knocking air from his lungs. His already blurry vision felt like he was looking through a tunnel, and he didn't even have enough breath to moan.

He watched as the old man towered over him, breathing in ragged grasps. The old man set his bloody sword on the table and knelt down in front of Jayson.

Jayson lay on the groaned, writhing and wondering if he would ever breathe again. His head felt like it was going to explode from lack of oxygen, and he was starting to black out. He longed for the peace of it but was terrified at what would happen next. Would he be killed? Tortured? Left for dead in the forest? What would they do to him if he blacked out?

The man knelt in front of him and wiped his brow with the back of his sleeve. He hefted the wooden cane and leaned forward.

A few seconds passed with only the sound of their breathing separating them.

In a soft voice, the old man said, "My name...is Alexander Robertson."

Then he brought the cane down, hitting Jayson right between the eyes. The world went black.

Chapter 6
Sector 1 – Axis
Abdullah Al Hakir

1

"Come on!" Eddie Boleman shouted, pumping his palm against the metal bench press. "You got this! Come on!"

Abdullah strained his muscles, blowing air in a tight stream through his lips. The weight bar moved up an inch and then stopped. It felt like he was pushing against a brick wall. He could feel the blood pumping through his skull, making him lightheaded.

All of his attention was on the weight, straining through his energy reserves and willing it to move. He grunted with exertion and pushed.

It didn't budge.

"Come on, God damn it!" Eddie growled, leaning over the bar. He looked angry and frustrated. And he wasn't even the one trying to lift the damn weight! "*Lift* the damn thing!"

Abdullah struggled for a reply. Something like 'how stupid can you be to think that helps?' or 'shut up, moron.' Something clever. Instead, he groaned in exhaustion, which didn't have quite the same impact.

The weight bar slipped an inch lower and his arms threatened to give way. That vein in my forehead is going to explode, he decided. Blood will start spurting, and everyone will run away screaming. Then I'll drop the bar on my neck and suffocate. And Eddie will finally stop bugging me about always going to the damn gym.

But no blood spurted out. Nor did the bar move. Abdullah groaned through the fog that was his mind. An eternal second slipped past...

And that was it: the heavy bar plummeted down, thudding hard against his chest and knocking the last bit of air free. Eddie was slow in catching it.

"Damn," Eddie muttered, helping to lift the bar off his bronze skinned friend. "I thought you had it that time."

Abdullah drew in a ragged breath, then another. It hurt. His heart had climbed up into his head and was working to punch its way loose.

"So did I," he managed to gasp, sitting up. The world spun in confused circles before reorienting. "But my arms disagreed."

"You were so close."

"If by 'close' you mean 'never stood a chance,' then yes. Yes, I was," Abdullah said. He accepted the offered towel and wiped sweat from his face. His arms were tight, on the verge of cramping.

"One more set?"

Abdullah stared at Eddie like he was crazy. Eddie raised his hands in surrender. "Okay, okay. How about we get lunch instead?"

"Sure," Abdullah agreed. Eddie lifted Abdullah to his feet by his left arm like he was a pillowcase instead of a one-hundred-kilogram man. Eddie was twenty-two, several years younger than Abdullah, still enjoying the boisterous energy of youth.

His real name was Alonso Edward Boleman the Third. He was a trust fund baby with golden locks of hair and a smile that melted girl's clothes off. His body was rippled with muscles, and his eyes were an intense shade of green.

Those were good reasons for hating Eddie. The problem was, Eddie was also one of the nicest guys Abdullah had ever met, friendly and outgoing.

Abdullah was a few inches shorter than Eddie, and his body was built stockier. He had to work to keep himself in shape. If he even looked at food too long he gained weight.

And it didn't go to his arms or legs but settled right in his abdominal region. He shaved his head in anticipation of the receding hairline his grandfather left him, and his eyes were plain charcoal. Walking anywhere with Eddie was equivalent to being invisible.

Eddie was his closest friend. He had abandoned the life of privilege to join the military, planning to earn everything.

Abdullah finished wiping off his face and checked his watch. Late morning still. Normally he would be on duty this time of day, guarding the armory. But, after Captain Schmidt died they were all given a few weeks of leave to relax.

It had gone past the point of being a pleasant vacation. Abdullah had run out of things to do.

"How long do you think until we get moving again?" Abdullah asked. His nerves were settling back down. His muscles had set into a dull ache of mixed pleasure and pain.

"Another week at least," Eddie replied.

"*Another* week?" Abdullah asked incredulously. He had to remind himself that Eddie was only guessing. There was no official word from higher up about when Denigen's Fist would start out on its patrol routes again.

He hoped like hell that Eddie was wrong: another week of downtime would have him rocking quietly in his quarters muttering about potatoes.

They walked through the second-floor gym heading to the exit. They passed by various pieces of shoddy or well-used gym equipment. This was an enlisted soldier's gym, which meant that it wasn't well taken care of or cleaned despite being one of the busiest on the ship.

The entire room smelled of stale sweat and body odor. It was mostly empty and had been since leave started. Most of the crew were down on Axis partying and blowing their hard earned cash on alcohol.

"You really think it will be that long?"

"At least," Eddie said. He waved his hand in front of the sensor and the door sprang open. They strode into the silver and white hallway. "They still have to do the Pass of Command ceremony. And that's only *after* they pick the new Captain."

Abdullah groaned. Eddie smirked and kept walking.

The Central Walkway stretched off in both directions, running the length of the ship on all floors with various elevators for the crew to move up and down. Right now the two men were near the middle, one level above the engines and two levels below the midshipmen crew quarters.

Normally, the CW would have been packed beyond capacity and they would be swimming through a sea of bodies. Engineers, enlisted men, soldiers; all of the lowest level crew used this hallway to go about their daily lives.

That meant a good twenty thousand crew shared fifteen percent of the ship's space. That was when Denigen's Fist was at half capacity. Abdullah was terrified that the ship's budget would grow and they would hire on the rest of the crew.

About half a kilometer farther down the CW, the hallway opened into a chamber called the Borough. The Borough was a six block open-air structure resembling a city-center. It contained house sized structures built into the walls and a gated Arboretum. It was premium space for the highest ranking crew, Captain, diplomats, and Ministerial Envoy.

It was entirely off limits to most of the crew unless they were assigned guard duty, of course. Abdullah had been there twice and saw the shops and theaters. It could have housed fifteen thousand soldiers with very little effort. Last ship census put its population at eight hundred. It was a comfortable place, filled with important men and women.

On the opposite end of the ship was the equivalent chamber for working men and women. That area was less than a quarter the size of the Borough and contained a few shops selling cheap trinkets with three dive bars. It was affectionately called the Belly of the Beast. Everything was for sale if you knew who to ask.

Abdullah hated the separation between enlisted men and officers. High ranking crewman and diplomats considered themselves nobility. They couldn't empathize with the soldiers who served them. To do that would make them aware of the impoverished conditions of their crew. And that would make them feel bad, and everyone knows it is a tragedy for a rich person to feel bad.

The men and women down here were the lifeblood of Denigen's Fist. Abdullah had dreamed about the Imperial Navy as a child. He believed in the promised glory and honor. He bought the propaganda wholesale and signed on for a three-year contract. One day, he promised his mother and father he would be a great man. One day he would be important.

He'd never imagined just how wrong he could be.

No one gained rank in the military through skill or ability. Status was bought with blood, the kind flowing in veins, not spilled in combat. If someone was born into the right family, then he or she could make something of him or herself. For everyone else…

They lived in the Belly of the Beast.

"Who do you think they'll get to replace Captain Schmidt?" Abdullah asked. They diverged off the CW onto a side hallway.

"Dunno," Eddie said with a shrug. Their footsteps echoed down the silver luminescent walls. "Someone just like him, most likely."

Abdullah snorted. "There's no one 'just like' Captain Schmidt. At least not one that could make Captain."

"True enough. They'll replace him with an old ass-hat arrogant enough to think God chose him for the job."

"Yeah," Abdullah agreed. "And we need it."

Eddie coughed, then laughed. "What?"

"Schmidt was soft-spoken. He treated us well," Abdullah explained, "And things were bad."

"How so?"

"Training, preparation. If we were attacked tomorrow, how do you think we would handle it?"

Eddie shrugged. "No idea. We've never been attacked."

"That's just blind luck."

"No, not blind luck. Peacetime," Eddie argued. "We don't need a war general. We need another lazy bastard like Captain Schmidt. So what if training goes to hell? So what if we can't fight our way out of a wet paper bag? We don't need to be ready to kill people."

"If you want peace, prepare for war," Abdullah said.

"If you prepare for war, then you plan to start one," Eddie replied. "If you have a powerful new weapon, you want to try it out. The problem with training for war is you get good at it. And when you're good at something, you want to do it. Writer's like to write. Singers like to sing. And killers like to kill."

"No one likes to kill."

"Bullshit," Eddie said. "A lot of people like to kill. A lot more would if they ever got the chance."

"I disagree."

Eddie shrugged. "Even if you do, will you risk me being right? If you're wrong, we get fat and lazy. If I'm wrong, a lot of people will die."

"We're disciplined to *not* start killing people," Abdullah replied, "just because we can."

"True. But keep in mind that the human race is notorious for self-deception and denial. We would never go to war just because we can. Yet, if we want to start a war, we will look for any reason possible to justify it. If we prepare for war, we'll find one."

"What if one finds us?" Abdullah asked. They turned another bend in the hallway and ducked into a stairwell. There was an elevator going down, but it was closed for repairs. It had been out of commission for the last three years. "What do we do then if we aren't prepared?"

"War with whom?"

"The Union," Abdullah said.

Eddie laughed. "Not going to happen."

"Why not?" Abdullah asked.

"They aren't a threat."

"They could become one."

"Not a chance," Eddie replied. "Darius doesn't want open war. He wants what every good dictator wants: money and respect. Let him be King of the misfit planets for all I care. He isn't a threat to us."

"That doesn't mean we shouldn't be prepared in case he attacks," Abdullah argued. "He might."

Eddie shrugged. "Then we'll deal with that when it happens."

They headed up a flight of stairs off the main roadway. Six flights of stairs left Abdullah winded and starving. Once they reached the floor of deck two they stepped into one of the agricultural centers.

Machines whirred all around them, lifting and raising acre-sized platforms of dirt with various fruits and vegetables growing in them. The air smelled faintly of manure and pesticides and was quite warm. There was a constantly rotating system, fully automated. It stacked the pallets either in shadow or under powerful lamps that simulated sunlight from twelve different ideal suns, depending on the plant type. The cavernous chamber was half a kilometer wide and twice as long, spanning the length of the ship.

Other than the plants and machines, though, the room was empty. The domed ceiling and curved walls stretched up and around them like a cocoon, reminding Abdullah of the domes down on Axis. The ceiling even had the faint appearance of a sky above them. Though, unlike the domes on Axis, Abdullah could tell that this was all fake.

"This place gives me the creeps," Eddie said, echoing Abdullah's thoughts. He rubbed more sweat from his forehead and started walking faster. Eddie lengthened his stride a bit to keep up.

"Especially when it's empty like this," Abdullah agree.

"Definitely."

"It sounds irrational, but..."

"You don't have to tell me," Eddie said. "Any robotic machine that can lift several tons of dirt this easily can't be trusted."

Abdullah chuckled. They were about halfway across the floor when Eddie suddenly stopped. Abdullah went a few more steps and then glanced back curiously.

"Sweet onions," Eddie explained, wide-eyed. Abdullah cocked his head to the side confused. "We *never* get those."

"Yeah, so?"

Eddie pointed off to the left. One of the enormous pallets sitting out in the open was full of short green stems sticking out of the soft dirt. "There are thousands of them."

"Thousands of crew, too," Abdullah said.

Eddie made a beeline toward the pallet. "They won't miss a couple."

"What if there's an alarm?"

"Then I guess," Eddie said, kneeling down and grinning wolfishly, "that you'd better get ready to run."

He grabbed a few of the stems and gave them a quick yank, ripping three sweet onions out of the dirt.

Abdullah couldn't help himself: he cringed. He expected a high pitched alarm to blare overhead, bringing guards running to defend the crops.

But nothing happened. It was quiet. Eddie dusted the onions off on his gray shirt and stepped back. He cocked his head to the side and looked around curiously. "Do you hear that?"

Abdullah cocked his head. "I don't hear anything."

Eddie peeled the wrapper on one of the onions and took a big bite out of the center. It crunched. "Exactly. No alarms."

He tossed one to Abdullah, who caught it deftly, frowning. "This is stealing."

"It's only stealing if we get caught."

"No. it's still stealing even if—"

"Oh would you lighten *up*, Abdullah," Eddie said, a faint red tinge coloring his cheeks with anger. "Sometimes you should just shut your mouth and eat the damn onion."

Abdullah hefted the onion in his hand and finished wiping off the exterior. Eddie took off again, munching on his onion and heading down the aisle. Abdullah had to admit, it looked good. They were ripe, fresh and juicy, and he loved onions. And, they *were* one of those treats that enlisted soldiers only occasionally received. The best vegetables were reserved for the tables of higher ranking men and women.

And Eddie was right: they would *never* notice a few missing.

With a sigh laden with regret, Abdullah carefully reburied his onion in the pliable dirt and hurried to catch up with his friend.

2

Abdullah scooped some more of the spaghetti into his mouth, wishing for some cumin. Or paprika. Or hell, just about anything that would give the lifeless paste some flavor.

"That's the worst part of being on this ship," Abdullah said, holding up his fork with some noodles twirled on it. Eddie was leaning over his own plate, shoveling food—that would immediately burn back out with his high metabolism, the bastard—into his mouth. He paused and glanced up, waiting for Abdullah to finish. "If food isn't bland and unexciting, they won't serve it to us."

"You kidding? This stuff is great. It's just like my old nanny used to make."

"I thought you said your nanny couldn't cook."

"Exactly," Eddie said. "Tastes like home."

Abdullah chuckled and pushed his plate away. That was the other thing about the military. They gave him about two thousand calories more than he needed with every meal.

"My mom cooked once," Eddie said thoughtfully. "It was one of the six occasions in my life I even saw her. You know: when she wasn't away on a business trip."

"Oh? What did she cook?"

"Some fish with lemon seasoning. It was actually really good. I let my sisters have the leftovers to be nice. One of my biggest regrets."

"You're such a saint."

"Hey, this was back when I thought my mom loved us. I never knew it would be the only meal we got from her," Eddie said. He slid his plate away and let out a long burp. "What about you? Your mom, did she ever cook?"

"All the time. But you would have hated it."

"Why is that?"

"It was only on the rarest of occasions that she mixed food in with her peppers," he said. Eddie laughed.

"Yeah, you're probably right. I don't handle spicy food very well."

"After a while," Abdullah said, "you can't taste the spice anymore. Or the flavor. Then the only way to enjoy food is to spice it even more. It's like a drug."

"One day you wake up with curry on your face and two days missing from your life and you think, 'was it all worth it?'" Eddie said with a laugh. He leaned back and yawned. "Holy crap that spaghetti was heavy. I think I need a nap to digest."

"Lazy."

"I'm going to go sleep the rest of the day away."

"All right," Abdullah said, standing up and carrying his tray toward the trash can. "I'll see you tomorrow then."

Eddie nodded. Abdullah headed back out into the hall, then after a few quick turns ended up back in the Central Walkway. It was still early in the afternoon, which meant he had the whole day ahead of him, but nothing to do.

He considered heading for the Belly of the Beast. He had some money he could spend. He knew he shouldn't—he was a habitual saver, putting all of his money into accounts for when he retired. It might have been a bad choice to join the military, but he was going to be damned if he got nothing out of it. Yet, even then, spending a few credits here and there couldn't hurt.

In the end, though, he decided it wasn't worth it. He wasn't big on socializing in bars, preferring to spend his leisure time on side-projects or studying. He had some books he liked to read: non-fiction historical textbooks, mostly. Fictional stories were about as useful as video games.

He was about halfway down the CW to his quarters when he heard a buzzing sound. He scanned in both directions. The hall was empty of passengers, and it took him a moment to spot the noise. A little gray robot hovering about four feet off the ground was making its slow way down the hall. Abdullah moved to the side to let it pass.

It didn't, though. It stopped and hovered in front of him, rotating. He heard a clicking sound, reminding him vaguely of the sound chickadees make in large groups. Abdullah frowned and tapped his ear, turning on the translation device in his ear. It didn't work very well, being one of the cheapest models.

"...your data pad," the device translated.

"I'm sorry," he said to the robot. "Can you repeat your message?"

"Yes, of course," the robot said, this time using a voice modulator. The robot's voice sounded like a young woman, clean and crisp pronunciation with no noticeable accents. "I am here to deliver your invitation to the Pass of Command ceremony, which will happen two days hence. It is contained here upon your data pad."

Abdullah frowned. "You must have the wrong person. I am Abdullah Al Hakir."

"I'm quite aware, sir," the robot said.

"Then maybe there has been some mistake. I shouldn't be getting an invitation."

"Nevertheless," the robot said. An envelope-shaped object slid out of a thing opening along the side of the robot. "Please, take the device."

Abdullah grabbed the thin device and pulled gently. It slid out of the robot. It was a data pad, one of the most expensive models. It would be several months of paychecks at Abdullah's rate.

"This is some kind of..." he said, but when he glanced back up, the robot was gone.

He sighed and swiped a finger across the glossy screen. It shot to life, illuminating the invitation. The robot was correct: it was to the Pass of Command ceremony, and it was for him.

Maybe it was a prank. He thought for a few seconds, but couldn't imagine anyone playing a prank like *this*. It would be dangerous if they got caught and at the very least expensive. The high ranking officers would certainly not consider it funny.

But if it wasn't a prank, and it wasn't a mistake, then what was going on? He was about as low ranking as the officer pool went. He shouldn't be getting an invitation like this.

He could worry about it later. He slid the invitation in his pocket and continued trekking down the hall.

Chapter 7
Sector 1 – Axis
Captain Kristi Grove

1

Kristi Grove adjusted the rigid fabric against her hip with a growl. *Won't this elevator move any faster?* She picked at one of the blue straps digging into her skin, deciding that as soon as this wretched party was over she would burn it.

Jamar, her assistant, had insisted she wear it, explaining that it could be seen as an insult to show up to the Nolantis household in military garb.

Quite frankly, she considered it more of an insult to *her* that she had to show up in a stupid dress. Misogynistic. Why must women be expected to wear dresses? *Because they are the fairer sex,* was Jamar's response each time she asked.

Which pissed her off even more. 'The fairer sex' was a chauvinistic descriptor used to further subjugate women into complementary roles. Emphasize base instinct qualities of attraction and then associate them with worth.

Unfortunately, women could be just as much the problem as men. It was Georgette Nolantis, the wife of famous diplomat Timothy Nolantis, that Kristi was here to impress. Women were backbiting and manipulative where other women were concerned. Especially women like Kristi, who didn't fit their worldview.

The darkest corners of hell were reserved for women who scorned the achievements of other women.

But that was neither here nor there. She was here to make a token appearance at Georgette Nolantis' house party and nothing more. The Nolantis family had been good to her, especially with the most recent promotion. She had to maintain alliances.

At least, that was what Jamar said, and she usually deferred to him in matters of strategy. Personally, she would have had no problem burning bridges.

The invitation was for Commander—*Captain,* she self-edited—Kristi Grove, plus guest; she doubted that the Nolantis family meant she could bring her servant along, but the plus one was hers to decide. She didn't care. Jamar Paskin might be shorter than most men. And fatter. And balder. But he was an invaluable asset. If she were a modest woman, she would admit that she wouldn't have attained all she had without him.

Jamar stood next to her in the elevator wearing a charcoal tuxedo and white gloves. His receding hair was combed back, and he wore gold-rimmed glasses. His left hand rested on his ample stomach and the right was folded behind his back. His smile was an easy one, well-practiced and inviting.

Her cheeks hurt just watching him smile.

"I'm surprised," she mumbled just loud enough for him to hear. "You are normally dressed so extravagantly. To see you in something so...plain...it makes you seem almost human."

"Sometimes the simplest attire speaks the loudest," he said, raising an eyebrow at her. "My attire stands as a backdrop to make you all the lovelier," he spoke loftily, like a noble. "Though I can only do so much. Be sure to smile. And arch your back. You have ample assets. Put them to good use."

She scowled at him. "'Assets'? I'm not here to find a husband, Jamar. I didn't even intend to come until you talked me into it."

"It would have been an offense not to," Jamar reminded her. She snorted in response. They were passing the eighty-seventh floor. The top thirty levels were all penthouses, and the Nolantis family owned the entire ninety-fourth. "Rest your left hand on your hip as casually as possible."

"Sometimes I wonder," Kristi said, "why you don't treat me with more respect. You are my servant. And yet you dare give me advice?"

"I am here to make sure you purport yourself with dignity. You hired me for a reason."

"No, my family hired you," Kristi replied.

"And with good reason," Jamar repeated. "They are worried that you'll snap without guidance. You're like a walking time bomb."

"Careful," Kristi replied. "Bombs are dangerous for people who stand too close to them."

"When you walk," Jamar said, ignoring her, "be sure to sway your hips."

Kristi sighed. "*Why* would I sway my hips?"

"Men like to watch swaying hips. It's all about where you want attention to be. Some women want to draw it to their faces. Some their bosoms. And some try to draw eyes...lower. For you, I recommend lower."

"You are saying I shouldn't want people to look at my face?" she asked.

He shrugged. "On the contrary, your face is quite pleasing. Except your nose. It is too big. My point is, you exercise regularly, so your ass is marvelous."

She rolled her eyes. "Any more suggestions?"

"If you truly want my assistance," Jamar said, eyes twinkling, "then I would dilate your pupils, remove your brassier and rub ice on your nipples. Then I would teach you how to pout properly."

Kristi stared at him in shock for a second and then narrowed her eyes. "I don't pout."

Jamar held up his hands in conciliation. "Hence, we'll have to be satisfied with a few minor corrections. Arch your back, sway your hips, and please, please, please don't speak unless you absolutely have to."

Kristi bit back her retort and turned back to face the door of the elevator.

"Jamar?"

"Yes, ma'am," he asked.

"Remind me to kill you when this is over."

The elevator buzzed and slid open. Kristi walked smoothly into the crimson hallway, hearing a drawn out sigh from behind her.

"Yes, ma'am," Jamar said.

2

"You're stiff as a board," Jamar mumbled, sipping a martini. "Try to relax."

"I'll relax once we leave."

"Ten more minutes."

"Five," Kristi said.

"Ten," Jamar reiterated, "or after the first party leaves. We cannot be seen exiting first. That would not do at all."

Kristi sighed. They were standing against the back wall. The main room where the party was being held was enormous, which was quite impressive. On Axis, space was at a premium, and this location must cost a few million credits each month.

A chandelier hung in the center with candles.

Kristi hated it here amidst the fancily dressed people. Milling. *Milling.* Even the word was annoying. Shake a few hands. Allow men with no skills and creepy smiles to kiss her knuckles. It was disgusting.

"That group," Abdullah said with a discreet nod, "is making its way toward us."

"What?" Kristi replied. She glanced over the group. "They aren't even moving."

"They'll be coming here next to speak with you," Jamar said.

She squinted at them. "How can you tell?"

"Don't squint," Jamar said, still staring straight ahead. He sipped his drink. "Their body language screams it."

"Do I know any of them?"

"You've met one previously. Kathryn Quinlan in the red dress. You met her three years ago at her father's factory. Ask her if she approves of the gift you sent her father last month and inquire after his recent hospitalization."

"What did I send him?"

"An old model hunting rifle, modified and engraved. The family collects them. Jacob Wellington is her guest with the red bowtie. He works for her company and is from a merchant family. Let her introduce him but don't shake his hand."

"Why not?"

"His family is too low."

"The other woman?"

"Rachel Gates. She is the guest of Consular Peter Gavriel."

Kristi narrowed her eyes. She knew of the Consular but had never met the man personally. He was a soulless calculating murderer and smuggler. "That's Peter, in the tuxedo?"

"We aren't here to fight," Jamar chided.

"He's a scourge on the Republic. A cancerous cell spreading corruption."

"He's also rich and has lots of friends," Jamar said. "That scourge could destroy you in an afternoon."

"When I'm Captain, he will have no power over me."

"And until then he can destroy you. Play nice."

Kristi stared daggers at Jamar and then blew out a breath, willing her anger to go with it. She forced a smile on her face.

"Stop smiling," Jamar said. "It makes you look constipated."

She sighed.

The group was moving toward them, talking amongst themselves. Jacob Wellington was a handsome man with wavy hair and a thin face. Kathryn was a frumpy woman in a saggy dress.

Rachael Gates was supermodel pretty, standing a full three inches above Kristi with blonde hair and green eyes. Her expensive silver dress dropped to her ankles, but it included a cut all the way to her thigh on the right side. It was modest while still showing plenty of skin.

Peter Gavriel was a thin, black man with perfectly white teeth and silver rimmed glasses. His lips were curled in a half-smile, and he wore a charcoal gray suit.

Jamar drifted away, too low born to be introduced, leaving her alone with the approaching group. She waited until they had come up to her and then turned first toward the frumpy little woman. "Kathryn, dear," she said with as much honey as she could muster. "How are you?"

"I am flourishing," the frumpy woman said, delighted. "I didn't know if you would recognize me."

"Of course," Kristi admonished. "Your family has been of great assistance to me and I consider you a closer personal friend. How is your father? Did he like the gift I sent him?"

"He *loved* it," Kathryn said.

"Has his health improved? I nearly died when I heard he was in the hospital!"

"Quite a bit. He had a bout of pneumonia some weeks back but recovered from it quite well. Thank you for your concern."

"It's nothing. I'm happy to hear it."

"And this gentleman is Jacob Wellington, my guest for the evening," Kathryn said. He started to extend his hand. Kristi nodded politely at him but turned her attention to the Consular. Jacob got the message and dropped his arm.

"And how do you do, this fine evening?" she asked, working to keep anger from her voice.

"I am most excellent," the Consular replied, smiling at her. He reached out toward her and Kristi forced herself to offer her hand. She hated him. She hated everything *about* him and the thought of touching him sickened her. But to refuse would be discourteous, which would be tantamount to suicide among these people.

He took her fingers in his hand and knelt down, brushing his lips across her skin. Shivers of displeasure danced up her spine, but she imagined that instead of him kissing her knuckles she was punching him in the face. The thought brought a smile to her lips.

"Congratulations on your promotion," Kathryn said as the exchange was completed. "We were all delighted to hear you would be taking over Denigen's Fist. It was always one of my father's favorite vessels. Did you ever have the chance to serve on it?"

"Ten years ago," Kristi said, "before I was promoted to Commander. This is something of a homecoming for me.

"I am sure you will purport yourself with the highest of honor," Peter Gavriel said.

"Thank you," Kristi replied curtly, aware that she was scowling. She doubted that looks could kill, but was determined to try.

Kathryn, oblivious, smiled at the both of them. "Well it was wonderful seeing you, Ms. Grove, and I wish you all the best in your new position. Jacob, come along."

Jacob flashed his brightest fake smile at her and moved to follow Kathryn. All that was missing was a leash.

"I hope you enjoy your term on Denigen's Fist," Consular Peter said once the others were out of earshot. "Short as it is likely to be."

Kristi bit back her first retort. Then her second. And third. She tried to think of a Jamar-approved statement, and settled for, "Thank you."

"I'll be watching, waiting for you to fail."

She forced herself to take a deep breath.

"And when your world finally comes apart at the seams, I will be there to pick up the pieces."

"Is that so? Because I'll be coming for you to wipe out your very exis—"

"Commander, I believe Sir Nolantis was looking for you," Jamar said smoothly, slipping up beside Kristi and deliberately bumping into her. He turned to look at Peter Gavriel. "Oh, I'm terribly sorry, was I interrupting something?"

The Consular smiled. "No, our discussion has been concluded. I believe we understand each other quite well."

Kristi started to open her mouth. Jamar shot her a warning look and she closed it again. "It was nice speaking to you," she said. Peter grinned and turned to leave, his eye candy following.

"Two days," Jamar said in exasperation. "You need to survive two more days without convincing someone to kill you. And here you are making threats."

"He won't do anything to jeopardize my position. I have too much support."

"He doesn't need *any* support to hire a killer."

"I'm not worried about an assassin murdering me."

Jamar frowned. "And why not?"

"Because *your* job is to keep me safe," she said. "And if you fail, I'll be sure to kill you."

He sighed and pinched the bridge of his nose. "Good plan."

"I thought so. Can I leave yet? I've had enough ostentation for a lifetime."

"A few more moments. The Portman family will be leaving first. We can follow in their wake without offering offense."

"You seem quite convinced."

"I am," Jamar replied.

"How do you know they are going to leave?"

"The same way I always know at parties like these," Jamar said, picking his drink off a nearby table. He took the olive out and bit into it, savoring the flavor. "I slipped a fast acting laxative in Mrs. Portman's drink."

"You did *what*?"

"Only enough to make her uncomfortable. Unless I misguessed the dose. It was a horse laxative, and she looks to be about seventy kilos. It should be having the desired effect in—"

He was interrupted by the sound of glasses crashing to the floor. Everyone looked over to see a middle-aged woman with graying hair holding the hem of her dress and pushing her way through the crowd. A worried look was plastered on her face.

She was pursued by her husband, making excuses.

They disappeared into the hallway. Everyone watched the door in stunned silence.

Kristi fought back a chuckle. She couldn't successfully hide her grin.

"I think that is our cue," Jamar murmured, finishing his drink.

Kristi made her way over to the Nolantis family and thanked them profusely for the invitation. Then she headed into the hallway toward the elevators. She pressed the button and waited for her servant to catch up.

"Jamar," she said.

"Yes?"

"Have I ever told you that you are a horrible person?"

"Every day."

"Good," she said. "That's good."

Chapter 8
Sector 6 – Geid
Argus Wade

1

Wade stood outside the little gray house belonging to Traq and his mother, letting his friend think in silence. It was painful for him. He was talkative by nature, willing to ramble on and on about anything and everything. Vivian, on the other hand, preferred lapses of solitude, and he did his best not to interrupt her thought process.

Argus Wade wanted to get away from here, to leave Geid and return home to Axis. As much as he hated the Ministry, he loved the amenities afforded him. He'd sold the last bits of his cargo, but not nearly at the profit margin he had hoped to achieve. The people on Geid were poor. They couldn't afford to pay extravagant prices for commodities, let alone frivolities.

An eagle flashed by overhead, its enormous shadow trailing along the ground. Argus watched it disappear into the sky. It was quite a beautiful day though a little warm and humid for his taste. It would be strange, he knew, to live somewhere like this. Somewhere so...quiet. None of the ambient city noises he'd grown up with to occupy him. Just the wind and the trees.

He would get bored with it, he knew. The thing about the fast-paced lifestyle was that once you had a taste of it, there was no going back.

A naked child suddenly came sprinting out of the communal bathhouse, laughing and wet and chased by his angry mother. He was maybe three years old. Vivian jumped from the excitement, caught off guard and lost in her thoughts.

"Argus," she said, rubbing her temples. "I can't do this."

"You have to," Argus said. "There is no alternative."

"I don't know anything about children."

"I had some self-help books sent to the Cudgel. They are waiting in your cockpit. *Motherhood and You* seems pretty simple."

She gave him a cross look.

"I'm only trying to help."

She sighed. "I know."

"Keep him busy. See what he likes. I sent a full curriculum for him from the Ministry archives."

"For schooling?"

Argus nodded. "You won't have to worry about his education."

"It won't be enough," she said.

"It's the best of what the Ministry has to offer. A better education couldn't—"

"I'm going to teach him how to survive," she interrupted.

Wade hesitated. "How to fight, you mean."

"They are often the same thing," she said. "His life won't be easy."

"No," Argus said. "It won't. But he has the best person in the world watching over him."

"Flattery, Wade? Really?"

"I meant myself," he said. "But I guess having you around isn't bad either."

She smiled the tiniest bit.

"Just keep yourself busy, and I'll be in touch as often as I can. If you need anything, money, supplies, you let me know."

"We'll be fine," she said. "I think I found a good cover, as well."

"Oh?"

"Warships. They talk about enormous vessels twice the size of Capital Ships. At least."

"I heard mention of that on Terminus, many years ago," Wade said. "You don't think they are truthful, do you?"

She shrugged. "They might have some technologies we don't know about on them. From what I heard, they were lost centuries ago."

"If they exist, I'm sure we would have heard about them."

Vivian thought about that for a moment. "You might be right."

"I always am."

She ignored him. "Nevertheless, it still gives me something to do. An excuse for why I'm not returning alongside you."

"Thank you, Vivian," he said. "I mean it, from the bottom of my heart."

She glanced at him and nodded. "Take care of yourself, Wade."

Then she turned and headed into the small house.

Chapter 9
Sector 6 – Geid
Traq Lane

1

Traq was terrified.

When the woman—Vivian Drowel—had shown up at the door, she'd had a short conversation with Rica and then after a tearful and quick goodbye she'd taken Traq by the hand and led him away from his home. His mother packed him a bag and told him she loved him.

He was in a daze following Vivian through Averton. She was tall, a lot taller than his mother, with high cheekbones and dark hair. She held onto his hand with an iron grip and pulled him whenever he slowed to try to look over his shoulder.

His eyes were wet, but he didn't dare cry out loud. The first time he'd started sobbing she gave him a long look.

He'd heard stories about horrible witches eating little children when they misbehaved. He tried really, *really,* hard not to think about those stories.

They walked in silence. Averton was a place he knew by heart. A sprawling metropolis of narrow streets and bustling people. There were four open-air markets crammed with customers and goods. Dried fish hung from lines, and the entire city smelled of fermenting fish. In a few weeks, workers would slide the bones out of the mushy meat and pound it into a salty paste.

They navigated around a vendor pouring fruity drinks from his cart that were laden with sugar. Farther along the roadway, a teenage boy offered to sell Vivian a pair of cheap sunglasses, and still farther a dog hiked his leg against the corner of a salon, watching them pass.

Traq watched it all but saw none of it. He couldn't really believe he would leave Averton behind forever. Let alone his planet. It just seemed so unreal, like a dream.

Or a nightmare.

A carefully tended garden surrounded a golden shrine. A lot of people knelt in front of it. Once, a few months earlier, he'd asked his mom why she never prayed at the little shrine. She told him that it didn't belong to *their* God. He wasn't really sure what that meant.

Outside the city, it was a twenty-minute walk, yet it seemed to take only seconds. Vivian led him to a large parking lot for factory workers. There was a massive silver spaceship resting in the center.

"What is that?" he murmured.

She didn't reply.

Probably a spaceship, he decided, curious despite his terror. The ship was enormous and sleek, at least four times bigger than his house. The strange metal gleamed brightly from all different angles, catching sunlight in some spots and reflecting it in others. He wondered how it flew. He couldn't imagine something that big lifting off the ground.

But they didn't go in. Not that one. Vivian took him instead to a much smaller and older ship. It was resting in the shadow of the larger vessel, hidden in the corner of the lot.

He felt an intense pang of fear. Where the first one was wondrous, this one was terrifying. It looked like a death trap.

"Climb on board," Vivian said.

Traq eyed the loading ramp apprehensively. The paint was fading and he saw weird shapes and letters on the side. His mother had begun to teach him how to read, so he recognized a few of the letters but some of them were completely foreign.

This ship was basically a big box with rounded edges attached to a smaller box jutting out the front.

"Is it safe?" he asked.

"It's old, but still flies. The engines were replaced a few years ago and all of the safety systems meet Engineering Standards."

Traq had been asking about the ramp—it didn't seem to have any supports keeping it off the ground—but nodded anyway. Slowly, he started walking up the metal platform, gaining confidence as he went.

Vivian guided him to an enclosed room near the back without talking, her boots making metallic thuds against the floor. Traq's own shoes were soft-soled and caused only a whisper. The inside was cooler than outside. It was almost cold.

She gestured to a pile of blankets and clothing in the corner of the room. "Stay here during takeoff," she said.

Then she disappeared, the door sliding shut behind her. Traq was surrounded by crates and the walls were angled differently than his house, making it feel cramped and uncomfortable. And he was alone.

There were no windows either. The air tasted stale and bitter.

A humming sound grew from underneath him and the floor felt like it was vibrating. He didn't like it. He felt like a rat trapped in a cage.

With no alternatives, he sat down on the blankets: the floor was made of latticed metal. He doubted it would be comfortable to lay on for more than a few minutes.

After about an hour he started sobbing.

It was still another hour before he gained enough courage to leave the cramped room to explore.

He wandered through the small ship absently, marveling at how different it was. The walls were polished metal, not wood or concrete. Bright lights dominated the narrow hallway. He'd been in cars, had even heard about ones that hovered, but nothing like this. The houses in Averton weren't fully sealed or climate controlled. Inside this ship, however, he felt...stuck. Enclosed.

Trapped.

There was an alcove with an exit hatch near the front. A window on the side showed a star-filled canopy beyond. It was like looking at the stars in the middle of the night.

To his left a ladder dropped into a dark room. There was a loud grinding sound and hiss, not very inviting.

The last things he saw were a pair of sliding doors along the wall on his right and another door straight ahead. He didn't go near them. He was afraid of getting in trouble if the tall woman came back.

Instead, he went back to the cargo hold and sat down.

About ten minutes passed before she finally returned. He heard footsteps clapping toward him. He huddled in the blankets, terrified. Vivian stepped into the room and stared down at him, standing in the doorway. The lights were behind her, framing her in shadows.

"Do you have any questions?" she asked. Her words were clipped and strange, and he had to struggle to understand her. Her accent was nothing like what he'd heard before.

He asked, "Where are we going?"

"Mali."

"Why?"

"Business."

"Are we going into space?"

"We are *already* in space," Vivian replied.

Traq looked up in surprise. "I didn't feel anything..."

"It's a decent ship."

Traq closed his eyes and tried to see if anything felt different. The floor was vibrating more, but everything else seemed the same.

"I can't leave?"

Vivian shook her head.

"Is my mom coming?"

Again, Vivian only shook her head.

Traq couldn't help it. He started crying. She was silent for a moment, and then said, "The restroom is through the cockpit to the left. Stay out of the engine room." When she saw he didn't understand, she stepped back and pointed to the ladder. "Don't go down there. At least not until I can show you what is safe."

"Is this my room?"

A slight smirk curled the edges of her lips. "This is the cargo hold. You'll use the room on the left once I clean it out. It's where I store medical supplies. Go and shower, and when you come back I'll have your room ready. You can sleep. We'll be arriving on Mali soon, so get plenty of rest. Any last questions?"

Traq rubbed his eyes and looked up. "Why am I here?"

Vivian didn't respond. She just stared, those dark gray eyes studying him. He tried to stare back but couldn't. He ended up looking down at his hands, wondering if he had made her mad. When he looked up, she was gone.

Chapter 10
Sector 1 – Axis
Abdullah Al Hakir

1

"What we waitin' for?"

"The new Captain," Abdullah replied quietly, waving his hand for his companion to lower his voice. "She's supposed to arrive today and assume command of the Fist."

He glanced around the conference hall, making sure none of the well-dressed and bored looking officers were listening in on their conversation. No one was. Good.

The Bridge Officers were all engaged in their own conversations or milling about with annoyed expressions on their faces. It didn't seem anyone was interested in what he or Mikael had to say. *And why would they be?*

Abdullah ran a hand across his short stubble of hair and blinked, trying to ignore the hum of overhead lights and hushed conversations. He was miserable, but he didn't dare show it.

So what the hell am I doing here?

Most of the officers in the conference hall were taller than he was, built thinner and more athletic. But that didn't bother him. He could take any two of them in a fight. What did bother him was their professional standing onboard Denigen's Fist. To say they outranked him would be a monumental understatement, which was what had him on edge and sweating. These were the Fist's highest ranking officers, the kind that never left the Command Deck, and he was little more than an enlisted man.

For him to be rubbing elbows with the elite seemed unreasonable. No, it didn't just seem unreasonable, it *was* unreasonable. They knew it too. They gave him and his friend Mikael—another enlisted man not usually invited to important ceremonies like this—a wide berth and cruel glares, refusing even casual association.

They seemed to take Abdullah being invited as a slight on their honor. Maybe it was. But when Abdullah received that personal invitation from the new Captain two days ago, he didn't dare refuse.

"Are we s'posed to eat the food?" Mikael asked. With his thick Daer accent, the word *food* sounded more like *fudd,* but Abdullah had no trouble understanding him. They'd been casual friends for a few months now.

He would have preferred to have Eddie with him—Eddie grew up in this lifestyle, so he wouldn't be out of sorts—but he would take what he could get. At least, he had Mikael to watch his back.

"What?" Abdullah asked, distracted.

"The food. Do ya think they'd be offended if...?"

Abdullah chuckled. "Why would they set out food if we weren't supposed to eat it?"

"Iono, I was just thinkin'..."

He didn't finish. He didn't have to. Abdullah understood completely. It felt like they were being watched, their every movement sized up and judged. The feeling came from the officers, sure, but it was more than that. The opinions of these men didn't bother Abdullah much. They were several classes above him on the social and military ladder, sure, but after today, he would probably never see them again.

But the Captain...

These Bridge Officers could have Abdullah kicked out the fleet, possibly with a dishonorable discharge, if he pissed them off. But Captain Kristi Grove could have Abdullah killed. And if she did, no one would speak a word of objection.

"I'm sure it's fine to eat," Abdullah mumbled, gesturing toward a group milling near the table. "See? They're eating. I doubt anyone would even notice if we tried the finger foods."

A long moment passed.

"I'm not hungry," Mikael decided.

Abdullah almost laughed, but in his current state of anxiety-bordering-on-terror he thought he might sound hysterical. He kept his mouth shut, focusing on the other officers instead. Some he recognized—Rodriguez Montes, the Lieutenant Commander, Patrick Dalent, Master of Gunnery—but many more he didn't know at all.

Even in his awe of the circumstances Abdullah had to admit a lump of bile and disdain at the back of his throat. These gathered men and women all had two things in common. First they all came from well-to-do families in the Core that bought their way through school, training, and into their current ranks.

The second was that they had too high an opinion of themselves. They avoided enlisted crewman as if they were plague carriers. A good leader, Abdullah knew, would seek out those under his charge and develop a relationship. These officers kept to themselves with pretentious dignity. It was as though God himself had given them their station on board Denigen's Fist.

But the worst part was that, in a certain way, Abdullah had to admit it felt that way. They had the First Citizen backing their every move, and the First Citizen represented the opinion—loosely as only a dictator can—

of trillions of people. The haughtiness of such spoiled nobility was fully justified and proudly displayed.

"Who's the new Captain?" Mikael asked, clipping the word *Captain* to become *Cap'n*.

"A woman named Kristi," Abdullah answered. He'd heard a lot about her in the last few weeks, but the reports were nothing more than conflicting rumors. Those rumors quickly became folk tales, and already the new Captain was eight feet tall and a butcher.

Some claimed she was beautiful and generous. Others said that she was horribly scarred from long years fighting and terrible to look upon. Laser bolts out of her ass when she farted had even come up on occasion. Other people thought she was just a normal woman, maybe a mother and probably a good leader. Abdullah knew the power of prejudice and how it could affect relationships, so he reserved judgment until he met her personally.

Something he never really expected to do.

"Why ain't she 'ere?"

"Her ship hasn't arrived."

"But then why'd she call this meetin' already? Why not wait 'til she gets 'ere?"

"We aren't going to question our Commanding Officer," Abdullah said roughly, scanning the conference hall again to make sure no one overheard the last bit. He took Mikael roughly by the arm and stared the scrawny man in the eyes. "And if you say another word like that, I'll have no choice but to report you for misconduct."

Mikael was taller than Abdullah and had creamy blond hair and blue eyes. His skin was pockmarked, his eyes sunken and bloodshot. Mikael had a piercing intelligent expression, but it was often vacant from the Limpid White he so enjoyed losing himself in. Abdullah knew that if he rolled Mikael's sleeves up he'd find dozens of track marks.

Abdullah had been friends with Mikael for months. The scrawny drug addict was brilliant with technology and had saved Abdullah's ass more than once with deadlines by fixing his data pads. But if Mikael wasn't going to keep his rambling mouth shut he would get himself into trouble. And if that happened Abdullah might get in trouble just by proxy.

The tension and anxiety of waiting around was wearing on the entire group. It had been four hours of waiting on edge in a cramped conference hall. Even seasoned veterans of on-ship politics were struggling to remain patient. More than a few had begun pacing.

Whoever Kristi was, she was trying to make an impression.

He eyed Mikael for a long minute and then pointed once more at the table of food. It was piled high with a variety of expensive delicacies. Most of them were local from planets near Axis, but some were rare delicacies from smaller worlds out in Sectors Two and Three.

"Let's get some food," Abdullah said, "and stop worrying about the wait."

Mikael itched his arm and seemed about to respond. Instead, he wiped the cold sweat from his forehead and nodded, following Abdullah to the table. They loaded plates up with finger food and nibblers and poured themselves glasses of a blushing sweet wine.

Their last Captain—Schmidt—would have balked at the idea of anyone drinking on board Denigen's Fist at all, let alone on duty. But wine was the only offered beverage at the table, the spread lacking even water. Abdullah wondered if that was a test to see who would drink a prohibited beverage, but he shrugged the idea away. It sounded like a rather petty method of judgment, and it was more likely Kristi simply didn't stigmatize the beverage as much as her predecessor.

They had just arrived back to their corner of the hall when the green double doors opened. Abdullah quickly set his plate down on a nearby polished table, finishing a cracker smothered with green paste and chasing it with a mouthful of wine before snapping to attention.

The officers formed two lines facing the door, subconsciously ranking themselves from left to right per actual position on the ship. Abdullah and Mikael were at the far right in the back line.

Abdullah smelled his breath and cursed, suddenly angry for eating the food. The paste was thick with garlic and hot spices.

The entourage poured in: first through the door were a pair of uniformed men—standard grey-blue, but without the emblem of the Fist on their sleeves—carrying a heavy wooden pedestal. They placed it in front of the wall.

Once they were finished they disappeared to a back corner of the room. A stream of important looking individuals came in next.

They were led by a tall woman in a dark gray uniform with flowing silver hair and a smooth face. She carried herself with impressive dignity. The other people in her congregation seemed timid in comparison. *That must be Captain Grove*, Abdullah decided.

She walked to beside the platform but didn't climb atop. Instead, she folded her hands behind her back and stared at the line of twenty officers gathered before her. Another man with a thick belly and balding head climbed onto the pedestal. He had gold-rimmed glasses and was holding a data pad in hand. He had a baby face and looked to be sweating.

The other ten members of the procession filtered to the sides.

The fat man looked bored, waiting for everyone to finish settling down. A floating metal disc hovered in the air nearby, recording everything so that the rest of the crew could watch the ceremony later.

It was a full minute before he spoke.

"On behalf of his Esteemed Grace the First Citizen Jozef Benedict, the Third of his name, I declare this vessel to be under the Command of Captain Kristi Harkin Grove. With God as my witness may it be so."

The man waited after speaking, holding the data pad against his chest and eyeing the congregation slowly. It was as if he was waiting for someone to question the edict...or to catch his breath. It was hard to tell which.

Finally, he spoke again, finishing the second half of the well-known declaration, "With the will of the Republican people I hereby welcome Captain Kristi Harkin Grove to Imperial Vessel TX-55219, so-named Denigen's Fist. May she serve the people of our worlds with the dignity and diligence so deserved."

Abdullah ignored the speech—he'd seen it hundreds of times on vid—and focused instead on the woman. Her face was rigid and body tense. She looked to be in incredible athletic shape. Captain Schmidt had spent more time eating than exercising, huffing and puffing from the mild walk from his quarters to the bridge.

Abdullah didn't think this Captain would have a similar issue. She seemed relaxed through the declaration, eyeing the crew with only mild curiosity. He doubted she would even say anything today. These transfer of power ceremonies were formality more than anything else.

And now that it was over he felt the tension slipping away. It was done, nothing had gone awry, and Abdullah could relax. She must have invited Abdullah and Mikael here just to show that she was different. Captain's always wanted to differentiate themselves from their peers.

Kristi must want to impress the enlisted men. Having low ranked people in the crowd said she wasn't only going to cater to her high ranking commanders. She would, of course, cater to them exclusively. But it was always good PR to make it seem like she was shaking up the status quo.

In a few minutes, the ceremony would be concluded and the group dismissed. Then it would just be waiting for orders to come in.

Normally Abdullah would hear that speech played over the intercom. It would play three times—once for each rotation of guards—over the next day and that would be the end of it.

This was the first time he'd actually seen the Pass of Command performed outside a televised recording. They were always so dull on vids, and he was depressed to find out that they were just as dull—

"Lieutenant Commander Rodriguez Montes, Corporal Mikael Wilson, and Sister Portia Nace step forward," the announcer on the pedestal said suddenly. His voice cut the silence with a sharp edge, ripping Abdullah from his thoughts. A few of the other officer's exchanged glances and Abdullah blinked.

What...?

He hadn't been expecting anyone to be singled out during the ceremony. That never, ever happened. He glanced over at his terrified friend: Mikael was wide-eyed with his mouth hanging open.

Abdullah made a clicking noise at him. Mikael glanced at him, and Abdullah nodded toward the front. *Go,* he mouthed.

Mikael nodded, his eyes as big as saucers. He gingerly pushed past the front rank officers and followed Rodriguez and Portia to the front. They stood in a line before the podium at attention. None of them looked comfortable, and no one seemed to know what was going on.

Abdullah noticed one of the members of Kristi's entourage step to the side and walk behind the three named guests. He took position between the three and the rest of the officers, facing forward.

To his credit, Mikael didn't glance around, staying perfectly still.

The announcer turned to face the first man in the line, Rodriguez. "Lieutenant Commander Rodriguez Montes, you have been charged with the crime of selling goods and property of his Holy Grace the First Citizen without permission or knowledge. You have been found guilty of said crime, as well as the crime of consorting with disreputable traders on the planets Daer and Vinn. Your punishment, as per Military edict one-fourteen-dash-twelve, is death."

The hush that fell over the room was palpable. There was a hesitance in the room as Rodriguez looked up slowly.

"Wh...what?" he asked, the word barely above a whisper.

A flash of motion broke the hesitation. The man behind the three officers drew a small pistol from a hip holster and placed it against the back of Rodriguez's head. The motion was smooth, well-practiced. There was a small pop—the weapon was small caliber—and Rodriguez collapsed to the floor. Blood pooled gently out of the wound.

His body twitched once, then went still.

The crowd held its collective breath, stunned. They had no choice but to stare in morbid fascination. They came unarmed, as per instructions, but even if they all had assault rifles at the moment they wouldn't dare use them. Not against their Commanding Officer.

Even as she killed one of them.

Mikael didn't share their hesitation. He turned and tried to flee, but just as fast he was grabbed and held in place by two members of the Captain's entourage. He was begging and struggling but couldn't break free.

Rodriguez's lifeless body was ignored.

"No, please! I have children!" Mikael lied. "I have a family..."

"Corporal Mikael Wilson," the announcer began, ignoring his pleas, "you are found guilty of the crime of ingesting and injecting illegal substances banned by Military edict seven-dash-four-twenty-six while serving actively in the military for the First Citizen Jozef Benedict the Third of his Name. The punishment for this crime is death."

The gun went up, and this time, the pop made Abdullah wince. Mikael was a drug addict, but he was also a friend. Abdullah couldn't object, though. Not if he wanted to stay alive.

But it still hurt watching him die. Mikael was the only friendly face in the room, and he'd never done anything wrong to anyone.

What the hell is happening? Abdullah wondered. *This definitely isn't standard operating procedure.* He'd never heard of anyone being killed at a Pass of Command Ceremony. It was unthinkable.

Only a few minutes had passed since Captain Grove walked on deck, and already Abdullah's world was turned on its head.

It felt like he was wandering through a dream. This couldn't be real. The gathered enforcers and executioner adjusted to box Sister Portia Nace in. She was shivering and moaning but hadn't tried to flee. She was muttering something, a prayer or chant, too low for Abdullah to hear.

"Sister Portia Nace," the announcer said, slower this time. "You have sworn your life to the Holy Ministry on behalf of his Eminent Grace the First Citizen and his Minister Givon Mielo. Your crimes are blaspheming against the Ministry and holding faith in false idols."

"I haven't!" she cried. "I would never stray the faith!"

Abdullah could only see the woman from behind, but he knew her rather well. Her rank on the ship meant nothing to the overall hierarchy. She answered to no one but the Minister. She was his Envoy, a coveted and well-respected woman, beloved by the crew. She was the spiritual leader of the Fist's onboard Ministry, often leading in weekly prayers.

Abdullah never imagined her to be anything less than a pure representation of the Ministry: apocalyptic and aloof, untouchable in her love of religion. He couldn't believe she would dishonor the Ministry and her faith. It was unfathomable to think of her worshipping anything other than her God.

But he wasn't about to point that out.

"Sister Portia Nace, your crime is against the Holy Ministry you deigned to serve and thus punishment was passed down on behalf of Conciliator Argus Wade and Minister Givon Mielo. Your crime is against God, not the First Citizen, so you will not be offered burial in space."

He paused, dabbing sweat from his forehead.

"You are to be thrown into the furnace and burned until dead."

"No!" Portia cried. "No please! I've done nothing. Please!"

The men took her by the arm, and the muscular executioner slid his pistol away under his overcoat, folding his arms behind his back. Portia thrashed against her captors, to no avail, crying and screaming incoherently. Abdullah watched them drag her to the exit, trying to make out her words, and suddenly he realized what she was saying:

Please kill me first.

And then she was outside. The door shut behind her and they were cast once more under a heavy blanket of silence. Abdullah couldn't even hear anyone breathe. The officers faced forward, and the Captain stared back, no one acknowledging the pair of bodies lying on the floor.

A long moment passed.

And then, "Abdullah Mohammad Al Hakir," the announcer called. "Step forward."

2

The voice was like a knife cutting through Abdullah's abdomen, and suddenly he couldn't breathe. His vision swam in front of him and he fought rising panic. *Focus, breathe, focus*, he told himself, counting his breaths.

I can't go forward...

...I have to.

They'll kill me if I go...

...They'll kill me if I don't.

A full thirty seconds passed before he could move. No one spoke. No one moved. His eyes were locked, and he felt lightheaded. He forced one foot to move, then the other, and muscle memory took over. His body was sluggish.

The officers parted easily before him. He doubted any would trade him places right now. He tasted garlic bile in his throat and fought to keep his knees from shaking.

If either the announcer or the Captain were aware of his trepidation they pretended not to notice. Captain Kristi only watched him with her cold gray eyes.

He forced himself to walk past the executioner and stand next to the body of his dead friend, holding perfectly still. *If I duck to the side and dive I might be able to tackle the man standing behind me and wrestle his gun away*, he thought, then forced the idea away. It was hopeless, utterly. If they wanted him dead, he was dead.

He tried to think of any crimes he had committed. There were several, but none so horrible he should be executed. He thought about the times he'd fallen asleep on duty, gambled with his fellow low-ranking officers while off duty, even times he had considered consorting with disreputable traders...if bartenders counted.

In his terrified state, he even thought about all of the times he had accidentally given the wrong order to a soldier or misspelled a word in one of his reports. Had anyone else done those things? He didn't know. Every misdeed felt like fair game in his heightened state of panic.

Oh God, I drank the wine...

"Abdullah Mohammad Al Hakir," the announcer said in his slow practiced voice, pausing to add grandiosity to his words, "on behalf of his Holy Grace the First Citizen you are hereby promoted to Lieutenant Commander of Denigen's Fist, effective immediately. You will begin performing the duties therein required from this day forth and answer directly to Captain Kristi Grove. With God as my witness may it be so."

Abdullah tried to absorb the words, but they were slippery. Lieutenant Commander? That wasn't even a promotion that was...what the hell does that mean? I barely hold rank at all. I'm a junior grade Lieutenant in charge of seven people. The Lieutenant Commander is in charge of half the goddamn ship of—

Sixty thousand.

Abdullah almost fell over. There had to be some mistake. He shook his head slowly and tried to formulate the words to object.

This couldn't be right. They must have selected the wrong person.

The announcer didn't seem to notice his sudden concern, turning back to the rest of the gathered officers.

"You are all hereby dismissed for the day to deliver messages and make preparations for travel. Enjoy the buffet and discuss for as long as you wish but make sure those under your command are fully informed of these circumstances: we will leave the central Sector tomorrow on a patrol route through Sector Two.

"Viewing services for Rodriguez Montes and Mikael Wilson will be held on deck three at twenty-two hundred hours followed by funeral services. The body of Rodriguez Montes will be sent to Axis per his family's request.

"Lieutenant Commander Abdullah Al Hakir, you are ordered to report to the bridge for debriefing."

Abdullah was still shaking his head and barely registered the order. He looked up, but the announcer was already walking away. As the door opened four more people flooded into the room to gather the bodies on long stretches. Body bags at the ready.

Abdullah found himself caught by the gaze of Captain Kristi. Her gray eyes boring into him, telling him nothing. She seemed almost bored by the entire proceedings.

It was for show, he realized. *She killed my friend because he was a drug addict, and she wanted to set an example. He didn't do anything to warrant death, but he doesn't have any family to object or complain. What kind of a cold and heartless bitch are you?*

He prayed she couldn't read his thoughts. They stared for a few more seconds before she nodded slightly and walked away, disappearing out of the conference hall with her entourage. The officers were alone once more, yet still no one spoke. All stood in stunned silence, exchanging glances and clearing throats.

He doubted anyone would touch the food. He glanced over at his plate on the far table and fought down a queasy feeling. He had to leave it for someone else to clean up. Right now he had to go to the bridge.

Suddenly, he had the urge to laugh sardonically. He bit it back.

Yes, the Captain certainly made one hell of an impression.

Chapter 11
Sector 6 – Mali
Vivian Drowel

1

The blocky merchant class spaceship Cudgel lowered slowly to the surface of the barren brown planet, landing with an audible *plop* that made Vivian wince. She'd searched for over an hour for a landing spot that wasn't a mud pit, but the best she could find would still leave her landing gear deep in sludge.

It had rained within the last few days, and with the planet's slow evaporation rate water would sit on the ground as a muddy paste for at least a month. It didn't rain often, but when it did it left things a mess.

Dry deserts, mud, and incredibly powerful winds were all the planet had to offer. It was stripped of its resources hundreds of years earlier by extensive mining operations and could barely sustain its modest population.

Vivian rose from her seat in the cockpit and stretched out her back. *A day,* she decided. *Maybe two.* With a sigh, she headed farther into her ship to find Traq.

2

"Why is it so muddy?" Traq asked. They were standing on top of the ship's ramp, looking out at the desert below.

"No foliage or evaporation," she replied, "so the water just mixes with the dirt and stays."

"Why aren't there any trees?"

"They were cut down."

"All of them?"

Vivian nodded. Whoever owned this planet, years ago, hadn't been concerned with preserving it. They stripped it bare of anything of value and left it a floating husk. They also left the workers who moved here years ago behind, those too poor to afford passage off this world.

In the Republic, many did the same thing. They would create enormous stations orbiting these planets, ship supplies up from the surface and then leave once the planet ran out of resources.

The only urban center left on Mali was an outpost-turned-city named Garran's Ridge. Population just over two million. Every other city and mining facility were either buried by constant sandstorms or destroyed.

"Why are we here?"

"To talk to the locals," she said. "Find out what they need so we can hopefully trade with them."

"What do they need?"

It was only a guess, but Vivian was confident in it:

"Water."

3

Vivian didn't even like pets, so what the hell was she going to do with a kid? Every step of the way, she felt his eyes on her. Watching her. And he wouldn't say anything, he would just stare and then run away, making her feel like maybe she had something on her face. It was infuriating, but she knew she would have to maintain her calm. He would grow out of it.

At least, that's what the books told her.

Wade's stupid, stupid books.

The funny thing was just how many there were. He sent her basically every parenting book they could offer. There were thousands of them. Some claimed children were little treasures, and others that they were little monsters. Each book had a silver bullet solution to raising kids, and none of them were the same. For the most part, all she had learned was that raising kids was difficult, and no one really knew how to do it.

Which meant, at the very least, if she screwed up it wouldn't matter too much.

The worst part was, her experience being a child wasn't much to draw upon either. From as early as she could remember, she lived at the Ministry. It hadn't taken her long to realize she was different, that something was wrong with her, and that her 'teachers' didn't care much for her. To them, she was an animal.

They beat her with whips when she disobeyed, training her to use her modest gifts and studying her. That was something she never wanted Traq to experience, and she resolved herself to take care of Traq in the best way possible.

Unfortunately, she was fairly certain that locking the kid in the cargo hold of her ship because he annoyed her was in the 'don't' section of most parenting books.

"I..." she said, then sighed. "*We* need to leave the ship for a little bit. We need to talk to some people."

His eyes went wide.

"We're on a different planet?" he asked.

Vivian grated her teeth.

"Yes. This is Mali. We're about two kilometers from a city called Garran's Ridge. We need to ask them about some things."

"What kind of planet is it?"

"The gravity is ninety-eight percent axis norm; the star is a Solar Analog to a K class star..."

His expression was blank. Oh, this is going to be fun, she thought. He doesn't even know basic science.

"We're going to have to walk, you might get muddy," said Vivian, turning and striding to the exit hatch. She did a quick check of her gear and punched the button to lower the ramp. She turned and glanced down the hall at the cockpit.

"We'll only be gone a few hours TM, just radio me if you run into trouble."

TM, her little robot assistant, walked out of the cockpit on her reverse jointed legs. She clicked an affirmative response.

Suddenly Vivian felt something clutch her leg. Her body went rigid.

Slowly, *ever so slowly*, she removed her hand from the hilt of her half-drawn sword. The Vibro blade was slung over her right shoulder—*careful Vivian*—and she looked down at the creature clutching her thigh.

Traq was shivering and staring at the robot, a look mixed between shock and terror plastered on his face.

Vivian had never thought of TM as particularly scary. She was a service robot, insanely useful, but without combat skills. True, TM had a small flamethrower mounted on her shoulder, but she insisted it was only for welding. Welding, and killing bugs. Vivian had never known a robot to have an aversion to bugs and assumed her engineer had a sardonic personality.

Gently, she extricated the child from her leg and looked at the robot.

"He didn't know you were on board?"

TM streamed a series of binary clicks. The robots voice software was turned off—Vivian didn't like having other people listening in on unencrypted conversations—and it sounded like a hundred or so chickadees singing. Her internal translator decoded the message for her.

"Good job then. Hiding was an admiral decision TM. Now he's not only scared of you, he's petrified."

TM clicked angrily in response.

Traq mumbled something incoherent and reached out to touch the robot, as though afraid it would scorch him. His eyes were wide, but the fear was replaced by curiosity.

"It is not my *job* to introduce you two," Vivian retorted. "Just watch the damn ship."

This time, TM clicked a high pitched long response.

"No, you would *not* do a better job watching Traq...yes but...I mean I *know* I forgot to feed him but he found that packet of crackers and...I can say whatever I *damned* well want in front of my passengers and—oh, forget it!"

Vivian turned and strode down the ramp, forgetting about the mud. She stepped ankle deep in a puddle just at the bottom and cursed in frustration.

4

Angrily, Vivian trudged off in the direction of the city her scanners had picked up. She walked light on the slick surface but set a brisk pace, her boots scrunching uncomfortably from the mud. She didn't know, or particularly care, if Traq was keeping up.

The sun was hot, but without intense humidity, it was quite a mild day.

Gale force winds blew across the landscape every few minutes. Each time she staggered to keep her feet and once slipped to her knee, muddying it. She knew that if the wind was hard on her, Traq didn't stand a chance. *Think of it as a training exercise*, she decided. *A really cruel training exercise.*

5

When she first radioed the planet from orbit, a man named Quinton informed her they didn't have a landing pad. Anywhere outside the city would do for landing, and they would meet her nearby.

There was a group of about twenty locals waiting for them just inside the city limits. They were all smiling, which was kind of unsettling. When people were this happy about Vivian's arrival, they either weren't used to off-world travelers or they were planning to kill her.

In her current mood, she wasn't sure which one she would prefer.

"Welcome to Mali," a man who could only be Quinton said, gesturing grandly. He had deep green eyes and white hair, though he didn't appear that old. Probably bleached by the sun. He was wearing a purple flannel shirt, blue denim pants, and a pair of sandals that made him look kind of like a piñata as he waved his arms.

It's a mud hole, she thought, glancing around. Not that impressive.

"It's windy," she said instead.

"You should see it at night," Quinton said, laughing heartily. "We don't receive many visitors, so this is a very special occasion."

Vivian glanced back and used her hand to deflect the sun from her eyes, trying to spot Traq.

Traq was about fifty meters back, head down and leaning into the wind.

The gale let up suddenly, and he collapsed face first into the mud. Vivian stifled a laugh and then shrugged away the shame it elicited.

Traq picked himself up and hurried the last distance to them before the wind whipped up again. He was wiping his face off with his shirt, smearing it more than cleaning it. Vivian introduced them and listened vaguely as Quinton ticked off the list of names of the others gathered around.

"You must be hungry, would you like something to eat?" Quinton asked.

"We would love a meal," Vivian said, glancing down at her side. Traq was covered in mud from head to toe. "And a place to clean up."

"Of course, please, right this way."

Quinton led them through the city and the congregation followed. A few were carrying weapons, she noted, but they were old model projectile pistols and rifles that had been put through extended use. She had the Vibro blade slung over her shoulder in easy reach and a heavy pistol tucked under her black tunic, but she wasn't concerned about safety.

Right now she was concerned about information. Something she could give to Argus to justify her absence.

Most of the buildings were primitive; patchwork monstrosities. Newer lean-tos created semi shelters, butting up against the older structures.

The people lived in abject poverty. A lot of windows were boarded up and people were crammed in close together. They walked slowly, hopelessly, eyes down.

Quinton led the group alongside an open sewer, high from the rain water. The smell curled her nose.

Every corner she passed she saw large ceramic basins overflowing. She saw locals dumping it on themselves and scrubbing their bodies with it, but she didn't see anyone drinking it. *Could be dangerous*, she thought. *Maybe acidic fall.*

All in all, her impression of the city wasn't positive. It was dingy and would have been nothing more than a pimple in a sector closer to the Core. Yet, to hear Quinton talk of it, this was one of the most beautiful and lively places to grow up in the entire galaxy.

After about twenty minutes, Traq asked if he could have something to drink. All conversation ground to a halt and a few people exchanged glances.

Quinton met Vivian's gaze and then his eyes flicked down to Traq. There was a brief pause and then he said, "Of course you can," and pulled a slim bottle from his pocket.

"We can't—"

Quinton shot the speaking man a look, which shut him up. The man was taller than Quinton, though not a lot, with ruddy skin and pale eyes. Vivian thought back and remembered that his name was Ralph.

He had a look about him that bespoke confidence and arrogance. He remained silent as the bottle was handed over to Traq, staring pointedly off down the road and patting his hand absently against his leg.

The spot he was patting was where a gun would be, she realized, but right now he was unarmed. Traq guzzled half the small bottle in two swigs, oblivious to the dirty looks their escort was giving him.

Traq slipped the bottle into his pocket and Quinton began walking again, talking more about the city. The atmosphere of the entire group was more subdued.

They traveled another ten minutes to their destination. At least, half the buildings were disused, but even these had people living inside them, curled up in entryways with tattered clothing. High population density with low quality of life.

Quinton led them to a large apartment building and stopped outside. Dust swirled in the air around them as the wind picked up, turning the road into a howling tunnel. It was getting dark.

"This is my home," Quinton said, then turned to the rest of the group, raising his voice. "Unfortunately, my wife would panic if I tried to feed you all!"

They chuckled and began to disperse. Quinton was left alone with Vivian, Traq, and Ralph.

"It's going to be a big one tonight," Ralph said. He was practically shouting to be heard over the wind. Quinton nodded.

"Make sure everyone gets inside on time. Send the men on rounds."

"You got it, boss," Ralph replied, turning to face Vivian. "Ma'am."

The look on his face was casually hidden disrespect. He turned and left, disappearing down the street the way they'd come.

The sun had all but disappeared, she realized. She couldn't believe it happened so fast. One moment it was a bright sunny day, the next the sun was gone. Already it was dark and forbidding, with shadows climbing up the walls.

The wind whipped at them in sharp gusts. She held onto Traq's coat and all three moved into the lobby. The wind died down, whistling through little cracks in the walls.

"You ration water?" Vivian said once it was quiet enough to speak. Quinton nodded, heading into a stairwell. He started up the stairs, talking over his shoulder. The inside was dimly lit.

"We have to. Some people," he said, "think we should be stricter. Keep population growth from outpacing our water and food supplies. For now, water rationing is enough."

"They want to use the water to control the population? Enforce eugenics for a better future?"

"Basically," Quinton said with a frown.

"I think most cultures have people who think that's a good idea," Vivian offered.

"We couldn't do that if we wanted," Quinton said. "People would revolt."

"What makes the water supply so low? Everywhere within an eighty-mile radius is drenched."

"Yes, but the water is undrinkable without filtration. Even when caught in basins. Too many chemicals in the air at higher altitudes. "

"Can't you drill for water?"

"We do, but that needs to be filtered as well. We have a few reservoirs that are safe, but what water is clean and drinkable is strictly regulated."

"I'm sorry," Vivian said, glancing at Traq. "We didn't know."

Quinton waved her concern away. "It's no issue. As mayor, I get a slightly larger ration anyway."

The ceiling was a lot lower than Vivian was used to, forcing her to bend as he led her through a dark and dirty hallway. Trash littered the sides. The lights—mostly cheap incandescent bulbs—flickered as the storm picked up in intensity, shaking the walls.

He stopped in front of a small door. "And here we are."

The door wasn't locked. A trusting man, considering his position. Trusting men rarely stayed in power for long.

The apartment was small and cramped, and there was a strong odor of sickness in the air. The first sound she heard was a crying child in a separate room.

"Excuse me," Quinton said, disappearing into the back.

Traq moved to follow but Vivian caught his shoulder. A groan came from the other room. It was the groan of a woman in anguish, struggling for a life that was slipping away. Vivian knew the sound better than she would have liked.

She scanned the apartment. It was sparse with a pair of oil lamps on opposite corners. She didn't see any refrigeration units, but she did spot a small gas stove along the left wall.

"It smells bad," Traq whispered. Vivian shushed him and took a seat on the floor, beckoning for Traq to take one of the chairs. He did, and after about ten minutes Quinton appeared, followed by what could only be his daughter. She looked to be about two years old with curly honey-colored hair.

She hid timidly behind her father's leg at first, then ran out suddenly and began hitting Traq repeatedly in the shoulder, giggling. Traq had no idea what to do and looked to Vivian for help. When the little girl noticed Vivian, she squealed and ran behind her father again, sucking her thumb and clutching his pants.

"This is Aliza," Quinton said, smiling sadly. "And my wife is Patricia, but she won't be joining us."

"We have medicine on my ship," Vivian said softly. Quinton shook his head.

"You have my thanks, but she's received the best possible care we can afford and it's too late to save her. Now, I just want her to have a peaceful goodbye." He rolled up his sleeves and opened a cupboard under the stove, pulling out a few wrapped packages. "I wasn't planning on visitors today, so the meal will be spare."

"That would be perfect," Vivian said.

It took about twenty minutes to prepare the food, which consisted of some sort of soft grain noodle and a meat she'd never tasted along with a sprinkling of spices. Vivian sat on the floor, afraid if she used the chair she would hit her head on the ceiling fan. Aliza sat on the opposite side of the room, eyeing her throughout the entire meal. The food was disgusting, but Vivian forced it down.

Traq didn't seem to agree, devouring his helping in a matter of minutes. No water was served, and when Traq pulled his bottle out of his pocket Aliza reached for it, making 'ugh' sounds and clenching her fingers repeatedly. Traq passed it over to her and she quickly emptied the bottle, making smacking sounds with her lips.

Once the meal was complete Quinton pulled out a package of cigarettes, offering one to Vivian. She shook her head and he lit up, standing near the window with it cracked just an inch. It was dark outside, but they could hear the wind howling its way down the street. It threw dust against the wall and glass. The repetition of the sound was quite soothing, threatening to lull her to sleep.

They sat in silence.

"I suppose it's best that I explain why we're on this planet," Vivian said. "We came here looking for any information you have about warships."

Quinton took a puff on his cigarette and leaned back. "You'll have to be more specific."

"You used to make them."

"Well, not me personally. They were made here, in orbit around this planet. But that was hundreds of years ago. Thousands maybe, more like a legend now. I wouldn't believe it myself but look around. We live on a world that's been depleted."

He paused, scratching his left eyelid with his thumb. "This used to be a beautiful world. We have images from millennia ago. It was vibrant and green. Dangerous chemicals were brought and used for mineral leeching. Species died off one by one. After a time, the damage was irreparable."

"Why don't you leave?"

Quinton chuckled. "Who would take us? What do we have to offer? We make do as best we can. Our vegetation has a harder and harder time surviving. With our water supply so dangerously low, I'm afraid that one day we'll just start dying off. And no one off-world will even know about it."

"Why not ask for water purifiers?"

"From who? Our satellites are down so we can't contact other worlds and we haven't had a space-faring vessel land here in months. When people *do* show up they take our metals and trade supplies or credits we can't spend. Our requests for aid fall on deaf ears. The merchants don't care about our plight as long as they get our minerals to sell on Terminus and Jaril."

Vivian glanced over as the room fell once more into silence. Traq was sleeping on the rug and Aliza had curled up next to him, sucking her thumb and watching Vivian bleary-eyed. *Doesn't trust me in the slightest, but Traq might as well be her big brother,* she thought. *Traq must have forgotten about the smell.*

It was a horrible thing, to get used to the smell of death.

"One day this planet will be nothing more than a husk," Quinton said, puffing on his cigarette and dropping the butt out the window. It disappeared with the wind down the street and he slid the window closed. "But you asked about warships. Space stations would be more accurate."

"What?"

"They only made six of them, from what I heard, and it was several hundred years ago. All six were lost or destroyed."

"How big?"

"Each had a minimum crew of one million," he replied.

She hesitated. "What?"

"That was just what they required to operate. The biggest could manage twenty million at full capacity."

"Holy hell," Vivian murmured. The biggest Capital ship she'd seen held a crew of three hundred thousand. At full capacity. If what he was saying was true, then Argus and the Ministry would be very interested in acquiring schematics.

"Are the records classified?" she asked. He shook his head.

"Not many people even remember the stations. It was so long ago, and they didn't last. Must not have been built very well."

"Can I take a look at anything you have?"

"I can pull it and make you a copy. They assembled most of the components in space. All of those records were lost with the ships, but we did put some of the frameworks together down here. You can have all of it."

Vivian nodded. "You have my thanks."

"If I can ask for something in return, I would ask that you deliver a message to Jaril and the Royal family. Things are...getting worse. And if we don't get water purifiers soon..."

He left the thought unfinished.

She hesitated. "I'm not sure what I can do. I can deliver your message to people in Jaril, but I doubt they will care."

Quinton nodded though his expression was downcast.

Another few minutes passed and Vivian felt the patter of the wind lulling her to sleep. Quinton yawned and stood. "You can sleep here tonight if you don't mind, or I can ask for other arrangements to be made up. I'm sorry that we don't have set accommodations for outsiders, but people rarely stay overnight. They don't like associating with locals," he added sadly. "This is one of the few buildings that maintains consistent power during night storms."

"Here is fine," Vivian said, glancing down. Aliza was passed out as well, still curled against Traq. They looked peaceful and she didn't want to disturb them, but that meant she would only have the corner of the room to herself. She wouldn't have much space to stretch out.

Quinton nodded to her and disappeared into the back. He returned a moment later with two blankets and a pillow. Vivian helped him gently put the pillow under the heads of the sleeping children and then draped one blanket over them. Quinton offered to get her a second pillow, but she declined. She doubted she would sleep long anyway.

Satisfied, Quinton turned off of the lights, locked the door, and disappeared into the room with his wife.

Vivian folded the other blanket and leaned it against the wall. She thought over the new information, wondering what it might be worth. A sinister thought had started creeping into her mind. If the ships ever existed, they were missing. But that didn't mean the same thing as destroyed. If Darius knew about enormous warships sitting on his doorstep...

Something like that could turn the tide of any battle against the Republic.

Doubtful, of course. Doubtful that the ships existed at all, and even more doubtful that Darius would know of them. Vivian fell asleep, worried what the future would bring.

Chapter 12
Sector 1 – Axis
Argus Wade

1

Argus Wade leaned against the cool metal railing, watching stars twinkle outside the deck's viewport. He was on the bridge of the Capital Class Warship named Denigen's Fist. Below the stars, he could see Axis stretching into the distance.

They were in high orbit, several hundred kilometers from the surface. Most planets across the galaxy showed a variety of different colors at this height: dim greens and browns of vegetation, bluish water, and swirling white clouds.

But not Axis. This planet was the center of the Republic's dominance, the homestead of the First Citizen and the Ministry. Axis was uniform gray, a metal ball in space. Much of the planet was covered in domes. The oceans were drained and pumped through enormous pipes.

It was beautiful, he knew. At least in propaganda pictures. It gleamed in the sunlight like an enormous jewel.

Unfortunately, all the splendor was lost on the surface by constant cloud cover and devastating weather. The domes were covered in layers of soot and dirt. Outside those domes it was unlivable: the metal reflected sunlight away from the planet, creating a cycle of cooling that left external temperatures excessively low.

Argus had grown up in one of those domes. Poverty and crime were a daily reality. He'd hated it and wanted to escape. But now, years older and wiser, he missed it.

Millions of ships traveled to Axis on an hourly basis. They delivered foodstuffs and necessities to the multitudes living under those domes.

The air was cleansed and tasted antiseptic. Oxygen and water were shipped in.

Axis was a testament to humanities control over his world. It existed by a giant engine of technology. The last census put the population at forty-seven billion. The estimated natural population should be four billion. A single day of missed shipments, a single *hour*, would cause millions to starve and die.

2

Argus was born on Axis thirty-three years ago in one of the poorer domes. It was one of those 'better than life' models with perfect weather, never too hot or too cold. He grew up craving rain and snow, wishing for seasons that never came.

As a kid, the tenuous balance of the planet never bothered him. The idea of a generator breaking down under his dome meaning thousands would die from dehydration or suffocation was inconceivable. He wasn't even taught about natural plant life on other planets until he was sixteen.

That was twenty years ago. Then the Ministry found him. Axis was one of the hardest places to hide children similar to him. They received a genetic test at school age, and if the proper genetic markers were discovered, they were given over to the Ministry for care. No questions asked.

There was only one aspiration for those like Argus; one chance of escape from imprisonment at the Ministry: become a Shield. A First Citizen hundreds of years ago was fascinated by the *Ordo Mens Rea* and ever since they selected the personal bodyguards from their ranks. It rankled the Ministry, but they couldn't refuse a request from the First Citizen.

Argus wasn't good enough at fighting to be chosen. He had no chance of becoming a Shield and defending the First Citizen. But he was good with numbers and people. From an early age, he showed aptitude, working his way up the ladder with more and more responsibility until he became indispensable to the Ministry. An important cog in a very, very large wheel. After a while, they forgot he was even a member of the Order.

Being forgotten was the greatest gift Argus ever received. He was careful not to remind them.

The gliding metal door swept open behind him on the bridge and a puff of cool air washed past. He turned and stood up straight, smoothing his black robes. Captain Kristi Grove strode on deck, raising a hand to single her entourage to wait outside.

She must not think I'm a threat, he thought as the door slid closed. He didn't know if he was more relieved in her trust or insulted by her lack of concern. Argus shrugged the thought away, bowing low to her. She nodded curtly and stepped beside him, looking past to the planet below.

"It's beautiful during the day," she said. Argus nodded.

"Quite."

"But I prefer it at night."

"Oh?"

"In the darkness, it takes the appearance of a sleeping beast."

"I believe we had some business to attend to?"

Captain Kristi turned to face him. "Not just yet," she said, turning and facing the entrance to the bridge. She crossed her hands behind her lower back and waited.

Less than a minute later, the door slid open again and a timid man walked onto the bridge. He had cropped black hair and deep bronze skin. He was built thick and muscular with a plain face. His uniform put him in the lower ranks, probably an enlisted officer. No one important.

The man hesitated for a second in the doorway and then strode onto the bridge with false confidence.

"Captain," the low ranking officer said, snapping to attention a few meters short of Kristi. His body was rigid and voice steady, but his eyes betrayed his trepidation. The pupils were dilated and fluttering. The bridge must be an intimidating place for someone like him, Argus knew. His first time on the bridge of a Capital Class Warship had been terrifying.

The bridge itself was one circular room. It could hold fifty to sixty people at terminals throughout with a raised platform in the center. There was an entrance for the High Officers onto the platform and an entrance for lower ranking personnel on the floor.

The bridge was empty right now, capable of running itself without human intervention.

"Lieutenant Commander," Kristi Grove said to the newcomer with a brisk nod. "Thank you for coming."

"Captain, I was wondering—"

"What's your opinion on the other officers?" Captain Kristi interrupted smoothly.

"Sir?"

"The other officers. What do you think of them?"

The man hesitated for a long moment before speaking. "They are excellent officers and leaders. Your First Officer Fredrick Penn is well liked; Chief Warrant Officer Vincent Belgrade is a brilliant tactician..."

His voice droned off as Captain Kristi shook her head. "Abdullah, if I was looking for a political assessment or resume I'd speak to the men personally. I want to know what they mean to the enlisted men. Are they respected?"

The officer—Abdullah—looked over at Argus for support, a terrified expression on his face. Argus kept his expression unreadable, glad he wasn't in the man's position. He'd known Kristi through correspondence for a few days now, but he had a healthy respect for her penchant for manipulation. She enjoyed her mind games.

Finally, Abdullah found his voice again. "Warrant Officer Belgrade is seen by the men as an overbearing fool and Frederick Penn a backbiter. Some think he killed Captain Schmidt in the hopes he would be promoted."

"Would he kill me?"

Abdullah hesitated again and then shook his head. "I have no idea, but if I were you I'd make sure he never got the chance." After he said this, he seemed to second guess his brash response and lowered his eyes to the ground.

"But you say he doesn't have the respect of the men?"

"He promotes for loyalty, not talent or ambition. His friends are power hungry and controlling. The enlisted soldiers won't speak against them for fear of punishment. It's happened before."

"If the men won't speak, then how can I verify what you say is true?"

"You can't," he said. "Or, at least, it would be difficult. My friends trust me, but they wouldn't say these things to other people who ask."

"So I've heard. People trust you, Abdullah, and you are a good man. That's why I promoted you. I expect competence and obedience. Don't second guess yourself. And never," she said, emphasizing each word, "ever, second guess me." Abdullah nodded his understanding, but the look of terror was still present. "Dismissed."

He saluted and turned heel, the tenseness in his body giving Wade the impression he was fighting the urge to flee. As the door slid smoothly shut Kristi shifted to face Argus once more.

"He seems intelligent," Argus offered. "But out of his depth."

"He came highly recommended by the previous Captain. He was up for a minor promotion before Captain Schmidt met his end."

"If what he says is true, why keep Fredrick Penn as First Officer? As Captain, you are well within your rights to replace him."

"I was afraid Penn held the respect of those under his command. He's been on the Fist for twelve years, and I didn't want to act rashly. But now that my suspicions have been confirmed, I can deal with him accordingly."

"You're going to have him killed?"

Kristi smiled, but only her lips curled. It never reached her eyes. "No. You are."

3

"Excuse me?"

"As Captain, I have the authority to kill anyone under my command. But my command is shared."

Argus didn't like where this was going.

"Which means that, if my *equal* seeks to have someone killed, I have no choice but to acquiesce."

"She's only a little girl."

"A very *powerful* little girl."

Argus was starting to feel sick.

"I haven't signed the paperwork yet..."

She laughed. "*You* sent the request to me, not the other way around, and I still have all of our correspondence on record. What happens if I send that to the Minister?"

"She's only a child," he said, his voice low.

"I am well aware," she said, just as low. "And she takes after her father."

4

"What do you want?"

"Nothing more than what is already offered," Captain Kristi said. "I merely don't like dishonesty. I have certain agendas I am hoping your daughter can help me accomplish, and I don't want you working against me. We should be on the same team."

Argus hesitated. "What agendas?"

"Cleaning up corruption. Battling evil. All well-intentioned goals, you would agree."

"Is having people put to death on that list of goals?"

The Captain was silent for a moment. "How many different sins are there?"

"Sins?"

"Over twenty, many of which are punishable by death. How often are such sinners put to death?"

"Never," he replied. "Those barbaric laws haven't been followed in years."

"Because the Ministry is weak," Captain Kristi said. "The Republic is weak. We have a cancer, eating away at our civilization, and we do nothing."

"There will always be bad people."

"And more when good people do nothing," she said. "Your daughter is in a unique position, able to judge the wicked with impunity, to right wrongs that are centuries old. She will be known as the greatest Minister in history."

Argus listened, aware that she was crazy. He had to admit, there was something tempting in what she was saying. He hated corruption as much as the next person.

"She will be safe?"

"This is the safest place in the galaxy," Kristi said. "You have my word that as long as you do not work against me, Givon Mielo will never have access to her or know of your involvement. She will never want for anything."

"Okay," Argus said. "Then we have an understanding. On one condition."

The Captain narrowed her eyes. "Speak."

"She will make her own decisions," Argus said. "About who and when to...follow your agenda."

Kristi thought about it and nodded. "I will advise her, but never force her. She is my equal, not my servant."

"Very well," Argus said, miserable but having no alternatives. He offered his hand, and the Captain shook it. "It was a pleasure speaking with you."

Chapter 13
Sector 1 – Axis
Abdullah Al Hakir

1

Abdullah strode through the empty Command Deck, heart thumping in his chest. His stomach was doing flips and his legs felt like rubber; all he wanted to do was lie down.

The Command Deck retinue was still on leave. Normally the terminals here were thriving with activity. Personnel pored over data and communications and filtered information for easy processing by the High Officers.

Tonight they would get their orders, and tomorrow they would flood back to Denigen's Fist. In a few days, they would be back on patrol.

Abdullah would have to send similar orders when he got back to his chambers. The thought was disorienting. How many of the soldiers he was in command of even knew who he was? A handful? Less? He would be delivering orders to over sixteen thousand soldiers on a daily basis. Most of his time would be spent on the bridge with the Captain.

He'd dreamed of one day acquiring a post like this, but that hope was unrealistic. He never actually thought it might happen.

A whisper of sound distracted him. He could have sworn he'd heard a voice.

There. It sounded like a child. He spun, trying to pinpoint the location in the empty hall. He saw a small light on the far side of the Command Deck. The Captain's private office.

Abdullah cocked his head and listened. Now that he'd pinpointed the sound it was easier to make out. It sounded like a young girl singing softly. The notes had an eerie echoing effect in the empty hall. Did the Captain have children?

It was by no means forbidden, but unexpected. Children had a way of humanizing people that no self-respecting Captain would tolerate. Many had children, of course, but they never brought them or their families onboard the ship.

But then again, he was the only person on the Command Deck today. Maybe he wasn't supposed to know someone was here.

He should leave. He had a duty to perform, and he didn't dare mess it up. Yet now his curiosity was piqued. He wanted to know if he was correct if the Captain was a mother. The thought was actually comforting. After everything else that had happened today, knowing that she was just a normal human with a family would do wonders for his psyche.

After a short internal debate, he walked to the cracked door. His heels clicked across the floor and he paused, wondering if he should knock.

Instead, he gently pushed the door open. The room was small and sparse. Old fashioned weapons hung on the left wall—Captain Schmidt had been a collector—and a faux fireplace glowed in the corner. The floor was carpeted in a maroon plush material. A one-way mirror gave vantage over the Command Deck behind him.

The only furniture was an ornate wooden desk with a rolling chair. A small girl, no more than six or seven, stood beside the desk. She held a doll in her hand and singing to it. She wore a sea green dress, and her brunette hair was done up in a ponytail. She didn't notice him come in.

She was holding the feet of the doll against her stomach and running her free hand through its hair, rocking absently back and forth on the carpet. Abdullah glanced warily around. There was no one to watch or supervise her.

"Hello," he said softly. He had to repeat himself before she glanced at him. She stopped dancing and clutched the doll to her chest, but her sudden look of fear was replaced by a wide grin within seconds.

"Hi," she said, looking shyly at her shoes. "I'm Abi."

"I'm Abdullah," he said, patting his chest. "Is your mother around?"

She shook her head. "No, my mother isn't here. My daddy is here, though. Do you need to speak to him? I can go find him."

"No, that's all right," Abdullah said, confused. The man on deck with Captain Kristi, most likely. Maybe he was replacing the deceased Sister Portia Nace as the onboard Minister.

If that was the case, Abdullah felt sorry for him.

"Do you like Betsy?" the girl asked. It took him a second to realize she meant the doll.

"She's quite pretty," he offered. Abi beamed.

"She's a mommy. But my dad wouldn't let me bring the other dolls. He made me put them in the trunk."

Abdullah nodded. "Do you have a lot of dolls?"

"Uh huh, I have lots. Do you have any?"

"No," Abdullah said.

"Oh," the girl said, looking back at her shoes. "My boyfriend has a lot of dolls."

"Who's your boyfriend?" Abdullah asked.

"Justin Tommy Miles," the girl said. The name sounded vaguely familiar.

"Is he a singer?"

"Uh huh. He said he's going to marry me one day. He said so."

"Mmhmm," Abdullah said. He decided it wasn't worth mentioning that the singer was probably three times older than the girl or that the young star had several other girlfriends his own age. "Is your father a Minister?" he asked.

"Um...I don't know," the girl said. "Do you want to hold Betsy?"

Abdullah shook his head. "No, she looks comfortable where she is," he said. "I need to go back to work. It was nice meeting you Abi."

"Nice meeting you too," she said, clipping each word with a nod and grinning. She spun and resumed stepping, humming to herself and rocking the doll in her arms. Abdullah watched for a moment, trying to wrap his mind around everything that had happened. The Ceremony, speaking with the Captain, and now meeting this little girl.

He couldn't. None of it made sense. With a sigh, he walked back out of the Captain's Office and away from the command deck. It was late evening, and he had orders to deliver.

Chapter 14
Sector 6 – Mali
Vivian Drowel

1

When morning came, Quinton prepared them a meal of vitamin enriched oatmeal and a loaf of stale bread. Vivian found the food distasteful, but once again Traq devoured his—and her—helping like a starving child. Vivian was grateful Traq was here. At the very least, their host wouldn't be offended. For whatever reason, Traq really did enjoy the food.

Quinton carried his still sleeping daughter to his wife's room. Vivian got her first good look at the sickly woman. She was small and slender and wrapped in a thick woolen blanket. Her face was drawn and pale. Quinton was right. She didn't have long for this world.

The sun was brighter and a deeper shade of red than she was used to when they headed out. It beamed down on them, promising to leave burns on her skin.

Children played a game with sticks. They all stopped to watch them pass.

Everything was different this morning. A thin layer of dust covered the city now and not many people were outdoors. Most of the water basins she'd seen the night before had lids covering them. Those lids were also covered in dusty clay.

Quinton saw her expression of distaste and chuckled. "Last night was just a light breeze. After a rain we don't have to worry about bad storms for a few months."

"I'd hate to see it during dry years," she said.

Quinton turned down a street. They passed more homesteads and apartments and a few shops just opening for the day. Meager wares and stale foodstuffs seemed to drive the economy.

Quinton led them to a squat three-story building. Out front, she saw four Jeeps—ancient combustion engines—and the first green plants in the entire city.

The greenery consisted of a well-tended garden. A few rose bushes, some dandelions, and a lonely persimmon. There were also a few undistinguishable bushes scattered around the flowers. It was pathetic compared to the carefully tended gardens she'd seen but made beautiful by proximity to so much dust and clay.

Vivian was impressed. "It's nice to see some things grow well here."

"My wife used to tend it," Quinton explained, an edge of pride in his voice. "But when she got sick..." his voice trailed off. He cleared his throat. "Some of the secretaries kept at it. A lot of people think it's a waste of water, but I think it inspires hope. I let them keep it."

"It is beautiful," Vivian said. "Maybe one day your entire planet can be like this again."

Quinton laughed. "Fill one hand with wishes and the other with..."

There was a sudden creaking sound. The door of the squat administration building burst open with a crash and a man stumbled outside, brandishing a projectile rifle. He pointed it at Vivian.

And here it comes, she thought. She'd been expecting this ever since the first walk through the city the previous night. She hoped to be gone before they found their courage.

She heard a shuffling from nearby as Traq crouched behind her and a whining sound, but she didn't dare take her eyes off the man as he spoke.

"We're confiscating your ship."

"Allen—" Quinton started.

"Shut up, old man!" the man said, briefly pointing it at Quinton before turning it back to Vivian. "You're too weak to do what is needed around here."

"There's no need for violence," Vivian said, keeping her voice low.

"Then you'll turn over the ship peaceably?" Allen asked, hope and suspicion on his face.

"I'm afraid I can't."

Allen's face hardened, and he drew the gun up. "Tell us how to fly it."

"She's going to help us," Quinton admonished. "Please lower the weapon!"

"Yeah, she is," Allen said. His grin was that of a feral animal. He was missing half his teeth. "All we need is her ship!"

It would take two seconds to kill this poor man. He wasn't trained, so he couldn't even understand how horribly outmatched he was. The rifle wasn't even aimed at her, but rather over her left shoulder. Vivian could draw her pistol, dodge his first haphazard shot, and one quick snap would end it. But she didn't want to do that. He was just a scared man with a rifle and no wits.

"I'll deliver your request for help to every planet I can," Vivian said. Allen started laughing, nearly hysterical.

"Like that would do any good. Those money grubbers wouldn't pull us out of the water if we were drowning."

"We can't take her ship," Quinton pleaded. "Allen, think this through. You have a family!"

"I said shut up!" Allen growled. Then his eyes narrowed and he spoke again. His voice thick with emotion, but Vivian heard every word. "We'll just figure the ship out ourselves. It can't be that hard." Vivian started to reach for her pistol.

Suddenly Allen's head disappeared, vaporized by a point-blank laser shot.

The hiss of the rifle came from inside the administration office. From their angle, they couldn't see who it was. Slowly the body slumped to the ground, thudding on its knees and collapsing sideways.

The shoulders landed in the garden, scattering dust into the air. Luckily the shot cauterized the neck, but there was a still a little fountain of blood spurting from the neck, drenching the white roses with droplets of blood.

Vivian let out a breath and glanced over at Quinton. The mayor stood frozen in place, staring at the body, all of the blood drained out of his face.

"Allen was one of my deputies," Quinton whispered. A man stepped out of the building with a rifle slung over his shoulder. This man Vivian did recognize.

It was Ralph.

"Sorry, I heard the commotion from inside and got here as fast as I could," Ralph said, leaning his rifle against the door and kneeling next to the body.

He's entirely too casual. This is definitely not his first time. I'm used to seeing death from my experiences as a Shield, but for most people the first death they experience is traumatic and—

Uh oh.

Vivian spun and glanced down the street behind them, letting out a long sigh and placing her knuckles against her temples.

I am really not good at this at all.

Traq was gone.

2

Quinton stood in the center of the street as the woman disappeared down the road at a full sprint. She was fast, and he knew without a doubt that he couldn't keep up for even a few seconds. She disappeared around the corner, and he realized what she was after.

"The kid must have gotten scared," he mumbled, turning back to the carnage. He felt sick. He felt old. He needed to be strong. He was in charge of this city, for God's sake. It wouldn't be good for him to fall to pieces.

There was nothing we could have done.

Allen made his choice. Thank God Ralph was there.

"Thanks," Quinton said. He moved over to Ralph, patting him on the shoulder. His legs were wobbly, but he could keep it together.

The roses were covered in little drips of blood. "My wife would kill me if she saw this."

Ralph Pearson chuckled. "That she would."

"We need to uh…" he said, then shook his head. His mind wasn't working. "We should…"

"Let's get him moved before people come around. His family shouldn't see him like this."

Quinton nodded, thankful Ralph was here. *I can never repay this debt,* he realized. He grabbed Allen's left side, fighting down his revulsion, and Ralph grabbed the right. Together they carried his torso and limbs back into the administration building.

A thin trail of blood followed them as they carried his deputy. First past the desks, then the staircase leading to the second floor. They traveled down a hallway to a storage room. Quinton's back strained from the load, like when they brought in grain from the silos or salt from the mines. This was just like that.

Except no matter how hard he wished, it was still Allen.

Don't fall apart. Keep it together.

They put the body in the storage room. It was the only thing he could think to do. Later they would have to move it, once he called the coroner. Probably in a few hours.

Quinton hated leaving Allen here like this, but he had to make sure the mess was contained before he could do anything about it.

"Thank you," Quinton repeated as they grabbed a pair of mops. He started scrubbing the line of blood that led back to the front door. A clear path. He still felt sick to his stomach, but it was as much from worry as it was from revulsion now. He didn't know what he was going to do, what he was going to say.

Especially to Allen's family. *He was a good man. He didn't deserve to die like this.* He took a deep breath and reminded himself to take things one step at a time.

"Thank God I was here," Ralph said while they scrubbed. "I didn't make it home last night with the storm coming on. Just slept in my office."

Quinton nodded. It took only a few moments to clean up the blood. They worked in silence, but when they were done he noticed Ralph staring at him. He was expectant, leaning against his mop.

"This wasn't isolated," Ralph said softly. "You know it wasn't."

"Allen always was too rash—"

"No," Ralph said, shaking his head vehemently. "The man's dead. He doesn't need us making a mockery of his life."

"He tried to kill us."

"His choices were bad. But the underlying problem is still there."

Quinton leaned in close, whispering, "We can't steal her ship. We aren't thieves."

"We don't need her ship," Ralph replied. "Allen was wrong. But we have problems. *Legitimate* problems. And we can't keep sweeping them under the rug!"

"Vivian promised she would get the word out. If we can get more water purifiers, then…"

Ralph was shaking his head. His eyes were cold. "No. Equipment won't solve anything. At best it will be a bandage. We need to address the problem at the source. They don't listen." As he said the last he waved vaguely out the door at the city beyond. His voice was gradually rising in anger as he spoke:

"If we just buckle down and fix our own problems, then we won't need anyone else's help. It is not their job to take care of us, Quinton. I might have pulled the trigger, Quinton, but you forced his hand. His death is on your hands. No one will help us unless we can help ourselves."

"Ralph..." Quinton said, "We can't stop people from using water."

"We can regulate it better. And the food."

"We can't—"

"We can!" Ralph said, throwing his mop across the room. "Stop hiding behind fear! Allen's dead because he thought you were weak. Maybe he was right." Ralph was practically spitting the words. He stared at him, then looked over his shoulder. His eyes narrowed. "We don't need *their* pity."

Quinton glanced over his shoulder and saw Vivian coming back to the building, holding hands with a terrified looking Traq. He was glad they'd had time to move the body out of the way.

By the time he turned back, though, Ralph was gone.

3

Traq hadn't made it far down the street before Vivian caught him. He was around the corner at a full sprint back toward Quinton's apartment, terrified. She'd put her hand on his shoulder to stop him. His sudden reversal of direction almost tripped her as he jumped at her. He clung to her waist, crying and sputtering.

Wow, I've had the kid for four days and already he's watched somebody get murdered in front of him. I don't need a book to tell me how bad I've screwed this up. Is there anything else I can ruin today?

She gently patted him on the back for a few minutes, trying to figure out what to say. What could possibly make this situation any better? Had Traq's mother ever taught him about death? She doubted it.

Vivian hadn't seen anyone killed until she was twenty-four. She'd seen animals killed for ritual and slaughter. But never people. What kind of effect would seeing a man get his head blown off have on a five-year-old?

It couldn't be good, but there was nothing she could do about it. Right now she had to get him off the planet before anything else went wrong.

"Let's go," she said, grabbing his shoulders and stepping back. He looked up at her, still sobbing, and she felt miserable. She took his hand and started walking back toward the building. At first, he struggled a little, but then he fell silently into step.

She saw Ralph and Quinton talking in the doorway and then Ralph disappeared farther into the shadows. There was still blood in the garden, but the body was gone, for which she was duly thankful. Quinton handed her a stack of data pads.

"I...this is all the data we have on those stations I told you about. It's not edited. Don't worry, we have copies."

She took them gently and slid them into a pocket. She didn't even care anymore. "You have my thanks."

"You should go," Quinton said, but he couldn't meet her eyes. "It's not safe here just now."

"I understand," she said. They shook hands.

"I can take you back to your ship," Quinton said, gesturing to one of the off-road vehicles. Vivian helped Traq inside and sat next to him as Quinton put the vehicle into motion.

They traveled in silence out into the deserted wasteland. It couldn't sustain, she knew. It was a fragile city slowly bleeding to death from multiple wounds. One misstep and they would all die.

She wished she could help. Right now, though, she wasn't even sure she could help one five-year-old child.

Once at their ship, Quinton said farewell as Vivian lowered the ramp. Traq disappeared from her side to his room and she went to the cockpit, firing up the engines.

She placed a call directly to the Office of Argus Wade. He answered quickly.

"Hello Argus," she said.

"Vivian," Argus Wade said, delighted. "How are you?"

"Terrible," she said.

"Oh?" he asked, arching an eyebrow. "Whatever could be the—"

"Stuff it, Wade," Vivian said. "I'm not good at this. It was a terrible plan."

"Kids usually are," he said. "And the worst part is, you can't give them back."

"This one I can," she said. He shook his head, his smile disappearing.

"No, Vivian. You can't. You're committed. Come Hell or high water, you are committed."

"I'm just making things worse. I screwed up, Wade. I screwed up bad," she said. Her voice sounded whinier than she would have liked.

"Oh, it couldn't have been—"

"He watched a man die."

A pause. "He what?"

"You heard me."

"Wow. I don't know what to say. Did you *have* to kill him?"

"I didn't kill anyone," Vivian said, offended. "I wouldn't do anything like that unless absolutely necessary."

"Well there you go," Wade said. "Just help him get past this and turn it into a lesson."

"What lesson, Wade, should a five-year-old learn that involves death?" she asked, and then sobbed. "Wade, I can't do this. I'm just going to drop him off somewhere safe and leave."

"If you do that you know what will happen," Wade said, his voice soft.

"I can't," she said, brushing a tear off her cheek.

"You can. Just be there for him and help him. You are a terrific person."

She sighed. "Okay, Wade. I'll try. But I'm telling you, I'm just going to make things worse. I've probably ruined him already."

She clicked a few controls, trying to guide her ship off the planet into space. It didn't move. Instead, a warning light flashed on and she scrunched her nose up in confusion.

Crap, are we stuck in the mud? Did something break?

"Wade, I'll contact you later. I have a problem."

"All right, Vivian. Just remember two things: you can do this, just be there for him."

"Uh huh, and what's the other thing?"

"I now have video footage of you crying," Wade said and then the screen went blank. Vivian cursed and stood up, wiping tears from her eyes. Despite Argus Wade's encouragement, she knew she was no good for the kid.

She could drop him off at an orphanage. Make them promise to take good care of him. She would just ruin everything for both of them if she took him in. *He doesn't deserve to be stuck with someone as terrible as me,* she thought. *I never was good with children.*

The warning was still blinking, and it showed the ramp was still lowered. The outside controls were deactivated, so the command had come from inside. She picked up her pistol and moved slowly through the ship, wondering if she had an intruder. *Another person wants to take my ship?*

She made it to the ship's ramp and saw Traq near the exit hatch, facing away from her and with something heavy clutched to his chest. She scrunched her nose in confusion, lowering her gun.

"Traq?"

He spun, almost dropping his armload. She saw that it was a large bucket filled to the brim with water from the ships sink. He saw her eyes go wide and looked down at the bucket, almost apologetically.

"They need water," he said. Vivian stood in the hall, staring at Traq. "So I was going to bring them some."

Suddenly it was hard for Vivian to breathe.

I was wrong, Vivian realized, stepping forward and gently taking the container from him. *I don't deserve someone as good as him.*

Interlude
Sector 4 – Tellus
Captain Lyle Queston

1

"What is the meaning of this?" Captain Queston asked, settling back into his chair and glaring at the monitor. On the other end was Captain Emilio Finch, traitor, and turncoat to the Republic. "You would dare stop my ships?"

"You've entered Union territory," Emilio said patiently. He was a big man, large lips, and freckles. "We don't want to attack you."

"Then move your ships!" Captain Queston growled angrily. "And there won't be a problem."

"This isn't Republic space."

"I know that," Queston muttered. He was in his own lavish personal chambers taking this call—he didn't want his men to know what was going on and perhaps ruin his plans—but it wasn't going as expected. He'd expected to show up to general fanfare and act as appropriate to resolve the situation.

Instead, he'd been greeted by a fleet of thirty ships armed and ready for a fight. He had four warships at his command (all warships, unlike some of the enemy vessels, which were merchant vessels or private ships) and was fairly certain he could survive an engagement. At least long enough to flee.

But he didn't want to flee. That would defeat his entire purpose in coming here, and he would *not* return without accomplishing his objective. This would make him a hero and seal his position for life. They might even consider giving him a promotion to war fleet command.

"I'm here to speak with Darius."

"On behalf of the First Citizen?" Captain Finch asked.

"On behalf of myself," Captain Queston said with a sneer. I have brought my ships and intend to swear myself to his cause."

It was a lie, of course, but one well told. Captain Queston prided himself on being a fantastic liar, and he wasn't concerned with someone as lowly as Captain Finch calling his bluff.

So he surely wasn't expecting the other man's response to be, "Why?"

"Why what?"

"Why would you swear yourself to our cause?"

So it's our cause now?

"I want to help create a better galaxy and be part of the rearranging of our political structures. The Republic has trod on the weak for too long, and it is time for things to change," he said. The words came out with confidence and clarity, masking the contempt just beneath the surface.

Captain Finch nodded. "You would be a tremendous asset," he said.

"Of course, I will be—"

"But that does not change anything in the short term. I cannot allow you to pass thus armed."

Captain Queston narrowed his eyes. "You are saying I must turn around?"

"We can escort your fleet closer to the planet and allow you to take a shuttle to speak with Darius, but there are conditions."

"What conditions?"

"Lower your shields, remove power from all of your weapons, and allow my men to come on board until things are resolved."

"Never!" Lyle growled.

"Then I suppose you must turn around."

"You're asking me to put my fleet at your mercy."

"If your intentions are honorable, then you have nothing to fear."

"Without a doubt, my intentions are honorable!"

"Then as soon as you have sworn allegiance I will withdraw my troops and allow you free reign in our territory."

"This is how you greet a senior Captain of the fleet?" Lyle asked bitterly.

"That is no longer my fleet," Captain Finch reminded him, his voice hard. "And it is my duty to protect this planet. If Darius accepts your oath of fealty, then I will be the first to congratulate you with a cold beer and pat on the back. But until then, you have heard my terms."

I could blast a hole through your pathetic fleet. I could destroy all of your ships and drop bombs onto Tellus and wipe Darius out of existence.

Except, he was fairly certain he couldn't.

Turning over his defenses was a terrible plan. If Captain Finch decided to turn against his ships, there was nothing he could do to stop him.

But it was the only way he was going to get any closer to the planet. All it would take was one conversation with Darius to prove his loyalty and then he would be free to move about and do as he pleased.

Like, execute Darius Gray.

"I accept your conditions," Captain Queston said, waving his hand in acknowledgment. "I will power down all but the core functionality of my ships and allow you to escort me to the planet. And when I have spoken to Darius you will see that my intentions are honorable and that all of this is an unnecessary mistake."

Captain finch nodded slightly. "We shall see."

2

Captain Lyle Queston strode through the entry hall with purposeful steps, conscious of the loud *click-clack* his hard soled shoes made against the marble floor. His three Keepers, on the other hand, passed with barely a whisper, wearing soft slippers and plain silver robes. They were gifts from his Ministerial Envoy, Maxwell Foor.

When they were first brought on board, five years ago, they terrified him. It was one thing to hear about the Ministry's punishment for those who deviated from the faith; it was quite another to see the effects first hand: three young women, all lobotomized as children, left to serve whatever purpose their addled minds could handle.

But, as time progressed, the Captain had become gradually more and more fascinated by them. They had a simple nature, lacking the petty animosity of their betters. Give them treats and they were happy, leave them alone and they were content. Maxwell enjoyed sending the three to wander the halls of Lyle's warship, a subtle warning of what could happen to people if the True Faith found them lacking.

Consequently, whenever he gave a sermon, the great Ministerial hall was packed.

Captain Lyle brushed a strand of hair from his forehead and straightened his coat. He was a handsome man with thinning hair. A well-maintained beard graced his high cheekbones, giving him an aristocratic look. He worked hard to maintain it. It kept the men serving under him loyal and made women blush.

He knew he was attractive and spent time cultivating his appeal.

Pillars of white granite flanked the central walkway every five meters. Outside the pillars, the floor was a shade of deep blue. Inside they were a dark shade of red.

Seventy meters from the door to the central chamber. The ceiling climbed two flights above, making the room feel spacious. Opaque glass sky-domes went even higher, spread every fifteen meters along the trek, spilling dull sunlight onto the floor.

It created an interesting effect. Lyle walked from shadow to light and back into shadow as he clicked his way down the hall. The walls were swirling blue, gray, and black marble, giving the entire hall an ostentatious and gloomy air.

He didn't have to make the walk so goddamned long, Lyle decided. What sort of pretentious bastard makes people walk seventy meters across an empty hall just to reach his throne?

And it *was* decidedly a throne, sitting atop a pyramid of steps in the central chamber. The throne was cut from more of the swirling marble, making it blend into the wall behind it. It was backlit by hidden globes to help it stand out.

The granite pillars ended at the edge of the circular chamber, and the throne rested in its center.

All that walking, and the room ends with a child sitting in the central seat?

Darius Gray was a small man, short by common standards and slim of build. He wore a silver goatee on his chin that matched his leather outfit. He couldn't have been over twenty years old.

Other than the goatee he was bald. His eyes were sunken and skin stretched, sallow. Captain Queston wondered if perhaps the youth had spent the better part of his life malnourished.

It would certainly fit the rumors surrounding him. Darius fought and killed the people who saved him from poverty and fled here to start a revolt. Out here, on Tellus, the people worshiped the very ground he walked on. He was going to save them from the First Citizen and Republic and give them everything they deserved.

Such silly nonsense. The only thing these people deserved was a bullet.

Lyle stopped in front of the throne, craning his neck to look at the child. *Maybe if I join Darius, the people will side with me instead of him,* he realized. The more he thought about it, the more likely it seemed. Why would they side with Darius, a child, over one of the greatest military minds the Republic had to offer?

It had been four years since this revolt began and the Union was born. Four years of defiance, and what did the little revolt have to show for it? Three poor little planets on the edge of Republic space, hanging on by a thread. Tellus was the only planet worth anything. The others were simply too poor to matter.

Lyle watched Darius on his throne, unimpressed. One of the keepers coughed. The air brushed against the back of his neck. The sound echoed down the hall and back to them several times before fading away.

He waited for Darius to speak.

But he didn't. Instead, he tapped idly on a data pad on his lap. If he even knew the Captain was there, he didn't show it. *Arrogant child.*

Captain Queston was used to dealing with his kind before—pretentious and overconfident as only a young man can be—and this would be no different. Darius sought the same things all young men seek: entertainment and glory.

And he's getting both. As much as the Captain hated Darius, he had to admit that his plan was effective. He had seen the effect of Darius's rhetoric personally when he landed his shuttle. The planet was in the middle of a revolt against the greatest superpower the galaxy had even known, threatened by a war they couldn't possibly win, and outclassed in every way that mattered. And yet, rather than being too terrified to act or think—as would have been appropriate—they had hope that they could win.

Hope. As though hope will protect them from the First Citizen's wrath.

But they were just civilians, easily molded and even easier to break. Darius could preach all he wanted about the glory of his cause, but he had no chance of actually accomplishing the quest he'd set for himself.

The arrogant fool would end up getting everyone who joined him killed.

3

Which wasn't why Captain Queston was here. Or rather, it was precisely why he was here. Captain Emilio Finch, the asshat who seized his ships, controlled three warships, none of which were Capital Class. When Darius and Tellus turned traitor, Emilio swore fealty to Darius. His punishment for such a crime would be an ignoble death.

Another thirty ships could join Darius tomorrow, and it still wouldn't be enough to make the galaxy worry. *No matter how big you build your marble seat, child, you'll never be able to fill it.*

Lyle stood before the marble stairs and waited.

A long minute passed.

Shooting Darius now was a decent idea. He'd been ordered by Captain Finch to come unarmed, but he'd slipped a holdout pistol through security just in case. They hadn't even searched him, the idiots.

But, if he shot Darius, he would be putting his ships at risk. They were flanked and outnumbered. Right now he would be hard pressed to make it off the planet into warp if he shot Darius. Better to finish this situation, regain control of his fleet, and strike at Darius when a better opportunity presented itself.

Darius tapped his data pad, the sound echoing in the room.

Lyle stared up at Darius with mounting rage. He wondered what was going through the young man's mind. Did he understand how offensive he was being to his elder? His *better*?

If Darius was even half as smart as people claimed, he was probably trying to decide how deferential he should be. Lyle was a veteran Captain. *Surely* Darius understood just how important Lyle's support would be to his cause? Captain Lyle would *legitimize* this piss-ant revolution.

Lyle was more decorated than any other Captain in the fleet. And he'd worn every one of his medals for this ridiculous occasion.

Lyle needed to have control of this conversation.

Why is it so hot in here?

Lyle tugged at the collar of his shirt, loosening its grip on his neck and then offered a thin bow.

"Distinguished Noble," he began grandly, more than willing to be the first to speak. "I come before you today to swear fealty to your cause. I would like to offer gifts on behalf of a future without the Republic."

He finished with a flourish and a bow and waited for Darius to respond. Time fluttered past with scarce notice. Darius stared at him as if bored and then tapped a few quick strokes on his data pad.

He seeks to throw me off guard, Lyle decided, still benevolent. He thinks that if he doesn't respond, I'll panic. But he doesn't understand the kind of people I've dealt with. He's nothing. A nobody. I've written Peace Treaties with Warlords. I can handle a little bastard child.

He gestured toward the three Keepers with his arm and continued, "As you can see, the gifts I have brought to you are exquisite specimens from my own collection, gathered at great personal cost. They serve in my Ministry—" still no reply "—and I have more than sixty-thousand men aboard four ships. All of them are ready to defect and swear fealty to your cause.

"In addition, I have gathered pass codes to defense grids protecting two Core Worlds that I would be willing to divulge...provided you accept."

Again Darius refused to respond. He looked thoughtful for a moment and then wrote another note on his data pad.

Lyle tugged at his collar again and fought down embarrassment and ire. To ignore him once was a calculated offense, but now Darius was bordering on insolent.

Was he actually *thinking* about whether to accept Lyle's offer? Four ships—all of which were more powerful than Captain Finch's pathetic offerings—was nothing to scoff at? These were warships, each capable of large scale engagements.

This proposal from Lyle was the best stroke of luck Darius could ever wish for. And that wasn't counting Lyle himself, the most distinguished Military Leader apart from General Nicolai himself!

"Surely you accept my oath, so I see no need to further waste your time. I'll have one of my Commanders send you a copy of—"

"Do you like Bakka?"

The interrupt was smooth. Darius spoke with ease and his voice carried weight.

Lyle stuttered. "...what?"

"Do. You. Like. Bakka?" Darius asked, slower this time. He emphasized each word.

Lyle was nearly shaking from the insolence. What the hell kind of question is that? Does he think me a petulant child? I could draw my gun and end his life in a second, ending this entire uprising in its infancy! Perhaps that would be for the best...

"It's a fruit pastry, local to Tellus," Darius continued, oblivious to Lyle's rage. "I had never tasted it before I arrived, and it was a piece of sheer luck that I picked Tellus as the world to help found the Planetary Union. The pastries here are quite delicious."

Lyle shook his head, seething. "I don't see how that relates—"

"See, my conundrum is this: keepers don't retain full faculties after the lobotomy, yet they still enjoy sweet foods. Most things don't affect them, given their state of being, but they react with great pleasure to sugar. I think it's an innate human feature that can never be taken away. Something hidden within the lizard brain, I suppose. Do you agree?"

The last words hung in the air between them, echoing softly off the marble as Lyle searched for a response. *Where is he going with this?*

Darius's tongue poked out the side of his mouth as he thought. He punched a few more times on his data pad and looked expectantly back at the Captain. Lyle rubbed his temples and blinked a few times. His mind felt fuzzy with...

Anger...?

Of course, he was angry, but...but he wasn't, was he?

He suddenly wasn't sure.

"Yes. I think I see where you are going...but if we can turn back to the business at hand..."

"Whenever I find Keepers, I kill them," Darius said, his voice flat. He could have been talking about the weather. "But not because I'm angry with them, you see? They are an abomination, but it isn't their fault. I don't want to punish them, and I certainly wouldn't make them suffer."

"Um...okay...?" Lyle said. He felt heavy, like a weight was resting on his mind, trying to drag him to the ground. He suppressed a yawn, and shook his head, trying to clear it. *What the hell is going on?*

"So I stuff Bakka with poison and let Keepers eat the sugary pastry. They gorge themselves on the sweet treats as their lives ebb away."

As he said the last part, another section of marble separated along the right wall, revealing a door. It sunk into the frame.

A woman—she couldn't have been more than seventeen—walked out of the hidden doorway. Her mouth was curled in a sweet smile, and her hips swayed as she walked.

She was carrying a silver tray in her left hand. It took him a minute to recognize the little pink pastries, and when he did his mouth hung open. Bakka. Lyle recognized it as a childhood treat popular on most worlds among the wealthiest of families.

Suddenly he found it difficult to breathe.

4

The young woman had to be one of the twin sisters who fled the church with Darius, either Maven or Alyssa. Lyle didn't know a lot about them except that they were in Darius's inner circle. They had allegedly become generals in his army.

He found that to be a stupid decision. They were untested. You don't put a novice in a veteran's position and expect greatness.

Doubtless Darius's decision was based purely on his adolescent need for the woman's approval. She was beautiful by any standard with blue eyes that danced with amusement.

This was probably Alyssa. Rumors claimed that Maven was difficult to look upon. She was scarred at birth with some sort of accident and he'd always imagined a girl with a tail. Or gills.

This sister wore her jet black hair at neck length. Evenly cut bangs fell down her forehead to just above her eyebrows, framing her smooth face.

She wore a mini-skirt that barely reached her thighs and a white v-cut blouse. Both her face and chest were dotted with freckles.

She walked over to Lyle, smiling lasciviously at him, and offered the tray to him. Lyle felt sweat dripping down the back of his uniform and fought the urge to adjust his collar again. He stared at the pastries with mild fascination and tried to think through the ramifications of what was happening.

Things weren't going as planned. Not at all. He wasn't even considering how to regain control of the conversation. Now he just wanted to get out of here and never look back.

"Would you like a pastry?" Darius asked politely. His words carried, slapping Lyle like a wet towel. Captain Lyle blinked a few times, forcing his thoughts to coalesce. They were jumbled, as though they'd been pushed out of order in his head.

"What? No...no...no, thank you," he mumbled, clearing his throat.

Darius gestured and Alyssa shifted a few steps, offering the tray to the Keepers. Lyle fought the urge to slap the tray out of her hand. Instead, he watched in horror as the blank-eyed Keeper grabbed a thick pastry and shoved it in her mouth, barely chewing. She swallowed a huge mouthful.

Lyle watched in awe, expecting the lobotomized girl to keel over at any moment. *That's crazy. This is crazy. Darius wouldn't poison my Keeper in front of me, would he? That's murder, even against such partial-people.*

But he still expected it to happen. A moment passed. The Keeper chewed. Nothing changed.

Alyssa walked up the stairs to Darius. He took an offered pastry from the tray and waved her away. She glided to the bottom and stood off to the side, watching Lyle with a calm expression on her face.

Darius bit into the pastry and then let out a sigh of pleasure.

"Delicious," he said, wiping his mouth and setting the pastry on the edge of his marble chair.

"It...uh..." Lyle managed, but he couldn't think of anything to say. It was too hot. The world was practically swimming.

"Now, let us talk business. You offer me your pledge of four ships. But you could have brought four *hundred* ships if you so desired. Perhaps even thousands would join if you truly intended to defect. But you don't, do you?"

"I...of course, I..."

"So the only real question we have to resolve is, "Who else knew you were coming here to kill me?"

5

"This was a lone wolf kind of decision, wasn't it?" Darius added. "You asked Nicolai for permission to attack me, but he denied you, so you came of your own accord. You figured killing me would propel your standing, and once you'd accomplished the task Nicolai would have to forgive and reward you."

Lyle took a step backward, hands shaking. He looked around, hearing a pounding on the walls. No, it was in his ears. He considered trying to run away but knew it wouldn't work. The grand entrance hall had seemed long on the way in. The trip out would be impossible.

"But there were some things they didn't tell you, weren't there?" Darius said, apologetic. "Like who I really am? Where I really came from? And most important, what I can do. I doubt even Nicolai himself knows the half of it."

Lyle felt his mind closing in panic. *He can't know that's why I'm here. He's bluffing. He has to be. Any fool would think I might have wanted to kill him, but he can't know for sure!*

Darius stared at him for a long second and leaned back, waving his hand dismissively. Suddenly, everything changed. It was like a cool breeze washed over him, wiping away his headache. The pressure he hadn't even realized was there disappeared. The world felt lighter, cleaner.

What just happened? What the hell just happened?

"No matter," Darius said. "You don't need to tell me *everything*. I have other ways of extracting the information I need. Without you, though. I don't really need you, anymore. I suppose you are just as useless as I feared."

"The...uh...codes," Captain Lyle said, rubbing his forehead and taking another half-step backward. "I know codes that can bypass..."

"These?" Darius asked with a light smile, holding up the data pad and turning it to face Lyle. Even if Lyle could have read the numbers from this distance they would have been too blurry to understand. His vision was swimming in terror. "They were at the forefront of your thoughts. You shouldn't offer up your bargaining chips so easily."

"I would serve you..." he whispered, right hand gliding slowly toward the holdout pistol in his pocket. Could he draw it before Darius's guards took him down? *I should end the uh...the um...resistance...in the name of...that person...the one I serve...*

No, he wouldn't be able to, he realized. Whatever was happening was something he didn't understand. He'd come here sorely ill-prepared. He moved his hand away from the gun and used it instead to wipe his forehead.

Darius watched his motion and made a *tsk*-ing sound. "You brought a *weapon*, even after we agreed that you would come unarmed."

"It's not loaded!" Lyle insisted, fighting down panic.

"Isn't it?" Darius asked. Lyle felt his hand jerk down of its own volition. It grabbed the gun and yanked it out of his pocket. Then his arm rose ever so slowly toward the side. The rest of his body was still under his control, but sluggish, as if he were lying under several tons of mud.

He watched in helpless horror as the gun took aim, zeroing in on the temple of a red-haired keeper. The vacant young woman stared forward, not even registering his change in posture.

"You say it isn't loaded," Darius said, leaning forward in his throne. "Let's find out."

Lyle couldn't stop it. He felt his finger pull the trigger.

The loaded bullets were hollow point, a personal favorite. There was a resounding *crack* in the air, followed by a miniature explosion. That was followed by a splash as droplets of warm blood hit Lyle's exposed hands and face.

The young Keeper stayed standing in the same exact position, minus half of her head. The crash of the gunshot reverberated through the dim hall violently, ricocheting painfully off walls and bouncing back. The pain in his temple from the noise was nauseating, and he heard a ringing that came from everywhere and nowhere. Gore splattered the floor, wall, and pillar behind the Keeper.

Time froze.

The body slipped to the floor.

Captain Lyle Queston let out an agonized sob.

"A lie?" Darius said, his voice soft. "Dear Captain, you can't expect me to trust a liar, can you?"

As if in a dream, the gun reversed direction and he felt the muzzle touch against the side of his head. *This can't be possible. He's just a child! He's just a goddamned child!* The barrel scalded his skin from the last shot.

"Please..." he managed to sputter. "*Please...*"

He pulled the trigger.

And then it ended.

Chapter 15
Sector 4 - Tellus
Darius Gray, Alyssa Ophidian

1

Darius rubbed his temple's and let out an exhausted sigh. His head hurt, the same way it always did when he exerted himself.

The ringing wouldn't stop. He should buy a sound dampening system, something so that at least high frequency sounds like gunshots wouldn't echo so damn much. Or at least he could invest in some earplugs.

Not that it would matter if he wasn't given time to put them in. He hadn't been expecting the gunshots; they weren't part of his original script, but he considered them a good improvisation under the circumstances. And Alyssa had followed along perfectly with her puppet master impersonation. She was a firebrand.

That's what he loved about her.

The ringing finally diminished. He brushed the half-eaten pastry off the armrest, no longer hungry, and pressed a button on his communicator. "Send someone in to clean up this mess," he said. "And two glasses of water."

He didn't wait for a response before clicking the communicator off again. He stretched and looked down at the Captain below. The man's blood was pooling. Bits of his brain matter and gore from his skull were covering the remaining pair of Keepers, who were cowering. Darius walked down to them and eyed them slowly.

"I thought we *weren't* going to kill him," Darius said.

Alyssa shrugged. "Not originally."

"I thought he would serve as an example. Send him back to the First Citizen properly cowed. A warning. What changed your mind?"

"He wasn't worth the effort," Alyssa replied. "He was a coward. It barely even took a suggestion to get him to do it." She was sitting at the bottom of the stairs now, rubbing her temples. "He didn't even fight back. I could have made him dance before shooting himself."

"Did you make him wet himself?" Darius asked, glancing down and stepping around the mingling puddles.

Alyssa chuckled.

"No. He did that by himself."

"You're right, though. He was easy to read. I got all of his passcodes and command sequences. Did we secure his ships?"

"The entire crew is being checked already. They surrendered almost immediately. Our logistics officer said he thinks fifty thousand soldiers might remain loyal after his 'vetting' process. It should take a few months, though, to accomplish."

"So many?" Darius asked. He'd expected about twenty thousand to make it through his rigorous tests. He needed to stamp out problems. He didn't like the idea of executing so many, but he needed to make sure that he only kept soldiers he could trust.

And that he made his point. The point was everything. These men might be loyal from pride or trust one day. In the meantime, fear would have to do.

"That's just an estimate. He'll give you final figures in a few weeks."

"What about your sister? Is she making any progress? It would be nice to recruit some loyal troops and start causing real damage. I'm sure they would be more than willing to fight."

Alyssa stood up and sidled over to Darius, wrapping her arms around him. "So curious about my sister? Perhaps I can take your mind off of dear Maven."

"Perhaps," Darius agreed.

Already a cleaning crew was assembling waiting for them to back away from the mess.

"Can you believe he tried to offer us Keepers as a gift?"

"I thought everyone knew you hated them," she said with a chuckle. "What an arrogant ass, to not even look into your history before coming here. What will you do with them?"

Darius half turned and cocked an eyebrow. "You have to ask?"

She shrugged. "It seems like such a waste to kill them."

"It's draconic, I know. But they terrify me. It's a chilling reminder of what the Ministry had in store for me."

"Murdering them seems a rather extreme punishment, though. *They* did nothing wrong."

"You have a better alternative?"

"Let them live. They are simple. They will never bother you."

He turned sharply toward the rest of the servants. "Clean these bodies up. I don't want a speck of blood left," he ordered. They sprang into action, grabbing the bodies and swiping mop heads across the floor. He turned to Alyssa. "They will *always* bother me. Send me a report on your sister."

2

Alyssa glided down the hallway, struggling to keep her face and raging emotions under control. Sometimes she hated Darius. Hated the way he would ignore her. The way he treated her. The way he looked at her sister.

She walked with purpose, heading through the lobby and servant quarters to a war room they had prepared in the back. She passed several holographic projectors, each showing a different speech Darius made in the last six years throughout Sector Four. Those speeches were getting common viewership even outside Sector Six.

She stepped into the war room and glanced around. One of her lieutenants was leaning over a table, his scraggly beard hanging from his chin and sweat pouring down his face as he typed furiously on a data pad. She doubted he'd worked so hard in his entire life.

"Adrian," she said, her voice sharper than she intended. The man turned to her, a haggard look in his eyes.

"Yes, ma'am?" he asked, standing up and rubbing his forehead with a bandana.

"How are the preparations coming?"

"We have seized all four of Captain Queston's ships and begun logging inventory. I must say the munitions depot is rather more stocked than anticipated. There are more than sixty-two class G light cruisers in the hangar of the Lady Falla alone. Which is regrettably more than we have of pilots, so we will have to begin training—"

"Sixty-two?"

Adrian looked mildly angry at the interruption but said nothing. "Yes, ma'am."

"How big are they? Do they have warp capabilities?"

Adrian gestured in frustration. "Big. Several hundred tons apiece. And, yes, they can warp. They are docked inside the warship."

"But they can also land on planets?"

He made and humph sound. Alyssa considered wiping the condescending look—the *why are you asking stupid questions?*—off Adrian's face, but decided against it. Right now she was angry, and if she let even an ounce of that frustration out to play, she might not be able to stop.

"Bring one down here."

"Here?"

"Yes, here!" she said vehemently. "And if you question another order I will force you to tear off your own testicles. Bring two, in fact. I want one stored close by. Look for a large abandoned building to hide it, and make sure no one can find it. The other will be my personal transportation. Mark sixty on the report."

"Can you fly it?" Adrian asked, his eyes went wide as he realized what he'd said. "No, no, what I meant was do I need to find a pilot to train you as well."

"Yes, a pilot to train me would be excellent. Find one who is suitable. Both ships need personal crews to maintain them and keep them in peak condition, in case I have to—" she almost said *flee* "—leave the planet in a hurry."

"Is there anything else you require?" Adrian asked.

Alyssa thought for a long moment and then let out a long sigh, cursing under her breath. "Yes," she said. "Send me an update on my bitch of a twin sister."

Chapter 16
Sector 6 – Jaril
Maven Ophidian

1

Maven groaned as the beeping receiver woke her up. She rolled to her side and threw her pillow at the far wall of the officers' quarters at the sound. It did no good. The beeping continued.

A glance at her clock told her that eleven hours had passed since she went to sleep. *Eleven hours and no one woke me up or killed me in my sleep? I suppose the crew will be loyal yet.*

But even if her mutinous crew aboard Evelyn's Grace wasn't suffocating her in her sleep, *someone* was trying to wake her up.

She staggered off the plush bed and over to the view screen, rubbing bleariness out of her eyes. She brought the image into focus. It was her sister, Alyssa.

Maven groaned. If there was anyone she didn't want to talk to right now, it was her pompous and arrogant sibling.

She stumbled to the restroom, letting her sister wait. Eventually, Alyssa would give up and record a message. Voice, of course. Not text.

But that was neither here nor there. Right now Maven was more concerned with dressing and getting out to visit her crew—had she really slept eleven hours?—and see how much damage they had caused.

None of them liked her. Until a few months ago they all served the First Citizen. When Captain Finch rebelled, he took them with him. Many were loyal to Finch rather than the Republic, and most of their families lived out on Tellus anyway. For them, not a lot changed in their Chain of Command.

But it was still a large change. They went from having cozy military jobs in a peaceful era to being enemy number one; couple that with being ordered around by a sixteen-year-old girl who wasn't even *in* the military six years ago and they became quite disgruntled.

But *that's why Darius sent me*, she thought with only a touch of bitterness. *No man out here would respect Alyssa. She's too pretty. But they see my oxygen mask and listen to me struggle to breathe; they* imagine the terrible scars that lie beneath my hood. They envisage the horrible misshapen creature that I am, the exact antithesis of my sister's ravishing beauty, and they fear me.

Right now she needed that fear. It was what kept her in charge if nothing else. And she needed to be in charge. Oh yes, she needed it badly.

Horrible misshapen creature that she was, she had big dreams.

2

When she was finished preparing and putting her breathing mask on, she finally clicked on the communicator. "Alyssa? What do you need?"

"Is that how you greet your sister?"

"No, but I thought I'd be polite today."

"Darius wants to know how it's going."

"And you as well?"

"I don't particularly care."

"You can tell him it's going fine. We arrived at Jaril this morning. They won't let us land yet."

"Then attack them," Alyssa said. "Enough barrages and they will be loyal."

"Enough barrages and no one will be left to be loyal," she said. "Kind of defeats the purpose."

"Just take the damn planet. We gave you a warship."

"You mean *he* gave me a warship," Maven corrected.

"Just take the planet, Maven," Alyssa said. "We need more soldiers."

"How did the meeting with Captain Queston go?"

"He's dead."

"Oh?"

"Self-inflicted. I might have had something to do with it."

Maven laughed. "Well then, I suppose things are going well."

"What happens if next time they shoot instead of talk? What are we going to do then? We need more ships."

"I'll get *us* more ships," Maven replied. "But I'm going to do it my way."

Then she hung up, smiling to herself. She could imagine Alyssa on the other end, scowling.

"My way," she reiterated with a sigh. "The *right* way."

Chapter 17
Sector 6 – Jaril
Vivian Drowel, Oliver Atchison

1

"This is merchant vessel KMV1 Cudgel requesting permission to land," Vivian intoned into her headset, fingers flicking over the ship's controls. A few moments passed, followed by a click and then a young woman listed off docking coordinates.

Vivian dropped her ship through the atmosphere and lowered down to the surface, landing in her designated hangar. Traq sat next to her on the copilot's chair, eyes wide open as he took in the sights beyond the viewport.

The city was comprised of muted grays and silver. Skyscrapers reached into the clouds and the roadways were congested with innumerable vehicles. A greasy haze hung in the air, the result of burning fossilized and natural fuels. Primitive technology, low in efficiency, but for many planets it was all they could afford.

The city reached for the horizon, a good twenty-mile sprawl. It was impressive. Especially to someone like Traq, who'd probably never seen a single building more than twenty stories, let alone an entire city of them.

The ship came to rest in the dock. Vivian sat still in the pilot's chair for a few moments, wondering why she was here. It was an impulsive decision, and one likely to get her killed.

She still felt good, however. Other than his current disbelief at seeing Jaril for the first time, Traq seemed to be relatively unscathed by their recent misadventure on Mali.

They hadn't talked much on the flight from Mali to Jaril, and she'd spent most of her time poring over her books. She was determined to learn every scrap of knowledge she could.

Her communicator flickered to life, and Argus Wade's face appeared on the console. Traq disappeared, still not used to the giant head appearing on screen.

Wade watched him disappear from view and then chuckled.

"Poor kid has so much to learn."

"He definitely does," Vivian said in a resigned tone.

"So you're going to take care of him? After last time we spoke..."

"I'll train him, but I'll never harm him the way they harmed us," she said. "What's the worst that can happen?"

"Was that rhetorical?" Wade queried, grinning. Vivian chuckled.

"I wasn't expecting to hear from you. You disappeared last night, and I couldn't reach you. Anything going on I should know about?"

"Personal business. Nothing major," Wade said offhandedly.

"About your daughter?"

"Yes."

"You dropped her off personally?"

"I wanted to get a feel for the new Captain. See how it would go."

"And?"

"Everything seems fine," he said. Vivian could tell he was lying. "But I saw your message as soon as I got back. We've been friends a long time, so don't take this personally: have you lost your mind?"

"Quite possibly."

"It's too dangerous to approve you going to Jaril," Wade said. "It's dangerous because you're from the Ministry, but it gets worse. A Capital Ship is heading to Jaril now, sent by Darius."

"Evelyn's Grace?"

"That's the one. Captain Finch's flagship. How did you know?"

"It's already in orbit."

"Damn it, Vivian. Don't go there!"

"It's too late, Wade," she said. "We're already here. I used the trade warrant you sent me to land."

"Damn it, Vivian!"

"It's just one ship. They won't even know I'm here."

"What if they bombard the planet from orbit?"

"They haven't yet."

"That's because they know they can't take the planet by force," Wade said. "So they are trying diplomacy."

"I got in easily enough."

"Getting out is the trick."

"Why would you send the Hummingbird? I said I needed transport, not your baby."

"This kind of request will have to go past the Minister's desk for approval. He isn't keen on sending anyone into a war zone."

"Warzone? That's a little melodramatic."

"That remains to be seen," Wade said.

"Tell him it's related to the information I found on Mali. I uploaded it to you earlier."

"He'll want to know more. What are you going to Jaril for?"

"Information."

"Information can wait. He doesn't appreciate stupid people, Vivian, and right now you seem like Queen of the idiots. What could possibly be so important on Jaril that it couldn't wait until Darius left?"

"Nothing," Vivian replied.

"Nothing?" Wade echoed. "The Minister would castrate me if I tried to run *this* past him."

"Then make something up. Tell him I'm looking for some rare new element that only exists in this Sector. Maybe I'm after a new energy source. Or don't tell him at all."

"That's your suggestion. Try to hide something like this from the Minister?"

"Are you saying you can't?"

"I'm saying I shouldn't," Wade said, rubbing his face with his hands. He sighed. "Fine. I've got a merchant ship. A little old beater that shudders when it slips into warp. I'm betting I can talk Traq's uncle into using personal leave time to come get you."

"I appreciate it, Wade."

"Do you really plan to sell your ship?"

"It's the only way to get enough credits."

"I can send you credits."

"From a Ministry account? That seems like an even worse plan if the Minister finds out. The Cudgel is my personal vessel, so no paper trail."

"Fine. The one I'm sending you will hold you over until I can send you something better. It's old but with some work, it'll last. I was going to scrap it."

"Thanks."

Wade's expression turned serious. "Where are you planning on going after?"

"To fringe worlds mostly. Dangerous places. You said I should teach Traq things I know, and that's what I know. I'll teach him how to survive and how to fight."

"Excellent," Wade said. "The galaxy could use a few more good murders."

"Wade..."

"I know. I know. I look forward to hearing all about it. I'll call Jack. Good luck."

They ended the call. She picked up her Vibro blade and wondered if she should leave it behind.

Having the weapon hanging over her shoulder made her feel safer, and she could keep the weapon under her cloak. It would be difficult to reach if things turned dangerous, but carrying it made her more comfortable. She also kept a holdout pistol tucked into her right boot. She was trained better with blades.

She couldn't think of any rational reason not to travel armed. She doubted many people on Jaril did, but that just meant she had to hide the weapons well. It was better to go to the planet with protection and not need it than the alternative.

"Traq," she said while the ramp lowered. "It's important that people don't know I'm from the Ministry. If anyone asks, I'm a merchant pilot and you're my son. Okay?"

"Okay," Traq said. They walked down together and Traq coughed, covering his nose with his hands. He was practically gasping for air. "What's that smell?"

Vivian chuckled. "It's just how this planet smells," she remarked. "Every planet has its own unique mishmash of ecosystem and technology. Don't worry, you'll get used to it."

"I don't want to get used to it," Traq stated, still sputtering.

"Would you prefer staying on the ship?"

He looked up at her in shock. "No way. I want to see everything."

She nodded and set off. "Then you'll have to get used to it. Smell is the weakest sense, so it will pass shortly."

"Will it be like this on other planets?" Traq asked. His voice was getting weaker as he struggled to keep up. He was trying as hard as possible not to breathe. She thought back, wondering if the smell of other planets used to bother her so much.

"Everywhere. It's the same if you go onto a new spaceship. Each has its own smell, but after a while you'll stop noticing it as much," she said. Then added, "And it's also not polite to point out."

They passed out of their hanger into the spaceport. It was bustling with activity, bodies pressed together. No one seemed too terribly upset about the Union ship in high orbit. Most of the ships she saw were merchant's vessels. Few went off the planet.

The Union ship hadn't communicated with the populace and was probably working with the Royal Family through negotiations. They hadn't started a blockade, but Vivian had little doubt they could. Any ship trying to fly past would be shot down once they declared a blockade.

She just had to be off the world before that happened.

She used her data pad to find the nearest market and then led Traq out into the sunlight. The exit of the spaceport was dominated by a sprawling park filled with trees, flowers, and walking paths. It was packed to the brim with picnickers and wandering pedestrians.

There was a pond at the center of the park and a garden that ran alongside the spaceport. Walking paths crisscrossed their way through the area and trees dotted the landscape, offering shade for picnics and the like. The weather was pleasant and warm, so a lot of people were outside.

To the west ran a brick walkway flanked by enormous granite statues. It connected to the main avenue. The statues depicted ancient heroes in a variety of poses, some holding primitive weapons or leaning on staves. Probably a line of deceased kings and queens. Or perhaps important nobility.

"This place is weird," Traq whispered, looking up at her.

"It's just different," Vivian said.

"The people dress funny," he observed. "Why is her skin like that?"

She almost laughed when she watched Traq point at a short woman with tinted blue skin. She quickly grabbed his hand and lowered it to his side.

The woman was not amused. She carried herself away with the air of a well-to-do noblewoman. She looked at Traq with her eyes narrowed, then huffed and brusquely walked away with a shake of her head.

"It's not polite to point," Vivian said. Traq blushed. "As to why people dress like that. Or why someone would do that to their skin, I couldn't quite say."

"Excuse me!" a voice said. It was a deep baritone. She glanced over and saw a uniformed man rushing toward her. He was black and handsome in a silver uniform.

"Hello?" she said. The man ignored her, heading straight for Traq and lifting him in a big bear hug. Traq started laughing and giggling.

"Bart!" Traq said, hugging the man awkwardly from his raised position.

"Hey kiddo, haven't seen you in a long time." He turned back to Vivian. "Name's Bartholomew."

"Vivian," she said, biting back an angry response. "You were expecting us?"

It wasn't a question. "I was. Jack called me a little bit ago to have me keep an eye on this little guy."

"Jack Cartwright?"

Bart nodded. "Knew him from back in the day, before he went to Terminus and joined the Republican Fleet. I signed up with the Admiralty here instead, but we've stayed in touch. He asked me to keep an eye on his nephew and help out."

"You live here?"

"Nope," Bart said, "but I used to a long time ago. I actually landed yesterday, and I'm heading out tomorrow. Lucky timing. I said I'd make sure you got here safe and had a place to stay. Jack wants you to stay near the spaceport, and he said he should be here in a couple days. The establishments are somewhat... prejudiced...against outsiders, so I took the liberty of getting you a room and renting a ride."

He handed her a pair of primitive swipe keys. "We couldn't possibly..."

"I insist. Jack's a friend. Any friends of his is a friend of mine." He checked his wrist watch. "Now is there anything else I can get for you? Directions maybe?"

"I'm looking for a vendor."

"Food? We have some excellent dishes—"

"Equipment. Specifically water filtration systems."

His face scrunched up. "That's an odd request. I'll have to think about it. I don't spend much time on the planet or know many people, but I'd be willing to ask around. How about you go to the hotel room and relax. I'll come meet up with you after I find something?"

She thought about it. She would like to take a more active role in finding the equipment. But, on the other hand, Traq was starting to get tired and overwhelmed, and without knowing where to start searching she would have no better chance than Bart would.

"All right," she agreed.

"I'll send you my number if you need anything," Bart said, setting Traq back on the ground.

She nodded. "You have my thanks."

"No problem. How much were you planning to pay?"

"Well, I was hoping to trade for it."

"Trade what?"

"My ship. I've got another one on the way."

Bartholomew laughed. "All right then. I'll look into it for you. See you in a bit."

2

Oliver munched his slice of bread idly, watching the group split up and head their separate ways. He'd spent the last five minutes studying one woman in particular. She was tall with raven dark hair and a heavy cloak. She was definitely an outsider. Had he met her on Terminus? No, that didn't sound right.

And she was armed. That was what first caught his attention. A pistol in her boot was one thing, but he'd wager a month's salary that she had some sort of bladed weapon strapped to her back. Maybe a Vibro sword. She was trying to keep it hidden but in his years of seedy dealings Oliver had learned how to spot the smallest details.

But her face...why did she look so damned familiar?

He stuffed the last bit of nom in his mouth, wiped his hands, and hurried up the road. He disappeared into the crowd and weaved his way down a few alleys. He didn't dare approach the woman directly. Not until he knew more about her, or what she might have worth stealing. But the soldier, on the other hand...

After sidestepping a few people and ducking around a corner, he stepped out just as the naval officer turned down his street. Oliver glanced back over his shoulder and intentionally bumped into the tall black officer, pretending to be distracted.

"Sorry," he mumbled, stumbling to the side.

"It's no problem," the soldier said, helping Oliver catch his balance. Oliver nodded to the man, then his eyes went wide in mock recognition.

"Oh," he said, taking a step back. "You're an officer."

"Yes?" the man said, irritated.

"You wouldn't happen to serve aboard the Urden, would you?"

The man looked puzzled. "Yes. Do I know you?"

Oliver shook his head. "No, sorry, it's just...You serve under Admiral Hektor Menschen?" The man nodded. "Well, then it's my lucky day. My name is Oliver Atchison," he added, offering his hand. Tentatively and with suspicion on his face, the man shook it.

"Bartholomew Grace," the officer said. "If you'll excuse me, I'm in something of a hurry."

"Of course," Oliver said, falling into step as the man walked off. His mind played through possible ways of gaining the man's trust. He'd helped a friend deliver a shipment of goods to the Urden earlier this morning, and he still happened to have the paperwork in his pocket.

He rolled the details of his lie into place and began casting his net, "As I said, it was lucky I bumped into you. The port crew never showed up this morning to pick up the crates of ammunition."

He pulled the folded envelope out of his pocket and handed it to the man.

Bart stopped walking and a grimace crossed his face. "None of them?" He opened the envelope and saw that none of the details had been filled it. Oliver didn't feel compelled to tell Bart that it was only a copy.

"How many men should there have been?"

"Four," Bart said. Oliver shook his head. Six had shown up, he remembered.

"No. No one showed up and we weren't sure what to do," Oliver lied.

Bart sighed. "This is going to cost us half a day. If those bastards are out getting drunk..."

"I was on my way to the spaceport now to send a message to your Munitions Officer. I wanted to see if it was okay to have my own men deliver the crates to the Urden," Oliver said. He added a little extra lie, just for effect. "No shipping charge, of course. Since you're an officer, I hoped maybe you had the ability to authorize that without unnecessary paperwork."

Bart nodded. "I do, and I appreciate it. What's the soonest you could have them brought up?"

Oliver grinned. "Actually, I sent them up this morning, but I'm relieved to have the little details sorted out. I didn't want to cause your ship to leave late on account of my goods being delayed."

Bart blinked. "Oh, the crates were already delivered?"

Oliver nodded. *By your own men nonetheless*, he didn't add. More than likely those men would get reprimanded now for supposed dereliction of duty. But Oliver didn't care. All he had to do was fudge the paperwork that was send to the Urden later.

"Yes, they were. Would you mind signing there on that line for me?"

"Of course," the man said. He scribbled and handed the paperwork back to Oliver, who stuck it back in his pocket.

"Thanks very much for your time, Corporal," he said, bowing and starting to turn away. He hesitated just long enough to make sure the officer could get another word in.

"Wait," Bart said, fishing in his pocket. He pulled out a credit data pad. "This was my bonus for last month. You've saved me quite the hassle, and I would be much obliged if you split this with the men that delivered the goods," he said.

"That's very kind of you, sir," he said solemnly, slipping the pad into his pocket. It was turning out to be a profitable day. Bart scrunched his face up and thought for a moment.

The effort made him look kind of like a giraffe, Oliver decided.

"You wouldn't happen to know anything about...water purifiers, would you?"

Oliver almost shook his head. Almost. He knew nothing at all about water purifiers.

Instead, he hesitated, wondering if it had something to do with the raven- haired woman.

He shrugged. "I know a bit."

"Any idea where I could purchase them?"

So that was it? "How many are you looking for?"

"Several," the man admitted. Oliver spent a moment processing the information and trying to decide how to use it.

He *did* know a lot of merchants in the city, and he was confident that he could track anything down if given enough time.

Plus, if it turned out those purifiers had nothing to do with the woman, he could just pass the contact along to one of those other merchants...for a fee, of course.

So he lied.

"You know, I think you might be in luck. My partner and I recently acquired an as-is warehouse from a failed business venture. I haven't read through the entire manifest yet, but I thought I saw water purifiers on the manifest. I'm not sure how many, but I'm guessing, say—" Oliver decided to go big: "—twenty."

Bart's eyes widened. "That many?"

Sure, why not. "Yeah, I believe so."

"Any idea how much they run?" Bart asked.

Oliver rubbed his chin. *Hmm...* "I'm not an expert, but I'd say around eighty thousand credits apiece," he said, deciding that sounded reasonable.

Bart nodded, considering. He hesitated as though trying to make up his mind about something, and then asked tentatively, "Would you be willing to trade for them?"

"Um..." Oliver said, wondering how deep the hole was he was digging for himself. "Trade what?"

"A KMV1 merchant vessel."

Oliver almost fell over. "A what?" he asked, the words slipping out.

"It's a starship," Bart said. "Merchant class, excellent cargo space."

Oliver knew that; he was just completely caught off guard. "Can I have some time to think it over?" he asked, composing himself. Bart nodded.

"How about you come meet my friend in a while and we can discuss it?" he said.

"That sounds fine," Oliver said, sure he meant the woman.

"Meet me at the Grand Hotel at eight," Bart said.

"All right," Oliver said, shaking Bart's offered hand again and disappearing into the crowd. He glanced at his watch. It was six now. That gave him two hours to figure out what an actual water purifier cost.

Chapter 18
Sector 6 – Jaril
Maven Ophidian

1

Maven Ophidian stood on the bridge of the newly renamed Crusader Class Warship Eisle, formerly Evelyn's Grace. She'd picked the name that morning, hating the name 'Evelyn.'

She was looking out at the world, Jaril, with mild disdain. It was a beautiful place, she had to admit. Pleasant but backward. It would be a nice acquisition for the Union. When they swore allegiance.

She stood in the center of the Captain's deck, ignoring the bustling activity around her. The officers gave her a respectful berth, but she knew that was more to do with her reputation than anything else. Many years ago she learned that her attire put people on edge.

She eschewed the gray uniform Darius suggested she wear. He thought that if she wore the same outfits as the crew they might accept her. She disagreed. Standing out was the best chance she had of being taken seriously. Instead, she wore crimson and black robes to hide the oxygen tank she carried. A tube ran to her oxygen mask, inflating and deflating in a rhythmic fashion.

When she defected from the Ministry with her sister and Darius Gray, she became a General in his new army. She was skilled in using her implant—telekinesis, like her sister, but considerably more powerful—and was not averse to using it as a show of force. If she remained with the Ministry she had no doubt she would have been chosen as a Shield.

Not her sister. Her.

"Sir," a voice said behind her. She held up a gloved hand, signaling for the messenger to wait and then counted to fifty. She had to be in control of every conversation she entered if she wanted to cull respect.

Finally, she turned to face the man. He stood a full head taller than her, standing at attention and staring at the wall over her shoulder. He was handsome in a pathetic drone sort of way.

"Yes?" she asked, her voice altered by the modulating speaker inside the oxygen mask. The end result sounded coarse and deep, nothing like the soft voice she was used to in private.

"You said you wanted us to scan for vessels that aren't local," the man said. He was tall with sharp features that never betrayed even the slightest hint of fear. His cologne was overwhelming, and she wondered if he was trying to impress her.

"And...?"

"We found one," the man said, unflinching.

"Of course, you did," Maven said, turning back to the view screen and crossing her hands behind her back. There was no hint of surprise in her voice.

She had ordered the scan of every ship entering or leaving the atmosphere. Most shared similar ID tags, but some would have to be off-world traders. Probably from Terminus.

"It landed near the capital, Mys," the officer said. "Should I send a team down after it?"

"No," she said. "It is probably just a trade ship. We're still trying to be civil with the authorities. Keep an eye out for when it tries to leave, then catch it. Dismissed."

"What if..." the man started, then hesitated when he realized he was talking out of turn.

She turned slowly, hands still behind her back, and stood perfectly still. All the activity on the deck had stopped and all eyes were on her. She waited, making sure she had everyone's attention and then brought her gloved right hand from behind her back, holding it in view.

"What if..." she echoed, holding up her hand as if admiring her nails. The man swallowed.

"What if they speak make their presence known? That would break the treaty we've established." the man said, his voice barely loud enough to be heard.

"I doubt they will. However, your concern is noted. It is a bridge we can't cross until we reach it," she said, lowering her hand and letting the budding energy dissipate. Then she added, more forcefully this time, "Dismissed."

The man saluted and rushed back to his post, shoulders slumping with visible relief to be out of her presence. She unnerved him, just as she unnerved most of the crew.

She had to take things one step at a time. She doubted this treaty would last—it was Darius's stupid idea, agreeing to keep all outsiders off of the planet while negotiating—and even if it did work it wouldn't get the results she needed.

She needed to keep her eyes on the bigger picture. The long-term prize. Bombing the planet from orbit—Alyssa's more stupid idea—would destroy the very resources they were trying to acquire.

Chapter 19
Sector 6 – Jaril
Vivian Drowel

1

Vivian paced impatiently in the modest hotel room, waiting for Bartholomew to arrive. She was impatient. Evelyn's Grace was up in orbit above, and no matter how confident she acted in front of Wade, she understood what it meant.

If they found out she was here, they could kill her without breaking a sweat.

And if they knew *who* she was, they would.

When the knock finally did come at her door it was everything she could do not to run and throw it open. As promised, Bartholomew stood in the doorway. He was accompanied by a thin man with pale skin, blonde hair, and blue eyes.

"May we come in?" Bartholomew asked and then noticed Traq was asleep. "Actually, out here should be fine."

Vivian stepped out into the hall and gingerly shut the door behind her. "Who might you be?"

"Oliver Atchison, at your service," the other man said, bowing low. "I heard you were trying to buy water purifying equipment?"

"And you're here to sell it?"

"Yes. I have several units I'm willing to part with."

"I want to deal in trade," Vivian explained.

Oliver nodded. "Bartholomew told me. You want to trade for your ship."

"It's in dock B-7 right now."

"That's an older model," Oliver asserted, rubbing his chin. "But I'm not terribly picky. Would you be willing to let me see the ship first?"

"Of course," Vivian said. "Though I would like to be present."

Oliver nodded and glanced over at Bartholomew. "I appreciate you directing this my way," he said.

"Not a problem," Bart said. "I'm just glad I could help."

"Just curious," Oliver said, glancing at Vivian. "What are you planning to do with all of the purifying equipment once you buy it?"

"That's part of the deal. I need it dropped off at Garren's Ridge on Mali."

"And that's it?"

"That's it," she said.

"Sounds a little too good to be true," Oliver said. "But I'm willing to float in the shallow end of the pool. Give me a day to talk to my business partners."

"We can meet tomorrow to discuss it."

"Of course. Thanks for your time." Oliver shook hands with her and Bart and disappeared down the hallway, humming to himself. Vivian watched him step into the elevator, wondering what bothered her so much about him.

He was handsome and spoke with a practiced ease. That alone flagged him as unsafe. He was the kind of person who could lie about which planet they were on without even a tremor in his voice.

Vivian hated people like him. On principle. But then again, her animosity was on a personal level. If he was interested in making a fair trade, then there was little she could complain about.

She turned to Bart. "Can I trust him?"

"Oliver? He seems nice enough. Just chance I ran into him on the street."

Chance doesn't exist with people like him

"Your ship is worth a little less than a million?" Bart continued. Vivian nodded; she'd never had it formally priced, but that sounded right for the model. "He's willing to give you one million and a half credits worth of equipment in trade. It's difficult finding anyone willing to sell ships on Jaril, and he'll have an easier time selling the ship at a high markup than he would selling purifiers."

Vivian nodded. It made sense and made Oliver sound like an enterprising businessman...still, something didn't feel right. Maybe it was something he said or did during the conversation. It was like he'd been...studying her. "Was he the only person you asked?"

Bart shrugged. "Didn't think I'd have to ask anyone else, especially with time so short. What's the likelihood of someone else being able to come up with twenty purifiers in a few days? Why, do you want me to do some more digging?"

She shook her head. "No, he seems fine." Actually, Oliver seemed like the common underworld scum that took advantage of people. He was handsome and smart, and he knew it. Maybe that was why she didn't like him.

But she wasn't in the Republic, and right now his sort of underworld scum was exactly what she was looking for. At least, if she wanted to make a quick deal. "I'm going to get some food and turn in for the night. I really appreciate the help."

"I told you, it's no issue. I'll come by when Oliver contacts me tomorrow."

Bart shook her hand and disappeared down the hallway, leaving her alone. She went back inside and sat in her armchair. She had a faint feeling of unease as she unclipped her weapon and set it on the table, but it was the same feeling she'd had all day.

Buy one-and-a-half million credits worth of purifiers in trade for a one-million credit ship? She'd always believed that if a deal sounded too good to be true, it usually was.

Chapter 20
Sector 4 – Alderson
Jayson Coley

1

Jayson awoke to agony. He groaned and clenched his eyes, willing himself back to unconsciousness. It did no good. His body ached, but that was nothing compared to the throbbing in his head. It felt like someone had grabbed his skull on both sides and tried ripping it in half.

For all he knew, someone had.

"He's awake," someone screamed.

"Don't yell," he mumbled. Or tried to. The words came out 'ooh ell.' He had cotton mouth and the back of his throat burned with stale bile. He must have vomited in his mouth. Yesterday. He swallowed, but that just made it worse.

"What?" the person screamed again. It was a man. "Here."

Jayson felt his head lifted forward and the edge of a rough bowl touched his lips. Cool water drained into his mouth for a few seconds. He managed to swallow some of it but ended up coughing as it burned down his throat.

He reached up and swatted the bowl away. Another fit of coughing wracked his body and he drew in a ragged breath of air. "I said, 'don't scream,'" he mumbled again, opening his eyes. The world was bright, painfully so, and swam in front of him. After a few seconds, he made out shapes: the base of a tree, some fallen leaves, and branches, underbrush.

Jayson cocked his head to the side and saw Richard Dyson kneeling beside him. The other man's clothes were torn and dirty and he had a bandage wrapped around his injured foot. His eyes were haggard, and he looked a full ten years older than he had before.

"I'm barely whispering," Richard said.

To the left Jayson saw Tricia Jester. She stood at the edge of the little clearing he was lying in, lips pursed and lines creasing her forehead. Or as much of her forehead as he could see; the top of her head was wrapped thickly in strips of cloth. Her skin gleamed with stale sweat and her amber eyes were studying Jayson. She still looked lithe and beautiful despite the dirt and exhaustion lining her features.

"So, we're alive," Jayson said. He wasn't sure how he felt about that.

"For now," Richard replied.

"How long was I out?"

"Almost two days."

"Holy crap."

"I know," Richard replied. "He did a real number on you. Shallow cuts mostly, but you lost a lot of blood."

Jayson took a deep breath and sat forward. His head spun for a few seconds from the exertion. He glanced down at his leg. His pants had been ripped open and his leg was wrapped in a bluish green strip of cloth. "Bandages?"

"Shirts," Richard replied. Jayson glanced at him: Richard's shirt—which matched the color of the bandage—was missing the bottom six inches. Tricia's was ripped as well; showing a generous portion of her well-toned stomach and perfectly smooth skin. "We got the bleeding to stop with pressure, but if you move too quickly you might open it again."

"Thanks," Jayson replied.

"Don't mention—"

"We need to move," Tricia interrupted. Richard glanced over at her.

"Not yet."

"We've wasted enough time already," Tricia argued. She took a few steps closer, folding her arms over her ample chest, steely eyes locked on Richard. Richard stood up, holding his hands up as if trying to calm an angry animal.

"It wasn't wasted if it meant keeping Jayson alive."

"It wasn't time we could—"

"...and we can't move until we know his wound won't—"

"—waste. We don't even know what's out here and—"

"Hey!" Jayson said, raising his voice. It hurt his throat, but they both stopped talking and stared at him instead. He drew a deep, ragged breath. "Thank you. Both. For keeping me alive. I mean it." He turned to face Richard. "But she's right. It was a bad idea to stick around in the open like this."

"You'll need time to recover," Richard said. "We aren't even sure if you *can* move yet."

"So you should just leave without me," Jayson replied. He lay back down on the dirt, feeling dizzy and weak. "I'm useless like this. Even if I could walk, I'd only slow you down."

Tricia made a clicking sound. "He's right."

"Bullshit," Richard replied. "He's delirious."

"I'm fine," Jayson said. "And I can take care of myself."

Richard ignored him. He faced squarely at Tricia. "I'm not leaving him."

"You'll have to. We can't spare the effort of protecting him."

"Look, Trish, they don't *want* us to leave him."

"Don't call me Trish," she replied, narrowing her eyes.

He ignored her "or else why would they have left us all here together? We woke up less than ten feet from each other. We're supposed to stick together as a team."

"You don't know that."

"But it makes logical sense," Richard argued. "Why else leave us together like that? Why not just dump us kilometers away from each other if their goal was to let us die?"

"The exact opposite could be true," Tricia replied. "They might have left him here to be an anchor around our necks if we're dumb enough to stick around."

"Maybe," Richard admitted. "But both options can't be true. And one involves abandoning a man to die in the woods. Could you live with yourself after that?"

"Yes."

"Bullshit."

"I'll leave you as well," said Tricia coldly, "if you don't come now."

Richard sighed. "Then go."

A long moment passed. Tricia didn't move.

Richard said, "See, Trish, you aren't going to leave us. If you were, you would have left yesterday. Or the day before. But you stuck it out." He knelt down next to Jayson, checking the bandages. "So stop pretending to be the heartless bitch you want us all to think you are. Either help figure out how we can move *with* Jayson, or sit your pretty little ass down and wait."

She narrowed her eyes. "When we get out of this," she said. "You and I will exchange words."

"I'm looking forward to that," Richard replied, still not looking up. "I like words."

She made a disgusted sound and headed into the tree line. Jayson let out a breath of air and willed his head to stop throbbing. He was lying in the dirt and his body felt pathetic. It was a combination of pain, weakness, and stiffness.

"She's right. You should leave me," he said. "I'm no good like this."

"Just shut up," Richard said gently, examining the bandages. "We put two days into keeping you alive. I'll be damned if we went through that just to leave you here to die."

"Why?"

"Why what?"

"Why would you keep me alive?"

Richard thought about it. "We had two problems when we woke up. One was intractable, so we solved the other. Keeping you alive was easier."

"Two days? What about nutrients? Did you feed me?"

"Tricia pre-chewed your food. I whispered sweet nothings in your ear to get you to swallow."

Jayson coughed. "What?"

"Relax, I'm kidding," Richard said. Then, "I helped chew too."

Jayson chuckled. It hurt, a lot. "So then what's the intractable problem?"

Richard smiled sadly. "What the hell do we do now?"

2

Tricia returned a few minutes later with a Y-shaped tree limb. They tested it and found that Jayson could use it as a makeshift crutch: a few inches too short and miserably uncomfortable, but at least it made walking a possibility.

The next problem was that after only a few steps he was exhausted. His body was lethargic and weak from blood loss and prolonged unconsciousness. He sat on a log, gasping for air and willing his pain to subside. Tricia looked at Jayson like he was something she'd scraped off the heel of her boot.

"I'm not usually this pathetic," he said after the third such rest, struggling to catch his breath. "Sorry."

"It's going to take some time for your muscles to loosen up," Richard replied. "But you should recover your strength quickly once your body limbers up."

"We don't have time for this," Tricia muttered under her breath. It was just loud enough to be overheard.

"You need food," Richard said, ignoring her. "Are you hungry?"

Jayson nodded. "And a little nauseous."

He fished in a pocket and handed Jayson a strip of dried meat. "It's fish."

Jayson sniffed it. "How old?"

"Caught it yesterday and smoked it over the fire. It's not bad."

Jayson took a bite. It was rock solid, but the taste wasn't bad. He let it dissolve in his mouth, swallowing flakes. "You said I was out for two days?"

"More like thirty-six hours," Richard said after a thoughtful pause. He scratched his beard, which was already starting to look scragglier. "We tried waking you a couple of times, but you were lights out to the world."

"What he means by 'wake you,'" Tricia said, nose in the air, "is he threw sticks at your head to see if you would react."

"What!?"

Richard nodded solemnly. "I had a scoring system and everything. Thirty points if it landed on your nose." He knelt down, conspiratorial. "Trish refused to play. I think she knew I would win."

Tricia made a disgusted noise.

Jayson took another bite of the fish. It hit his stomach and spread with warmth. He started feeling better within minutes. "So you've been living off of fish?"

"Not entirely," Richard replied. "Tricia made a few traps. Managed to catch a little squirrel-like creature. Cooked him up the second night. Actually tasted pretty good."

Jayson tucked the last bit of fish in his mouth and took a deep breath. "Okay," he said. "Let's walk."

Richard helped lift him under the arm and got him back to his feet with a groan. They set a glacial pace toward a nearby creek where Tricia and Richard had been getting water.

Jayson could hear it bubbling behind the trees and brush before he could see it. It was two meters wide and about a meter down at its deepest point. It was also icy cold. Jayson lowered to the ground and settled on his hip. He took a long and rewarding drink, using his hands to cup the water.

"Oh, that's good," he said.

"Uh huh," Richard agreed. "Now strip and get in."

"What?"

"You heard me. Strip. And clean your clothes too."

Jayson hesitated. "I think I'll be fine without—"

"No offense, but you *smell* terrible," said Richard. "Actually, no, I take that back. I *mean* to give offense. Now get in the damn water."

Jayson couldn't help but glance at Tricia.

Richard groaned.

"Seriously? You're twenty-something and *still* worried about cooties?" Richard asked. "Who do you thinks been keeping you clean *thus* far?"

Jayson hadn't thought about it. He didn't particularly like to either.

Still, he hesitated. Some habits were hard to break. Richard sighed in exasperation. "I'm telling you, she's seen *plenty* of those before. She doesn't care."

"I know that. I just..."

"Would you prefer that I stripped first?" Tricia asked.

"I would," Richard said without even a moment's hesitation. Tricia glared at him.

"No," Jayson said, shaking his head. It sounded entirely silly, after all of this, to worry about something as trivial as being naked in front of strangers.

He began stripping his shirt off. Shooting pain roared through his body, but he did his best to ignore it.

Richard helped with his pants where the blood had dried and caked the cloth to his skin. Naked, Jayson gradually lowered himself into the cool running water. It was freezing and he shivered; his teeth chattered.

"Stop being such a wuss," Richard said. Then he splashed water onto Jayson's upper body. It shocked the skin where it hit and made him shiver even worse. But he began adapting after only a few moments. After a minute, it felt good. He started scrubbing his skin.

The shallow bath was invigorating, washing the last of his sluggishness away. It was the difference between day and night after being in the water for only a few minutes. He couldn't remember any bath or shower ever being so rewarding. It was a euphoric, almost religious, experience.

Once he'd finished cleaning himself—as best he could under the circumstances—he turned his attention to his clothes. They were caked with blood and sweat. Richard was right: they smelled terrible.

He found a suitable rock and scrubbed them clean as best he could. He wished for soap, but the water was better than nothing. As he finished Richard hung the wet clothes on a tree.

"How long will it take to dry?" Jayson asked.

"It's windy," Richard said. "And not very humid. So I'd say...an hour?"

"Are you guessing?"

"Yes, but it's an educated guess. We washed and dried our clothing yesterday," Richard said. "I never really expected to spend time washing my clothes out in the wilderness somewhere. One of those skills I left off my resume."

"Then maybe it's time to add it on," Jayson said. He relaxed into the water. "What next?"

Richard was leaning against a tree with his eyes closed and Tricia was sitting on a rock, idly rolling a stick between her fingers. Neither seemed thrilled at the prospect of tackling that question.

"We move," Tricia said.

"Where?"

They were both silent.

"Where are we?" Jayson asked.

"No clue," Richard replied. "Same planet. Maybe same continent. There are mountains nearby but no distinguishing features."

"So they just dumped us off in the middle of nowhere after hurting us badly enough that we can barely travel?"

Silence again.

"Why?" Jayson asked.

"My guess," Richard said, scratching his beard, "is to test us. They want to see how long we can survive on our own."

Jayson splashed some water on his face. "So like a test?"

Richard snorted. "Something like that. Yeah. They want to see which of us are worth the effort of training. If we can't survive this, they don't want us."

"So how long do we have to make it?"

"Until they come and find us."

"No," Tricia replied, shaking her head. "No one is coming. We have to make our own way back to the Academy."

Richard laughed. "See Jayson? This is why we kept you alive. We need a tie breaker."

"What?

"Trish here—"

"I said don't call me that."

"—thinks we should move and try to find our own way back to the Academy. I think the point of this exercise is to survive. So we build a structure, find food. Lay low. Then, when they are happy, they come and find us. What do you think?"

Jayson shrugged. "No idea."

"You have to have *some* idea," Richard said. "Even if it's a bad one."

"If we don't know where we are, how do we find our way back?"

"Exactly," Richard said.

"We're close to the Academy," Tricia argued. "The trees are all the same. And those *are* the same mountains."

"Let's say they are the same," Richard replied. "Even then, it would be no good to go trekking to them."

"Why not?"

Richard laughed. "Do you understand the concept of a *range* of mountains? There might be hundreds of them, each several kilometers apart. It could take us weeks trekking up the first one to find out we picked the wrong mountain. We'll be dead before we reach the second."

"Doesn't mean we shouldn't try."

"No that's *exactly* what it means. We should just stay here and—"

"Staying here is the same thing as *dying* here," Tricia said, "because no one is coming—"

"—build up our shelter—"

"—to rescue us. And we have no choice—"

"She's right," Jayson interrupted. "I'm siding with Tricia."

Richard trailed off and let out an exasperated sigh.

"You sure? We aren't really in shape to be moving right now."

"That's *why*," Jayson replied. "If they're going to test us, they're going to make it as hard as possible. We're injured, no supplies, not at all prepared for travel. So that's what they expect us to do."

"But we don't even know where to go!"

"We have, as you pointed out, a mountain range to follow."

Richard's jaw fell open. "Maybe *you* don't understand the idea of a mountain *range*—"

Jayson held up his hand. "I know, and if we pick wrong we're probably going to die before we realize our mistake. But, we have a few advantages on our side.

"First we can assume whoever left us here wanted to make this trek difficult. But they don't want to kill us. If picking the wrong mountain will get us killed, then most likely they won't make it a hard choice. The nearest one is most likely. And second, we can figure out which one is right before we climb any of them."

"How?" Richard said. "The Academy was a long way up. We won't see it until we're relatively close."

Tricia blinked in realization and then chuckled. "The train tracks."

Jayson nodded. "It's no wonder they used something so low tech to bring us out here. They're meant to help us find our way home. It's part of the test."

"Well, then what the hell are we waiting for?" Richard said, then made a tsking noise at Tricia. "And *you* said we should leave him to die."

Tricia sighed.

3

They walked.

Morning turned into afternoon. They aimed for the mountains. Tricia climbed trees every once in a while to make sure they were on the right path. Jayson was only capable of short spurts of energy before his leg hurt too badly to continue. They stopped frequently to rest and recover, something Tricia didn't like. But she didn't complain.

The forest closed in around them, sheltering them from the sun and keeping them cool despite the humidity. They chose their paths by least resistance, avoiding thick areas of the brush but keeping an easterly route.

No one talked. Well, no one except for Richard, who didn't shut up.

"I think I'll put my summer home over there," he said as they passed a waterfall. "It's beautiful out here."

There was no response.

They walked some more.

"I wonder if we'll stumble into any animals doing there...you know...business. Or mating," Richard said. "Anyone want to wager on which?"

No response.

They continued walking. Jayson focused on his feet. Left, right, left, and right. And then repeat. He supposed he should be thankful that the only things his mind could handle during that first day were motor skills. It meant he wasn't thinking about their predicament or the fact that the water might make him sick with dysentery or the problem that they might not even find more clean water. Instead, he focused on left, right, left, and right.

The ground was relatively flat, for which he was grateful. And the cut on his leg, while painful, wasn't debilitating. The more he walked on it, ironically, the better it felt. After a few hours, he started using the crutch as a walking stick.

He must not have looked healthy, though, because he heard Richard whisper to Tricia, "He's not doing very well. Maybe we should stop for the night."

"There's plenty of light left," she whispered. "We can cover more ground."

"Breaking down now will do more harm than gaining those few kilometers," Richard replied, looking casually over at Jayson. Jayson pretended he couldn't hear them. "Plus we're out of food."

"Out?" Tricia asked.

"We didn't exactly have a lot left this morning."

"We had three fish!"

"Breakfast, lunch, and dinner. It goes fast, Trish."

She made a disgusted sound. "Lasted longer with just the two of us. Fine. We can stop here for the night."

As soon as Richard told him, Jayson found a comfortable looking spot and collapsed. Richard woke him up, once, to give him some scavenged food and water from their makeshift bowl. It was dark. The meal was comprised of berries and some stringy meat.

Jayson decided later he should have asked Richard if they were poisoned berries. Or if Richard had at least tested them to make sure they were safe. But at the moment, he was too hungry and tired to care. He devoured the berries, spreading blue stains all over his face and hands, and then fell back into a stupor for the rest of the night.

It wasn't until the next morning that he realized another possibility: he probably *was* the test subject to make sure the berries were safe for Richard and Tricia to eat.

He couldn't decide if that bothered him or not.

They walked throughout the next day. And then the one after that. Gradually, they increased the distance they traveled as Jayson's body recovered. They went past fallen logs swarming with insects and through thick foliage where the sun pierced through the canopy with only the greatest reluctance. They crossed streams and forded a fast moving river sometime during their fourth day.

Tricia gathered pliable tree branches and vines as they walked. She used them to make traps and tools, increasing their arsenal of supplies. She managed to locate a knife shaped piece of rock. She chipped a few pieces away and turned it into a jagged weapon.

Each night she set out her traps in a circle around the camp. Little rope snares using fruits, vegetables, and bark as bait. And each morning she checked them for any animals they might have caught. More often than not, the traps were empty.

When they were, she would search out a rock or log for insects. She would flip it over and scoop up as many crawling things as she could find. Then she would declare it a meal.

Jayson didn't dare refuse. His body was recovering rapidly, but he needed to get as many calories as he could to keep healing. He grabbed the bugs that looked least likely to sting him and popped them into his mouth. Some of them squished, some were chewy, a few even wriggled after he bit into them. He made sure to chew those ones until they stopped before swallowing.

"I bet you did this kind of thing even when you had plenty of food," Richard remarked, stuffing a worm into his mouth. Tricia didn't reply. She rarely did.

They walked. Another day breezed past. And then another. Each night they sat in a circle. Some nights they had a fire. Some nights Tricia couldn't get one started. On two of the nights it rained in heavy cold sheets and they huddled close together.

Sometimes they talked—never about themselves—and sometimes they listened to Richard talk. He told stories about his life before coming here and the heroic things he did. A couple of times he sang a song off-key).

All of his stories were made up, but that didn't matter. After long days of walking and very little external stimuli, just hearing someone speak was enough.

Jayson was losing weight, but a lot of that was excess mass he'd put on before this 'excursion.' His body didn't need those pounds for a hike like this, and if anything he felt healthier as he got leaner.

The scenery never changed. More trees. More streams. The occasionally scurrying animal or snake or spider. The days began blurring together. Tricia estimated they were making six to eight kilometers a day through the thick forest, and Jayson couldn't dispute the claim. They could have been walking in a circle for all he knew.

The only sign they had that they were making any progress at all was when Tricia climbed the trees. The mountains were getting bigger, she informed them each morning. Jayson was beginning to suspect she might be lying.

4

They found a stream swimming with fish and crawdads after about a week. Richard insisted they stop and rest for the day.

"We should keep moving," Tricia replied. "It's only midday."

"This is the perfect opportunity to stock up on food," Richard replied. He scratched his scraggly beard, which was already enough to hide most of his face. "I, for one, don't like wondering if we're going to eat dinner. We've missed, what, eight meals since we started?"

"Coming from someone who's probably never missed a meal in his life," Tricia said, "forgive me if I don't seem to care."

"I've been hungry before," Richard replied defensively. "What do you think, Jayson?"

He shrugged. "It's more we'd have to carry."

"But less time we will spend foraging," Richard said. Then he bowed to Tricia. "But I'll defer to your wisdom, oh fearless leader."

She narrowed his eyes. "Are you mocking me?"

He looked aghast. "I would *never*."

She clearly didn't believe him. "Fine. We can stop. But catch your own damn fish," she said, then turned and disappeared into the forest.

Richard grinned at her. "I think she's starting to like me."

Jayson chuckled. "So how are you planning on catching these fish?"

"I'll use my shirt like a net," Richard said.

"Will that work?"

He shrugged. "That's what Tricia did at the last stream we stopped."

Jayson eyed the water skeptically. "These ones look pretty fast."

"I'm faster," said Richard.

5

Twenty minutes later Richard reemerged, soaking wet and unencumbered by any fish. "Don't look so smug," he said to Jayson, plopping on the ground next to him. "You wouldn't have caught any either."

"I'm not dumb enough to try."

Tricia appeared, walking toward the water with a stick in hand. "You won't get any," Richard said, panting. "They're too fast."

It took a full thirty seconds for her to skewer the first fish. She tossed it at Richard. It landed with a wet *smack* against his chest and flopped into his lap.

He held it up, twitching. "What do I do with it?"

"Clean it," she said.

"With the knife, I magically carry in my pocket?"

"This," she said, pulling the jagged rock from her pocket. She tossed it to him without looking, and he caught it in his right hand.

He stared at it doubtfully. "Seems messy."

"Just shut up and do it," she said, picking her next target. She jabbed down, again, the stick breaking the surface of the water and scattering a pool of fish. This time, she missed.

Richard looked over at Jayson. "Warrior women are so hot."

Tricia glared at him. Richard held up the knife and studied the bottom of the fish.

"Are you looking for a diagram?" Jayson asked.

"There should be dotted lines on it, right?"

"Just make a shallow cut."

"I don't want to pierce the stomach, right?"

"It's not a deer," Jayson said. "Just give it to me."

He reached over and took the knife and fish. He cut into the belly and started removing the innards.

"You know how to gut a fish?"

"It's not exactly rocket science."

Richard sighed. "I really am useless."

"We know," Jayson replied with a small smile. He finished cleaning it and set it aside.

"I wasn't exactly expecting...this...you know?"

"This isn't bad at all," Jayson said, catching the next fish Tricia threw his way. "If they really wanted to kill us, they would drop us into a desert. Here there is plenty of food and water, not a lot of bacteria. That, or they inoculated us against any diseases we'd have to worry about."

"You think they did?"

"I think that germs and bacteria are better at killing humans than about anything else. If they didn't inoculate us, then we're getting really damn lucky."

"Yeah, that would suck," Richard said. "You spend a lot of time in places like this growing up?"

Jayson shrugged. "My planet was pretty rundown. Not a lot of places like this left. We overpopulated and then died out or fled. Trish," he said, gesturing toward the water, "knows a lot more than I do about this sort of thing."

Richard turned toward the water. "Yeah. Why is that, Trish?"

"Call me Trish one more time and I'll stab you in the eye."

Richard ignored her as usual. "Did you grow up in the woods? Come on, tell us something. Did you run away from home?"

She didn't reply.

"I know," Richard said, nodding to himself. "You were raised by wolves."

"Do you ever shut up?"

"Hypothetically," he said, "I'm sure that I do. But right now I'm more interested in knowing why you're here. I mean, I know why Jayson's here. Pretty sure I know why I'm here. But what went so wrong in your life to leave you stranded out in the middle of nowhere?"

Again no reply.

So Richard speculated:

"You don't seem like the mothering type. If you had a heart I'm sure we'd be able to chisel ice off of it," he said, tapping a finger against his beard and studying her. "You're...what...twenty-seven? That means you could have been in and out of the military already. But I don't think that's where you picked this stuff up. More likely you grew up on a planet similar to this.

"Your parents were hard on you, so you rebelled from that life. So even though you're good at this, you don't like doing it. Reminds you of home. Am I close?"

She glowered at him.

"I'll take that as a yes," he said.

The next fish hit him on the side of the head.

6

They spent that night building up a large fire to smoke the fish. Tricia had managed to catch twelve of them. She skewered them on a stick and dangled them over the fire. They spent the next several hours napping and listening to the crackling fire.

It was peaceful for Jayson. A chance to admit just how tired he really was. The trip was exhausting.

He fell into a light doze. When he woke up he saw Richard and Tricia sitting beside the fire, speaking quietly and eating little strips of fish.

"He lives," Richard murmured when he noticed Jayson moving.

"Barely," Jayson said. "That smells amazing."

"Thanks. I can't catch a fish, but I can cook them."

Jayson forced himself to sit up. Richard handed him a piece of white meat. Jayson took a small bite, letting the flesh dissolve in his mouth. He'd never tasted anything so delicious.

"I found some herbs nearby. But someone—not naming any names—wouldn't let me season the fish."

"They could be poison," Tricia said, nibbling her own piece of fish.

Richard shrugged. He took a sip of water from their little makeshift bowl and passed it to Jayson. "True. They could have been delicious too. Now we'll never know."

"Do you never shut up?" she asked without any bite.

"Never ever," he replied. "I just say whatever comes to mind. I have no internal filter."

"Then perhaps you shouldn't say anything at all."

"But then it would be quiet. And when it's quiet there's time to think. And when I think I remember that we were dropped off into the middle of a forest by some complete lunatics and left to die. And that if we do survive this, then we get trained by the same lunatics, which just sounds all kinds of bad. So I'd rather not think, which means I have to talk instead."

Tricia made a disgusted sound. "Fine, if you must talk, do so quietly."

"How about you talk instead?" Richard said. "Joking aside, where did you come from? Why are you here?"

"I don't want to talk about it."

"Did you make some mistake and get in a bad situation?"

"I said I don't want to talk about it," Tricia said, her voice firm.

Richard eyed her for a moment and then held out his hand. "Fine. I don't know who you are or why you are here, but I'm thankful that you are. I think I can speak for Jayson as well as myself when I say that we would be dead by now without you."

Tricia looked at the hand in surprise.

"Hey, speak for yourself," Jayson said. "I would have been dead the first night."

Richard shrugged. "Yeah, probably. But seriously. Thank you, Tricia."

She took the offered hand skeptically and shook it gently. "You're always so insincere; I'm not sure what to think."

"I don't know," Richard said, then yawned. "But right now I think it's time to get some sleep."

"Okay," Tricia said. "You can take first watch. Wake me up in a few hours. Jayson can take the final watch."

"Why do we need a watch?" Richard said, yawning again. He leaned back and folded his hands behind his head. "We've been out here for at least a week, and nothing's happened to us so far. The worst things we've had to deal with are blisters. It's not like there's a single dangerous thing out here."

Tricia sighed.

Jayson groaned.

Some people just can't keep their mouths shut.

7

The attack came two days later, just after they'd finished their midday meal.

Tricia froze in place, eyes wary. She scanned the environment, hefting her walking stick and falling into a defensive stance. That was about three seconds before the creature sprang from its hiding place. Jayson stopped walking too, but he didn't see or hear anything.

It pounced at them, aiming straight for Richard. It was fast, a lot faster than he would have expected, and Jayson had to fight down a quick wave of fear. His body still hurt, and he was still exhausted. They were definitely not in fighting shape.

Richard shouted, stumbling back off-balance. It looked like a wolf but was only about the size of a large dog. Its fur was dark gray, almost black, its eyes little pits of charcoal.

Tricia stepped up to meet it, stabbing at the wolf's face. The tip of her spear caught in the fur but wasn't sharp enough to penetrate its hide. The wood snapped. Shards went flying, but it was enough to knock the wolf off its path. It clipped Richard in the hip, sending him off balance and staggering. He landed in the dirt with a grunt and the wolf landed six meters away, growling at them and circling.

That's when the other three attacked.

Jayson was prepared now. Or at least as prepared as he could be. He hefted his walking stick and stepped up next to Richard. It was a heavy piece of wood, not as flimsy as the fish skewer. He used it defensively, trying to keep his weight on his good leg.

The first wolf that came close received a sharp crack on the nose for its trouble. It stumbled away and Jayson reset his stance.

The other three circled, snarling and looking for an opening. Jayson and Tricia stood back to back with Richard on the ground at their feet. He was just now sitting up. "Ow," he mumbled, rubbing his shoulder.

"If they attack in force," Tricia said, eyes on the wolves, "we're dead."

"I love your optimism," Richard said, his voice distant. "What do you suggest?"

"Show them we are not prey."

She hefted her broken stick, hesitated a second to give Jayson time to move into position and then screamed and charged at one of the wolves. It charged back at her, snarling. She raised her stick but used it only to deflect the wolf's attack.

It snapped, grabbing the stick in its teeth. It ripped it out of her hands and crunched. The wood snapped like kindling.

Then it jumped at her, going for her throat—

—and came right into contact with Jayson's swipe. He brought the stick down in an overhead attack. He hit it right on the side of the head. The wood snapped in half and the wolf hit the ground, falling onto its side.

The wolf staggered to its feet, shaking its head. After a few seconds, it began growling though its eyes looked wary now. Jayson lifted the two-foot long section in his hand. It was, at least, sharp and he could use it for piercing.

Another wolf came at Tricia's back, but Richard stepped toward it and bellowed. His yell rolled out over the area. *At least, that voice is good for something,* Jayson decided. The wolf backed away, snarling at Richard.

Jayson shot Richard a look, raising his eyebrow.

"What?" Richard asked. "You work with what you've got."

The injured wolf stumbled a few steps away and the pack shifted positions to defend it. "Back up," Tricia said, "but don't turn your back to them."

They did, forming into a tight group and taking short steps away from the pack. The wolves continued watching them but didn't pursue.

Gradually the distance grew until the wolves were out of sight.

Jayson let out a breath he hadn't realized he was holding.

"Hey Trish," Richard said, out of breath.

"What?"

"You are so hot right now."

And then he collapsed, hitting first his knee and then collapsing onto his back.

"You're bleeding," Jayson said, kneeling. Blood was pooling where the first attack had hit him just above the hip. Either a tooth or claw, it was hard to tell which. Blood was covering his pants on that side and running down his leg.

Luckily, it hadn't done more damage. The wound wasn't very wide. Jayson ripped a strip of his shirt loose and pressed it against the cut.

Richard lifted his head up and looked at it. His eyes were glazing over. "So I am."

"Lay still."

"Okay," Richard said, his voice woozy. He yawned.

"And keep talking," she said, putting pressure on the wound.

"I thought," he said, then groaned, "I thought I talked too much."

"Right now we need for you to keep talking. Stay with us."

"Not going anywhere," he said. His eyes slipped closed.

Tricia slapped him in the face.

"Hey!" he said. "What was that for?"

"For calling me Trish," she said, turning to Jayson. "We need to get moving. With him cut like this he's going to be a beacon for any predators in the area looking for a snack."

"We can't carry him," Jayson replied.

"I know," she said. "He's going to have to walk."

"*He,*" Richard said with a yawn, "is going to take a nap."

She slapped him again.

"Gah! Would you stop that?!"

"Help me lift him," she said. "Get him to his feet."

Jayson heaved. His leg was better and he had more energy now, but he still wasn't back to full strength. By the time they had Richard to his feet Jayson's lower back was throbbing.

Richard slumped forward and Jayson held him up. "Now what?"

"We go," she said.

They started walking. Jayson braced his left side with the walking stick and used his right to keep Richard up. For Richard's part, he did the best he could to move on his own. After a while, the wound in his side stopped bleeding, but he'd already lost a lot of blood.

His face turned ashen. Jayson did his best to keep moving at a good pace, but after a few hours, Richard started tripping every few strides. Jayson expended a lot of energy catching him as his legs gave out, and finally had no choice but to lower him to the ground.

It was getting dark, and Jayson could barely keep walking. His clothes—what hadn't been torn up or left behind—were soaked with sweat and he hadn't drank enough water recently.

"That's it," he said, collapsing beside Richard and panting. "We can't keep going. Not like this."

"We're close," Tricia replied. "The last time I climbed I think I saw railroad tracks. A few kilometers."

"It won't matter. Even if we make it to them, it'll be at least twenty kilometers to reach the Academy. And that's up the side of the mountain."

"We can't stop."

"We aren't," Jayson replied.

Tricia stared at him.

"We aren't leaving him," she said, her tone final.

"I'm flattered," Richard muttered, leaning sideways against a tree. The wound had reopened and was seeping blood.

"Shut up, you," she said.

Jayson sighed. "We aren't doing that either. We just need a plan."

She blew out a breath and sat down next to them. "Okay. What do we do?"

Jayson thought about it. "Do you remember the sheds we passed every few kilometers?" She nodded. "I think those are for storage. On Eldun, we use trains for a lot of public transit, and sometimes maintenance crews use trolleys to ride on the tracks. If we can find one of those, I think we can use it to get back to the Academy much faster without needing to walk."

"Okay," she said. "Should I climb a tree and try to spot one?"

"It's too dark," he said. "Go on ahead of us. Find the tracks. As soon as you do, start a fire. Pile some wood nearby for us. Then follow the tracks to the left."

"Away from the Academy?"

He nodded. "Go back toward the city, in case we hit the tracks close to one behind us."

"How far?"

"As far as you can. When it's dark, turn and run back to us. If you find one of the sheds, grab the trolley and anything else you can find and bring them to us."

"Okay," she said. "What about Richard?"

"I'll get him to the tracks. The fire should keep anything that wants to eat him away."

He didn't add, *I hope.*

She hesitated. "And what about before then? What if those creatures come back while you're on your way?"

"They won't," Jayson said. "But if something else does, I'll have the walking stick ready. If you don't find the trolley tonight, then we'll start out as soon as we have light in the direction of the Academy. We'll pick up a trolley as soon as we pass one."

"Good," she said. She frowned and stood. "Do you need help lifting him?"

"No," Jayson said. "I'll need to rest for at least a little while longer. But you need to go. The farther you make it tonight, the more likely we are to have transportation."

"Okay," she said, clearly not happy. "Are you sure you'll be all right?"

"No," he said. "But this is about all we've got left."

She stuck out her hand. "Good luck."

He shook it. "You too."

8

Four hours. Pure misery and exhaustion were his constant companions, but they were gentle compared to the last one: terror. Pure unadulterated terror.

He heard movement in the trees, flanking them as they traveled. Half the time he spent carrying Richard. Night came on. He found himself peering into the trees, ready for an attack.

The silence was the worst of it. Since the trek had begun, Richard had filled the environment with his presence. Now, with Richard staggering along too weak to take care of himself, the forest suddenly seemed threatening.

It went thus: they would move through a particularly dense section of the woods. His nerves were dancing on razors, sending adrenaline coursing through his body. They would finally make it through without being attacked only to repeat the process once more.

Four hours that could have been four years. That was how long it took to reach the campfire. He smelled the smoke in the air before he saw anything. The fire had burned to little more than coals, and it sat two meters from the tracks. He grabbed the entire pile of sticks and set them in a pattern on top. Slowly, he coaxed the fire to life.

Richard shivered next to him. The blood loss had slowed, at least when they held the shirt on tight, but it was still seeping through the bandage. Jayson didn't know what they could do about that without proper medical equipment. He also knew that if they didn't get some soon, Richard would be dead.

He might not even make the night.

The tracks were rusty with age. Jayson sat on the edge of one of them and watched the fire build. It bathed them in its flickering light, illuminating the area and releasing its light giving warmth. They would need more wood if they wanted to keep the fire burning all night, and they would need even more if they wanted to make it any bigger.

But that meant leaving the fire untended and heading into the dark woods alone. Right now he had neither the energy nor ambition. The woods looked threatening, an endless abyss of shadow and death. *There's nothing to be afraid of,* Jayson told himself. But he knew there was. If there were wolves out here, then they were other predators as well. Larger, more dangerous and deadly.

They'd been lucky to get this far. But that meant nothing compared to what stood before them. They were at least eighty kilometers from the Academy. Probably a lot more. That meant another ten days walking at least. They were exposed and out in the open.

Richard was dying, and there was nothing they could do to help him.

"Richard?" he said, his voice cutting through the deepening gloom. He could hear Richard breathing, lying beside the fire, but there was no response. He didn't like being here in these woods. And he damn sure didn't like being alone. "Damn it, Richard, wake up."

He had barely finished speaking when he heard a wolf howl in the distance. The beast's morose call filled the air around him, cutting him to the bone with a sense of deep gloom.

They wouldn't make it to the Academy. They *couldn't* possibly. Who were they trying to fool, trekking through the forest? This wasn't some macabre trial the Academy had set for them. They'd been left out here to die, abandoned to the wilds.

The call was answered by at least six mates scattered through the area behind them. Jayson held his breath as the sound enveloped him, and he heard Richard cough in his sleep. They wolves couldn't be more than a kilometer away.

The fire was already burning low as it devoured the small pile Jayson had offered it.

A few minutes later the wolves howled again. They were much, much closer.

Jayson couldn't decide if he should gather wood or pray.

9

By the time Tricia made it back the blanket of night had settled over the entire area. She walked up the tracks, exhausted with shoulders slumped. Jayson moved out to meet her and she stopped walking.

"Nothing?"

She just stared at him.

"Then we'll find something quickly in the morning," he said. He wasn't sure which one of them he was trying to convince.

"How is he?" Tricia asked.

"Not well," Jayson said. It wasn't worth lying. "The wound won't close without stitches, and we don't have anything to take care of him. He's going to keep bleeding until he's dead."

Tricia let out a long sigh.

"You think we should leave him?"

She bit her lip.

"Like you wanted to leave me?"

"He's the most difficult and annoying man I've ever met. 'Obnoxious' doesn't even begin to describe him," said Tricia, then she sighed. "But no, I don't want to leave him."

"Okay," Jayson said. "You get some sleep. I'll wake you up in a couple of hours. As soon as it's light we'll start moving."

"It could be a long way," she said.

"I know," he replied.

"Uphill."

"I know."

They began walking back toward the little fire. "We're low on supplies, and the fish won't last more than another day."

Jayson blew air out between his lips. "I know."

Tricia lay on the ground next to Richard. She checked his bandages, wincing when he groaned in his sleep. Then she lay her head down and closed her eyes. She was asleep in only seconds, her breathing getting deeper.

Jayson fought to stay awake, focusing on their surroundings. He thought he heard movement a few times out in the trees. Just outside the fire. But nothing approached the camp.

When he couldn't stay awake any longer, he tapped Tricia on the shoulder. She woke up blearily and nodded at him. Jayson took a spot near the fire after tossing some more wood on top and closed his eyes.

10

A few seconds later, Tricia shook his arm. "Wha...?" he mumbled, rubbing his eyes. "I haven't even fallen asleep yet."

Tricia only stared at him. It was light out. He groaned and sat up.

"Is the coffee ready?"

Tricia stared at him.

"I forgot, no sense of humor."

"I have a sense of humor," she said, standing. "You simply aren't funny."

Jayson groaned again as he lifted himself up. He brushed his pants off. "How's he doing?"

"Little change," she said. "His breathing is shallow, and he is pale. We need to move."

Jayson ate a strip of fish while Tricia woke Richard up. He was groggy but coherent. Jayson took him under one arm and Tricia helped balance his weight under the other, slinging his arm around her shoulders.

They walked alongside the tracks. It was slow going, but the ground was cleared of underbrush or roots. "This sucks," Richard said after about ten minutes.

"I agree," Jayson said.

"I thought you guys would leave me," he said, grimacing in pain. "I wouldn't have blamed you. I would have cursed you, hated you, and haunted your existence. But blame? No. Not my style."

"You wouldn't leave me," Jayson said. "So I'm sticking it out."

"That was all part of my diabolical plan," he said weakly, "to indebt you into saving my life."

"Then it worked," Jayson replied.

"But what about Trish?"

"I told you I would stab you if you ever called me that again," she said.

"I recall," Richard said, "that you were going to stab me in the eye. If I get to pick, can it be the left one? I never had much use for that one anyway."

"The right one it is," she said.

"I figured you'd be gone by now," Richard said. "But I appreciate you sticking around too."

"You're welcome."

"No," Richard said, his voice sounding a little weaker. He was quickly wearing out. Tricia through his arm over her shoulder to balance his weight better, keeping pressure on the wound on his side. "I mean it, Tricia. Thank you. I'm probably going to die before we ever make it to the Academy—"

"Don't say that."

"—but I want you to know that this means a lot. No one's ever really..." He didn't finish the thought.

"You're going to be all right," Tricia said.

He shook his head. "No. There's no way I'm making it out of this."

They walked in unhappy silence for a few minutes, watching the sun rise and following the train tracks. Richard could barely put any weight on his legs at all anymore. Jayson knew they were in trouble.

"Speaking of which," Richard said softly. "Since my arm is over your shoulder, and since I'm going to die and all, would you kill me if I groped your breast right now?"

"Without hesitation," she said, the ghost of a smile on her lips.

11

They stopped to rest twice. The second time Tricia went hunting for water and they finished off the last of their fish. Jayson hoped they were nearing one of the outposts. The mountain loomed before them in the distance, but it was still a long way off. It would take time to get there, and once they did it would take even more time to climb up to the height of the Academy.

That was time Richard didn't have. They couldn't afford days walking in his condition. They needed one of those trolleys so that they could keep moving without straining Richard. And, with any luck, the outpost would have some sort of reserve supplies too. Rations, water, anything.

By the time the sun was at its full height Richard was stumbling and nearly incoherent. Jayson and Tricia were exhausted and things were beginning to feel hopeless.

"Just leave me," Richard said after one of his falls. Jayson caught him but didn't have the strength to lift him back up.

"We settled this," Jayson said, gasping. "You didn't leave me."

"That was different," Richard replied. "You were hurt. I'm dying."

"If you weren't wasting so much energy talking," Jayson said, "you could probably run."

Richard chuckled. They hadn't spoken all morning, walking in focused silence. "I know. I have a problem. I'm seeing a therapist"

"We have to be close," Jayson said. "I wasn't paying perfect attention when we rode up, but I remember seeing at least twelve of those stations. That should put them no farther than fifteen kilometers apart."

"And we've gone about three kilometers already," Tricia said.

"Feels more like three hundred," Richard said. They stumbled a little farther. "I can't go anymore."

"I remember this section," Jayson said. The station is just around that next bend. We'll be there in five minutes."

"Good," Richard said.

They continued walking. When they rounded the bend, though, there was no station.

"You liar," Richard mumbled.

"No," Jayson replied. "I swear it was right here. It must be that next bend. Right up there. It'll be around there."

"Uh huh," Richard said.

"I promise. It can't be much farther. Five more minutes."

Once again, no station.

"The next one then," Jayson offered. "I swear, it's just past that next bend."

"Trish, can I borrow your knife?"

"Just a little farther, Richard."

"When this is over," Richard said. "I'm going to gut you like you gutted that fish."

"Wait," Tricia said.

"No, I'm not finished," Richard replied, grimacing. "Then I'm going to cook you over a fire and leave you in the woods for those wolves to find. And then I'm going to—"

"Shut up," Tricia said, "and *look*."

They did. A shed sat a few hundred meters in front of them, half hidden in the trees. A tree grew alongside it, hiding most of it from view behind a canopy of leaves.

"Oh," Richard said.

"Please let there be a trolley," Jayson mumbled under his breath.

With the shed in site, they sped up, pressing to reach it. They were all excited and hopeful. Finally, things were going their way.

Richard stumbled a few more times but they kept him from falling as they rushed toward the shed.

As they got closer Jayson could make out the features better. The track split about eighty meters before they reached the shed with a manual switch. The access track went to the large sliding door for one side of the shed and presumably through to the other side. The shed was some forty meters long.

The walls were comprised of rusted sheet metal, weathered with age. The sliding door wasn't locked, but it took Jayson several pulls to jar it loose. It hadn't been used in a long time. He threw it open, letting light spill in, and saw:

Nothing.

Jayson stood in the entryway, the excitement ebbing away. It was replaced with bone weariness. Just an empty shed, forgotten out in the middle of the forest. No supplies. No trolley. Nothing.

"What now?" Tricia asked.

"I don't know," Jayson replied.

"You keep going," Richard said. He slipped out of Jayson's hold and sat down on one of the rails. His face was pale, eyes sunken. "And I stay here."

"We already—"

"Bullshit. This is game over for me. We're making terrible time, and things are just going to keep getting worse. I'll be dead by tomorrow."

"Then we'll stay here. Look for supplies, fortify this place..."

Richard was shaking his head. "No," he said, then coughed. "No, it won't do any good. If there was a medical kit here, then maybe. But not now. This is a complete waste."

Jayson exchanged a glance with Tricia.

"Have a seat," Jayson said to Richard. "We need to rest anyway, and there's no better place to do it than right here where we have walls. We'll gather some wood and look for water and see what we can do about making this place comfortable."

"Comfortable place to die," Richard said, chuckling. The chuckle turned into a cough. "I suppose that's something."

"Just shut up, Richard."

Chapter 21
Sector 1 – Axis
Argus Wade

1

"What's he doing?" Yeol whispered, tilting his head to the side with a frown. His eyes were locked on the spectacle in front of him. His face was a mask of awe tinged with fear as he watched the robed figures move about the courtyard.

"It's a ritual," Argus Wade explained, straightening his black robes and pulling the hood back from his head. They were ritual robes, itchy and uncomfortable. Everyone was expected to wear them for religious holidays. "Something the church has done for thousands of years."

"What for?" Yeol asked.

"To pay homage to our ancestors. This shows our respect for the dead. Today, we ask for their guidance," Wade replied. He considered pulling Yeol away—children weren't allowed to take part in religious rituals until they were fourteen—and decided against it. Better to dispel his youthful illusions now than let them build over time.

"They ask a pig for *guidance*?"

Wade was silent for a moment. "Not exactly."

The porcine was snorting and squealing as a nimble, cloaked man led it to the center of a deep pit of sand. The pit was surrounded by several Ministry Officials, including the Minister Givon Mielo, as well as many of the high priests.

Behind them were students at the Ministry as well as low-ranking priests. Everyone was chanting, filling the courtyard with a quiet hum. Even the priests who spoke low of the Ministry were in high religious fervor today.

Which was reason enough for Argus Wade to keep his distance. As a member of the *Ordo Mens Rea,* he had a target on his back. Better to spend his day hidden from the people itching to form a mob.

It was a beautiful day on Axis—thanks to the domed structure forming their sky—and a lot of priests would visit. Some civilians would come as well to offer alms and pray.

Argus glanced up at the dome roof above them, looking for any signs of wear and tear. In some there were lines or imperfections, dispelling the illusion of open sky. A few were even missing lights or had broken machinery, making the dome shape obvious. Above the Ministry, however, the dome was perfect. Open sky above him. Except it wasn't. It was tons and tons of metal, trapping him like a rat in a cage.

He hated these holidays. He hated the rituals with a severe passion. His Order, the *Ordo Mens Rea*, had no rituals of its own. When they were adopted by the Ministry they were forced to give up their old way of life. They were forced to accept the Ministry's God as the one true God.

That had never really bothered Argus. It had been over two hundred years since so he didn't even know who their original God or Goddess might have been.

What he did care about was how ignorant the Ministry was. They were *proud* of that ignorance, reveling in it. Normally Argus didn't mind the life he'd been forced into. But it was days like today that made him truly hate it. If it wasn't for his unique genetic markers he would never willingly be associated with something this primitive.

He'd never even had a chance at a normal life.

He sighed and gently squeezed the young student on the shoulder. Yeol was turning eight in a few weeks. Like Wade his enrollment in the Ministry was not voluntary. He shared the genetic markers; as such he would spend many long years as a test subject and victim. He would be looked at like he was different, a freak, for the rest of his life.

The Ministry took him from his family at two months old and brought him here to live in an antiseptic plastic room with the other babies. He knew nothing about life except what the Ministry wanted him to know.

And if he ever, *ever,* stepped out of line, they would declare him a dangerous subject and lobotomize him. He would become a Keeper Then he would serve as an example, a shadow wandering the halls with a vacant look, terrifying the next generation of children brought in as human guinea pigs.

So no, Argus wasn't interested in protecting Yeol's fragile reality. Better that he understands early what would be expected of him. If Yeol didn't view the Ministry and the Shields through rose tinted glasses then he would have a better chance of surviving in this cruel, harsh world.

2

"You ready to go?" Argus asked. The cloaked man was leading the pig in circles, letting everyone see it. It snorted every few steps.

"Can I watch?" Yeol asked, looking up at Argus with big eyes.

"You shouldn't," Argus said. He'd been put in charge of Yeol and five other children as a mentor this year. The Ministry's sadistic program to give children the semblance of a parental figure. Wade hated performing this role and avoided the children as much as possible.

"But can I?"

Argus sighed. "A few more minutes," he said.

"Yay," Yeol replied, turning his attention back to the courtyard below them.

To think, only a few weeks ago Patrick Uhlren was down in that courtyard, impressing students with his virtuosic shooting skills.

Will ritualistic slaughter be as impressive?

The courtyard was comprised of cement flooring with two meters of dirt on top with grass and flowers growing out of it. It was constantly changing as the Church updated the selection to match the times. White flowers, pink, large green bushes. Once in a while, they even planted trees.

For the ceremony today, a garden dominated the northern side and an enormous circular pit of sand decorated the other. The walkways overlooking the courtyard were full with everyone who couldn't find room on the ground floor.

That pit of fine grain sand—imported from a planet in Sector Three for this occasion—was already stained red from the morning rituals.

An old woman stood in the sand, hunched over and frail. She wore long black robes and ugly white hair rested on her shoulders. A white bone mask covered her eyes.

She was the Ritualist.

Two other men came onto the sand with ropes. They slung them around the pig's neck and the three men took up a triangular position with the animal in the center. The Ritualist removed the hood on her cloak; her face was a mess of lines and wrinkles and she was anywhere between sixty and two hundred years old.

The grim smile on her face showed that no matter how many times she'd performed this duty, she still enjoyed it. A long jagged knife appeared in her right hand.

"What are they going to do?" Yeol asked, his voice taking on a note of apprehension. "What's the knife for?"

Argus let out a long sigh and held up his hands in defeat. He couldn't think of a better way to explain. "They are going to kill it."

The woman stepped forward, and with a smooth swipe of her wrist she slid the knife across the pig's throat. It squealed once, trying to jerk free, but the ropes held firm. The squeal was replaced with a wet wheezing sound as the pig slowly fell to the sand. Its eyes held a look of abject terror. Blood spurted.

A hush fell over the crowd.

Argus could swear he heard a *drip, drip* somewhere.

The creature thrashed against its ties for nearly a minute.

Yeol had a terrified look on his face and his body was shaking. "Why?" he mumbled.

"It's a ritual," Argus explained again, taking the child's shoulder and guiding him farther down the hall. The next part was to cut open the animal's midsection and drag its entrails out. The Ritualist would 'read' them.

175

No one in the Ministry actually believed she could see the future, but the rituals were still common whenever important events or holidays were coming up. It was a source of pride and solidarity with history.

And one which outsiders weren't privy to. There were no civilians allowed down there now. They would be allowed into the chapel, but they would never see this courtyard. Such barbaric rituals weren't discussed in polite company.

"What for?"

"History," Argus replied. "And respect. These are ceremonies that we enact to show our devotion to those who came before."

"Why do we do *this*, though?" Yeol asked. Argus couldn't think of a good answer. There was no sense in ranting to the child about the stupidity of people who held the power.

Once the pig was out of sight Yeol seemed to calm down. His body stopped shaking. The beauty of children, Argus knew, was in how fast they forgot traumatic events.

Or how well they repressed them. It was always hard to tell which.

They walked down the hallway, passing other students and priests and guests. Argus wasn't a teacher, but he was a respected member of the Ministry. Yeol was a good kid, ambitious and clever and very lonely in his new surroundings.

He supposed the reason he didn't avoid Yeol like the other kids was because he was the same age as his daughter—before he abandoned her on Denigen's Fist. Just thinking of his daughter made Argus's chest hurt. He was worried sick about her.

She was safe, he knew. The Captain had promised that Abi would be protected, and he didn't doubt that Captain Grove would keep her word. At least in that regard.

"We just do," he answered finally. He felt like he should say something.

"When did we start?"

"A long time ago," Argus answered. "Back when the Ministry was founded."

Yeol seemed to think this over. "What about *our* Order? The Order Mint Raya."

Argus smiled. "The *Ordo Mens Rea*," he corrected. "No, we never actually sacrificed any animals."

"Oh," Yeol said. "But we're part of the Ministry, aren't we?"

"Yes," Argus said. "But we didn't start in the same place. They...adopted us."

"Why?"

Because when they found us the first plan was to kill us all. They decided we would make a better weapon.

"Because they wanted to teach us about the True God," Argus said instead. "And because we could help them, too."

"How?"

Argus paused. The halls were mostly empty. He didn't like using his powers where anyone might see—they were expressly forbidden from using them publicly—and it was the fastest way to become a Keeper. He might be a priest on the official record, but here in the Ministry complex, he was as much a prisoner as if they'd used steel bars.

He guided Yeol into a side classroom. The door was unlocked, and he was careful to lock it behind him. He left the lights off and guided Yeol to the front near a window.

The room was plain and empty, lacking any wall decorations or posters that would be found in the typical classroom. The Ministry didn't allow the teachers to use any special teaching materials or posters.

He gestured at the board.

"Write your name."

Yeol looked at him curiously but did as he was told. He scrawled *Yeol Din* across the board in big capital letters. Argus waited until he was finished, and then did one more sweep of the room. He wanted to be completely sure that no one saw or heard anything. Especially if he was about to break one of the sacrosanct rules.

"Set the chalk down. Good. Now watch," he said. He closed his eyes, focusing on his mind and building energy. When he opened them again he cast out through his implant. The chalk lifted out off of the table, seemingly of its own accord, and floated to the board. He heard Yeol gasp in surprise but kept his attention on the board. He didn't want to lose his focus.

He scrawled *Argus Wade* in chalk on the board with the little piece and then pulled the chalk through the air into his hand.

"How did you do that?" Yeol asked, breathless.

"That was nothing. Here. Think of a number," Wade said. He stepped forward—he couldn't multitask with his implant—and handwrote '52' on the board. "Now a color—" *orange* "—and now think of any random thing."

Argus hesitated a second and scribbled *spaghetti* on the board. Then he set the piece down. Yeol's jaw was hanging open as he watched.

"How can you do that?" Yeol asked. "You can read my mind?"

"Surface thoughts," Wade said. He rubbed a bead of sweat from his brow and fought down the sick feeling that came whenever he used the implant. He wasn't good at it, didn't do it often, but it served very well for parlor tricks. "And I can move some objects. But they have to be really small."

"But how?"

"No one is quite sure," Argus said with a shrug. "We receive implants and then learn how to use them. Mental exercises. It's the only way we can do anything. But we don't know who invented them."

"Why not?"

"The Order didn't keep historical records," Argus said. "Just specifications. We aren't even sure what *planet* they came from. Some think it was on one of the moons orbiting Vitius. Some think it was outside the Republic. Maybe in Sector Nine."

Argus wiped the board clean of his scribbling and headed for the exit.

Yeol was silent, legs pumping furiously to keep up with Argus's easy stride. "How many people can do that? Like you did, reading my mind?"

"Less than one percent of people with implants," Argus answered. "And of those, very few could ever master it."

"Can I do it?"

Argus shrugged. "One day, maybe. When you have your implant."

"So I get to join?"

"In a few years," Argus said. "You *have* to join, technically."

Yeol thought about that. "Could I be a Shield?"

"Maybe," Argus lied. Yeol didn't have the natural talent nor the proper body type.

"If I don't get chosen," Yeol said, "can I go home?"

Argus hesitated, slowing his stride. "No," he said finally. Again he omitted his follow-up statement: *you'll never go home.*

Perhaps the only saving grace was that, since the Ministry took Yeol from his mother before his first birthday, he never knew a real home.

They rounded a corner leading to the Minister's office. Argus stopped and turned to Yeol. "I need to go into a meeting now. You should run along to your classes."

"There aren't classes today."

"I know. But I'm sure there's homework you could do."

Yeol nodded. "Okay."

"Have you been saying your prayers?"

"Uh huh," Yeol said, then recited, 'Through His Grace we grow strong.'

"Very good. Now run along."

The kid disappeared around the corner. Argus glanced back at the large ornate double doors. It was the archway into the office of one of the most powerful people in the galaxy.

Argus didn't want to keep him waiting.

2

"You wanted to see me?" Argus asked, hands folded behind his back and standing rigidly straight. His black teacher's robes hung loosely about his shoulders, swaying with every movement in the still air.

The Minister's office was twelve-by-twenty meters with a fifteen-meter high ceiling. It was lavishly decorated in a cream-colored motif. Rare hardwood flooring was covered with expensive woven rugs gathered from all around the galaxy. At great expense, of course. The value of the paintings covering the walls could have bought a large planet in Sector Three.

Ostentation didn't begin to describe it. In Argus's eyes, the artwork would have been better served in museums. *The things I could do with the money from selling those...*

A docked CPU decorated half of the desk with a rounded touch screen and holographic projector. Its value wasn't in the hardware it used, but the databases it interfaced with. The Minister had the same access to data that the First Citizen had: every detail about the trillions of people living in the Republic available at his fingertips.

Givon Mielo, the Minister, was an impressive and dignified figure, despite his advanced age. He sat behind the enormous desk, fingers intertwined before him. He appeared frail and diminutive in the oversized chair, but his eyes held a deep set and steady focus that belied any memory loss.

His hair was all but gone and his skin had the rough leathery texture of a well-used ragdoll. What remained of the fading white strands was pushed along the scalp in clumps, leaving gutters of pale, blotchy skin.

Argus felt bile in the back of his throat and suppressed the urge to pick his fingernails. A nervous habit he'd never fully broken. He did that whenever he was uncomfortable, and he was *always* uncomfortable in the presence of the Minister.

It's because he is always judging me. He doesn't even seem to be looking at me, but rather through me. He's looking through my eyes, into my soul. He sees what's inside me.

Luckily, Argus knew that the Minister had no such abilities. Givon Mielo was an intimidating man, but his power came from personality. He wasn't a member of the *Ordo Mens Rea*, just the Ministry.

Jealousy was part of the reason Givon hated Argus.

The Minister sat in his enormous ivory chair, raised several feet above Argus. No invitation was made for his guest to sit. Two child-aged Keepers flanked the man on either side of his chair, dressed in flowing blue cloaks and vacant stares.

Wade hated Keepers. He hated the entire concept. They had existed since the Order was first brought into the Ministry to humble them. In theory, they represented the forgiveness of the Ministry —they didn't execute anyone in the Order when they lashed out or rebelled, even their worst offenders—but it was just another method of control. There was no council to decide it, no overriding principles. It was simply at the discretion of the current Minister.

And there had never been a Minister so willing to make Keepers as Givon Mielo.

"Yes," the old man answered finally, staring down his beaked nose at Argus. Then he fell silent once more.

An old cuckoo clock chimed in the corner.

Argus resisted the urge to scratch his nose.

"I wanted to get clarification on a few things," the old Minister continued finally. He had the slow and emphatic cadence of a man deliberately choosing his words. The effect was contagious, and Argus found himself second guessing everything he thought to say.

"What things?" he asked.

"How long were you in Sector Six?"

"Nine days."

"Nine?" Givon echoed. "What made you leave?"

He can't possibly be serious?

"Warships were arriving from Sector Four. The First Citizen sent an Edict that all Republican Citizens were to leave. It was unsafe. So we left."

"I see," Givon said, resting his hands on the desk in front of him. "But it says Vivian Drowel of the *Ordo Mens Rea* chose to stay behind in a posting in the region. If it was dangerous, why would she stay?"

Argus hesitated. He was treading on thin ice. He didn't know how far he was willing to push his luck. He was already at risk with the Minister sniffing around the parentage of a certain young girl named Abigail. A new student who had conspicuously disappeared a few days earlier.

He didn't want to sell Vivian out, but he would if he had to.

"She thought a single ship could remain unnoticed, and she is hoping to wait until the Union ship has left to establish a post."

"Ah," the Minister said. "I see. And that's all it was?"

"Yes," Argus said. "That is all there was to it."

"I see," the Minister repeated, tapping his desk. "So it had nothing to do with a certain strange occurrence. A child...flying through the air?"

Argus felt his stomach sink. "A what?"

"A child. Jeremiah told me he saw a child fly through the air, perhaps propelled by another child."

"That would be impossible," Argus said. "No child out there would have had an implant."

"True," Givon replied. "But Jeremiah was quite insistent. He said you could corroborate his tale, as well as Ms. Drowel."

Wade shook his head. "I have no idea what he was talking about, but I saw no such occurrence. We did come across children who were fighting, but nothing strange happened."

Givon eyed him. "I see. But, had you witnessed such an occurrence, you certainly would have brought the child here?"

"Of course."

"As the law demands."

"As the law demands," Wade echoed.

Givon nodded. From his expression, Wade knew Givon didn't believe him. He would send people out there immediately to look for Traq, but it wouldn't do any good. "I will, of course, wish to speak with Vivian when she returns from her post."

"Of course," Argus lied. "As soon as she arrives on Axis I will send her to you immediately."

Wade had no intention of following through with that promise, but it seemed he was in the clear. For now. He would just make sure Vivian was always busy, and there would always be a ready excuse when the Minister asked. Eventually, the old man would forget.

"Very well," the old man said with a dismissive wave of his hand. "I thank you for the update and your continued service to our Ministry."

Argus couldn't have been happier for the dismissal. He hated spending time with the Minister. He knew he would spend the rest of the day exhausted from these few minutes of high tension conversation. It made him feel unclean, pathetic.

He bowed to the Minister and headed for the ornate double doors.

I'm in the clear. Now that Traq is safe and the Minister has no leads to follow up with I can finally relax...

He was only a few steps away, hand already raised to push open the door and escape, when he heard the Minister speak behind him.

"Oh, and Wade. Please keep me updated on how your daughter serves as my Envoy aboard Denigen's Fist. I am *greatly* interested in her success."

Suddenly, Argus felt sick.

Chapter 22
Sector 6 – Jaril
Oliver Atchison

1

"**Y**ou're sure?"

"That's the sixth time you asked me that question, Jim. Do I need to draw you a picture?"

"It seems implausible that she would break the agreement," Jim Crater replied. He was wearing a ridiculous green safari hat. Oliver wondered, again, why he'd bothered to make this trip.

Because I need money, and I need it today, he reminded himself.

That wasn't quite enough to justify working with Jim Crater.

"I doubt the woman knows there *is* an agreement. The Union and Republic don't exactly get along."

"You're sure she was from the Republic?"

Oliver sighed in exasperation. "Of course, I'm sure. I lived for twenty years on Terminus, and I know the difference between one of us and one of *them*," he insisted. "So are you going to loan me the money or not?"

Jim leaned back in his chair. He closes his eyes when he thinks, Oliver knew. But I already know how he's going to decide. Predictability is a nice quality in an asset.

Oliver knew he was reaching out on a limb here, but he needed the funds quickly if he was going to make this deal with Vivian work. He'd known Jim Crater as a casual acquaintance for over a dozen years. But the last time he'd seen him was two years ago. He'd changed since then, but not much.

What he did remember of Jim was a man with too much money and not enough sense. Jim was a military man, through and through, but instead of leveraging his family name and influence to become an officer, he'd jumped in at the bottom rung. He'd insisted it would make him a better soldier, hence, a better leader.

What it *did* make him was a pariah. He was mocked by the other officer's and blocked from any natural progression through the ranks. Five years of service and he grew disheartened. He quit the military and withdrew from society. Most people forgot about him.

Oliver didn't. Jim was one of the few people who had a lot of spending cash on hand that wasn't a bank. Oliver didn't like banks or paper trails. And if the deal was going to work, Oliver needed to buy the water purifiers *now*.

But right *now* all he was able to do was watch Jim think.

The kettle on the burner began whistling softly. Oliver moved it to a cool counter and waved the steam away from his face.

Jim Crater had inherited a deal of money from his family estate when his mother passed away. The family was deep into mineral rights, but their mines had run dry while Jim was in his teens. He'd inherited what was left, but with his stint in the military and unwillingness to listen to advice, good or bad, that money was slowly drying up.

Normally Jim was frugal with those credits, but he'd been spending them hand over fist in the last few days since the ship Evelyn's Grace showed up. Oliver was hoping that since Jim was in a giving mood, he might be able to cut a deal with the man.

The problem was, Jim wasn't spending as frivolously as Oliver had hoped. He was trying to kick start an underground movement. He wanted the Union to leave Sector Six for good.

The Royal Family, on the other hand, was greatly interested in a trading partner. It would solidify their grasp on the region. All they had to do was become good lapdogs for their new masters. So what if making a deal for themselves hurt everyone else?

To be honest, Oliver could sympathize. Eventually, the trade would happen no matter what. But he wasn't here to argue politics with Jim.

Oliver touched the side of the kettle. Still not cool enough to pour.

"Six hundred thousand credits?" Jim asked again. Oliver nodded. "That's the lowest you could get?"

"The ship is valued at a million. I'm getting it for just over half price and I'm splitting the deal with you."

"Splitting? It's my money," Jim said. "'Splitting' is a generous choice of words."

"I did the legwork," said Oliver. "And I brought the deal to you in honor of our old friendship."

It was true. Sort of. Mostly, Oliver's list of willing friends with enough money to make this deal was incredibly short.

Jim waited a moment and then nodded. "Fair enough," Jim agreed, leaning forward. "All right, I'll give you the money. I'll even give you half stake in the ship, but there is a condition."

"Name it," Oliver said, suddenly worried. He'd been expecting to get a twenty percent holding of the ship at *most* out of this deal.

"You mentioned that she was armed."

Slowly, Oliver nodded. "She had a sword of some sort and pistol."

"And she seemed capable of defending herself? If provoked, I mean."

Oh shit.

"That doesn't seem relevant—"

"No one has to die is the best part," Jim said, oblivious to Oliver's objections. "Create a distraction, she draws her weapons to defend herself, and the Royal Family has no choice but to declare the armistice with the Union broken."

"They'll turn our defenses against Evelyn's Grace," Oliver realized. "And end the discussions before any deals are signed."

"That's my price," Jim said, leaning back in his chair.

"Seems kind of cold-blooded," Oliver said, pouring the heated water over tea leaves to steep. "How will they know not a local?"

"If she's in a fight, they'll run her face against databases. Since she isn't local or even from the Kingdom, she won't show up."

"And if they don't run her picture?"

Jim shrugged. "Some things you have to take on faith."

"It's a risky plan."

"But if it works, we'll be better off for it," Jim said. "Sometimes you just have to bite the bullet and do what is necessary—"

There was a sudden knock on the door. Oliver sipped his tea and set it on the counter. "Who is that?" Jim asked, wariness on his face.

Oliver opened the door.

A ruddy man with pockmarks covering his face waited outside, nervous. Oliver gestured to come inside and shrugged at Crater. "I forgot to mention, I need that money *now*."

Jim's eyes went wide. "What?"

"Pay the man," Oliver said, sitting back down in his chair at the kitchen table, "and I'll do whatever you need me to do."

Jim grumbled, but he did offer up the data pad. The ruddy man typed in a few commands, Jim entered his passcodes and did a quick biometric scan and transferred the credits.

"Thank you," the broker mumbled, disappearing from sight. Oliver shut the door behind him and sipped his tea again.

Jim looked angry once the money was gone. "You *knew* I would take your deal," he accused. Oliver shrugged. "That's a lot of credits."

"It's a lot of purifiers," Oliver said.

Jim took his safari hat off and dropped it on the center of the table, running a hand through his receding brown hair.

"Well, I'm poorer by half a million credits."

"But richer by a ship," Oliver retorted, pulling a carefully rolled up handkerchief out of his jacket pocket and unrolling it. A pair of cigars rested inside. They were expensive but well worth the cost. Jim's favorite brand, Oliver remembered.

Oliver handed one to Jim, who was already perking up. "You went along with my plan, so I'll play along with yours," Oliver said.

"I'll call the Wrake brothers tomorrow morning and negotiate a price. A few well-timed shots in the air, make her think she's being attacked, and it'll be over."

Oliver nodded, mind working over the possibilities. The more he thought about it, in fact, the more he liked it. Evelyn's Grace had piqued the interests of the Royal Family. Whetted their appetite, so to speak, and their greed would not allow them to accept anything less than the profits they were promised.

Oliver knew how to trade, and he'd been to Terminus many times. He stood in the perfect position to slip his way into the vacuum being created when Evelyn's Grace fled. He would make a fortune; if he had his own ship and the ability to trade on behalf of the Royal Family...

Betraying Vivian, when he thought about it, seemed like a very small price to pay for half of a claim on a trading vessel. The money he could make doing his own shipping was well worth her animosity.

"Tomorrow, I'm going to the port to inspect the vessel we're about to trade for," Oliver said. "Then the next day we're making the transfer. Once a deal is struck I'll get her to the market and create your distraction."

"You think you can lead her on like that?"

Oliver almost laughed. "She won't have the slightest clue."

"Okay then. I'll hash out the other side of the plan. She'll never know what hit her."

"No," Oliver said. "No actual attacks. Scare her, sure. But don't hurt her. She might be just a normal civilian."

"She's armed."

"Just because she carries a gun does not mean she knows how to use it," Oliver said. "Maybe in a few days, this will all be over. A couple shots, her weapons pop out, and the treaty is broken. Evelyn's Grace goes home."

"What time should I meet you at the spaceport tomorrow?"

"Don't worry about it. You put the money in; I'll take care of the rest."

Jim shrugged, putting his hat back on and sliding a lighter from his pocket. "You know, Oliver, if things go right, then this time next week we could be heroes for sending the Union packing. We'll have to pick up a couple victory cigars." He flicked the lighter and held the flame across the table for Oliver.

"Or coffins," Oliver added, leaning over and puffing on his cigar.

"Yeah," Jim said, lighting and drawing deeply before leaning back in his chair and releasing a cloud of silver smoke.

2

The hangar was built in an old grain field several centuries earlier. Back when Jaril was still mostly farmland. A monarch built the structure while declaring this his home, and the city of Mys sprouted around it. Now it was the largest and most beautiful city in the entire Kingdom.

But it doesn't change the fact that the hangar is falling apart.

Oliver leaned against the concrete and rebar wall in bay forty-three. He was carefully avoiding a stripped wire hanging from the ceiling that might or might not shock him if it touched his skin. It was hovering about twelve inches from his left cheek and he would have sworn it chased him whenever he moved.

That wire had fallen loose from a ceiling light during construction and draped down to ground level through due to excess cable and shoddy workmanship. Oliver didn't even want to guess how long it had been like that.

Once I have my fifty percent of a ship, I'll have to put up with these damn deteriorating spaceports on a regular basis.

Suddenly a wrench hit the ground a few feet to Oliver's left. A man shouted down apologies.

Oliver carefully moved away from the wall.

He tried not to picture what he would look like lying dead on the floor, skull bashed in.

Vivian Drowel stood a few meters away, reading over the schematics of the water filtration system. Each unit came in four pieces. If the shoddy hangar conditions bothered her, she didn't show it.

She was thorough. He had to give her that. Luckily she didn't seem to know any more about water filtration than he did, and with prices fluctuating throughout the galaxy she would have a hard time proving he was cheating her.

He'd been hoping to leave the hangar a few hours ago, but Vivian insisted on going over each and every unit and make sure they were up to spec. A few of the units were old and she insisted on running water through them and testing it.

Traq was sitting on the ground a few meters away, looking bored out of his mind as only a five-year-old can. Oliver felt bad for the kid, wondering if he'd ever been that bored when he was young.

He doubted Vivian was the kid's mother—they looked nothing alike— but she was a lot more for Traq than Oliver had while growing up. His grandparents gave him a place to sleep sometimes, but for the most part, he lived in group homes for kids or on the street surrounded by miserable adults and thieving bullies.

"Are you satisfied?" he asked.

"Nearly," Vivian replied. "Are you in a hurry?"

The question oozed mistrust.

"Of course not, but they close the hangar in a few hours," he said. And I'm bored, tired, and frustrated. Also, by the way, I'm planning to betray you so that a madman can run you off the planet and break up a tentative treaty.

He decided to keep *those* thoughts to himself.

And people say I'm not diplomatic. Ha!

Oliver felt in his pocket and found the little good-luck coin he carried. It was a trinket he kept out of sentimentality...mostly. It was also (conveniently) an exact replica of the Admiral Medallion for Heroism. It was given by the Admiralty whenever someone went above and beyond the call of duty and was only rewarded once every few years.

They were, of course, quite easy to replicate.

Whenever he dropped into a local bar it was the perfect conversation starter. A quick story about how he risked his life to save his war buddy Chester in some galactic battle was a great way to make sure he didn't spend his nights alone. *I pulled him out of the burning wreckage, giving him my own oxygen supply until we got to safety. I don't think I'm a hero, but the Admirals...*

He flipped the coin over in his hand and knelt down next to Traq. "Want to see a magic trick?"

The kid looked up. "Sure."

"See this coin?" Oliver asked, handing it to Traq. "Feel it, it's totally solid." Traq turned it over in his hand and then gave it back to Oliver. He held it up again for inspection and then held out his hands, showing the fronts and backs. "Now watch, I'm going to make it disappear."

Oliver exaggerated the motion of pushing the coin into his fist for a few seconds. He had Traq's complete attention now, and when he opened his hands to show Traq that the coin was gone the kid's eyes went wide. Traq looked around on the ground and then up at Oliver, and Oliver couldn't help but grin.

"Where did it go?"

"I told you, I made it disappear. Now watch, I'm going to make it reappear." Oliver closed his fists, exaggerated the motion again with his right hand and then opened his hand to show the coin. Then he handed it to Traq. "See? Magic."

Traq held the coin up to inspection. "How did you do that?"

"A magician never reveals his secrets," Oliver explained. Traq handed him back the coin and stood up. Traq turned to Vivian.

"How did he do that?" he asked.

Vivian finally looked up from the schematics.

"Probably a fake coin," she said. Oliver flipped it to her. She caught it deftly and scanned it over. "Then some sort of adhesive." She tossed it back to him.

"You wound me," he said, "to even *accuse* me of tricking this youngster here with anything less than *real* magic. I'd like to see *you* do better."

Vivian sighed and turned back to the manifests.

Oliver held the coin back up in front of Traq. He whispered, conspiratorial, "I use a sticky substance called petroleum jelly to hold the coin to the back of my hand," he said, showing his hand to Traq. "And I press the coin against the soft part between my thumb and finger so that when I open my hands and show you my palms you can't see the coin."

"Oh," Traq said, looking at his own hands and slightly deflated.

"Unfortunately, magic isn't real," Oliver disclosed, aware that Vivian was still watching him overtop the manifests. "And before you ask Vivian, yes. That means I always carry a little container of petroleum jelly in my pocket. Just in case."

A few moments passed and then Vivian set the schematics down on the table.

"It's not a lot," she said. "Only twenty purifiers. In the Republic, we could get twice this many for the same price."

She's bluffing, Oliver knew. Her eyes told him everything. If she knew for certain, she'd never sign this deal.

"Never been there," Oliver lied. "So I wouldn't know."

"No," Vivian said, "I suppose not."

Oliver was glad she was in a hurry to leave the planet because only a few hours in the right markets would have been enough to call his bluff. "I suppose this is enough if you are willing to stipulate to the rest of my agreement."

"The delivery has already been organized, and the goods will be on Mali within two weeks. I've taken the liberty of plagiarizing a trade contract and making a few modifications for us to sign. I added your stipulations in the bylines."

"I want your word as well," Vivian said. Oliver affected to be offended.

"The people who need water, those are *my* people, even if they live on a different world. You have my word that your purifiers will make it there. And in addition, I also pledge that if I find others willing to donate food, supplies, or water to Mali, then I will deliver them as well in honor of this deal we've struck today."

Provided they pay, of course.

He still had to put up with a few more moments of her eyes boring into him before she relaxed. Oliver briefly wondered what she would have done if she didn't like his deal.

"I will come back one day to make sure you live up to that promise," Vivian said, rolling up the schematics. Oliver bowed.

"When you do, you'll be quite pleased," he insisted.

"Come back tomorrow, and I'll have the ship ready for transfer," said Vivian. Oliver bowed again, only a few inches this time, and then turned toward the exit. He waited until Vivian was safely out of sight:

"Layers upon layers of lies," he mumbled. "Oliver, I believe you'll get yourself in trouble one of these days."

Chapter 23
Sector 4 – Alderson
Jayson Coley, Alyssa Ophidian

1

Jayson heard the train before he saw it.

It started as a rumbling, just enough to shake the ground. He was sitting against the wall on the eastern end of the long shed so he felt it under his legs, waking him from a light slumber. He shook his head, clearing the sluggish exhaustion from his mind, and focused on the dirt beneath him.

It took a few moments to realize the source of the vibration, and when he did he sprang to his feet. Something big was coming down the tracks.

The vibrations rolled in from the west, opposite where they'd been walking during the day.

The train was coming from the city.

"Do you feel that?" he asked.

Tricia was resting near the eastern door of the shed, leaning against the rusty wall next to Richard. She looked haggard and weak in the dim light. She glanced up curiously at Jayson as he spoke.

Jayson rushed across the dirt floor, dodging a pair of low hanging chains and barely daring to breathe. He made his way to the old sliding door along that western wall. He grabbed hold of the rusty handle and yanked; it ground open with a mighty squeal, heavier than expected. He didn't stop but kept pulling until his muscles ached and the doorway stood open.

Outside the night was thick and cool with a breeze rolling across from the west, chilling his skin. It was also quiet and empty. He stared deep into that darkness, willing a train into existence. The fire Tricia built a few hours earlier was on the opposite end of the building, shining light to the east. They'd been so concerned with traveling *to* the Academy they'd never even stopped to wonder what was behind them. The fire was just past the eastern door that he couldn't see very far out this direction.

He could see enough, though, to wonder if he was going crazy: there was nothing out there except flying bugs and a few trees hidden in the gloom.

A minute of deathly silence passed. Jayson felt his stomach clench in anguish. He knelt and pressed his hand to the ground. Nothing. Whether his position was bad or the train wasn't real, he felt no vibrations through the ground. *Please let it be real,* he intoned silently. *It has to be real. Please tell me I'm not going crazy.*

A few seconds that felt like an eternity flowed past, and...

...nothing. The breeze picked up, causing his ripped and stained shirt to flutter, but otherwise, the landscape was unchanged. The tracks bent after only a few hundred meters in front of him, curving into the forest and out of sight. He couldn't feel any vibrations.

But...

But he could smell smoke!

"What is it?" Tricia asked, coming up alongside him. "What did you hear?"

"There's a train coming," Jayson said breathlessly, running back into the shed. "There's smoke through the trees. A few minutes away. Grab Richard, we need to be ready."

"A train?" Tricia repeated. "Thank God."

"Maybe."

"Maybe?" Tricia asked, confused. "They'll have food. Water. Supplies. We're safe."

"You're assuming they're here for us," Jayson said, kneeling down and lifting Richard up into a sitting position. Richard was ashen faced and exhausted, too tired to even groan from the pain. "But I'm betting not."

"They couldn't just go on by," Tricia said in disbelief. "Richard will die."

Jayson didn't reply. He lifted Richard to his feet and Tricia took his other arm. He wobbled but didn't fall. "What's up?" Richard muttered, eyes barely focused. "We going somewhere?"

"Yeah," Jayson said. "Home."

"You can't seriously think they will leave us," Tricia argued.

"The train is coming from the city. I doubt they even know we are here."

"So what do we do?" Tricia asked.

They stumbled their way to the west exit and into the night. It was quiet still, but now they could hear the train in the distance. In a few moments, it would come into sight. They had about a minute before it was upon them. It wouldn't be moving very fast, he hoped.

"Here," he said. They lowered Richard to the ground and leaned him against the outside wall of the building. "Keep out of sight for now so they don't—"

"Jayson," Tricia repeated, grabbing his arm before he could turn away. "What are we going to do?"

Jayson blew out a long breath. "Ever hijack a train?"

2

"I think I'm going to kill Maven," Alyssa mumbled to herself, punching an embroidered pillow lined with velvet and azure. It was expensive and pretty but terrible to lie upon. Which meant useless in her estimation; she hoped to soften the padding to make it more comfortable, sure, but if it doubled as stress relief when she hit it she wouldn't complain.

She tucked the pillow back behind her head and leaned into it. It was warm and itchy against the back of her neck and entirely too stiff to be comfortable. With a curse, she flung it across the way.

"Yep. Definitely killing her."

Alyssa stared out the window as the scenery flowed past. It was night, and the train had poor lighting, but she was well satisfied that she wasn't missing anything in the darkness.

"A tree. A tree. A tree. Oh look, another tree. Damn it," she growled, adjusting her black miniskirt. It kept riding up every time she shifted in the seat.

She'd decided to wear it in its matching blouse and boots because she looked cute as hell, but it was turning out to be a terrible decision. The material chafed her skin and she'd already decided to burn it once this trip was over. If she'd known, she would be wearing it literally all day she would never have put it on.

But that was a minor problem compared to how the rest of her day had gone. She was miserable on this stupid little planet. Damn Darius and his ill-begotten agendas. Why must he keep agreeing to Maven's ill-conceived and poorly thought out plans?

"Once Darius sees how *useless* this place is," she muttered, "he'll have no choice but to shut it down."

It had seemed like a good plan to discredit her sister. Maven had taken the academy as a pet project, wanting to train loyal soldiers with particular skills. Saboteurs, survivalists. Self-contained anarchists, they could drop off on a planet for one purpose: terror.

Maven had staked a lot of her credibility into how well this Academy functioned.

But she wasn't half as angry at Maven as she was her pilot. She'd ordered the useless bastard to drop her off at the Silvent Academy early in the morning. That was when she first arrived. He'd refused, stating that it would be both illegal and dangerous to attempt such an endeavor. The arrogant man had refused *her*.

And why? Because the Academy refused to allow *any* flights to pass through their airspace, and they had ground mounted cannons to back it up. Her pilot warned her that violating airspace restrictions would give the Academy authority the fire on her vessel and, no, it didn't matter who she was.

Which meant that the only way she could reach the Academy was to walk or ride the train; a train for which no trips were scheduled in over a week. Alyssa had wasted most of the day finding an engineer.

Suddenly the lights flickered out in the cabin, casting Alyssa into complete darkness. She could feel the train thrumming beneath her, but she couldn't see anything. "Damn it," she growled in frustration. Seemingly in response, the lights came back on.

They'd been doing that since the ride started. Every few minutes it lost power. The engineer explained that the train's electrical connections were faulty. He'd been planning on fixing them before making his next trip...but that wasn't for several days.

So she was forced to tolerate spotty lighting. It hadn't bothered her at first, but after a few hours she was getting more than a little annoyed.

The engineer had been in a bar called the Flying Duck drinking with friends when she finally tracked him down (which infuriated her). He was also ugly and short and bald (which also infuriated her) and he even tried to refuse passage to the Academy (which really, *really* infuriated her).

He explained that she needed a formal invitation from the Academy Master to visit. They were undergoing some sort of trial for new recruits, and there were to be no interruptions.

What would the point be, she argued, of an unscheduled audit if she had to schedule it? She actually considered, in her angry state of mind, just knocking the engineer unconscious and taking the train on her own. She would have if she had any idea how to operate it.

So Alyssa did the next best thing for venting off some steam: she dominated the engineer's mind. She'd cast out through her implant and taken control of him. Then she forced him to do what she wanted. He'd fought back, of course, which just made her utter control of him all the sweeter.

She'd cooled off since then. Now she was just tired as hell and angry.

There was a beeping on her communicator. She drew it out of her purse and flicked it on, a smile spreading her lips.

"Maven, it's good hearing from you," she said to her sister on the other end of the connection.

Maven looked hideous. She was wearing her stupid overly-dramatic self-conscious outfit: a black cloak sagged low to hide her face and a plastic breathing mask, fogging gently each time she took a breath. She didn't like to let people see her face and hadn't since she was a child. Since the accident.

Her sister had always been rather theatrical.

"Alyssa..." Maven said, her voice lilting in disdain. "What do you think you are doing?"

"Serving the council, dear sister," she said. "Performing an audit to ensure our funds are being spent wisely."

"At my Academy?"

"It *was* quite the investment."

"It isn't ready yet," Maven said. "You shouldn't be there."

"I just want to help."

Maven laughed and shook her head. "I know *exactly* what you want."

"Little sister, why do you insist on treating me like an enemy? I want to help you and be there for you. I've never done anything to hurt you."

"Sure," Maven said with a noncommittal shrug. "But I'm telling you, you shouldn't be there."

"And why not?"

"Because my students are undergoing a training exercise," Maven said. "It could be dangerous."

Alyssa laughed, holding her stomach. "Oh," she said through gasps, "that's rich."

Maven didn't respond. Alyssa couldn't see her face, but she knew her sister was angry. She could tell by the precisely controlled breaths through the breathing mask. She had the look of a wounded animal, weak and pathetic.

"You didn't ask," Maven said.

Alyssa smiled at her sister. "Easier to beg forgiveness than ask permission, dear sister."

Maven shook her head. "Alyssa, please just turn around and head back—"

Alyssa closed the communicator, ending the connection. She couldn't help but giggle a little. Her sister was such a stuck up little cow sometimes. It was nice to put her in her place.

Once she'd managed to embarrass Maven's Academy to the Council, they would have no choice but to close it down and withdraw support.

Alyssa's headache began to recede. The call perked up her spirits. After a while, she relaxed in her chair and closed her eyes. She was confident that the engineer wouldn't step out of line for the duration of this trip so there wasn't anything to worry about.

"It'll all be worth it," she reminded herself, "when I can close Maven's Academy for good."

3

Jayson waited on the tracks, tree limb dangling in his left hand and heart beating like a drum. He stood in a loose stance, ready to move if the train didn't slow. If the engineer was paying attention, he might even bring the train to a stop. That would make the job really easy.

But as the train drew closer it also grew larger. He started to rethink his plan. It wasn't traveling quickly, but it wouldn't take much speed to be faster than him. He felt like an ant standing before a charging behemoth.

He bit back nerves and anxiety and focused on the task at hand. His objective was to get to the engineer, subdue him, and bring the train to a halt. If he was lucky, the man would think he was a hapless stranger and offer assistance. That would make Jayson's part in the plan easy.

Tricia's job was to make sure the train was empty and locate medical supplies. Once they had things under control they would patch Richard up and have the train continue on its way, delivering them to the Academy.

It sounded easy. But he had to admit there were certain things he'd overlooked. What if the engineer didn't give up easily? What if the engineer was armed? Reasonably, why *wouldn't* he be armed? They were in the middle of the forest at night. What were the chances the guy would want to help them?

Jayson would have done just about anything for a real weapon. But wishing he was armed with more than a wooden stump wouldn't do him any good.

"Who the hell hijacks a train," Jayson said to himself as the train pounded closer, "with a stick?"

Twenty meters away, it became apparent that the train wasn't going to stop. The engineer either didn't see him or planned on running him down. That was okay, Jayson supposed. If the engineer didn't know he was there, all the better.

It was moving at about eighteen kilometers per hour, he guessed. He could sprint and keep up with it for a few seconds at least.

Jayson stepped off the tracks to his right letting it approach. It would breeze right past him only a few feet away. The engine compartment had five steps with handrails along the sides. It was built similar to trains he'd seen on Eldun, so he guessed the rails would be sturdy. His plan required that he catch hold of those rails and pull himself on.

A second flitted past.

The train's floodlights almost blinded him as the train barreled closer. He heard a shout as the engineer finally spotted him, but it was already too late. The train suddenly sounded louder as the engineer cranked up the speed. But it would take too long to build enough to outrun Jayson.

Jayson's body kicked into high gear as adrenaline coursed into his veins. The world seemed to slow down around him. It always shocked him, at times like this, just how fast the human mind *could* work. He could see, hear, and process information at a much higher level of functioning than normal.

Another second slipped past.

Jayson forced himself to breathe in deep steady breaths. He turned with the train still a ways off and began sprinting along the tracks, his pace slightly under that of the trains. It reached him and flowed right past, thunder filling his ears.

He reached out with his right hand and caught the closest handrail. It was smooth and ice cold to the touch. He clenched down on it, increasing his pace to fall into step with the train.

But he was too slow. The train was traveling faster than expected, and he missed a step. As a result, he tripped and banged against the side of the engine. His knee hit hard and exploded in pain, but he bit it back and focused on what he was doing. He dropped the stick and used his left hand to keep himself off the ground.

He barely kept hold of the rail with his right hand but managed to lift himself off the ground. After a few seconds, he caught the other handrail with his left hand and leveraged his body onto the step. His knee throbbed but he didn't think he'd done any permanent damage.

The engine door flew open, nearly knocking him off his perch on the steps. A short man in grease-covered overalls and a brown hat glared down at him. "What the hell?"

Jayson didn't answer. He forced himself forward, half-crawling up the steps, and hit the man about the waist with a tackle.

"Hey!" the man shouted, hitting his back hard against the panel inside the engine. He launched a punch at Jayson, but it was slow and off-target. Jayson caught the man's wrist and leveraged down, forcing him to sit. The engineer collapsed into the chair, raising his hands defensively with a look of horror on his face.

"How do you stop this thing?"

The guy stared at him like he was crazy. Jayson raised his fist and the man cowered. Then he nodded toward a double lever on the front control board. Overtop it was a plaque with the word 'brake' on it.

"Oh," Jayson said.

"Look, I don't want any trouble," the guy said.

"I know," Jayson said with a shrug. "It's nothing personal."

Then he slammed the engineer's head against a flat panel beside the controls.

4

Alyssa was on her feet as soon as the train began slowing down.

"What the hell?"

They were already moving at an abysmal pace, so why the hell was the engineer stopping? She didn't know where they were—the entire forest looked exactly the same—but she was certain they weren't at the Academy. It was supposedly all the way up in the damn mountains.

And she'd given orders to the engineer not to stop until they were there. Something must have gone wrong. Or at least, something *better have* gone wrong. If she found out the engineer was willfully disobeying ...

A second later the lights buzzed in the cabin, flickered, and went out.

"Oh, for crying out loud!"

She headed for the exit, determined to punish the short man for his insolence. There was only light from the stars above, so moving wasn't easy.

A few steps away from the door it suddenly slid open.

"You'd better have a damned good reason—"

A tall black woman rushed inside the open doorway. She had a long face, large lips, and curly black hair. She looked haggard, and her clothes were stained and shredded.

She also looked strong and intelligent with narrow eyes and a strong jaw. Alyssa was wholly unprepared. She cursed and stumbled back, grabbing for the holdout pistol in her boot. The woman pursued.

Alyssa ducked out of range. The gun came loose from her boot, but she didn't have time to draw and fire. She dodged a punch and kicked out with her right foot. She didn't hit anything, but that wasn't the objective. She was aiming for the woman's ankle, forcing her to give ground or suffer a debilitating injury.

She raised the pistol, trying to draw a bead, but the woman didn't hesitate. She stepped inside Alyssa's defenses and launched a kick at her stomach.

Alyssa managed to avoid the brunt of the attack but it still clipped her side. The hit rocked her and sent stars shooting across her vision. "Bitch..." she moaned, sucking in a breath.

Alyssa twisted her hips and swiped with her leg, tripping her opponent and forcing extra distance between them.

It bought some time, but not enough. Alyssa knew she was in trouble. She drew a short ragged breath of cold air into her lungs, but she could feel her body crying out for lack of oxygen.

The woman braced herself against one of the seats and bounded back into the fray. She caught Alyssa's hair and punched Alyssa on the wrist holding the gun with two sudden jabs. Hard. The gun fell, bouncing down the aisle to come to a rest near the open door.

That attack was followed by two more rapid strikes. The woman was fast and a lot better trained than Alyssa, and without her eyes adjusted to the lack of light she was doubly at a disadvantage.

The first attack hit her on the jaw. She took that one in stride, still in the fight. The second clipped her nose, sending an explosion of red through her vision. The cabin swam and she cried out in pain, stumbling back and furious.

Alyssa felt more than saw her opponent moving, heading for her gun. She was angry, as angry as she'd ever been. She channeled her emotions into focused determination, gathering it as energy in her implant. She knew the woman had picked up her gun and that she would use it without a moment's hesitation.

But Alyssa had no intention of letting that happen.

"Drop it," Alyssa growled, throwing her power behind the command. The words barely came out with so little air in her lungs, but they were just a pattern for her thoughts. What mattered was the mental bridge she'd built.

The woman tried to resist, but Alyssa batted her mental defenses away as thought they were a child's sand castle. This woman had never practiced mental defense. She'd doubtless never known how dangerous it could be to enter a battle of wills against someone like Alyssa. As a result, she was unprepared.

Most people were.

The gun clattered to the floor with a soft thud.

The cabin fell quiet. The only sound ragged inhalations as the two women struggled to breathe.

A rush of pride surged through Alyssa as she felt the woman mentally cower from her. Such utter domination of another human being was savagely empowering. Whenever she cast power through the implant it was a lustful, sinful experience. She loved every second.

"Walk to me," Alyssa purred, tasting blood on her lips. The woman did, only the slightest tremor in her steps. "Good girl."

As she grew closer Alyssa could see her eyes. They were wide with terror. The woman knew everything that was happening, but she could only watch. She had no control over her own body. The best part wasn't turning the woman into a mindless puppet; it was that the woman knew who was doing it to her.

"Kneel."

Slowly, the woman lowered herself to her knees, lips shaking.

Alyssa hauled her arm back and slapped the woman across the face, open handed. It stung her palm and a few fingers went numb, but she felt another surge of primal pleasure. She did it again. And again, this time with the back of her hand.

"You stupid hussy," she growled, hitting the woman one more time. She walked past the woman to her gun, swaying her hips. She was back in control, and it felt *good.*

She scooped the gun up, feeling its comfortable weight, and strode back toward the kneeling woman. She was screaming in her mind, thrashing to regain control over her body. But it meant nothing. She wasn't strong enough, and Alyssa held her mind in a vice grip.

"You picked the wrong fucking train, bitch."

She leveled the weapon at the back of the woman's head, savoring the moment.

Which turned out to be a bad idea.

She was so focused on killing the woman who'd hurt her that she didn't notice anything else. She never heard anyone else slip into the cabin. Never saw the figure come up behind her.

"Step off, whore," a man said. She cursed and spun, raising the gun and lashing out through her implant, but too slowly. Out of the corner of her eye, she saw him standing there. He had sunken brown eyes and a beard and was wearing dirt and blood covered clothing. He looked to be on death's door.

He also looked to be swinging what looked to be a very large tree limb...

...at the back of the head.

It was a wrecking ball against her skull. She heard something snap.

Suddenly she was on the ground. The world was spinning.

And everything went black.

5

Jayson heard a resounding *crack* from inside the passenger car as he dragged the unconscious engineer to the car. He cursed and dropped the man unceremoniously to the ground, rushing toward the sound.

The door was still open and there was a trail of blood on the ground that he followed inside. The lights were dim and flickering, but he could see well enough. Richard was lying near the aisle at the end of the trail of blood, groaning in pain and clutching a broken tree limb. Tricia was holding his head in her lap, crying.

Next to them on the floor was a woman he'd never seen before wearing a mini-skirt. Her face was covered in blood. She looked vaguely familiar but he couldn't place her from memory. She was attractive, minus the matted hair and blood staining her face and neck.

"Are you okay?" Jayson asked, kneeling next to Tricia. She didn't respond. "Tricia! What the hell happened?"

Still nothing. She opened her eyes, but they didn't focus on anything. Jayson glanced around and spotted a white and red medical kit on the wall. He hurried to it and jerked it down. It was heavy, which was good. That meant it was stocked. He unsnapped the sides and opened it.

He sighed in relief to see the clean supplies and set the kit on the ground next to Tricia. "Hold him. This is going to hurt."

She still didn't reply, but she did reach down and grab hold of Richard's hands. Jayson cut his bandages loose, revealing Richard's wound. Somehow—probably when he boarded the train—he'd managed to tear the wound open even farther. What the hell was he thinking, climbing on the train like that?

The cut was dirty and ugly with faint red lines tinting the edges. Infection, but only just begun. With luck, it wouldn't do any permanent damage.

Jayson coated a towel from the kit in alcohol and set to scrubbing the wound clean. With how bad off Richard was he barely moaned.

Once satisfied the wound was clean Jayson set about closing it up with clean supplies. He found stables and sealed it closed and cleaned the outside with a foaming disinfectant. He wrapped Richard's entire side with gauze.

He found some antibiotics in the kit and after a little struggle managed to get Richard to swallow them. There were also a few vials of painkillers, so he injected a low dose and laid him out on the floor at the front of the cabin. His eyes were closed but the grimace on his face loosened up as the medicine took hold.

Throughout all of it, Tricia barely moved. She was rocking gently and paying no attention to the outside world. Her eyes looked more haunted than normal, and he wondered what had happened to her. What *could* have happened to her in those few moments to be so devastating on her psyche?

"Take care of him," he said to her. "We need to get moving."

She still didn't respond. He grabbed her shoulders and shook her. "Tricia! We don't have a lot of time. Get yourself under control."

Tricia looked at him, crying and distant. "She...she took me...I couldn't..."

"Richard is going to die," Jayson said. "Unless we help him. We need more antibiotics to fight his infection, and we aren't getting them here."

Her eyes focused a little bit, and she looked down at Richard. He was breathing peacefully now, but shallowly. "He saved my life."

"Then don't let him die."

She looked up, unconvinced, but she did nod.

Jayson found another roll of tape in the kit and set about tying up the woman and the engineer. He did take a few moments to bandage the wound on the back of the brunette's head, just to make sure it wasn't too bad. He didn't know who she was, and Tricia didn't seem able/willing to tell him. Best not to let someone he didn't know die. At least not yet.

"Watch them," he said. Tricia didn't look at him, but she did nod again.

Then he headed back up to the engine. He took a few minutes to familiarize himself with the controls. There were a lot of knobs and dials, but after a few minutes of trial and error, he managed to get the engine up and running.

It shuddered to life and started grinding forward once more.

Jayson sat in the chair.

All at once the exhaustion hit him. The adrenaline poured out of his body, leaving him a weak and lifeless husk. He was starving, weak, and sore throughout every muscle.

But he still didn't have time to rest. He slowly brought the train up to speed, peering forward and watching the tracks ahead. The lights didn't go very far, and he couldn't see more than a few dozen meters.

"It's no wonder the engineer couldn't see me," he muttered.

A few minutes passed. He watched the tracks, but every few seconds he felt his eyes slip closed. They simply did not want to stay open. He felt miserably exhausted, past the point of caring where he fell asleep. All his mind cared about was that it could shut down.

"No," he muttered. "Can't fall asleep."

He fought for another minute or two, determined to stay awake until the train reached the Academy.

Naturally, he fell asleep mid-thought.

6

Jayson awoke with a start, disoriented and afraid. It was painfully cold and he was leaning sideways against a metal frame, almost lying flat. The world was tilted...or something...but he couldn't quite tell why. Whatever had happened was in his semi-conscious memory. All he knew was that something felt wrong, but he couldn't tell what it was.

A second later he could.

The left wheels of the engine thudded back down on the rails as the train flew around a turn. The motion jolted him to full awareness, almost throwing him out of the engineer's chair, and he cursed in fear and frustration.

It was light out, early morning, and the train was thundering down the tracks. What had seemed slow in the trees was now dangerously fast on the curves. They were up the mountain on switchbacks. A light snow had begun to fall, and the landscape was drastically different from where they'd just left.

Tight switchbacks, Jayson remembered suddenly, *and getting tighter*. They'd slowed down a lot before reaching this point on his first trip up the mountain. It was sheer luck, he realized, that the train hadn't capsized during that last turn.

He fought down rising panic, wracked his brain, and remembered the control scheme of the dashboard. He skimmed it over, picked a lever at random, and yanked back on it. The engine started shuddering on the rails, but they didn't slow down.

"Damn it," he said, glancing around. He quickly pushed that one back into position and picked another one. They were coming up to the next switchback, and this was far worse than the last one. They would capsize if they reached it at this speed.

He grabbed hold of the next lever and yanked it back. There was a loud screeching sound as the brakes engaged.

The train slowed to a crawl. They edged up to the next turn at a fraction of the pace. The next curve they passed went much smoother. The wheels stayed firmly on the tracks.

Jayson breathed a sigh of relief. He set the speed on the lowest setting and relaxed back into the chair, rubbing his hands and blowing on them. It was cold now, a lot colder than it had been the first time they rode up to the Academy, and he wondered how cold it got later in the season.

It took only a minute to realize he needed something to cover up with: a coat or blanket. He climbed out of the engine, dropped to the ground, and waited for the passenger car to catch up.

At the slow speed, it was easy to keep pace. He walked up, pulled the door open, and slipped inside the car.

Not a lot had changed. Tricia was still sitting on the floor with Richard's head in her lap. She had stopped crying and was idly twirling his curly hair. She looked exhausted and hurt, eyes haunted.

The other woman, the one he'd tied up, was still in her seat. Though now she also had a bag over her head. Jayson looked at it curiously and then at Tricia.

Tricia shrugged in reply. "I'm not sure if the bag helps," she said, "but it can't hurt."

"I see," he said.

Jayson went over to the med kit and dug inside. He checked over Tricia's previous head injury. It looked pretty well healed from their time spent in the forest, so he checked his own leg. The wound was scabbed over and rough, so he spent a few minutes cleaning it and re-bandaging it. Then he popped some painkillers.

The numb feeling spread through his body in only seconds. It was like heaven.

She shivered. "It got cold."

"I know what you mean," Jayson said sleepily. "I wonder if there are any blankets in here."

"There aren't. I checked."

Jayson nodded. Then he hesitated before asking, "What happened, Tricia? Why are you...?"

She was silent for a long second, then she shivered again. This time, it had nothing to do with the weather. "She was in my mind."

"What?"

"She was *in* my mind," she repeated.

Jayson shook his head. "I don't understand. What do you mean 'in your mind'?"

"I mean she was *inside* my goddamned mind," Tricia said angrily, tears streaking down her cheeks. The emotion was sudden, startling Jayson. "Controlling me. I wanted to *move* but she wouldn't let me. I could feel her in there, playing around like I was some toy, but I could only watch as she..."

Jayson sat on the floor next to her. He reached out and put a hand on her arm. "That seems..."

"Impossible," Tricia finished, grabbing his hand and squeezing. "But it's true."

"She's one of them," a voice said groggily. A gun appeared in Tricia's hand from nowhere, aiming at the engineer as he woke up.

Her hand was shaking.

"Easy," Jayson said, gently taking the gun, "it's the engineer. And he's tied up."

Tricia let out a deep breath and relaxed. "Sorry, I'm just..."

"It's okay," he said. He turned to the engineer. In better lighting Jayson saw that he was a plain looking little man, balding and fat. His face was very round and his eyes too close together.

Right now he was staring intently at the woman with a bag on her head, fear evident in his eyes.

"What do you mean?" Jayson asked. "What do you mean she's one of them?"

"What she did to your friend, she did to me too," the man said quietly. "You should kill her, now, while you have the chance."

"You mean she controlled your mind?"

The man winced and nodded. "Just for the fun of it, I think. But her sister is worse. Way worse."

"I'm not sure I understand," Jayson said. "What you're talking about just isn't possible."

203

"I thought the same thing until about a year ago. Then that bitch Maven showed up. And she...she killed..."

Jayson had heard the name before. She was all over the news, one of the twin sisters that came with Darius Gray when he rebelled. She was on his new Council, one of his Generals. Together, the newscasters proclaimed, they would help build a new world with fairness for all.

Darius was at the head of the new Union.

So, this must be...

"Shit," Jayson said, dropping his face into his hands. "You mean the sisters? This is one of them?"

"'Devils' is more appropriate," the engineer said with a shudder. He glanced over at Jayson. "They serve Darius. They have...powers. Alyssa can control minds. And Maven...Maven used her mind to grab me and squeeze."

"Squeeze?"

"Imagine being caught in a vice grip that's slowly tightening."

"Telekinesis?"

The man shrugged. "Call it what you want. I call it scary."

"Is Maven here?"

"No, Thank God. Alyssa is bad. Cruel. The other one, she's crazy."

"A crazy woman with special powers," Jayson said skeptically. "Forgive me if I have trouble believing you."

The engineer nodded grimly at Tricia. "Just look at your friend."

Jayson was still skeptical, but he had to admit it made a sort of logical sense. Tricia was rock solid in her demeanor, but she clearly believed that such a thing happened. Jayson didn't want to believe, but mostly because if he admitted something like that was possible...

"Does the Ministry know?" he asked.

"They'd have to," the man said with a sharp nod. "But here's the scarier question: did the Ministry do this to them?"

Jayson wasn't sure he wanted to know the answer.

7

"When I moved here, the Silvent Academy had thirty trainers," the engineer explained a while later. Jayson was sitting in one of the seats watching the snow fall. It wasn't clinging to the ground yet, so it was still early in the season. "And about two hundred students. They were the Hammers. Greatest soldiers you would ever see. I was proud to work here."

"I've heard the Hammers were genetically engineered," Jayson said.

The man shrugged. "Could be possible, sure."

"Genetic engineering is illegal."

"So is murder. It's unethical, and we can leave it at that. I won't make judgments one way or the other. I will say that these men and women were huge. Especially in those suits of armor. Looked like something out of a movie. Outside the suits, they were like normal men. Inside..."

"They were trained here?" Jayson asked. "But not anymore?"

"Their training facilities were moved to the Core. Closer to Axis. That was twenty-some years ago. After that, things out here died out. People left, the city fell apart. A few stayed on. Alexander Robertson was headmaster. He bought the land for pennies and kept the place open, but there weren't any students. I stayed on because I've got nowhere else to go.

"Then about a year ago Maven showed up. Alexander told me she was scarred as a little girl. The Ministry threw acid in her face to punish her for disobeying. Nearly killed her."

"That's horrible," Tricia muttered.

"If you met her," said the engineer, "you'd wish they finished the job."

"So she came to the Academy?"

The engineer nodded. "On behalf of Darius Gray. Said she wanted the place reopened. We said there were no students, so she told us she'd find some. Send them here. Alexander would train them and Darius would pay. It would be just like when he trained the Hammers."

"By dumping them into the middle of the forest?"

The man chuckled sardonically. "Hell no. I think Robertson figured out that he'd signed a deal with the devil shortly after. Maven told him how he would modify the training. *This* was all Maven's plan. She insisted on it. Said any training should be like the real thing. If all of you died, she'd just get a new batch of students. Sink or swim."

"If they don't teach us anything then it's not really training," Jayson said.

"Didn't I tell you she was crazy?" the engineer asked. "I don't know what the Ministry did to that little girl, but she's turned into a terrifying young woman." He glanced out the window, furrowing his brows. "We're about to the Academy. Who's up front?"

"No one," Jayson said. "It's cold as hell out there."

"Well, you're going to want to get up there soon. The tracks end after the Academy, and we'll end up in a pond if we don't get stopped in time. Make sure to throttle down to four before making the final turn and check the ELM gauge to make sure—"

"You do it," Jayson said, standing up and walking over. He cut the tape on the engineer's wrists. The short man rubbed them gratefully. "You aren't going to screw us, right?"

"Not a chance," the man said. Then he hesitated. "But I will give you a heads up: she's important. Like, major big league. And I'm pretty sure you pissed her off."

Jayson exchanged a glance with Tricia. "Do you think we should turn around? Head to the city instead?" he asked.

The engineer laughed. "Trust me, your best bet is to hold your head high and pretend you did nothing wrong. She isn't dead, just a little bruised. And you hit her in the head. If you get really lucky she won't even remember what happened."

"Encouraging," Jayson mumbled.

The engineer slid it open. A cool rush of air flowed inside along with swirling flecks of snow. The man paused. "Whatever you do now, though," he said, "don't take that bag off her head."

Then he jumped out and ran toward the front engine. Jayson slid the door shut behind him. He leaned against the door and let out a long sigh.

"This," he said to Tricia as he sat back down, "is turning out to be the worst two weeks of my life."

Chapter 24
Sector 6 – Jaril
Maven Ophidian, Jayson Coley

1

Maven sat in front of the terminal aboard the warship Eisle, stunned by the report she was receiving and trying really hard not to laugh.

"They did *what?*"

"They kidnapped the train," Alexander Robertson explained on the other end of the connection. His voice was terse, expression worried. *He thinks I'm going to be angry,* she realized. *He doesn't realize this is the greatest news ever.* "And they captured your sister, who was the only passenger on board. We arrested them, of course."

"What, why?"

The man's expression quickly became guarded. "Technically, they failed the test you set out for them. They did not arrive back at the Academy of their own—"

"Wait, wait, I want to hear more about my sister again," Maven said. "So they hit her in the back of the head, tied her up, and turned her over to you?"

Alexander looked uncomfortable. "She did not tell us she was coming in advance of her visit or we would have warned her of your test."

"Oh, I warned her," Maven said.

"The engineer said that when she showed up in town she was quite persuasive and unwilling to listen to suggestions."

Maven finally broke down, laughing and clapping her hands. "That is the greatest thing I've ever heard. Oh, my sister must be *furious.*"

"She has not awoken yet," the old man said, running a hand over his gray beard. "Shall I notify you when she does?"

"No, no," Maven said. "Just stick her back on the train and send her home. Drug her if you're worried she'll wake up early. I'll deliver a report to Darius that her mission was a *complete* success."

"What shall I do with the, uh, students?" Alexander asked. "The ones who failed the test."

"How many made it back?"

"Five," Alexander replied. "The others perished in the wilderness. But the three that arrived by train technically did not abide the rules you set forth—"

"A non-issue," Maven said, waving her hand in dismissal. "I consider kidnapping Alyssa to be a complete success!"

"Very well," Alexander said. "We will begin training immediately."

Maven clapped her hands again, excited. "I look forward to future reports."

They disconnected the call, and Maven burst out laughing. She fell out of her chair and collapsed to the floor she was laughing so hard. She couldn't shake the image of Alyssa tied up in the back of the train with a bag over her head. How that must have infuriated her pompous ass-kissing sister.

She couldn't wait to speak to her about it. At length. Many times. Alyssa would want to have the students killed, of course, but Maven knew it would not be a hard sell to convince the Council otherwise. After all, the students had effectively dealt with Alyssa even when they were wholly unprepared for her mental abilities.

How useful would they be with adequate training?

2

Jayson was asleep within ten minutes of the train stopping.

Alexander Robertson met them outside. If he was surprised to see the train rolling to a stop in front of his Academy, he didn't show it. The three bedraggled passengers stumbled out into the cold wind and snow flurries.

Richard was immediately shuffled off to the infirmary, and Tricia went with him. That left Jayson alone with Alexander.

Jayson told him what had happened over the last few weeks, as well as whom their prisoner was. Robertson didn't say a single word during the entire explanation. When Jayson finished, Alexander nodded in response, led Jayson to a nondescript room on the second floor of the Academy, and disappeared. Then he locked the door behind him.

The room was plain and gray. The bed was hard. He'd never been so content.

He awoke at some point later. His body ached, and he was exhausted. He tried to remember what woke him up and decided it must have been someone knocking. He stumbled to his feet and shuffled to the door, rubbing the sleep out of his eyes and containing a yawn.

It opened a second later, and he saw Robertson waiting for him. The old man looked tired, especially around the eyes. He was leaning on his cane in a white suit with his gray hair combed backward.

"Hello, Jayson," he said.

"Hello," Jayson replied with a nod. "Is this my prison cell?"

"It was."

Jayson pondered that for a second. "That could be interpreted in quite a few different ways. Several of which are not positive. Are you planning to execute me, Alexander?"

"Headmaster," Robertson corrected without malice. "And no. You are now one of my students."

"What if I'm not interested?"

Alexander Robertson didn't reply. Jayson hadn't really expected him to.

"What happens next?"

"Training. Survival. Our benefactor is expecting you to be useful within a year and fully trained within three."

Jayson bowed his head. "Useful," he said, shaking his head. "As a Hammer? Or whatever Darius's equivalent will be?"

"Not exactly," Robertson replied. "The Hammers were trained to be paragons of humanity, to be better, stronger, and more resilient than any enemy they might face."

"Oh?" Jayson said. "Then what are we being trained for?"

Alexander Robertson smiled, but it was a sad smile. "Get some sleep Jayson," he said, turning away from the room. "You'll need it. We will begin tomorrow, and once we start, we won't stop until you are done or dead."

"You didn't answer me," Jayson said, grabbing his arm as he turned to leave. "What does she expect us to be? Spies? Assassins? Soldiers?"

The headmaster let out a long sigh, closing his eyes. When he opened them again, Jayson saw defeat in his eyes. When he spoke, the word was almost too low to make out.

"Terrorists."

Chapter 25
Sector 6 – Jaril
Vivian Drowel

1

Vivian watched the equipment vendor, a heavyset man with three chins and fading hair as he disappeared into the spaceport crowd. He'd just finished setting things in order for the final goods to be loaded onto the Cudgel. He seemed nice enough; unlike Oliver, *he* didn't rub her the wrong way.

Though she had to admit that Oliver was efficient. She'd only been on the planet for a few days and already all of her deals had been settled. She looked around at the equipment filling up the hangar and was more than a little impressed. To be honest, she hadn't really *expected* anything from a swindler like Oliver.

But then again, that was her personal bias bleeding through. He was too smooth by half, and with a clear and even cadence while speaking he reminded her of an actor spewing well-rehearsed lines.

And the way he did his trick with the coin. That irked her. He had Traq wrapped around his finger, and a more paranoid person might have assumed he was taunting her for her inability to communicate with the child effectively.

Of course, a less paranoid person wouldn't have given the exchange any thought at all. It was just someone trying to impress a kid with a magic trick.

But she would have to come to terms with it if she wanted this deal to work at all. It would take days to finish loading all of the water cleansing equipment onto the Cudgel. And even then it might take multiple trips to ship it all to Mali. She couldn't afford to stick around that long. Not with everything else going on.

She glanced over at Traq again, glad that he was here. He was why she was about to lose the Cudgel—a ship she'd bought and held onto for over ten years—but he'd also reminded her that some things were more important than money or wealth.

There was a beep from her communicator. She flipped it on. Jack Lane, Traq's uncle, appeared on the projector. She heard a sharp intake of breath from beside her.

Traq ducked behind Vivian with a squeal as the image coalesced, but gradually reemerged when he realized it wasn't going to hurt him. "Jack?" Vivian said.

"Don't worry, this line should be secure. I will be arriving on planet sometime tomorrow to pick you guys up. Did Bart find you okay?"

She nodded. "He met us at the spaceport. And he's been rather helpful."

"Then did you manage to successfully...uh..." Jack scratched his head. "What was it you planned to do?"

"Yes, we were successful."

Jack nodded. "And then we can head to the Ministry."

"Yes," she lied. "That is our next destination."

She would have to figure out something to explain why she wasn't taking his nephew home, but that was a conversation for another day.

Traq stepped nearer to the image, gathering courage as the conversation continued.

"Hey Jack!" he said, waving.

"Hey, kid. Are you having fun with Vivian?"

Traq nodded. He was grinning ear to ear now that he knew the communicator was safe, and Vivian couldn't help but smile as well. That was something she'd come to like about the little kid: his moods were contagious, and everything excited him. She couldn't remember the last time something as simple as a long range transceiver had excited her.

"I'll land around midday tomorrow and meet you both at the pond outside the spaceport. That work?"

Vivian nodded and disconnected the call. She decided to spend the rest of the day taking Traq around to see the city. This was the capital world of his home Sector, after all. Once they left tomorrow and reentered Imperial space she didn't know if they would ever come back. One day, she knew, these memories would be important to him.

But for now, she just wanted to find some dinner.

2

Vivian was engrossed in her books when Oliver showed up at the Mys hangar late the third morning. She found that she was in a tremendously good mood. A crew had shown up early to load the water purifying equipment onto the Cudgel, and already they were halfway done.

The equipment broke down in such a way to be space saving and she was pleased to see that they were going to be able to load it all onto the Cudgel in one trip. She might even convince Oliver to forward a message from Mali after dropping off the equipment. It would save her from worrying about it.

Traq was curious about everything. He was starting to get less homesick and kept asking random questions. Vivian discovered that the hardest questions to answer were the ones about her own past.

She didn't like talking about herself, and she was frustrated when she found the chapter about being open and honest. Lying wouldn't work, she read, and would only cause the divide between them to grow even wider. What did it matter if Traq knew what the planet she was born on?

Apparently it mattered a lot, but she wasn't about to start worrying about that right now. She kept her answers simple and cryptic; she could focus on his education once they made it to Terminus and she decided where they would go next. Wade told her it wouldn't be a good idea to go back to the Core, but the galaxy was enormous. Plenty of hiding places.

She heard the elevator coming to a stop behind her and stood to see Oliver walking into the hangar. He was wearing a bulky coat with gray pants and his hair looked like the wind had been blowing it around all morning. Compared with yesterday he looked positively disheveled.

"You wouldn't believe how hard it is to get a transfer deed for a spaceship put together in a day," he said. "I've never actually looked into it before, but apparently we have strict policies on Jaril. Who knew?"

"It isn't a problem, is it?" she asked. He shook his head.

"I tracked down a few attorneys and banged on some doors at two this morning, but everything is taken care of. Rush transfer and I can take the ship off planet tonight. With luck, I'll have your water purifiers delivered to Mali in two days."

"That's impressive," she said.

"Necessary, actually. I already picked up a shipping job next week, so I'll need to get a move on." He hesitated. "I suppose I should have asked earlier, but it slipped my mind...what are you planning to do now? You weren't expecting me to give you a ride...or...?"

She shook her head. "It's already been taken care of. You have the deed?"

He nodded and pulled a data pad out of his pocket. She signed her name and input a few codes for the ship, and then he handed her the contract that obligated him to drop off the equipment for her.

She knew it was nothing more than fluff. There was nothing in the deal to force Oliver to uphold his end of the bargain, but she did appreciate it. It was better than nothing.

She signed her name, and he signed his. He looked relieved and his face opened into a wide grin. "Well, ma'am, it's been a tremendous pleasure doing business with you. Let me buy you both lunch."

"That's not necessary," she said.

"I insist," he countered, turning to Traq. "Hey little man, what do you want to eat?"

Traq bounced up. "How about Nom and Korrin?"

Vivian had no idea what that could be, but Oliver seemed to light up at the suggestion. "Absolutely. I know a little kiosk that makes great Nom."

Oliver started toward the elevator and Traq fell into step beside him, leaving Vivian no choice but to follow. Traq rambled on about the planet, the weather, the smell, and a variety of other things as they walked. He seemed invigorated, and Oliver talked to him smoothly, as though the child's inane ramblings made sense.

As they walked, Vivian began to realize that this was the happiest Traq had been since he left his home. Why was Oliver so easily able to elicit a response from him? What did he do that she didn't?

She watched them talk for a few minutes as they walked through the space station, and by the end of the conversation she was even more confused. Evidently Oliver just had some way of dealing with people she would never understand.

Oh well. Her job was to take care of Traq, not be his friend. They exited the spaceport and wandered into a nearby market, enjoying the weather. It was a sunny but cool day, making it very comfortable. She checked her watch and figured they had about an hour before they should go meet Jack Lane at the pond in the park.

They walked past the line of granite statues for another few minutes before stopping in a food court. It was filled to the brim with groups, each engaged in their own conversations. The smells emanating from the various stalls ran the gamut from enticing to disgusting. Oliver turned to her and pulled out a credit stick. "Ever had Nom before?"

She shook her head. "Haven't even heard of it."

"It's a special holiday dish on Geid, but it's too popular to only be served once a year. It's a kind of bread with dipping sauce and Korrin is a sharp cheese. But I would say have the cheese served separately if you aren't used to it. It's an acquired taste."

She nodded and followed him to one of the counters. The line was long but moved quickly, and within moments, they were seated. Traq dug right into his food as though he was starving, and she was glad for Oliver's recommendation.

The cheese was terrible. When she nibbled on a piece she decided it tasted like mold. The bread, though, was soft and warm and covered with some sort of seeds that added a spicy flavor and strange texture. The dipping sauce was oil based and sweet.

It was delicious, maybe the best bread she'd ever tasted, and she made a note to see if it had spread to the mishmash culture of Terminus yet. Something this good, if it could be made with non-local ingredients, would inevitably become quite popular elsewhere.

Once Traq was finished, she saw he was eyeing her cheese, and she gratefully passed it over. He devoured it as well and leaned back in his chair, yawning. Oliver chuckled and glanced at her. There was just a slight note of apprehension in his eyes, and she felt a pinch of worry.

He glanced around, as though looking for someone. But when he looked back, he seemed to have collected himself and appeared calm.

"So when are you two leaving?" he asked.

"Later today," she said, eyeing him carefully. *What is he looking for?*

"Then I wish you the best in all of your future travels."

"Would you be all right with my contacting you in a few days to verify the equipment was delivered?"

"Oh, absolutely," he said. "That will save me a lot of worries as well. Excuse me," he added, grabbing up all of the trays and disappearing into the crowd.

"Are you ready to go?" she asked Traq, suddenly in a hurry to leave. Traq nodded.

"Are we going to see my uncle?"

"Yes. He's taking us off the planet. I'm sure he's landed by now."

Traq spun. "Aren't we going to wait for Oliver?"

"I'd rather not..." Vivian started to say. Her voice trailed off when she saw Oliver walking back with three drinks in a carrier. He set the container on the table and handed a drink to Traq.

"We ate some food from your world, and now it's time you tried something native to mine," he said to Traq, then smiled and handed a second drink to Vivian. She looked at it skeptically. *Did he drug it?*

Why would he drug it?

Hadn't he made out like a bandit already? What more could he want?

She thought she was being paranoid but knew she wasn't. His eyes told her everything. Something was wrong.

"This is a local drink called Parles. We use three different kinds of fruit and the milk from a—"

"Hey Traq!" a voice called. They turned to see Jack across the food court, waving his hand in the air and pushing through the crowd. Traq jumped up and looked around, then took off at a sprint when he spotted his uncle. Vivian tried to catch him, not wanting him to get far away, but he was already gone.

She turned around, but Oliver was gone as well, having disappeared in the other direction. She scanned for him, didn't see him, and cursed. Jack came up to the table, wearing a civilian outfit and carrying Traq with one arm. Traq looked thrilled, but Jack's face tightened when he saw Vivian's expression.

"What's wrong?"

"Did you see which way he went?" she asked.

"Who, the guy you were with?"

"Yes."

"What? Why? Who is he?"

"I don't know, but we need to leave. Now."

3

Oliver rubbed the sweat off his forehead. *Why haven't they started shooting yet?* He wondered. He'd done his job perfectly, getting the woman to the food court and surrounded by a crowd. They should have opened fire already.

Vivian was beginning to get suspicious, and when Jack showed up he knew he was in trouble. He'd made his exit, figuring he'd done enough.

He heard a persistent beeping sound and realized it was his comm. It had probably been going off for a while now, but he was too frustrated to care.

"What?" he mumbled, answering it.

"They are moving," Jim said. "Following you."

"Me?"

'Yes, you."

"Why aren't the brothers shooting yet?"

"They never showed," Jim said. He sounded calm, which baffled Oliver, who was sweating bullets.

"All right, then we'll scrap the plan and think of—"

"They are gaining ground, speed up."

Oliver started walking faster, pushing his way through the crowd. "How far—"

"You wore armor today right?"

"Just the vest but—"

Oliver didn't get to finish. He felt something hit his chest, hard and then pain arced up his body. A split second later, he heard thunder. He felt all the air rush out of his lungs and was suddenly on the ground, staring up at the sky.

Vaguely he was aware that the crowd was panicking around him. He mildly hoped they didn't trample him.

Luckily they seemed to be scattering *away* from his position. Someone was shouting in his ear but he couldn't make out the words. The world was spinning. There must be a storm coming because he could hear thunder. He saw the flash of a figure standing overtop him for a few seconds, casting him in shadow, and then that too was gone.

Slowly the world reoriented itself, and he could breathe again. He dragged in a few breaths of air and then forced himself to sit up. The food court was mostly empty, but he could see the occasional patron hiding under a table.

The ground and walls were torn apart from gunshots and blasters. The smell of burnt gunpowder and ozone hung in the air. Apparently, a lot had happened in the last few seconds.

He picked up his communicator and realized it was still connected. "Jim?" he said, but the word sounded like a whisper. He cleared his throat. "Jim? You still there? What the hell is going on?" A long moment passed with no response.

He slowly stood, wincing as pain raced down his chest. His shirt had a giant hole burnt into it and his body armor was dented and smoldering. Luckily, the shot hadn't passed through. "Hey, Jim. Come on. Tell me something. What is happening?"

There was still no response. Off in the distance, he heard the screeching siren of security officials, and farther away he heard the sound of gunfire. He heard a whirring sound and saw a hovering war robot with six mounted rifles pass by. It swept along a road perpendicular to his position about twenty meters south, oblivious to his presence.

The robot was on a beeline for the space station. Cursing, Oliver stuffed the communicator back into his pocket and hobbled down the avenue in pursuit, wanting to find out what was happening and groaning with every step.

4

Vivian ducked down another side street, Vibro-blade in her right hand and pistol in the left. She wracked her brain, trying to figure out what could have gone wrong, but kept drawing a blank. Jack kept pace beside her, a pistol in hand. His arms wrapped around his terrified nephew.

Traq was clutching his uncle with his face buried in Jack's shoulder, lost to the world. The street was clear before her, which was lucky for pedestrians and stray fire, but it also meant that the authorities would be on her much faster.

"Which way?" Vivian asked. She spun and lashed out through her implant. The security official rounding the corner behind was thrown backward by a blast of energy. He thudded against the wall several meters away, hitting heavily against the cement wall. It wasn't hard enough to break bones. Or at least, she hoped not. At this point, she wasn't sure how much she cared.

"This way," Jack said. "I picked up your TM walker and put him on my ship before looking for you. Can you call him?"

Vivian pulled the communicator unit out of her pocket and flipped it on, then tossed it to Jack. Another two guards in a green car rounded the corner ahead of them, rifles already firing in their direction.

She shoved Jack out of the way and raised her pistol, squeezing the trigger. The right guard dropped back into the car with a hole in his arm. The other managed to duck aside, but the car kept coming.

Vivian rushed forward and leapt into the air, landing on the front of the car as it barreled down the street. She slashed down with her blade. The curved tip sliced into flesh, cutting a tendon and disabling the man's arm.

The rapidly vibrating weapon dug deep into his flesh, shredding everything in its path. The poor security officer screamed in agony and tried to raise his gun at her. His arm was shaking.

She didn't want to kill him, only wound him badly enough that he couldn't pursue

"TM, you there?" Jack asked. There was an affirmative click from the other end. "I need you to get the ship prepped for launch. Get ready to hack their network if you have to. We're going to need a clean escape."

They were only about a quarter mile from the spaceport now, but the sirens in the air around them made it seem a lot farther. Security was gaining on them quickly, but at least the bystanders were out of sight. "Go faster, Jack, we need to get out of here," she asserted.

Jack didn't answer, but he shifted Traq and slung him over his shoulder, holding onto his legs. Traq looked like a sack of rice bouncing on his uncle's shoulder as Jack took off sprinting for the spaceport. Vivian kept pace about a step behind, firing her pistol to deter the occasional pursuer.

She saw the spaceport hangar rise in front of them as they rounded a corner, then she realized to her dismay that the bay doors were closed. It was a blast door, not particularly thick, and the panel next to it still had power.

She could rewire the system and open it. But that would take time and the area around the door was open and exposed. A line of statues ran along the sides of the walkway out front, but there was nothing directly in front of the door.

But they didn't have any alternatives. She glanced behind but didn't see any immediate pursuit. She turned back toward the doors.

"Cover me," she said, cutting the front of the panel off. She tossed Jack her pistol and with a practiced flick of her wrist the blade stopped vibrating. She used the tip to remove the faceplate from the door controls.

Jack set Traq against the wall behind a statue to the right and then leveled the pistol. It was small and low caliber, but he wielded it with practiced ease.

Vivian heard him fire off a few shots but focused on rewiring the controls. She had to hope Jack would keep her safe, especially considering none of them were wearing armor.

"Three coming," he said over his shoulder. "Hurry up."

She didn't bother to answer. She was almost done and had to hope that the door to their hanger wasn't closed as well.

"They backed off," Jack said. "Must be planning to flank us."

A few more seconds passed and suddenly Vivian felt something grab her shoulder and yank her to the side. She hit the ground hard and rolled to her knees.

A second later gunfire opened up from the street behind them, tearing into the statues and sending plaster flying in the air. Jack stood next to her, shrugging apologetically.

"A war robot," he said.

Vivian managed to peek around the corner to see the robot but had to duck back almost instantly. It was a mammoth creation, over six meters tall and hovering in the air on thrusters.

It had six mounted guns, two of which were laying down suppressive fire. She understood now why the security team hadn't been in such a hurry to chase her. Why bother when they had this at their disposal?

"We have to neutralize that," she said. "Before the rest surround us."

"Okay," Jack said. "How?"

Vivian had no idea. She wracked her mind for a plan, but nothing came. The situation was slowly going from bad to worse. She waited for the shots to slow but realized they probably wouldn't.

At any given time two rifles were firing, which meant the other four had time for the barrels to cool off and reload. She doubted it had great armor shielding against her vibrating blade, but that meant nothing when she couldn't get close. Similar robots were known to carry thousands and thousands of rounds of ammunition.

"Can your weapon cut through the wall here?" Jack asked, picking Traq back up. She looked it over and shook her head.

"It's a reinforced base. It will be too thick for a Vibro-blade to cut through."

"Then what do we do?"

She considered their situation and realized the longer they waited the more hopeless it became. "You'll have to go through the door. It's almost open, just finish cutting and splicing the last two wires and it should open. Then make a run for the ship and get off planet."

"We aren't leaving you."

"That isn't the plan. I'm going to try and work around these statues and take out the robot. But if I'm not right behind you, don't hesitate. On the count of three—"

She broke off suddenly when she heard a loud explosion. The assault rifles stopped firing. She peeked around the corner and saw the war robot careen into the building beside it. One of the propulsion legs at the bottom was smoldering, trying to reignite and realign the thrusters.

She spotted someone in the distance behind it, firing a pistol at it. He fired off another two shots and then took off running. She thought it looked like Oliver, but it was hard to tell from this distance.

The robot stopped spinning in place and leaned against the building beside it, opening fire back in the direction it had come. Not about to waste the opportunity, Vivian rushed out and finished splicing the wire on the control panel.

"Move!" she said, waving Jack through the opening. Jack scooped Traq up and carried him through the door, disappearing into the dimly lit antechamber beyond. Vivian started through, then hesitated.

The robot had almost repaired and reignited its propulsion leg. She wasn't sure who helped them or why, but she also knew that once the robot got moving it would cause that person serious trouble.

She stood on the roadway and drew her Vibro-blade. A quick flick set it vibrating again. She hauled back and sent it careening down the street.

She'd been right about its armor, and the curved blade cut the robot cleanly in half. The top section tipped forward and collapsed to the ground.

Her blade hit the ground behind the robot, sinking a foot deep into the asphalt, then began thudding like a jackhammer.

She ignored it and rushed into the spaceport. Jack was already running through the entry hall, about forty meters ahead, but she quickly caught up.

All of the people that weren't evacuated from the spaceport had found hiding spots. No one stopped them as they rushed to Jack's hangar.

TM waited at the top of the ramp, clicking angrily as they approached.

"Close the ramp," Jack said, ignoring the robot and handing Traq to Vivian. She punched the control button and carried Traq to the cockpit, strapping him into the copilot chair as Jack lit the engines.

"Where are the guns?" she asked, looking around frantically.

"Guns? This is a transport ship, Vivian."

She sighed.

"TM, can you get it open?" Jack asked. The little robot clicked the affirmative. The hangar door started grinding open above them, and a few moments later they were heading into the air above.

She looked through her control port and saw a few hangar doors opening and more ships taking to the sky. "We have company," she said. Jack didn't answer but she felt the ship pick up speed, heading straight into the atmosphere. "Looks to be four ships and—" she broke off, eyes going wide. "And the Cudgel. It's chasing after us too."

The Rey broke through the atmosphere and she looked up, seeing the Union warship above them. "The planet's prepping to fire. They just sent out a message," Jack said over the comm.

"Those guns hit hard but don't have much accuracy. We're too small for simple targeting. But if they land a shot, we're done. What was the message?"

"It wasn't sent to us. TM is deciphering it now," Jack said. "Two ships just dropped out of warp six thousand kilometers away."

"What?" Vivian asked. She glanced down and saw the pursuant ships pulling out of the atmosphere below them and then a moment later she saw the first shot from the huge planet-mounted blaster cannons tear into space. The shot went wide. "They missed," she said.

"No," Jack said. "They weren't aiming for us."

5

Maven Ophidian heard the message play over the bridge with mild amusement. It was ordering her ship to leave or they would be fired upon.

"Time to leave," she said.

"We can fire on them!" a man said. "Why would we flee?"

Maven had expected some response and wasn't about to forgive this time. The officer was in the air instantly, hovering in place and crying out in pain.

She sent pressure through her implant to squeeze against the man's rib cage. There was a cracking sound as several ribs snapped. He screamed, a blood curdling horrible sound and then fell silent. Maven never moved as his broken ribs pierced into his heart and lungs. He floated in the air, held by her will alone.

"Need I repeat myself?" she asked softly. She fought the urge to rub her forehead. The exertion of using her implant gave her a severe headache.

No one offered an argument. All they had to do was look at the dying man on the floor, blood pooling around his body.

6

"That went way better than I expected," Oliver said, leaning back in the co-pilots chair and closing his eyes. He struggled to stop his heart from doing flip flops.

"I got shot!" Jim said. He was lying on the floor of the cockpit, wincing in pain with his back against the wall. His boot was burnt from where a bullet tore through into his foot. He'd wrapped it tightly with tape. He'd also taken some drugs to dull the pain, but they were starting to wear off. Oliver glanced down at him and narrowed his eyes.

"So did I, if you recall," he said. Jim waved his hand in the air.

"I shot you in the chest. No permanent damage. Barely even dented your armor."

"You didn't know it wouldn't go through!"

"I suspected. And hey, it worked perfectly. Why would she shoot you if I already did? My plan was flawless."

"Well we did both get shot," Oliver said. Jim could only shrug.

"That we did. I knew she had a gun. But from that distance, I never imagined she'd be so accurate."

Oliver lowered the ship—his new ship, that was—down to the surface of Jaril near the hospital. He requested and received clearance to touch down on the roof. The other security vessels were going back to the spaceport, and he was pleased with how things turned out.

No one was quite sure what happened, but it hadn't taken long for reports to target the woman as an outsider. The media was running loose with the idea that she had started the attacks.

Oliver just hoped that no one knew their involvement. Getting arrested at the hospital would ruin his day.

The Royal Family had no choice but to declare the treatise over with the terms broken.

And, Oliver had been glad to see, Vivian escaped as well. He hadn't particularly enjoyed deceiving her, but he also didn't particularly care. After all, he'd shot the war robot and damaged its thrusters to help her escape. He considered them even.

All that mattered was Jim was happy that the Republic and Union were flushed out of the Sector, and Oliver was happy that he had half of a new ship.

A crowd was gathering on the roof as they touched down, and after a moment, he realized more than half of them were reporters. To be honest, he hadn't really expected it to succeed, or worst case scenario he wouldn't be in the middle of it.

"Looks like we've got a fan club," he said, pointing at the gathered crowd. Reporters were always better than government officials.

"I told you, Oliver, we're going to be famous," Jim said, chuckling. "Just remember, when anyone asks. I'm Captain of this little piece of crap."

Oliver shrugged. "All right with me. And, if they ask, *she* shot me, right?"

"Right," Jim said.

"Okay then. But don't get too caught up in the fame just yet. We still have to go to Mali in a couple of days."

"What? Why?" Jim asked. Then burst out laughing when he remembered the deal. "To deliver those goddamned water purifiers? Yeah, I guess that's the least we can do."

Chapter 26
Sector 3 – Daer
Abdullah Al Hakir, Kristi Grove, Ike Oreman

1

Abdullah stood in the conference hall in front of his seven chosen officers, arms folded behind his back. He surveyed their uniforms to ensure they were pressed and clean. Pristine. The four men and three women he'd selected stood at perfect attention, myriad faces impassive; eyes staring straight ahead.

Are they respecting me or ignoring me?

He didn't know. *He* would have offered respect for any High Officer on board Denigen's Fist. But then again, he'd never had to deal with a situation like this from their perspective: an upstart jumping to the top of the ladder.

Only a few hours ago, Captain Grove had given him the order to select and prep his own team of officers. Jamar, her manservant, gave him a recommendation list, but he quickly scrapped it. The suggested officers were all high-born, but none of them offered anything particularly unique or helpful to Abdullah. With the new accommodations, Abdullah needed all the help he could get.

These were enlisted officer's, all hand selected by Abdullah. He'd known some of them personally before his promotion three days ago, but a few he knew only by reputation.

Eddie was his only friend among the seven. Abdullah didn't have many friends.

But, he liked to keep track of good soldiers on board Denigen's Fist. These were some of the best he knew of. They were skipped over for promotions because of low birth but scored top marks on all proficiency-based examinations.

They were all near his age, either the late twenties or early thirties. Not much younger than Abdullah, who'd just passed his thirty-eighth birthday. Even then, he doubted they would consider him a peer.

Not anymore, at least.

Abdullah's life was in upheaval. The ship was in upheaval. And here they were, in Sector Three, trying to find new normalcy amidst insanity.

Thankfully most of his communications were sent electronically. There was a staff ready to relay any order to the correct location at all times of the day. Without them, Abdullah wouldn't have had a chance. They would have realized him for the fraud he was.

They might anyway.

2

"We picked up something on long range scanners," the officer said, hands flying over the control console, tapping out a series of commands. "A shipping vessel, ID signal jammed."

"Get me a spec readout and lock onto their tracers. If they go to warp go after them."

"Should we hail them?"

Kristi thought about it for a moment. If the ID signal was being jammed, that meant most likely this was a smuggling vessel. A smuggling vessel or one of those goddamned pit fighting ships. In either case, it was involved in illicit activities.

And it sat here, floating in orbit above the trading planet Daer. Daer was known for its black market trade industry and corrupt officials.

Her first duty as a Captain of the Republic's Fleet was to protect and secure the galaxy against external threats. The likelihood of galactic war was minor, so her secondary purpose was to regulate and protect the citizens.

She *wanted* to do her job, but it was made all the more difficult by corruption running rampant through the entire system. It stemmed from the top, from people like the Consul Peter Gavriel. He bought officials and forgave criminals. He'd even bought Captains, Kristi's peers.

The thought sickened her.

The people of the galaxy deserved better. They deserved more than corrupt politicians who took bribes in back rooms and sold civilians to the highest bidder. They needed to know that they were safe and that there were people on their side; they needed to understand that people who did terrible things wouldn't be tolerated.

"Hail them, but no threats. Keep it civil and keep them occupied."

"Yes, sir."

"We want them to decide to flee. After it's too late. Move us closer, but slowly. We don't want them to think they are at risk."

The pilot nodded and began relaying the orders to the engine controls. The communications officer opened a channel and hailed the smugglers, acting confused and seeking reverification on everything.

Kristi stepped over to the railing and glanced down at one of the officers sitting at the terminals below.

"Where is Lieutenant Commander Al Hakir?"

"He is on deck twelve, sir," the officer reported.

"Tell him to ready the crew. We're going to board."

3

Abdullah was handed a data pad. It contained all of the information he would need.

To make his decision...

About how best to board the enemy ship...

As soon as the alarms started blaring, a young soldier found Abdullah and led him to a station where he could deliver orders from. He'd walked in a daze, struggling to stay calm.

"Sir?" the young woman asked. She was sitting at a terminal, waiting to relay his orders.

Abdullah stared blankly at her. Alarms were blaring all around him. People were shouting.

"Sir?" she repeated. "What are your orders?"

I don't know, Abdullah almost said. *I have no idea what I'm doing. What I'm supposed to do. I don't even remember what your name is. Sally. Or Susie. Or something. Why are we attacking smugglers? Are we sure they are smugglers? What kind of ship is this?*

But he didn't dare ask those questions. The data pad would include all of that information, he knew. It would also include the list of all the boarding teams. Twenty members apiece. Or maybe it was twenty-two.

He wiped his sweaty finger across the screen. Nothing happened. He tried using the cusp of his shirt to dry it off. His entire body was covered in a sheen of sweat.

If I mess this up, is Kristi going to execute me?

"Sir?" the young woman repeated, a concerned expression on her face.

Will they execute her, too?

He felt someone touch his arm. He glanced to the side and saw Jamar Paskin, a mildly bored expression on his rotund face. Abdullah remembered him as the man who spoke in the conference and Kristi's servant.

"Here you are, Sarah," Jamar said, handing a data pad to the young girl. "The Lieutenant Commander asked me to hold onto these for him. It must have slipped his mind. If you would be so kind as to relay the messages?"

The girl nodded and accepted the data pad. She turned back around in her seat, sliding a pair of headphones over her ears, and began relaying orders. Her fingers flashed over the screen at the same time as she rambled off a series of alphanumeric codes.

Abdullah watched for a second, having no idea what was going on. Jamar put his hand on Abdullah's shoulder and led him away.

"We'll let her be for now," Jamar said.

"Were those my orders?" Abdullah asked.

Jamar nodded. "And they were excellent, my friend."

Abdullah allowed himself to be steered over to the door of the bridge. They dodged several other officers and assistants before finding a quiet place to stand. Jamar removed his hand from Abdullah's shoulder and then swept it across in a dramatic motion.

"This," he said, "is like a well-oiled machine."

Abdullah watched people scrambling around him. Lights flashed. Sirens blared. A soldier slipped and fell only a few feet away, hitting his arm hard on a rail. Only Captain Grove, standing on her raised platform, seemed relaxed. She could have been on a beach somewhere, she was so calm.

"It looks chaotic," Abdullah said.

"Indeed," Jamar agreed. "But there is beauty in chaos. If you can control it...harness it...why: there is no telling what you might accomplish."

Abdullah didn't know what to say.

Denigen's Fist rocked suddenly, followed by a loud roar.

"Did we just fire the plasma cannon?" Abdullah asked. Jamar nodded.

"You just disabled their engines. Your next shot will damage their hanger to keep anyone from fleeing. The third shot will take out the bridge. You're certain the battle will only take three shots and are hoping to minimize loss of life."

"What about drop pods?"

Jamar held out his hands. "Four ships are deploying between the smuggling ship and the planet. Any pods they cannot capture are to be destroyed."

"What else did I order?"

"Twenty ships will board from four entry points, entering with concussion grenades. A broadcast is playing in four languages over their speakers promising to take anyone prisoner who lays down arms. The ship has been split into quadrants so that the enemy cannot regroup in a centralized location."

"Is that all?" Abdullah asked.

"Not by a long shot," Jamar said. Another shock reverberated as their massive cannon fired off another shot. Jamar headed for the door leading from the bridge and gestured for Abdullah to follow. "But we don't have time for the minutiae. You're expected down at Hangar Four to oversee prisoner transfer."

They stepped onto the Command Deck. It was packed, unlike the last time he'd been through. Hundreds of people typed away at terminals. The drone of conversations echoed throughout.

"Prisoner transfer?" Abdullah asked. "You think they'll surrender?"

"They already have," Jamar replied. "They just might not know it yet."

"I need to be there?"

"You *should* be there," Jamar corrected. "It is an ideal place for the men to see you. A good first impression."

Abdullah glanced down at his shirt. The armpits and neckline were a darker shade of gray from sweat. "I'm not sure what kind of impression I will make."

Jamar opened up his bag. He drew out a gray shirt, folded and pressed. He handed it to Abdullah. "There's a restroom by the exit. The Nano-fiber material of this uniform is more comfortable than anything I'm sure you've ever worn. Still, I'd recommend wiping yourself down first. Just in case."

Abdullah accepted the shirt, rubbing it with his thumbs. "You've thought of everything."

"Always plan for the worst. You'll never be caught off guard."

"Why are you doing this? For me? Wouldn't it be easier to just let me fail?"

"Yes," Jamar said with a chuckle. "It would."

Then he disappeared, stepping back into the chaotic crowd around him. Abdullah hesitated for a second and then made his way to the restroom. He stripped his shirt off and threw it in the trashcan. He dried his chest off as best he could and then put the shirt on. It felt smooth on his skin and weighed almost nothing.

As an afterthought, he folded up a few pieces of toilet paper and put them between his sleeve and armpit.

He paused to look at himself in the mirror. His skin was paler than normal and his eyes looked slightly glazed. He splashed some water on his face, took a few deep breaths, and exited the restroom.

4

The battle, if it could be called one, was over in only a matter of minutes. Kristi ordered for the Gunnery Officer to target the engines as soon as they were in range. After only a few shots the smuggling vessel was disabled.

Alarms blared all around her. Officers ran from one terminal to the next. People yelled, shouted, and cheered as events progressed in the confrontation. Kristi stood unmoving with her hands folded behind her back, an island of clarity against the raging storm around her.

She was most pleased by how quickly and efficiently the ship was boarded. Any doubts she had about promoting Abdullah Al Hakir were abolished as the smuggling vessel was overrun and taken. Reports were still coming onto the bridge from the front lines, but she knew the crew casualties from Denigen's Fist could be counted on two hands.

She watched her twenty drop ships attach lines to the other ship and haul it closer to Denigen's Fist. Several smugglers were shot during the engagement, but the soldiers managed to secure the enemy bridge and round up all of the crew.

That crew numbered almost four thousand. Traitors and thieves all. *Men and women who have turned their backs to the First Citizen.*

Normally, after securing the vessel it would be hauled to a nearby planet. Each smuggler would be given a trial. Despite being a Captain of the Republic Fleet, Kristi Grove was *not* within her rights to judge the smugglers. She could not judge anyone outside of a military court.

However, there was a problem: the nearest world was Daer.

An officer handed her a data pad. It listed casualties.

The alarm system powered down, casting the bridge into silence.

On Daer, the smugglers would see only a modicum of justice. Of the four thousand, only a handful would be found guilty. And those would be given short prison sentences in lieu of the harsher penalties possible.

If anything, it would help them gain more friends and ties in the criminal underbelly of Daer. The most corrupt members of society were the ones running it.

The thought of racketeers and criminals judging smugglers and murderers boiled the Captain's blood. If she had her way, she'd wipe the establishment clean, fix the corruption at its source. But that was a fight for another day.

Today was all about the message.

Thankfully she had an alternative. She could not judge the prisoners for civil crimes, but she *could* turn them over to the Envoy for justice.

The Ministerial Envoy had the full backing of the First Citizen and Ministry. In Republic space, an Envoy's word was law. They could judge any criminal activity and deliver the appropriate punishment in the First Citizen's name.

Such action was not common. Normally the Holy Ministry avoided political or economic endeavors. The little priests were taught to dispense with justice only in the worst of situations. They certainly weren't willing to go above and beyond the call of duty and make examples of criminals, and when criminals *were* turned over for judgment, they were often forgiven by the Ministry.

However, turning the criminals over to the Envoy was greatly preferable to turning them over to Daer.

Plus, she had great confidence in the new Ministerial Envoy aboard her vessel. Abi would make the right decision, Captain Grove knew. She nodded to her First Officer and exited the bridge.

She strode to a meeting room off of the command deck where her Minister was waiting.

Animal paintings and crayon drawings decorated the walls.

A tiara hung from the door handle.

The room stank of youth.

Why did I let her keep so many toys?

Abi was playing with a large stuffed bear when Kristi entered, but she broke into a wide grin and ran to the Captain, throwing a hug around her mid-section. "Thank you, thank you, thank you!" the little girl repeated. Kristi extricated herself.

"You like the bear?"

"I love it."

"What's his name?"

"Argus," the girl said shyly, grinning ear to ear. "I named him after my daddy."

A knowing smile creased the old woman's lips.

"That's very nice of you. Have you been reading the paper I gave you?"

Abi blushed. "Yes."

"Don't lie to me, Abi."

"It's too *hard*! I don't even know what the words *mean*."

"You don't need to know. You just have to recite it. It has to be perfect, okay Abi?"

"Okay," the little girl said sadly. "I promise I'll practice."

"It will be in a few hours, and afterwards, I promise you can play with Argus for as long as you want."

That made her happy again. "Thank you!" she said, smiling widely.

Kristi was smiling as well. One more piece falling into position.

5

The next several hours were a blur. Soldiers watched as a procession of prisoners was brought aboard Denigen's Fist into a hangar bay. Several High Officers congratulated Abdullah, a few going so far as to pat him on the back. His strategy was brilliant, his attention to detail superb. How had he managed it so cleanly after only a few days on the job?

Abdullah took it all in stride. Or at least, he hoped he did. To be perfectly honest, he was glad he managed to make it through the day without fainting. By the end of it, even the second shirt was covered in sweat and he had sticky little balls of toilet paper covering his skin.

This was his first taste of leading a warship: simultaneously euphoric and terrifying.

They had attacked and captured a smuggling ship. Two had been in range, but Kristi was only interested in taking one.

The escaping ship was a large merchant vessel known as the Screaming Lady, and it was owned by a man named Immanuel Lefelenzo. He wasn't a smuggler but operated a number of fighting pits and slave rings.

Too bad he got away.

Things had calmed since the frantic battle, and now Abdullah wanted nothing more than to collapse onto his cot and fall asleep. He had a dull headache behind his eyes and felt utterly drained.

But that wasn't possible. Instead, he returned to the meeting hall where his seven soldiers waited. No one said a word about his absence. He wondered if they'd been here during the entire battle. Probably. They wouldn't dare disobey an order from their Lieutenant Commander.

"You are all being reassigned," he began finally. "To work for me. At ease."

The officers relaxed. Eddie was at the end of the line to the left, but his expression was as blank as those of the others. It was as if he was refusing to acknowledge that he knew he Abdullah was.

"Do you have any questions?"

"No sir."

"Good. There is going to be a lot of information sent to your quarters over the next few days. I expect you to know all of it. Understood?"

"Yes sir," they all said.

"And one last thing," he said, deciding to keep the meeting short. "I expect you all to be honest with me. Never withhold any information, for any reason. I've picked you all because you're the best at what you do."

He looked them over one last time and then waved his hand. "You are all going to report for duty tomorrow at—"

"Lieutenant Commander," a voice interrupted over the intercom system. "Your presence is requested by the Captain."

Abdullah glanced behind him at the speaker. *Again?*

"Now?"

"Yes, sir. Hangar four."

"Not the bridge?" he asked, surprised.

"No sir," the voice said. "Hangar four. Captain Grove is expecting you immediately."

Abdullah looked back at the soldiers. "Then I better not keep her waiting. You are all dismissed for the day. Report at my office tomorrow at oh-eight-hundred, and we'll discuss everything. Read every single paper you get. Dismissed."

The seven saluted and filed out of the room. Abdullah watched them disappear and then picked up his jacket, folding it over his arm. *Will I ever get to sleep again?*

He doubted it. Hangar four? That's where the prisoners are being held. Kristi must be planning to deliver a speech to the new prisoners.

And then Captain Grove would drop them off on Daer and be done with it. It was the nearest planet, only half a day away. Dropping off the prisoners would take a week, and it would be tedious. But that would give him time to relax and recover.

The sad fact was Daer harbored criminals. Captain Schmidt had never taken a smuggling vessel this close to Daer. It was a rookie mistake, the kind that would make Kristi a lot of enemies. They would all be back out in a month, looking for a new ship to work on with a score to settle.

But she *was* a new Captain. Prone to making mistakes. She couldn't have known that Daer would free all of her prisoners.

And, the more he thought about it, the better it seemed overall. The other officers were impressed with him—even if he had nothing to do with the orders—and the men and women under his charge respected him more now. They knew he could do the job.

The next time we flag a smuggling ship I'll be ready.

6

Lieutenant Commander Al Hakir made his way through Denigen's Fist. He passed through one of the gardens. Above him was an enormous glass dome, and beyond that only stars. It was beautiful, one of his favorite places on the ship, and one he hadn't known about until his promotion.

He rode the elevator from level twelve to level four. The halls of the Fist were bustling with activity and excitement. He heard a few soldiers mention the prisoners. Already rumors were spreading.

All of the whispers stopped as he passed, which was disorienting. Most of the men saluted or nodded to him. He was surprised that they recognized him at all. People stared at him with expressions varying from respect to frank amazement. *Why you?* they seemed to be asking. He wished he knew.

"Lieutenant Commander," a voice called as he stepped off the elevator.

He glanced around and saw Jamar waiting. The man had a data pad clutched in his pudgy hand. He wore an easy smile on his face as Abdullah approached.

"Yes?" Abdullah asked.

"I am to inform you that the Captain will be running a few moments late. She asked for you to check on the Minister's Envoy and see that she is prepared."

"She?" Abdullah blurted before catching himself. Jamar smiled wryly and narrowed his eyes.

"Yes. She is in the conference hall to your left. Currently, she is preparing her speech."

"The Envoy is making a speech?" he asked.

Suddenly, it clicked.

"We're turning the prisoners over to the Ministry," he said.

Jamar nodded and then said professionally, "It has been decided that the Minister shall decide the fate of our six thousand captured smugglers. May the Lord light the heathen's path, yadda yadda. Have you any further questions?"

Abdullah shook his head. "I will check on her."

Jamar smiled knowingly. "I believe you are already acquainted."

"Huh?" Abdullah said. "I don't think I've met any new Ministers."

"It has been a whirlwind of days. You might not remember. Just please make sure she leaves her dolls behind."

Luckily, Jamar walked away without waiting for a response from the new Lieutenant Commander. He never noticed the horrified expression on Abdullah's face.

7

"Daer is the closest planet," Ben said, rubbing his chin and yawning. "And my cousin works at the district office there."

"For all the good that does you," Ike Oreman said, his voice bitter.

"You kidding? I'll spend a few hours in prison. At most. With this many people all dropped off together, they'll cut most of us loose as soon as this old Junker leaves orbit. Denigen's Fist. What kind of name is that? Who the hell was Denigen?"

"You think they'll let us go?" Ike asked hopefully.

"I know they will," Ben said. He was in his late thirties. Ike was only seventeen, so he didn't know the ropes yet. Ben had been captured five times like this if you believed his stories. "Why do you think we fly so close to Daer? Our boss knows what to do. Most of the time they don't even mess with us. They know the score."

"But they trashed our ship."

"It happens," Ben replied with a shrug. "A few people will go to jail. As an example. Truth be told, it does us a favor: cleaning out the trash. But everyone else, they'll just let go. Ain't worth the hassle."

"Will they let me go?"

"This is your first time in trouble. No rap sheet. I'm sure they will. Just be polite. And tell your lawyer you have a sick family. He'll take care of the rest. We'll both be free in a couple of weeks. Then we can sign on to another ship. Something smaller, so we get a bigger share of the profits. Most of 'em are looking for new blood."

Ike was silent, looking over the amassed bodies around them. There was barely enough room to move his arms. At least, he wasn't claustrophobic.

Though he was cramped and miserable. The air smelled of sweat and body odor. The atmosphere was tense.

But not as tense as he would have expected. Most people seemed to share Ben's optimism. Soon they would be dropped off on Daer, and not long after they would be free. This was just a hitch in the process. The owners would lose profits, sure, but that was their problem. The people here, in this hangar, they were the small fish.

It seemed like a waste.

"Why would they attack us?"

"Huh?" Ben asked, cocking his head sideways. He had a bum ear and could only hear from the right.

"Why did they shoot us down in the first place? What was the point?"

Ben shrugged. "No idea. Heard it's a new Captain, so maybe that's it. Brown nosing, probably, or just plain dumb." Ben hacked into his sleeve and wiped his mouth. "If the Captain keeps doing dumb stuff, she'll end up dead. If she figures it out, though...well, there's money to be made."

Someone bumped into Ike. "I just want off this ship."

"Me too, kid," Ike said. "Me too. But don't worry, it won't be long. The Captain's going to come out, give a speech, and then we'll be on our way. Ever been to Daer? It's one hell of a place."

8

"Abi?"

The little girl looked up, a wide grin on her face. "Dulah!" She held up a small plastic doll in a white dress. It was eerily detailed to resemble a woman. Abigail had covered it in layers of clothing, and it had the vague resemblance of a clown. "Betsy missed you!"

Abdullah coughed. "How...are you doing?"

"We are about to have a tea party. Would you like to join us?"

Abdullah felt sick. "No, not right now. You have a...speech...right?"

Her face fell. "I don't want to do it," she said, crossing her arms and pouting. "I don't like to read, and we have our tea party! Argus is going to come too."

Argus the doll? Gods, what is going on?

A child as the Minister's Envoy? This is crazy.

Abdullah had never heard of it happening before. He couldn't imagine the Minister sanctioning such a decision.

Not that it mattered. Abdullah was in no place to question the Ministry, and he certainly wasn't going to question Captain Grove. If she wanted the little girl to read a speech, then it was his job to make sure she did it.

But how the hell am I supposed to do that?

"Do you like tea?" he asked.

"Uh huh," she said. "And we already started preparing the table. Our guests will be arriving soon and Betsy and I have to prepare."

Abdullah hesitated, thinking. "Can I come to your party?"

Her face lit up. "Sure Dulah, you can come!" She ran to the corner of the room where all of the chairs had been pushed to. "But now I need another chair!"

"I can get a chair," he said. "And we can have our tea party. But first I need you to read the speech."

She narrowed her eyes at him. "I don't want to."

"But if you don't read it, the Captain won't let me come to your party. And I really want to."

He felt like an idiot, but Abi seemed to be considering it. "Will you be there with me when I read it?"

"I'll be there, right beside you the entire time. And as soon as we are done we'll all have tea. Okay?"

She thought a moment longer than nodded. "Okay, Dulah."

The door opened behind them. Jamar stepped into the room carrying a folded black robe. Red lines ran along the neckline and sleeves. "Are you ready? You need to put this on."

Abi touched the material. It shimmered under her touch. "It's beautiful," she said breathlessly. "Is it for me?"

"It's all yours. Come with me."

He led the little girl to a side room, and Abdullah let out a long sigh.

Captain Grove followed her servant into the small office room a few moments later, arching an eyebrow at Abdullah. "Did you convince her?"

"She'll do it, I think," he said. "Whatever it is you want her to do."

Captain Grove smiled, but it didn't reach her gray eyes. "Good. Better we don't drug her for this. It's important that she trusts us."

Us? Abdullah thought but didn't dare voice the concern.

"How did you convince her?" Kristi asked.

"I...uh...promised I would go to her tea party after."

This time, the Captain didn't smile. "Then I suppose you'd better not let her down," she said, turning and disappearing out of the room.

9

"Where is this asshole? It's been hours," Ike said, holding his arms up. His elbows were the only defense he had to keep a little breathing room. The crowd was milling tighter with pent up energy as more people were forced inside.

The room was well beyond packed, and he couldn't see anything other than a sea of bodies. He wasn't even sure how the life support systems were keeping enough air in the same location.

"Won't be long now. We're all here," Ben said. "And you better not be too uncomfortable. We're going to be here for a few more hours until they can get us to Daer and drop us off."

"What?" Ike groaned. "Hells bells."

"This is our *real* punishment. Just think of it as a growing experience. This will make you stronger. And remember kid: this time tomorrow we'll be free."

"I just want to get the hell out of this cargo hold and—"

"Shut up," Ben interrupted. "The door is opening."

Ike glanced ahead and confirmed what his friend said was true. The bay door was sliding open. Several men strode inside, clearing the area and pushing prisoners back. They were all armed and armored. Ike peered up at the rafters and saw more guards posted above.

"Shit," Ike said, pointing up. "They are carrying launchers."

Ben glanced up and hesitated. "Missile launchers," he said. "Must be crowd control."

"Crowd control involves blowing us all up?"

"Bean bags is my guess," Ben said, but he didn't sound convinced. "Or ball bearings. Riot gear."

"Probably."

Ike glanced back to the front and saw that the men were setting up a stage. It was raised about eight feet off the ground, high enough that anyone on top could easily be seen. Another few minutes passed as the guards pushed the perimeter back.

Finally, a small contingent came out of the door.

"The hell?" Ben said. "They brought a kid? What the hell are they doing?"

Ike watched the group climb onto the platform. A hush had descended over the hangar and all eyes were faced forward. The lights dimmed. Ike lowered his elbows and felt a chill run down his spine.

Something was wrong.

The aforementioned little girl was in black shimmering robes that dragged the ground. She stood in the center of a trio of people on top of the stage. To her right stood a woman in a well-decorated uniform and to the left was a bronze-skinned man with sharp features and short-cropped hair. He was holding the little girl's hand.

She looked up to him for support. The man nodded to her and she stepped forward, opening her mouth to speak. Everyone strained to listen, which was unnecessary. Her voice—shrill and rapid—echoed throughout the entire hangar by speakers.

"You have been gathered to face your crimes. In the name of the Minister, Givon...Givon Mielo, you have been judged," she looked up at the man beside her and he nodded his approval. The little girl turned back to the crowd. "Seek penance with God."

The crowd stood in stunned silence as the trio climbed off the stage and exited the hangar.

"What...what does that mean?" Ike asked, glancing over at Ben. "What the hell does that mean?"

Ben's jaw was hanging open and all the blood drained from his face.

10

"How did I do?"

"You did great, Abi," Abdullah said, holding her shoulder and steering her away. His heart was racing and he could barely breathe. "So good."

"And now we get to have our tea party?"

"Uh huh," he said. Captain Kristi had stopped, watching through the window the multitude of faces within. So many people crammed into one place.

Not for long.

Captain Grove gave him a long look and beckoned him over.

"Go ahead and set up," Abdullah said to Abi. "I'll be right in."

The girl ran to the office, all smiles and excited energy. She looked so small and innocent, her too-big robes flopping around her tiny frame. He watched her go and faced the Captain.

She was peering through a one-way window into the cargo hangar, hands clasped behind her back and a pensive expression on her face.

Abdullah glanced past her, wondering what she saw in those clustered faces.

"Captain?" a voice said over the intercom. "Shall we proceed?"

The moment dragged on. People inside the hangar had figured out what was going on and were pounding on the door. Some were climbing on top of each other. But there was no escape.

Abdullah felt a lump in his throat as he stared at the Captain. She turned to look at him. "You disapprove."

Abdullah couldn't hide it. It was written all over his face. "Dead men learn no lessons."

"You assume this lesson is for them."

He forced a ragged breath. "Who is it for?"

"We are in orbit over Daer. Once we leave this area, the only gravity strong enough to affect the smugglers will be the planet. And each other."

"They will clump together and plummet," he surmised, shaking his head. "A harsh lesson."

"But necessary."

"Will the Ministry be offended?"

"Their own Envoy gave the command," Captain Grove said, her voice making her meaning clear. "They cannot speak against her without speaking against themselves."

Abdullah's skin felt clammy and he felt like he was standing on thin ice. At any moment, he might fall through. "Then," he said, his voice barely above a whisper. "We have no choice but to honor her decision."

The Captain studied him for a long moment and smiled, her cold gray eyes boring into his soul. "No choice at all." She turned back to face the door. "Vent the hangar."

It happened quickly. Abdullah couldn't hear anything through the thick doors, could only see the terrified expressions. There was a sudden rush as people were dragged toward the exit and out into space, along with the hangar's air supply. But with bodies so tightly packed the air only managed to pull the ones closest to the exit out into space.

The rest scattered about in the hangar, the liquid in the air freezing solid in seconds. Abdullah watched them stop moving, horrified and wishing he was anywhere else.

Six thousand dead, he thought. Most of the bodies will burn up on impact with the planet's atmosphere.

But they don't have to hit the surface to make an example.

"I'll have guards clean up the mess before we reestablish atmosphere. I don't want any thawing out on my ship," Captain Grove said, peeling her eyes from the spectacle and glancing at Abdullah. The edges of her lips curled.

"Don't you have a tea party to go to?"

Epilogue

Argus

Argus Wade received the report only a day after it happened. He was in his private chambers on Axis. The words were clear and easy to understand, but he had trouble processing them just the same.

It was a report of what had transpired in Sector Two aboard Denigen's Fist. The entire Republic was up in arms about it, with constant newscasts condemning the actions of Captain Kristi Grove.

The actions of the Ministry.

It was a firebomb dropped into his lap, and he was terrified to think that he had orchestrated the events. He was responsible for the deaths of all of those people: criminal or not, they didn't deserve to die.

His daughter didn't deserve...

"Oh God, what have I done?"

There was a knock on his door. It opened after a few seconds and an attendant stuck her head into the room. "The Minister would like to speak with you."

"Did he say why?" Argus asked, a hollow feeling in the bottom of his stomach.

"He did not," she said. "He is waiting in his office."

Then she disappeared, leaving Argus alone. He fought down his panic, taking deep breaths and forcing himself to relax. He knew the Minister would receive word of the events that had taken place aboard Denigen's Fist. Events performed in his name and the name of the Ministry.

The walk to the Minister's office felt like miles, but before he knew it he was standing before the double doors. Hands shaking, he pushed the door open.

"Ah, Argus," the Minister said, smiling at him and setting aside a paper he was holding. "I'm glad you could join me."

"Of course," Argus said, hoping his voice wouldn't crack. "I was told you needed to speak with me."

"Yes," Givon replied. He didn't offer for Argus to sit. "I received a report recently about Ministry actions taken against criminals."

"Yes," Argus said, "and I assure you I will speak to Captain Grove regarding the events that transpired and make sure it never—"

"I approve," Givon interrupted. Argus trailed off.

"You what?"

"I approve of her actions completely," he said. "It is about time people came to understand that the Ministry isn't a spineless entity leading sheep. It is past time they realize just how important faith is in these faithless times."

Argus floundered for words. "I see."

"I wish to release a statement fully sanctioning the actions of the Captain and our young Minister aboard Denigen's Fist."

"I understand," Wade said. "I'll draft up documents and have them sent to you immediately."

"Good," the Minister said, smiling and picking up a piece of paper. Wade thought he was dismissed and started walking toward the door. "It seems that your daughter is going to have a long and fruitful career aboard her new vessel. You made a *most* excellent decision, my friend."

Argus Wade felt the words cut into his stomach, but he didn't dare show his emotions. "Thank you," he said.

Then he left the Minister's office, drenched in sweat and wondering if the world would ever stop spinning.

Jayson

It was a few days before Jayson was allowed to visit Richard in the infirmary. His friend was heavily bandaged and still looking pale, but they'd already been informed that there would be almost no time to rest. They would begin training soon, and their days would be long and arduous.

Part of Jayson was thrilled at the prospect...the other part was terrified. He didn't know just what he'd gotten himself into and was hoping he might find a way to get himself back out.

"How are you," he asked, sitting in a chair near Richard's bed.

"I'm all right," his new friend said, then coughed. "Apart from the excruciating pain and constant nausea."

"Training starts tomorrow," Jayson said.

"That's what they said," Richard said. "Think they'll go easy on me?"

Jayson shook his head. "No."

Richard coughed again. "No, I don't think so either."

"But, we're past initiation, so things can only get better from here, right?"

Richard stared at him. "I've seen a lot of things, and been to a lot of places, so I know something about how things work. Things are going to get a lot worse before they get better."

"Aren't you optimistic?"

"Just a regular ray of sunshine," Richard said. "Kid, you've got some talent, and maybe the pain is making me sentimental, but I wanted to tell you: don't let them break you. They're going to try and you just have to be strong."

"Sure," Jayson said. "I won't let them break me."

"Good," Richard said. "There might just be hope for you yet…"

Richard trailed off as the drugs kicked in, slipping back to sleep. Jayson sat with him for a while longer before heading back to his chambers.

The academy would be where he would stay for the foreseeable future. He would train and learn, but this would never be his home.

Vivian

Vivian settled the ship down at the hangar in the city Fasbend on the planet Eldun. They had been traveling for a few days and Vivian was sorting her feelings and emotions out after everything that had happened on Jaril.

She hadn't spoken much to Traq, and he had stayed in his room. She knew he wasn't handling things very well, but he was only a child.

"Children are resilient," she said aloud. She knew it was true, but she was afraid that such resiliency wouldn't be enough.

The life she had thrust him into when she took him from his home…it wouldn't be easy. He would always be at risk, and if the wrong people knew he existed, they would stop at nothing to retrieve him.

Dead or alive.

She stood and moved to Traq's room aboard her ship. She knocked on the door, waited for a second, and then pushed it open. He was sitting on his bed, head down and despondent.

He looked up as she came in. "Where are we now?"

"Eldun," she said.

"Why?"

"This is a lawless backwater planet, constantly on the verge of war. Which means it's dangerous."

He scrunched his face in confusion. "Shouldn't we go somewhere else if it is dangerous here?"

She looked at him, so small and fragile on the bed. He had a good heart, so full of life and hope. He didn't understand how bad things would be, and without help, he wouldn't stand a chance in the world.

"We're here because it's dangerous. Your training starts today."

Kristi

"Have you never heard of patience?" Jamar asked.

Kristi looked over at him, frowning. "I have been more than patient all of these years. It is time some things changed."

"You don't need to accomplish everything all at once," her servant explained. Sometimes it is best to let the dust settle."

"Every day there are more problems. More dust. If we let things settle how they may, then we will be picking up the pieces of this Empire in only a few years."

"It isn't an Empire."

"Isn't it?" she said. "A rose by any other name..."

"Then what do you propose?" Jamar asked. "We attack every lowlife and despondent we can get our hands on and single-handedly clean up the entire galaxy?"

"I'm not proposing anything," Kristi replied. She stood up, towering over Jamar. "Last I checked, I'm Captain of this vessel. My word is law."

About the Author

Lincoln Cole is a Columbus-based author who enjoys traveling and has visited many different parts of the world, including Australia and Cambodia, but always returns home to his pugamonster puppy, Luther, and family. His love for writing was kindled at an early age through the works of Isaac Asimov and Stephen King and he enjoys telling stories to anyone who will listen.

https://www.LincolnCole.net

Intentionally Left Blank

Intentionally Left Blank

Intentionally Left Blank

Intentionally Left Blank

Intentionally Left Blank